DEMI-DIETY

DEMI-DIETY

CHRONICLES OF KIERAFREYA™ 05

MICHAEL ANDERLE

THE DEMI-DIETY TEAM

Thanks to our JIT Readers

Dave Hicks
Deb Mader
Diane L. Smith
Dorothy Lloyd
Jeff Eaton
Kelly O'Donnell
Larry Omans
Peter Manis

If We've missed anyone, please let us know!

Editor
The Skyhunter Editing Team

*To Family, Friends and
Those Who Love
To Read.
May We All Enjoy Grace
To Live The Life We Are
Called.*

PROLOGUE

The air was filled with the acrid stench of sulfur. Poisonous black clouds darkened the skies, puffing in small bursts from the open mouths of vents littering the land.

A land that stretched on for infinity, a kind of limbo differentiated only by towering rock formations. Rugged things that broke free of the land and reached for the sky like fists from the grave.

The creature walked on.

His head hung down in shame, every footstep dragging, his mind lost in a darkness reflective of the land around him.

He came to a river. The water lay thick and black like motor oil, greasy rainbows staining the surface. A boat appeared in the water, its captain a blankly staring skeleton. It waited patiently.

The imp smirked. "How much to take me home?"

The skeleton gave no reply. Fukmos clambered in and took his seat as the skeleton placed a long paddle into the dark waters and maneuvered them into the heart of the river.

The ride was smooth despite the choppy waters. After a stretch, the water began to gently bubble and roll. Steam rose in billowing clouds, and through the fog, Fukmos could see the dead swimming in the river, heads breaching the surface like dark dolphins.

He placed a hand in the water, the skeleton at the front of the boat paying no attention as he continued to paddle.

Several hands reached for Fukmos', passing straight through it. He grinned, enjoying the teasing of the dead. Even in death, the souls of mortals had no effect on the forms of the gods.

He returned his attention to the boat, surprised to see that the skeleton had paused, paddle half out of the water, and was now staring at him.

"What's the matter? Am I not allowed to pet the animals? You didn't say 'hands and legs inside the ride at all times,' did you?"

The skeleton continued to stare for a time, the intensity of its gaze unnerving. Fukmos looked into the pits of the skeleton's eyes and was sure he could see something in there, watching him. Some other intelligence studying Fukmos from afar.

Who was he kidding? Of course, *He* was.

The skeleton's bones creaked and its focus returned to rowing. The boat passed into the yawning mouth of a cave that plunged them both into unholy darkness. It was only when Fukmos snapped his fingers that emerald-green flames appeared at intervals along the cave's wall, balancing precariously on small torches.

The river wound ever deeper into the cave. The skeleton guided them down forks in the river without hesitation.

A little farther on, the water began to quicken its pace. Fukmos knew this place well, having spent many of his formative years tracing and exploring the waters of the Underworld, and he knew that a little farther down that route would be a waterfall, the largest Obsidian had to offer.

A waterfall so large it made the Angel Falls look like a ripple in a stream.

At the bottom of the fall was a series of dagger-like rocks. Those condemned to suffer in the Underworld would tumble over the waterfall, plummeting thousands of miles to their inevitable re-death, then appearing back at the start of the falls and tumbling again. It was the ultimate punishment for the worst the world had to offer.

Fukmos shuddered. That sounded terrible even to him. But his father had his ways, and the god of death was hardly going to hug and squeeze people into oblivion.

They pulled up on an ashy shore. Fukmos exited the boat, then tipped an invisible cap to the skeleton. It wasn't paying attention. It was already slipping the boat back into the water.

Fukmos started to climb the steps that spiraled into the higher reaches of the dark cave. After the first few, he realized his efforts were futile. He sighed, rolled his eyes, and melted into shadow, saving himself the exertion of the climb. Increasing his pace, he slithered up the stairs and rose ever higher.

He returned to his true form when he was a few steps from the top. A pair of shadowy sentinels in dark armor adorned with rusty spikes guarded the door but made no movement as Fukmos walked past.

He was expected, after all.

He strode across the large open chamber, stopping at the bottom of a short staircase. An imposing figure shrouded in a mist of darkness and shadow that writhed and coiled around his being like a serpent sat in silence on the dais. Eyes like blue flame flickered beneath his dark hood. The throne was decorated with the bones of folks long since passed.

Fukmos fell to one knee, sliding his eyes from the blue flames to the black rock on the floor. "Father."

"Fukmos. You have failed."

Fukmos swallowed hard. He frantically nodded, knowing how futile it would be to deny all that had occurred.

"A minor setback, almighty Dark One. A simple glitch in the plan is all. It's nothing that can't be fixed—isn't already being fixed. Trust me, I don't—"

"Trust is difficult to earn," Asros interjected, his words cold and measured, "but it is very easy to lose. You have lost any semblance of trust that you might think you have."

Fukmos continued his frantic nodding, his hands twisting together near his stomach.

"Understood, Dark One. But please, if you'll just give me another chance, we can win this. The girl is still missing a piece of the armor. The biggest piece of all. And it is locked away. If we can keep that piece hidden, buried, and lost with the ancients, she is doomed to roam the world incomplete for the rest of her life. The threat will pass, the problem perish—"

Asros' hands clutched the arms of the throne as he leaned forward angrily, eyes blazing. *"The problem will not perish until the problem has been exterminated!"*

He stared for a moment into Fukmos' eyes. They had never been what anyone would consider "close" as a family, yet Fukmos had always felt a strange admiration for his father and hated to disappoint Him. He cowered and whimpered into his hands, waiting for his moment to speak again.

Asros leaned back impassively.

"As long as the girl exists, and as long as she carries the fallen goddess, we risk the unraveling of it all. Our little secret. I cannot allow this to happen."

Asros raised a hand toward Fukmos. The imp was lifted off the ground, the air around his throat clamping like a physical force. His legs kicked as he began to choke.

"Fix it!" Asros roared. "Find a way to fix what you've done. I will not tolerate any more failures. Do you understand?"

Fukmos nodded, his body flailing in the air. The next thing he knew, he was in a crumpled heap on the floor. "Understood, O Dark One. Understood. No more failure. I can do this. You'll see. I can do this."

Fukmos got up, then bowed so low his nose touched the floor. He turned and strode back toward the stairs, freezing when he heard his father say, "I know you can."

Fukmos spun.

"Because this time, you'll have assistance."

Asros clicked his fingers. A burst of smoke coalesced on either side of him, forming the shape of two girls. Although they looked child-like, Fukmos knew better. He had been around them for the better part of several millennia.

The girl on Asros' left stepped forward. Her hair was long and black and flowed around her body as though she were underwater. She hovered several inches off the ground, and her eyes were vacant pools of white. "Of course, he does. Don't you, Fukey?"

Fukmos' nostrils flared and he glared at the girl.

"Oh, now, don't tease, Myaris," the second girl, Dryana, said. Where her sister's hair was long and flowing, hers was short and thin. There were clumps of it missing from her scalp, and her skin seemed to be poxed, not that it seemed to pain her. "You know he only likes *causing* the mischief, not receiving it."

"Too bad," Myaris replied. "I thought we could have some fun together on the surface world for once. It's been terribly boring down here without you."

"And to think, all that time up there wasted," Dryana teased. They giggled like schoolgirls, although there was an emptiness to their tone. "Weeks and weeks, and nothing to show for it."

"We slowed her down," Fukmos flared. "The host...Valoric-what-ever-that-bitch's-name-was. We slowed her down. Created a challenge."

"Oh, really?" Myaris laughed. "As I understood it, you collected the armor *for* her, then delivered the goods on a silver platter. Isn't that what you told us, Father?"

Asros sat silently, watching with a studious eye.

Fukmos frowned at the pair. "Mistakes were made. It will not happen again."

He turned back to the stairs. His eyes were dark, his pride bruised. He walked briskly, hoping he would be allowed to exit without the nuisances following. The girls had caused him untold torment and irritation in their formative years when the world was young.

Before he reached the third step, a cold voice spoke.

"No. It will not," Asros crooned. "Remember, I made you. In failure, you can be undone."

Fukmos nodded, then sped down the stairs, chased by the haunting giggles of the dark-haired girls as they followed him.

CHAPTER ONE

Therese planted her feet. The edge of the forest was in sight. All around her, she could *feel* their presence, but the damn creatures had once again camouflaged themselves within the shadows.

"When there's something strange in your neighborhood..." she murmured, shield ready in one hand, hammer in the other.

Huk shifted uneasily. "Who you gonna call?"

He stood a few feet behind Therese, his goblin eyes scanning the forest. The setting sun shone through the trees, its final rays bright enough to impair their vision and leave blank spots in their eyes.

Gideon sighed. "Are we really going to do this?"

"Ghostbusters." Ben grinned, his bowstring creaking as he held it taut.

Something moved in the corner of his eye. He released the string, letting the arrow soar through the trees and find its mark. There was a groan of pain as the projectile took a large chunk of the creature's health.

"Bingo," Chloe said, her **Dark Vision** identifying the ghouls dotted around the group.

Several of them rushed out of the trees in unison.

They were strange creatures. They looked like severely malnourished hags with thin, bracken-like arms and legs, and forms that could melt into their surroundings. Their skin was marbled blue and black, their eyes dark orbs in their faces.

"To the right," Veronica shouted.

Chloe whirled, an **Ice Shard** forming in her hand. She threw the missile and pierced the ghoul's shoulder. The ghoul was knocked back but continued coming for her.

Ben was ready. Casting **Double Shot,** he loosed two arrows, one taking its place in the ghoul's cheek, the other skimming its skin and finding the one behind it.

The first ghoul went down, crumbling into a heap. Its body evaporated into the forest floor.

"Left!" Talbot called. "Big ones, too."

"Spread-eagle!" Chloe shouted.

The team took their positions, putting their training into practice.

The "spread-eagle" tactic was simple, involving the team positioning themselves in a tight cluster with the warriors and clerics in the center (in this case, Talbot, Huk, Leonie, and Veronica), flanked by the two mages (Chloe and Gideon).

The tank took front and center, blocking direct oncoming attacks with their shields (Therese), while long-range fighter (Ben) took the rear.

Hovering around the edge of battle, ready to charge when required, was—

"Blueballs!" Chloe shouted after the lumbering blue toffet, already bounding on his powerful paws toward several ghouls that had materialized in the woods beside them. He was already gnashing his razor-sharp teeth, ready to take down the enemies.

"He's got it, Chloe," Gideon called back, summoning his **Volt Shock** spell and shooting sparks ahead.

He took a few steps forward, opening up the formation for the warriors to attack. Chloe completed the maneuver on her side, the cluster of players spreading out like the wings of an eagle.

Chloe held her sword high, imbuing the blade with **Deic Light**. KieraFreya's mythical sword was incredible—light, sharp, and able to maneuver at her every whim to cut down the enemies ahead of her, not that she expected anything else from the personal armory of the goddess of retribution.

"A little higher," KieraFreya whispered into Chloe's ear, the magical armor taking a life of its own. Chloe's sword swiped at a ghoul and created a deep cleft in its stomach, which oozed thick, dark liquid. "I personally find that if you go for the head, you only need one chop."

"Thank you for that." Chloe decapitated the ghoul with the next swing.

"You're welcome. Maybe one day you, too, will become a fearsome warrior, as I once was."

"I'm a *Battle Mage*."

"Oh, yes. I forgot. You're one of *those*," KieraFreya teased.

Veronica, who had been darting between the players, casting **Healing Hands** to keep each player topped up to full health, overheard. "I told you Battle Mages were frowned upon. Finally, someone else in the group sees it."

Chloe smirked, not wanting to show Veronica that she was getting to her. "Yeah? Well, at least I can do *this*!"

Chloe poured additional energy into her blade. Four ghouls came out of the shadows, sprinting toward her. She broke free of the group, her sword lighting up the shadows. She twirled the sword in one hand as she summoned the etheric in her mind and prepared for what was to come.

"Watch out!" someone shouted.

Chloe grinned. The ghoul's arm reached for her and missed by an inch as she stopped and turned in a full twist around the creature. She swung her sword behind her and opened the ghoul's back in one swift motion, then used the momentum of the blade to stab the next ghoul's shoulder blade.

The ghoul cried out in pain as the other two came from either side.

Chloe released her grip on her sword, leaving it embedded in the ghoul's shoulder, and spread her arms wide. With one hand, she focused on her **Shadow Tweak** ability, feeling a smug sense of satisfaction when the shadows snaked toward her, creating a small wall directly in front of the ghoul on her left.

With the other hand, she summoned **Creepers Crawlies**, bending the plant life to her will and pulling down several vines that formed a block in front of the ghoul on her left.

She raised both hands, and the spells lifted higher.

The ghoul on her left tripped over the wall and fell on its face. A blanket of shadow appeared and cloaked its body, keeping it pinned to the ground. The ghoul on her right groaned as the vines coiled around its legs and dragged it into the air, suspending it several feet up.

With deliberate slowness, Chloe sauntered over to the second ghoul and retrieved her glowing sword from its back. She kicked it away, assessing its health with **Creature Identification** and seeing the bar now on zero.

She turned to the suspended ghoul and drove the blade into the part of its body where she presumed its heart to be; she couldn't know for sure. Either way, the area was glowing ever so faintly, thanks to her **Monster Slayer** skill, which showed her the weak points of the monsters they battled.

In a final maneuver, Chloe sawed the blade through the shadow blanket and finished off the last of her ghouls.

Veronica and Therese stared at her in stunned admiration. Behind them, Gideon, Blueballs, Huk, Ben, and Leonie were engaged with half a dozen ghouls of their own.

"Oh, this?" Chloe said, raising an eyebrow and wandering back toward them. "It's nothing. Anyone can do this. Y'know, master the sword *and* the etheric."

"Can *you* do that?" Therese muttered out of the side of her mouth to Veronica as Chloe laughed and moved to join the rest of her party in battle.

Veronica's face soured. "Shut up."

There were more ghouls on the other side now, coming in droves from deeper in the woods.

"We must be near a nest," Ben called to the others. "They just keep coming."

"A nest could be fun," Chloe said, appearing behind Ben and slapping him on the back before sprinting into the fray.

Ben shook his head and grinned. He brought his eyes back to his bow and continued raining arrows on the ghouls.

Although Huk, Leonie, Gideon, and Ben were doing a great job holding the ghouls back, Blueballs was the star of the show. His arms pinwheeled in a blur of blue fur, bowling through the creatures and weakening them for the others to pick off. Chloe could see him, a short distance into the dark, powerful arms sweeping the ghouls off their feet and hurling them against the trees.

The area lit up in a flash of blue as Gideon shot electricity from his hands.

"You might find life a bit more fun if you played with your other powers, y'know," Chloe said.

Gideon shrugged. "I like electricity, okay? It's...cathartic."

"I see."

"Besides, how else can I get the spell to level 5?"

"Level..." Chloe's voice trailed away. She quickly scanned through her spells-dex. "That's not fair. My best is **Telekinesis** at level 3."

"Maybe train that one a bit more?" Gideon suggested. "Looks like it's easier to level up one skill if you keep using it."

Chloe shrugged. "Fine. But not now."

Her hands lit up with the great spheres of crackling purple fire of **Purple Blaze**. Gideon stared at her wide-eyed. "We're in a forest, the whole thing will be set ablaze!"

To his surprise, Chloe was laughing. The orbs shrank to nothing. "You should have seen your face. Of course, I'm not going to throw fire at them. I remember what happened last time, doofus. What do you think I want to do, kill one of our party?"

The party tracked the ghouls to a clearing in the trees. Ghouls piled out, one after another.

The nest.

In the clearing was what looked like a large moss-covered rock. A hole led down into a dark tunnel. Even now, more ghouls were crawling out, reaching toward the KieraSlayers.

Huk wrinkled his nose. "It's like watching a cow give birth."

"How many of those have you seen?" Leonie asked.

"Enough."

"Shall we block the hole? Find a way to stop them from coming out?" Gideon suggested.

Chloe tilted her head to try to get a better look inside the shadowed tunnel. "Unless we want to explore their hole and see what we find?"

"You sound like Ben after a few too many drinks," Therese quipped.

"Hey!"

"We won't fit in there," Veronica crouched and ducked her head. Blueballs squatted at the cave's entrance, bashing the skull of any ghoul that dared to crawl to the surface. The action reminding Chloe of the Whack-a-Mole game she'd seen at arcades. "It's too small."

"Huk could go," Leonie suggested.

"You want to bet?" he replied.

"Or Therese?"

Therese scoffed. "I'd sooner lick Blueballs' backside."

Blueballs cocked an eyebrow.

"Oh, no offense, pal."

"Okay, well, blockage it is, then," Veronica said, clapping. "Who's going to do the honors?"

They turned to find Chloe already focusing on the tunnel. Her hands glowed with etheric energy, and soon they could hear the rock sinking into the ground. The cave entrance closed, looking more like a clamshell than the hole it was.

The cries of the ghouls quieted to a soft mumble as Chloe finished focusing on her **Telekinesis** spell. "There. Problem solved."

They all nodded, each taking a second to stare at their notifications and allow Veronica to heal any wounds they might have acquired.

Chloe stared at her own menu and saw the updates in bright letters.

Enemy defeated: Ghoul (Lv 7)

+530 exp

Enemy defeated: Ghoul (Lv 9)

+590 exp

Enemy defeated: Ghoul (Lv 8)

+550 exp

Enemy defeated: Ghoul (Lv 8)

+550 exp

Enemy defeated: Ghoul (Lv 8)

+550 exp

Chloe was also pleased to see that her two spells had leveled up.

Spell power increased: Creepers Crawlies (Lv 2)

Now that your spell has leveled up you can—*you guessed it*—control vines and foliage with a greater level of efficiency. A wider range of plant life is available for your manipulation, too.

Requirements: n x 17MP per second (where n is equal to the number of seconds taken to cast the spell)

Spell power increased: Shadow Tweak (Lv 2)

Ever thought of producing puppet shows? Just an idea. I suppose there are better ways to manipulate the shadows (extra points for creativity and innovation).

Requirements: n x 12MP (where n is equal to the number of seconds taken to cast the spell)

Not bad, Chloe thought. *Maybe I should try harder to level these bad boys up.*

Not that she hadn't already been trying. Spells seemed a lot more reluctant to grow than her other skills. She wondered about their increased potential, making a note for herself that when she had a quiet moment, she would experiment with her newfound etheric skills.

Finally, scrolling through her menu, she looked up her skills and stats, curious to see how close she was to obtaining her next character level. She had a hunch something would happen at level 15, but she wasn't sure what.

After her review, Chloe was pleased to see that she wasn't far from reaching level 15. Thanks to the KieraSlayers' journey from Killink

View toward the mountain city of Hammersworth, they had encountered a whole host of local monsters and enemies that had boosted their experience.

Which was perfect, considering she now had one final obstacle to face before she finally reunited all of the pieces of KieraFreya's armor: finding and taming KieraFreya's noble steed, Shikora.

Who knew what dangers lay along that path, and what strength they would need to complete the last of KieraFreya's mission? With their party down two men, they needed all the bonuses and benefits they could get. It had been bad enough losing Jessie in the battle for the armor, but to have to leave Tag safely guarded in Killink View while they continued on their travels without him?

That had been a tough pill to swallow.

Even now Chloe could picture his lifeless body on the bed in the sleeping chambers of the Twisted Spire inn. The real Tag was logged out and radio silent since the loss of his digital girlfriend.

They had left a note with the innkeeper, and Ben continued to try to communicate with Tag in the real world, but they couldn't stop and wait while Tag dealt with his demons. They were a party, and they had a job to do.

When they emerged from the trees, the group blinked stupidly at the bloody sunset beyond the vast stretch of the Yoren mountains ahead. Fields and streams covered the several-mile stretch between them and their destination. Small villages and farmhouses littered the land that bordered the legendary city of Hammersworth.

"Is that it?" Veronica asked, coming up beside Chloe.

Chloe shielded her eyes. She could see the high white stone walls encircling the city, which was half-tucked into the mountainside, reminding her of her first sight of Killink View.

She nodded. "I don't know what else it could be."

"And do we really think he'll be there?"

Chloe took a deep breath; the description of the man Prince Gilligan had told them about was still fixed in her mind, their only lead on this wild goose chase across Obsidian.

"Dear God, I hope so," Chloe replied. "Because if he's not, we'll have come all this way for nothing."

"Not for nothing," Gideon said.

Chloe raised an eyebrow.

"Every step we take together brings us closer as a party. No time is wasted in *Obsidian*."

Chloe smiled, pride swelling in her heart. She looked ahead and took her first steps onto Hammersworth's farmland.

CHAPTER TWO

Killink View was large, but Hammersworth put it to shame.

The largest city in Obsidian, and often considered the realm's capital, Hammersworth was the oldest inhabited city, its history stretching back thousands of years.

The walls surrounding the city were of thick, impenetrable stone. The houses and buildings inside were a mix of old and new, most of them constructed from the same rock that made up the city's walls. Every inch of the city was built to last.

Flags and trebuchets marked the walls at intervals, and dwarven guards were posted at the gates.

That was the first thing Chloe had noticed after they had ridden in and been granted entry: the number of dwarves populating the place. Talbot had informed the party that Hammersworth had once been the foremost mining town, way back in the days where resources were few and the world was growing.

Now the city continued its tradition, tunneling deeper and deeper into the mountains from which the city spread. Many dwarves still called Hammersworth home.

"You must be in paradise," Chloe said to Therese.

"I'll be honest; it's nice to outnumber you guys for a change. Everywhere you go, it's humans, humans, humans."

"You say that like it's a bad thing."

"Have you *met* your kind?"

They spent their first day in Hammersworth getting their bearings and laying low. The city was divided into four main sections, and they soon found themselves a comfortable place to stay in the residential quarter while they hunted for the mysterious man Prince Gilligan had told them of.

As with Killink View, it took a while to convince the innkeeper to let Blueballs stay with them. They'd expected nothing less, having learned that toffets were a rare breed, found only in the depths of the Heartwood. Even there, there seemed to be few of them left, considering Blueballs was the only one they'd crossed paths with.

After some gentle monetary persuasion (coin taken from the reward the king and queen had given them after the party's assistance to the Killink monarchy), the innkeeper had yielded.

"Prince Gilligan said he'd be hanging around stables, or anywhere, really, that had animals," Chloe said to Gideon as they made their way through the cobblestone streets. "Apparently he has quite an affinity for them."

They passed a great many dwarves, as well as a number of humans and elves. There were also some locals whose race confused Chloe. They were wide like dwarves but almost as tall as humans. Chloe wondered if there had been any incidences of cross-species breeding in the city.

"Well, that should be easy, then? Surely?" Gideon replied, eyes lingering on an apothecary shop as they passed. It featured a cage with a rather lively bat hanging from a hook on the outside.

Chloe laughed. "We'll have time to go shopping later." Gideon's ears flushed. "Once we've found this guy, we'll be able to grab the horse, complete the quest, and bathe in the riches of the mythical rewards. We'll be back to exploring and hunting for adventures like you used to do in your other games."

Gideon gave a half-smile.

"What's wrong?"

"I'm not sure I want it to be like any other game," Gideon said. "It's because this hasn't been like any other game that I love playing so much. In *Relic Hunter*, it was always the same: gather items, slay the dragons, and level up. This is the first game where I've felt a sense of purpose. I didn't realize being a mage could be so much fun and bring so much to the team. Being a warrior never gave me that. I was just another brutish busybody with a sword and a lust for blood."

"You? A lust for blood?" Chloe winked. "I couldn't imagine such a sweet-hearted guy could be so…"

"Reckless?"

"Sure, let's go with that," Chloe replied with a smile. "Oh, excuse me!"

Chloe ran over to the dwarf who had come around the corner. In his hands he held several leads for the llamas he was currently trying to drag through the streets. The creatures were stubborn, their hooves planted as though the last thing they wanted to do was follow him to his destination.

The dwarf grunted, his face turning red as he pulled, gaining inch by painful inch.

"Excuse me," Chloe repeated, closer now.

The dwarf looked at her with angry eyes. "Not now, girl. Can't you see I'm a little busy? Come *on*, Felicia. You're setting the example for the others."

Veins bulged on his biceps as he pulled.

"Maybe we can be of some assistance?" Chloe said. "You see, we're looking for people around here who know about animals—"

"I don't need any help." The dwarf grunted, eyes closed as he strained. "I've gotten them this far, haven't I?"

"Gotten who where?" Gideon asked.

The dwarf stopped straining, took a breath, and massaged his shoulder with his other hand. "What do you mean?"

"Well, you're saying that you've gotten them this far, but we really have no frame of reference. If you've dragged your llama friends from way outside the city walls, then that's something we can applaud. For all we know, you've dragged them from there," Gideon pointed toward a junction between buildings, just twenty feet away from where they stood, "to here, in which case, it's not as impressive."

Chloe tried to hide her smile but failed.

The dwarf looked as though he'd just been kicked in the face. "Look, *mage*. I'll have you know that I'm one of the strongest damn dwarves in this city. I can haul a rock twice my bodyweight and bench-press my goddamn wife until she falls asleep. I don't need your wise-cracking logic or your approval of my strength to get these goddamn animals to the stables."

"I meant no offense," Gideon said. "Your comment was just ambiguous, is all."

The dwarf couldn't believe what he was hearing.

"Look," Chloe said, stepping between the two and moving closer to the llamas, "let's put a stop to this demonstration of wits versus strength and look at the problem at hand."

The dwarf opened his mouth to protest, but before he could, Chloe continued.

"Sure, you *could* continue to drag these beasts across the city, straining and struggling to make any distance. You could. You definitely could.

"*Or* we could help you on your way and make the whole thing easier. We're not challenging your pride, and we're not saying you *can't* do it, we're just saying it might be easier with some help. How about that?"

The dwarf considered for a moment, curling a finger through his thick beard. A wry grin crawled up his cheeks. "Fine. Let's see how *you* motivate these blockheaded beasts."

Quest unlocked: Stubborn Llamas

This dwarf is having trouble getting his llamas to cooperate with him. Maybe a little gentle persuasion could yield a generous reward?

Difficulty: 1/10

Rewards: 500 exp

Accept quest: Y/N

He offered a lead line to Chloe, but she had already selected Y and was walking to a llama's side. The frontrunner stepped back as she approached, its eyes wary.

"Shhh," Chloe whispered, hand trailing down the thick fluff on its neck. The llama tensed, took another step back, and spat at Chloe.

The spit hit her helmet and dripped down the metal onto the ground. Chloe, however, wasn't fazed.

Chloe searched through her spells-dex and found a spell which might work, something she had learned back in Killink and had yet to try.

This seems as good a time as any.

Chloe closed her eyes and, resting her hand on the llama's neck, she focused on hunting through the mystical etheric swirls in her closed vision, searching and scanning for her familiar, who would act as her gateway into synchronizing with the magical force.

The small rabbit appeared and bounded toward her eagerly. The horn nubs on its head looked like they had grown since the last time she had cast a spell.

Chloe breathed slowly, her hands glowing a warm red as the spell left her fingertips and began to pass into the llama's coat.

"What's she doing? She's staining my livestock!"

Chloe heard Gideon hush the dwarf as she focused, feeling a sudden connection open between herself and the llama. Her **Whisper of the Wild** spell allowed her and the llama to communicate on a very basic level.

She felt anger and frustration, annoyance, and mistrust. With only her thoughts to guide her, she set about injecting positive emotions into the beast, the red aura that surrounded them both beginning to shift ever so slowly from red to orange to yellow, morphing now into blue and then green.

When she opened her eyes, the llama was staring at her, its body completely relaxed.

The dwarf cautiously pulled on the lead and, instead of planting its feet and protesting, the llama took a few easy steps forward.

"What did you do?"

Chloe smiled. "Nothing much. I just took a second to calm her down rather than try to drag her where she didn't want to go. Here, I'll show you again."

Chloe used **Whisper of the Wild** on the other two llamas, leaving the whole pack calm.

"Try it now."

The dwarf did, his eyes widening as the llamas came along willingly. She could see he was already preparing for the battle to continue, but they trotted with him, guided easily by the dwarf. They walked farther in ten seconds than he could have dragged them in ten minutes.

"I...I guess a 'thank you' is in order," the dwarf said, leading his pack through the crammed streets.

The sounds of braying and various animal calls hit their ears almost as soon as the smells did. Located just outside the main gates, the main stables housed a whole range of animals. Chloe was glad to see she was familiar with many of them, only a few being strange adaptations of other animals she had seen.

The dwarf led them deep into the large barn, passing several pens housing horses, deer, and more llamas. He ushered the llamas into the pen, shut the gate, and locked it tight, before wiping his sweating brow on his forearm.

Quest complete: Stubborn Llamas

You did it! Wow, was that one easy. Still, every good deed deserves a reward.

Rewards: 500 exp

"You guys really did me a solid," he said. "If it wasn't for you, I'd still be back there trying to get these beasts in here. The name's Burdock, by the way. I'm not sure I gave that to you.

Chloe smiled. "Chloe."

"Gideon."

"It was nothing, really," she continued. "Happy to help."

"What were you doing with llamas in the city anyway?" Gideon asked. "I can't imagine a scenario in which you'd need animals like these inside the gates unless they were…" His voice trailed away, not wanting to say the rest.

Burdock finished for him. "Dead? Chopped up on a platter and grilled?"

Gideon nodded.

Burdock pulled a dirty cloth from his pocket and rubbed his hands. "There are those within the city who believe that llamas bring certain kinds of luck."

"What kinds of luck?"

"Virility, mostly." Burdock grinned. "Some folks believe that making love in the presence of a llama is a surefire way to make sure a bun appears in the oven. For years, the city has had a problem with illegal llama breeding, particularly in the poorer districts. Some of the rich people will actually pay pretty handsomely to…borrow…a llama in order to improve their chances of conceiving with their wives."

Chloe snorted. "You're kidding?"

"Nope. It's true."

"That's absurd," Gideon said. "Do *you* believe that's true?"

Burdock shrugged. "Who's to say? All I know is that I breed and look after llamas for a living, and me and my missus have ten beautiful children to show for the eighteen years we've been together. I'm not saying that's proof, but…"

"Impressive," Chloe said.

"Thanks." Burdock clapped and startled the animals around him. "Now, how about, as thanks for your assistance, I get the missus to brew up some delicious herbal tea and share her famous bread with you both?"

Gideon's stomach rumbled loudly, the mage only just realizing how hungry he was. "Sounds fantastic."

"Sure," Chloe agreed. "Why not?"

Burdock and Reyner lived in an adorable little house not too far from the stables on an acre of land. In contrast to the stonework of the city, the house was built entirely of wood, with a small porch at the front that overlooked the various pens and enclosures in which their livestock roamed.

"I wasn't expectin' you home for hours," Burdock's wife Reyner said, a look of utter shock on her face when she opened the door.

"You say that like you have a boy toy inside and I interrupted you." Burdock stuck out his tongue.

Reyner flicked a towel affectionately at his shoulder, then invited them all inside.

She busied herself in the kitchen with the drinks, boiling water in a pan and adding her particular blend of herbs. Soon she came through with a tray laden with thick loaves of bread and cups filled with the most sweet-smelling liquid Chloe had ever encountered.

"This is delicious," Chloe said after taking her first bite of the bread. "And the tea...dee-licious."

Gideon nodded in agreement.

Chloe swallowed her bite, then said, "I thought you said you had children? Are they upstairs?"

"One of them is," Reyner said. "Has his nose in his books, as usual."

Burdock chuckled. "The rest of them are out and about, doing their chores. I'm not sure how family works where you're from, but folks in Obsidian tend to be put to work pretty young. As soon as they can put their hands to labor, they're a part of society, helping keep the great cogs turning. They'll likely be back around suppertime, but for now, it's just young Durton upstairs, studying every damn sentence of those books we got him last winter.

"Can you believe the guilds were tossing out their stock? Getting rid of the old editions to make room for the new?"

Reyner shook her head. "What a waste."

"And what about you two?" Burdock continued.

"What about us?" Gideon asked.

"Two young adventurers like yourselves must be on some fascinating quest, am I right? No offense, but the folks of Hammersworth certainly don't dress top to tail in armor unless they've got questing to do."

"Yeah, we're on a quest, all right," Chloe confirmed. "Me, Gideon, and our party. That's actually why we're here in Hammersworth; we're searching for someone who we've been told might be able to help us. When we saw you struggling with those llamas, we actually thought you might be able to lead us to him."

"I *knew* you'd need help," Reyner said, smacking Burdock on the arm. "You and your pride…" She leaned toward Chloe and Gideon. "I offered to come with him, but did he want my help? *Nooo.*"

"Reyner," Burdock hissed, "can we do this later?"

His wife sat back with a smug expression on her face.

Burdock rubbed a hand over his tired face. "And who is this man you're looking for? I mean, I'll try to help if I can, but we tend to keep ourselves to ourselves on the outer edges of the city."

"We've been told he's known as 'The Wrangler,'" Chloe said, remembering the description Prince Gilligan had given them before they set off from Killink View. "A large man who dwarfs…I'm sorry, I mean, who makes others seem tiny and has a reputation for wrangling animals and studying them."

"Do you know him?" Gideon asked.

Reyner and Burdock looked at each other, eyes narrowed.

"A tall man who's good with animals?" Reyner mused.

Burdock stuck out his lip, his head shaking gently. "Doesn't ring a bell. I know the Chestertons across the way deal a lot in more bovines, and the Yolans specialize in fowl."

Reyner clicked her fingers. "What about that gentleman Doris Yolan mentioned last time we invited them over for supper? The bear-like man who showed interest in her peacocks?"

"Hmm…maybe."

"What did she say, Mrs. Reyner?" Chloe asked, intrigued.

"Oh, please. Reyner is just fine," the woman said. "She said he appeared late one afternoon as the shadows were lengthening. Knocked on her door and inquired after her prize peacocks. I don't blame him, of course. They are something to behold. She was frightened out of her wits, but after a short conversation, she learned that he had no ill intentions. She showed the peacocks to the man and told him all about her history with breeding them, and after a short time, he left."

"Where did he go?" Chloe asked.

Reyner shrugged. "I don't know. You'll have to ask Doris. She should be home about now if that's of any use to you?"

Chloe and Gideon finished their drinks and bread and followed Reyner's directions to the small house on the east side of the outer wall, where an old woman was busily hoeing the garden.

"Can I help you both?" she asked as they approached.

They told Doris they had been sent by Reyner and filled her in on their discussion.

"Oh, I remember that man. Terrifying to behold. Thick, muscular, large."

Gideon swallowed. "How large are we talking?"

"Oh, *huge*," she said, studying Gideon. "At least twice your height, and thrice your girth."

"Do you know where he went?" Chloe asked.

Doris eyed her suspiciously, peeking through the slats of Chloe's helmet and straight into her eyes beneath. "You two some kind of bounty hunters or something? Did I do wrong, talking to the man? He never gave me no trouble, I assure you. Just appeared, studied my precious peacocks, and went back off into the night. I never had nothing else to do with him, I swear."

"Relax," Gideon said. "We're not bounty hunters, we're just on a hunt for a man who matches your description. You're in no trouble, Miss Yolan."

"It's *Mrs.* Yolan," she said. "Well, if that's the case, he went over yonder." She pointed across a field to the tree line, toward a break that indicated the road which passed through.

"Are you sure?"

Doris nodded. "Positive. I remember because I watched him for what felt like hours. Usually when folks head toward the forest, after a short time, you can't see them anymore because they've disappeared over the horizon. But this guy I remember watching. I kept expecting him to disappear, but his great shape was visible for a long time, and that's the way he went."

"Well, that's very useful," Chloe said, rising to her feet. She stared out the window toward the forest. "He didn't say where he was going, did he?"

Doris shook her head. "No."

Chloe and Gideon thanked Doris for her help and paused a short way away from her property. The sun was still high in the sky, the fields around alive with activity as the locals worked the land and tended their livestock. As they stared toward the forest, they heard footsteps shuffling behind them.

"Wait," Doris said, out of breath from the short journey from her yard.

Chloe and Gideon turned, watching the woman walk-jog toward them. "There is one more thing."

Chloe waited expectantly.

"The man you're looking for? He spent a great deal of time looking at my peacocks." She turned toward a pen where several large brown birds were pecking at the ground. "He admired their beautiful plumage. Said he'd never seen anything like it. To be honest, most folks who see my peacocks say the same thing. I don't think they breed in any other part of the land."

One of the peacocks raised its tail, its feathers brown and dull.

Gideon cocked an eyebrow.

"Oh, not those," Doris laughed. "My pride and joy, Fernando. He's the one strutting out of the coop now."

They all stared at the dazzling blue and green bird descending a short wooden ladder. He made his way to the females and shook vigorously, then fanned his tail in a spectacular array of multi-colored feathers.

"He is really something, isn't he?" Doris smiled.

"He sure is," Chloe agreed. "But what has this got to do with your tall man?"

"Well," Doris returned her attention to the others. "Before he left, he mentioned that he might swing by before the next full moon to catch another glimpse of Fernando. He had a large bag of coin strapped to his belt, and I got the feeling he was considering purchasing my baby boy from me at a later date."

"Wow. Would you sell him?"

Doris shook her head. "Not in a million years."

They thanked Doris once more, letting her know that they'd be by to visit again. They asked if she would be able to find a way to let them know if she got wind of the man, and she agreed to send a raven should there be a sign.

They gave their address at the inn, then headed back into the city. They had a while to go before they would be meeting the others, but they felt as though they'd made progress toward finding their target.

"Where to now?" Gideon asked, filing past the gate guards and scanning the streets.

"Arizona mentioned something about a mages' school here. Do you think we should go explore? Maybe see if they've got any Guardians here we could potentially learn from?"

Gideon nodded. "Definitely."

His hand clutched his stomach as it rumbled loudly again.

"Maybe we should get something to eat first?"

"Already?" Chloe laughed.

CHAPTER THREE

The sounds of celebration filled the air.

Veronica heard it from afar—the drums, the trumpets, and the cheering. Even from the small maze of alleys she found herself lost in, she could hear the festivities.

"What have these people got to be so cheery about?" Huk's gravelly voice croaked. "A city with no working plumbing or chocolate? I'd have killed myself years ago."

"Why don't you go ahead and do it, then?" Therese smirked.

Veronica found herself smiling as she ushered the others through the streets.

For the first time since joining the KieraSlayers, Veronica found herself alone with her original party. Well, not party, exactly, given that the group had never quite had enough members to form an official party.

They had been one person short when the exclusively party mission to defeat the dreyda had been announced and they had tagged along with the KieraSlayers out of desperation, wanting the experience of completing the mission.

At the time, Veronica had agreed reluctantly, wanting to remain the leader of her group, but she soon found that life was good under

Chloe's leadership. The groups had bonded and learned from each other. Chloe had a way of leveraging everyone's strengths and overcoming their weaknesses, and the party had become a well-oiled machine.

Still, it was nice to go back to basics and spend some time with Huk, Therese, and Leonie.

"This way," she called, squeezing through the crowded streets.

There was confetti in the air, and the music was louder now.

All around her, people craned their necks and rose on their toes. She might've worried that she'd lose Huk and Therese, the goblin and the dwarf being several feet shorter than the warrior and the cleric, but the rest of the crowd was comprised primarily of dwarves, with the exception of the odd human or elf.

Then Veronica saw it ahead. She paused at the thin rope holding the crowd back and marveled at the horse-drawn carriages working their way through the streets. Riders cloaked in gold held their heads high as those being driven waved out the windows.

A smile crept onto her face. "What the hell is going on?"

"It's Union Day!" A person Veronica mistook for a small girl shouted to her. She realized a moment later it was a female dwarf.

"What does that mean?"

"These are suitors for the king!" The dwarf clapped giddily.

"A whole year since he became king, already?" Her friend replied. "I can't believe it's gone so fast."

The first dwarf sighed. "I wish *I* could be in those carriages."

Veronica chuckled. The dwarven maidens sat sullenly inside the carriages, shadowed by their enthusiastic chaperones.

Something tugged Veronica's sleeve.

"Excuse me, miss. I can't see."

Veronica moved to step out of the way. "Oh, sorry, I—"

She stopped when she saw Therese bawling with laughter.

"You!"

"Come on," Huk said, trying to hide his own chuckles. "With any luck, the shrine will be empty, with all these people standing around in the street."

Veronica reluctantly turned away, heading back the way they had come. The music played behind them as the procession continued, dwarves and other locals passing them as they worked their way out of the crowd and took a right at the next intersection.

They had been looking for the shrine all morning. Despite the four-part structure of the city, Hammersworth was a large place, and there were no maps to make their hunt easier.

They paused and asked for directions. What they received was mildly helpful if a little vague and confusing, and soon they found themselves standing between a series of large fountains on a white-washed path leading to a large temple.

Leonie tucked a lock of blonde hair behind her ear. "I was beginning to genuinely think we'd never find this place."

"I never doubted it for a second," Therese shot back.

"Liar." Huk snorted. When Veronica asked him to explain, he was silent.

They made their way up the stairs toward the temple doors. It was calm around them, the music of the parade lost in the city. Clerics and other classes roamed in reverence, pausing at the fountains and occasionally closing their eyes to just breathe in the air.

Inside the temple, it was much the same, an even larger fountain taking center stage. A large basin at the bottom caught the overspill of an upper basin ten feet above it. Taking pride of place in the center was a carved tableau of every god imaginable.

Veronica recognized a few of them, but she hadn't had the chance to learn about every god the game had to offer. It seemed there was someone for every element of life, and with just a quick glance, she could guess what a few of the gods embodied.

"Impressive, isn't it?" a soft voice said from beside her.

Veronica snapped out of her thoughts, surprised to see a robed woman. She was as wide as she was tall, and her face was friendly.

"How many are there?"

"There are different tallies, depending on who you choose to listen to. Me? I choose not to number the immortals, for there can never be an end. The gods have bred and multiplied since the beginning, and who knows what great divine plan is in place to bring upon us more guardians?"

The woman smiled, radiant warmth emanating from her presence. "Hi, I'm Elisia, the Elder of this temple."

Veronica introduced herself and the others.

"What brings you all to our little slice of paradise? I remember every face that has entered this hall, and I'm confident that I've never seen you folks before. Adventurers, judging by your attire and demeanor."

"Oh, she's good," Huk whispered.

"We are just visiting," Veronica said. "We are new to the city and wanted to get our bearings. My first ports of call are always the temples and shrines. There's no better way to get a grip on where you are than to associate yourself with the shortest paths to the gods."

Elisia smiled. "Amen."

"We'd also *love* to take advantage of your fast-travel spot," Therese added rather abrasively.

Veronica looked mortified. "'Take advantage' is a crass term. She means we would love the opportunity to make use of the facilities. We've traveled a long way, and we'd hate for our journey to be for naught."

Elisia chuckled. "No offense taken. I understand entirely. We've had a lot of blessed pass our way recently, so I'm no stranger to your ways. Come, let me show you around."

Elisia led them around the temple, passing various open arches leading to shrines dedicated to the different gods. Once they had connected with the fast travel spot, she asked to whom they would each like to pay their tributes.

Since Huk and Therese had never aligned themselves with a god and didn't plan to make a decision then and there, they said they would wait outside in the sunshine for the others.

Leonie, on the other hand, asked to pay her respects to Meruer, knowing that, for warriors, paying tribute to the God of War often granted temporary boons and enhancements to their attacks, strength, and ability to level their swordsmanship at a faster rate.

Veronica watched her leave, wondering what she would find when paying homage to him.

"And you?"

Veronica considered this, wondering if she was really making a wise decision. Ever since leaving Killink View, she thought about her alignment with the gods and who best to try to communicate with to improve their prospect of success in their mission.

For well over a week, she had tried to communicate with Meruer. As KieraFreya's father, Meruer seemed the likely option to try to discover more about KieraFreya's path and the rocky moments before KieraFreya had been divided into pieces and thrown back down to earth.

But she had had no luck. There had been no response whatsoever. It was as if he simply refused to pick up on the call.

Or maybe you just aren't strong enough to communicate with the gods at will?

"I'll be honest, I'm torn," Veronica stated. "I've paid homage to a great many gods, and I'm still undecided about who best to dedicate my life to."

"Well, sweet one, you know that only through true dedication can a cleric grow her skill set and develop in her class. Ambiguity and indecisiveness are no paths to take. What is it that holds you back?"

Veronica chewed her lip. "See, I'm struggling to feel a true connection to the goddess of my choice, KieraFreya. In prayer and contemplation, she evades me entirely, and her father, Meruer, is just as evasive."

Elisia nodded in understanding. "The gods can be slippery, which highlights the need for sole dedication. Perhaps they sense your doubt and anguish."

"Perhaps. Maybe I just need to find members of the family who *will* communicate."

"The families of the gods are tight-knit and small," Elisia explained. "The trick is to not explore the family ties and beat around the bush, but to be specific. Target. Find out what elements appeal to you most, and see what you can bring out of yourself to further their influence on this world."

She grasped Veronica's shoulders, peering deeply into her eyes. "Tell me, what do you desire more than anything else in the world?"

Veronica was caught off-guard. She felt light-headed. Without hesitating, she said, "Love."

Elisia chuckled, breaking her gaze. The spell lifted off Veronica. "As I suspected, and a wise choice, too."

She placed a hand on her back and ushered the cleric toward a room with an arch decorated with roses and flowers. Around the bottom of the walls were brightly-colored flower arrangements, many shaped into hearts.

Elisia stopped in front of this room's fountain, which featured a carved man and woman naked and locked in the throes of lovemaking above the tumbling waters.

"Oella is the goddess you seek. The mother. The founder. One of the sovereigns. It is through her open embrace that you will find what you desire.

Veronica stared silently at the fountain. She had heard of Oella, Goddess of Love, along her travels. The sovereign gods were the most important for new and budding clerics to become familiar with, but she had never thought of aligning with a goddess who was centered on such a fleeting emotion as love.

"Are you certain, Elder?" Veronica asked, realizing that Elisia was already at the doorway behind her.

"Oh, yes, child, I'm certain. Who better to guide you toward your clerical specialization than KieraFreya's mother?"

When she saw Veronica's shocked face, she added, "Maybe you'll have more luck reaching *this* goddess."

With that, she silently exited the room.

CHAPTER FOUR

Demetri woke up to an empty bed and the sound of frantic typing.

He blinked stupidly in the glow of the morning sun, wondering why his alarm hadn't gone off. He'd had a night filled with the strangest dreams, and felt like he'd been in bed for hours.

A quick look at his clock told him that it was 6:55am, five minutes before the alarm was due to ring.

Shaking away his grogginess, he reset the alarm, then sat up in bed and stretched, remembering it was his day off. One of those rare days on which he was out of the office for the entire day, which took place once a week at most.

He pulled on his pants and a crumpled tee and found Mia at the kitchen counter, her laptop open, her eyes wide and glued to the screen.

"You look frazzled," Demetri said, planting a kiss on her cheek as he made for the coffee pot and began brewing a fresh pot. "You've been up all night."

"I know, I know," Mia said, waving Demetri's comment away.

"Again."

"Mmhmm."

When the coffee was ready, Demetri poured some into the cup, then pivoted and rested with his back against the counter. "You know, you used to bitch at me for doing that."

A pause. "What?"

"Working too much."

Mia looked over the top of her screen, eyes shadowed and dark. "Don't start."

Demetri held up his hands in surrender. "I'm not."

He watched her for a few minutes, moving the mouse around the screen, occasionally jabbing fingers at the worn keyboard. Her phone would flash and draw her attention, then something on the screen would draw her back.

Demetri let out a long breath and made his way back over to Mia. He stood behind her, lacing his hands around her waist.

"You know you can take a break, right?"

Mia didn't reply.

"Sweetie?"

Mia finished typing the email she was working on, then hit Send. The email flew into the corner of the screen, leaving behind a black background with various lines of multi-colored code on it.

Mia exhaled, rubbing a hand over her eyes. "I'm sorry, it's just… there's so much to do. There's not just the AI versus the gods situation to look at, but I'm being contacted by every friggin' inferior in the company, asking for advice and solutions." She turned to Demetri and kissed him on the lips. "Five more minutes, baby. I promise."

She joined Demetri almost an hour later. By that point, he was watching Chloe on the projector in the study, scrolling through the comment boxes and checking out the latest ratings and standings of *Obsidian* and its key players on his laptop.

Mia hovered in the doorway.

"Well? Are we going?"

Demetri laughed. They had arranged to spend the day walking around the city park, and maybe stopping at Mia's favorite restaurant for lunch.

Demetri raised his eyebrows.

"I'm sorry," Mia said, realizing how she had sounded. "It's just…I'm so tired."

"C'mon," Demetri replied, leading Mia to her coat and shoes. "The fresh air will do you good."

They were outside for the better part of half an hour before Mia complained that she needed to go home. Her eyes were drooping as they walked, the fresh morning air doing nothing to wake her up.

They made their way back to the apartment. Demetri took a seat in his study chair, and Mia collapsed instantly as her butt touched his lap.

"I don't know if I'm cut out for this," Mia said. "I was sure that Devlin was a shitty manager, and now I'm learning that his role was impossible. I'm just as bad as he was."

Demetri thought back to the weedy, up-his-own-ass jerk who had attended the meeting at the Lagarde offices with Mia and him. The guy who did no work and took all the company benefits he could.

"No way," Demetri assured her. "You're not a terrible manager. You're a *new* manager."

"That's the difference?"

"A new manager hasn't yet learned to delegate. You know how you used to complain about Devlin never doing work? That was because he passed it all down to you guys. When you take over from a manager, you have to be strong and not take all the work that gets pushed back up to you. If you take up everyone's slack, you'll have no time for your own work."

Mia nodded. "I *am* getting a lot of questions and issues."

"So delegate. Put someone else in the line of fire. You're a *manager* now. Free your time up to work on the stuff you're meant to be doing. The important stuff."

Mia nodded slowly, realization sinking in. "I *am* on the cusp of something big with the AI; I can feel it. I found an entire sheet of code that had self-generated a few days ago. It could be big, but I haven't had the chance to analyze it properly yet. Too busy putting out fires."

"Hire a fireman."

Mia looked up at Demetri. "You could be my fireman."

"I'll be whatever you want me to be." He smirked.

They kissed. Something moved on the screen, and Demetri's attention was pulled to the image of Chloe and Gideon standing outside a small farmhouse, with a pen in the background that had some kind of birds roaming around.

"Funny," he mused. "The ebb and flow of video games. One minute, their lives are on the line, and there are fires and monsters and armies. The next, they're sipping herbal tea with old ladies in the wilds. I wonder what the drinks taste like in Obsidian? Do you get to program taste, too?"

Demetri's voice trailed away as he looked down and saw Mia snoozing quietly on his lap.

Chloe and Gideon shielded their eyes as they exited the mages' school.

They had spent several hours studying in the dim candlelit gloom of the school's library, and now their eyes struggled to adjust.

It had been a fruitless afternoon, the books on the shelves yielding little in the way of history and lore that might help them track down KieraFreya's missing companion.

Chloe had hoped they might find something that detailed the powers of the gods and how they related to the etheric, but instead, she and Gideon had been distracted by the array of spells and incantations they had found in the books, the pages of which nearly all were torn and damaged.

"If you want pristine resources, try going to the Mages' Academy," a surly mage had grumbled to Gideon after he had asked what had happened to all the books. "We do what we can."

"Perhaps there's another library? A public one with resources on the ancients?" KieraFreya suggested as they made their way back through the city. "The mages' educational facilities can't be the only places with books."

"We'll try tomorrow," Chloe replied. "We promised the others we'd be back ten minutes ago. Maybe they've had more luck than we have."

Chloe fell into thought as they traveled back, not in the least disappointed that they hadn't found what they were looking for but wondering why they hadn't stumbled across a single Guardian at the school.

A small part of her had hoped they would find Hammersworth's equivalent of Arizona. Someone who would be able to help them further harness their etheric powers and teach them even greater control.

In Killink, Arizona had spoken of levels of magedom, and a small glance at her teachings had made Chloe hungry for more. What she wouldn't give to have her here right now!

After several wrong turns and a lot of asking for directions, they eventually made it back to the inn. They found the others sitting on a bench outside the door to the inn, each with a drink in their hands.

"Hey, you made it, then? Thought you might've got caught up in the festivities." Huk laughed, raising his glass at their arrival.

"Shut up." Therese chuckled, waving them over. "Come on, we got your drinks already. Good thing they ain't coffee or tea since they'd have gone cold ages ago."

Chloe and Gideon took seats.

"What do you mean, 'festivities?'" Chloe asked. "We've seen nothing going on."

Veronica explained about the parade they'd seen in the center of the city. She asked how Chloe and Gideon hadn't seen it since they had been heading that way to start with.

"We got waylaid," Gideon replied.

"As usual." Therese grinned.

Leonie turned in her chair. "Okay, what happened?"

Chloe and Gideon proceeded to tell them all about their excursion with Burdock and Reyner, including the information they had found out about Doris and her visitor. When they were done, Leonie leaned forward and said, "How weird."

Ben, who had been quiet until that point, nodded in agreement. "It does sound pretty strange. He's an elusive character. Even the Rangers' Guild has nothing to say about him, other than they've heard of his arrivals. He's like a whisper in the breeze, a man of myth who keeps to himself."

"No," Leonie said. "I mean, it's weird that peacocks are rare here. Where I live, they breed them like chickens and roosters. They stand on shed roofs and scream at the morning sun."

"How the hell are we supposed to find him, then?" Therese asked. "This whole thing is just another wild goose chase."

"*Peacock* chase," Talbot said, chuckling into his glass and stopping only when Gideon finished their tale by telling them that Doris was expecting him to return before the next full moon.

"So, what?" Huk asked. "We keep an eye on the old hag until the man appears again?"

Chloe elbowed Huk. "Don't be like that. She's a lovely lady. And that's not what I'm suggesting. She's a breeder of fowl and birds, and has messenger ravens she'll send to this address when she hears from him again. Until then, we can either go off on our own adventures into the forest or hang around the city and hone our skills."

"I vote for both," Ben said. He looked worn out, as though a good sleep wouldn't be too far away. "The Hammersworth Rangers' Guild is close-knit and specialized. I've gained more experience with them in one day than I might have in a week elsewhere. They have masters who are willing to teach, and I am willing to learn."

"Then how is that 'both?'" Leonie asked. "If you're gaining skills with the rangers, you're not looking for the Wrangler."

"Where do you think the rangers train?" Ben asked.

"You mean—"

"Yep."

"Then it's decided," Chloe said after draining the last of her drink. "Hammersworth is home, for now. We all need to improve our skills while we have a chance. Considering the last showdown we had, I have a feeling any additional bonuses and boosts we can get will be absolutely vital for survival. Remember, we had a god working against us. Imagine what our next obstacle might be?"

Everyone nodded in agreement, then started chattering about their day and what they were hoping to achieve tomorrow. A short while later, they began peeling off one by one to go to bed as the sky grew dark and the air turned chilly.

"Chloe?" Veronica asked, grabbing Chloe's arm before she broke free of the group.

"Yeah?"

"Can we talk?" She nodded to those still on the bench. "In private?"

Chloe followed Veronica to her bedroom. Once she was inside, Veronica closed the door and offered Chloe a seat on the ottoman at the bottom of the bed.

Chloe accepted.

"What is it?" Chloe asked.

"So, I found something out today. Something pretty big that might be of some use to your mission."

"*Our* mission."

Veronica tilted her head. "Come on, we might all get the experience, but we know it's your mission. You were the one who kicked it all off, the one who united us all. Just admit it's yours."

"What did you discover?"

"Yeah," KieraFreya said, "stop beating around the bush. We're all pretty tired, here. Aren't we?"

KieraFreya's words had the opposite of the desired effect on Veronica, who was still not used to the enchanted armor talking to her.

"Well?" Chloe encouraged.

Veronica took a breath, then told Chloe about her visit to the temple. Told her of her experience with Elisia, and the information she had received about KieraFreya's parentage.

Chloe gasped.

"My...mother?" KieraFreya wondered. "I can't believe I forgot who my own mother was!"

"Come on, KF," Chloe reassured her. "We're piecing you back together. We'll get there, I promise. Don't take it personally that you forgot something like that."

"Would you forget *your* mother?" KieraFreya asked.

Chloe considered. On some level, she would rather forget the woman who had turned cold and discordant during her lifetime. Maybe then she could imagine a warmer and more nurturing upbringing.

But would she *truly* like to forget her? Probably not.

"No," she said quietly.

"Exactly," For the first time, they could hear genuine frustration in KieraFreya's voice. "I can't even remember her right now. I can't picture her face. I can't imagine what my upbringing must have been like. I try and try, and all I see are dark clouds."

Chloe nodded. "I can confirm that."

"Well, you're in luck, because I think I can fill in some of the blanks," Veronica said.

"Are you telling us that you managed to patch through to Oweylo?"

"*Oella.*"

"Sure, her too."

Veronica nodded. "I did."

"Well?" Chloe rose to her feet, her armor pushing her forward excitedly. "What happened? What did she say?"

Veronica went into the story, describing her experience of prayer in the temple. After fifteen minutes of silence, Veronica had been about to give up trying, but just as she was about to leave, Oella answered her calls.

"Her voice was kind and sweet. Husky and nurturing. Every syllable filled my heart with a warmth I've never felt. A love that only a parent could give."

"Lucky for you." KieraFreya sneered.

Oella spoke to Veronica, asking what questions she had to ask and how she could help within her limitations. Veronica mentioned Chloe's and KieraFreya's quest, eliciting a sharp intake of breath from Oella. The goddess was elated at the news of her attempted reassembly and offered encouragement and luck to bring her home to her family.

"I asked her if she could help. If she had any knowledge of the location of your horse or the reason for your banishment."

"And?" KieraFreya urged. "What did she say?"

Veronica sighed. "She said that knowledge remained locked away with your father and that she was bound not to divulge any information that could either jeopardize or further the quest. She told me that as much as she loves and misses you, she could not violate what has already been signed and sealed."

"'Signed and sealed?'" Chloe mused. "Do you think that has something to do with the agreement you made with Fukmos?"

KieraFreya shrugged Chloe's shoulders. "I don't know."

"Was that it? Was there anything more…helpful?"

Veronica gave a small nod. "She said that while she was unable to help us find what has been lost, she could confirm that you are on the right path."

"Useful," KieraFreya grumbled.

"She also said that as long as you believe in the nine, your mission will be successful, and you will find your way home."

"The nine? What the hell are the nine?"

Veronica shrugged.

Chloe sighed. "Well, thanks, Veronica. At least we made some kind of contact with the almighty beings above."

"Yeah," KieraFreya whined. "Great use that is."

"There was one last thing," Veronica said, stopping Chloe from leaving the room mid-turn. "She said that as long as you keep your courage, your mission will be successful, and you will find the home you seek."

"Gee." KieraFreya snorted. "Thanks, Mom."

Veronica shook her head, staring into Chloe's eyes. "She wasn't talking about you, KF."

CHAPTER FIVE

Ben took a deep lungful of fresh, clean air.

The forest was peaceful, calm hanging across the leafy canopy. All around them were the sounds of birdsong as they trod silently through the undergrowth.

There was a flicker of movement. Ben looked beside him, where Anok, a fellow ranger of the guild, motioned him over with a series of complex hand signals. He nodded, following his gestures to where three more blurs of green moved stealthily ahead.

Ben's smile grew wider. He loved the outdoors, and as much as it pained him to admit it, he preferred traversing the forests to trundling around stone cities for days on end. Give him his bow, the fresh, clean air, and the sounds of nature any day of the week.

The rest of the party could explore and hunt for answers in Hammersworth. Ben was where rangers belonged.

A bird call reached his ears, musical and rich in tone—the leopard-spotted warbler. Not from a real bird, no. It was the agreed-upon signal of Rogan, the head of the party, as he led the others ever deeper ahead.

The rangers were a complicated class. Often, they enjoyed solo exploration, roaming the land and communing with nature. The rangers of Obsidian were the guardians of the natural world and took their cues from the animals and plants that inhabited the earth.

Yet, occasionally, the guild would come together on group missions. They were the best when it came to hunting, able to take down their targets with minimal damage to the carcasses. When they worked together, they could bring down even the largest, most fearsome predators.

That worked out very well for the stomachs of the city's monarchs, who had acquired a certain taste for the unusual and exotic.

Anok offered another signal. Without a sound, Ben ducked behind a tree, mimicking the signals to the rangers following behind, a mixture of NPCs and blessed. The most experienced were at the front and back, with those who were in need of additional support and training in the middle.

Ben was near the front of the party, having gained several ranks within the last twenty-four hours.

With a nod, the rangers obeyed Ben's signal, blending perfectly with the trees.

The call of the warbler again. Ben closed his eyes, listening to the sounds of the forest. The whispering call of the wind, the utterances of the leaves in the trees.

A twig broke nearby, and he knew they'd found their target. The bulky creature was somewhere ahead. Maybe fifty feet, if he had to guess.

The party of rangers remained still. Ben chanced a peek past the bough and saw a shadow moving some distance ahead.

The call of the warbler was replaced by another sound—sharp, shrill tweeting. Ben watched as several rangers began to shinny up the trees, the only indication of their presence the blur of their cloaks as they ascended.

Ben's adrenaline began to kick in, his battle instincts already psyching him up for the struggle.

Another tweet.

The sound of a body falling.

"Ooof!" came the exhalation of a ranger behind him. The sound echoed loudly around them.

Ben turned and saw the blur of green as the young ranger scrambled to his feet, the expression on his pale pink face one of embarrassment and shock. Ben recognized him as one of the newbies to Obsidian. Kurt, if he remembered correctly. The kid hadn't even specialized yet, but he was putting in the time to learn the craft and improve over his level 10.

Kurt's lips spoke a silent, "I'm sorry," and he began to clamber up the tree again.

But it was too late. A second later, a large blur of dark fur sprinted past Ben, finding its way toward Kurt and leaping up the tree. Kurt cried out as several rows of small but sharp teeth found the flesh of his leg and tugged him down.

"Now!" Rogan shouted.

The creature's eyes grew wide as arrows rained down from the canopy. Ben stepped out into firing range, loosing his arrow and marveling at the creature, which was now thrashing around on the spot, kicking its legs and snapping its jaws at every ranger it caught sight of.

It was large, about twice the size of a horse. It stomped and pivoted on four canine-like legs, its neck longer than it should have been. Across its spine, thick, bristling fur made its way toward a ravenous maw, its jaws dripping saliva as it tried to get its bearings.

"Remember your instructions," Rogan shouted over the snarls and growls. "Aim for the eyes!"

Ben closed one eye and placed his focus on sending the arrow directly at the creature's face. Arrow after arrow from his bow bounced off the creature's tough hide, just a few burying themselves an inch or so, the arrows not quite able to pierce the warg's body.

The shot was almost impossible, made even harder by the warg's constant thrashing. Its thick brow hung over its eyes like a protective canopy.

Ben would have to get closer to make the shot.

Kurt cried out in fear, retreating toward the bushes, using his good leg to kick his way there. His groans attracted the attention of the warg.

The creature snarled, licking its lips. It ducked its head, its eyes now out of sight of the rangers in the canopy. It closed the gap quickly, wanting to grab its prey and disappear. Its defense mechanisms relied on dragging the broken and frail to a quiet place to dine.

Ben sprinted forward, aware of someone running beside him.

"Don't think you're going to get all the glory, fresh-blood." Anok grinned, matching Ben's stride.

"Two heads are better than one," Ben replied, returning Anok's smile. "It's good to have you at my side."

"Remember, you're at *my* side."

Ben returned his attention to the warg, distressed to see that creature had Kurt's leg back in his mouth. With a burst of speed, he leaped, grabbed the bough of the nearest tree, shinnied rapidly higher, and kicked off with one leg, soaring through the air toward the beast.

He landed on the warg's back, one leg half-hanging off the side. The creature noticed the new arrival and turned his head, snapping glistening jaws at Ben, who twisted, grabbed a tuft of fur, and held on for dear life.

"A little help?" Ben called as an arrow flew toward him, bouncing off the creature just a few inches away from the ranger's hand. "Come on!"

"I got you!" Anok cried. His movements were a blur as he charged toward the warg, kicking out his legs at the last minute and sliding beneath the creature's belly.

The warg roared in frustration, undecided who to attack first. Ben took advantage of the distraction, swinging back onto the warg until he was atop its broad back.

The creature kicked and bucked. Ben held on, unaware that beneath him, his comrade had withdrawn his elven knives and was now desperately attacking the creature's underbelly.

The knives made slow progress. Anok had to continually take breaks to roll and slither around to stop the warg from chomping his flesh. The only real compensation at that moment was that several other rangers had rescued Kurt and dragged him away.

Ben scooted forward, working his way toward the warg's neck. Progress was slow, but he made it. When he reached the place where the neck joined the shoulders, he clutched a large tuft of the dark hair running down the center of the beast's neck and tugged as hard as he could.

The warg shrieked, its neck curving until it was facing the sky. At the same time, it felt the knives finally break the skin of its stomach.

"Fire at will!" Ben shouted, biceps bulging with the effort of holding the warg in place.

A volley of arrows rained from the trees, several of them finding their way into the warg's face. Its eyes were the first to go, and a handful of arrows found their way down the creature's throat.

The creature relaxed, its legs started to buckle.

"Anok, get out of there," he called needlessly, discovering a second later that the blood-covered Anok stood beside the warg's shaking body.

The monster went down with a crash, and there was a chorus of cheers from several of the newer additions to the team. Even Ben laughed, clapping his hands as he dismounted.

"Not bad," he said to Anok.

Anok nodded. "Not bad yourself."

"You stink."

"I've smelled worse." Anok laughed.

Ben looked at the other rangers, curious about the few who refused to clap and celebrate their kill.

"What's with them? Don't they know how to have fun?"

Rogan appeared from behind the trees. An ugly scar ran from his nose to his chin. His voice was deep and authoritative as he said, "Oh, they do. They celebrate when the job is done."

"What do you mean?" Ben asked, confused. "We caught one. We took it down and can now deliver the meat to the king, right?"

A crooked grin reached Anok's face.

"What?" Ben asked.

Rogan indicated that Anok should speak. "You haven't encountered wargs before, have you? Taking one warg down doesn't do a whole lot. They're pack hunters that work in teams. Why do you think so many of us gathered today to take them down?"

Them?

Ben heard the sinister growls of several more wargs. He could now count seven of the beasts surrounding them, each as huge and loathsome as the one they had taken down.

Rogan snorted, grimacing. "Right on cue."

"Positions!" Anok called, and the surrounding rangers wasted no time in finding their formations. Those who were halfway down the trees scrambled back up, glad to have drawn the long straws in this fight.

Game on, Ben thought.

The wargs crept closer, clearly in no hurry to rush their prey. Their leader, a warg with night-black fur and battle scars on its flank, stood taller than the others. It sniffed the air, its maw leaking viscous fluid.

Ben slowly nocked two arrows. If he was right in his thinking, he might just be able to take out both eyes with a single shot. He'd have to time it right, knowing that they were now playing a game of chicken, each side waiting for the other to make the first move.

The dark warg crouched, its muscles tensing, ready to leap. Its tongue danced across its lips, eyes fixed on Ben's.

Ben's breathing was steady and calm, prepared for whatever was to come. His fingers began to relax on the string, the arrow ready to fly…

Suddenly the air was filled with the strange cry of a creature they had never heard before. The noise sounding like an elephant trumpeting, only brought down to deep bass notes, and it had the rumbling vibrato of a lion's roar.

The wargs' ears pricked, their heads turning toward a dark figure who stood some distance away. It looked like a man, but it was difficult to discern.

The dark warg spared a longing glance back at Ben before snapping its jaws and signaling to the others. It led the way, turning on its heels and leaping into the forest.

"What the…" was all Ben could manage.

Anok returned to Ben's side, staring at the dark figure, who appeared to have morphed into the shape of a colossal bear.

"What is that?" one of the rangers asked, his voice a breathy whisper.

Ben became aware of Rogan standing beside him, eyes narrowed. "He goes by many names." He turned back the way they had come. "Come. Pick up the carcass, and let's return. We've come as far as we can today."

The rangers wordlessly obeyed. Ben, however, couldn't help but spare one last glance toward where the figure had stood, only to find that he was now gone.

***

"It had to be him." Therese stroked her chin thoughtfully. "Who else could it have been?"

Leonie spoke up. "No one said anything about him being able to *control* animals. That just seems absurd."

Ben shrugged. He took a long draught of his drink and placed it back down on the table. He had been happy with the experience he had gathered on the rangers' expedition today, but he had to admit that he was all kinds of confused by what had happened out there.

"It's not impossible that someone can control animals," Gideon mused. "There are spells and incantations that can influence nature." He glanced at Chloe. "You calmed the llamas yesterday. Do you remember reading anything in the original spell book about advanced versions of **Whisper of the Wild** ?"

"Llamas are slightly different than friggin' wargs." Talbot scoffed. "Give me a glob of spit in the face over the saliva of a hungry warg any day."

Gideon and Chloe giggled, remembering the llama who had spat at Chloe's face. "I'm not so sure," the battle mage said.

"Even so." Therese brought the conversation back around. "What does it matter? So, we know he's in the woods? He *might* or *might not* come back to Doris' house by the full moon? What can we do with that information? It doesn't bring us any closer."

Talbot raised a hand. "Not exactly true. While you've all been off doing…whatever you've been doing today, I've been studying. Asking questions. Trying to find out more about this city and its legends…"

"Oh, here we go." Huk rolled his eyes. "Nerd alert."

Talbot carried on as if he had heard nothing. "Turns out the people of the city believe a great spirit guardian looks after the forest, appearing to those who need it most and helping to control the predators who lurk in the shadows."

"Like some kind of grizzly Robin Hood?" Leonie asked.

"Nah, *he* does crap with money, right?" Huk answered.

"Did you ever see the Disney movie? Therese said. "One of my favorites. That one's a classic."

Chloe laughed. "Can we focus, please? Talbot, you were saying?"

"Yes, well… All this talk of the Wrangler's appearance and the tales of the forest protector got me thinking. Why don't we stage something to draw him out of hiding?"

Ben nodded. "That might work. We use someone as bait—get them lost in the woods and about to be mauled by ravenous wargs— and when the big guy appears, invite him for a quick chat and a cup of tea."

"That sounds like sarcasm," Talbot said.

"You think?"

"It's not a bad idea," Chloe chipped in. "It's worth a shot, I suppose. Lure him out of his abode and grab the chance to speak with him. The only real question is who we put forward as bait."

As one, all eyes turned to Therese.

"Oh, come on. Seriously? Me?"

"Who better to stand their ground and fend off maulers than our very own tank?"

Therese rolled her eyes and drained her drink. "Fine. Makes me really wish Tag was here right now. Maybe *he* could've been bait."

Chloe felt a small jolt of emotion. Tag's name had hardly been mentioned since they'd arrived, and it was a sore spot for her. She hadn't enjoyed having to leave him behind, but they'd had no choice. She certainly hoped he was okay, and that he would come back to join them all soon.

"One thing we haven't asked ourselves," Leonie added, drawing attention away from Therese. "If this guy guards the forest and protects those who are in danger, why didn't we see him when we were attacked by an army of ghouls?"

"Because we were never in any real danger," Ben replied. "With the wargs, there were many of them, and we were caught off-guard. It would've been one hell of a battle, with many casualties on either side.

"With the ghouls, they never stood a chance. Not really. Particularly with Blueballs on our side. We could outfight them easily."

Blueballs growled in agreement.

"So, what we need to do is put Therese in some real danger," Veronica said, placing a hand on her companion's shoulder. "Oh, this could be fun!"

Therese grumbled and disappeared inside to refill her drink.

CHAPTER SIX

Chloe,

How goes the hunt for Shika...Shikroko...KF's horse?

It's still so crazy watching all that you're doing on the big screen. The study's projector definitely offers a better cinematic experience for Mia and me. I can't imagine all the kids and geeks watching your adventures on their mobile devices. They're missing out on so much of the picture!

As requested, attached are your latest reports on Praxis Ltd. as well as your royalties and earnings in advertising from Fractured Reality. They keep sending us packages with official merchandise (presumably to keep you from suing them). Seems they've finally caught up with the trend.

To give you an overview before you deep-dive into stats and figures, you're doing *very well* from this whole venture. I have to admit, I'm impressed. Not only are you making a fortune on your investment in the fastest-rising gaming company in the history of the digital world, but you're only a few points off being the top-watched player in *Obsidian*, and that comes with a *lot* of financial benefits also.

To answer the other questions you sent over yesterday:

- Your parents are doing fine. Your whole family is doing what they do best—ignoring each other and getting deep into their own businesses. Henry and Henrietta have gone quiet, which could be a good thing, but in this line of business, you should always be wary of silence.

- Mia and I are doing well. She's working all hours of the day and night at the moment with Praxis and coming to grips with management. She'll do great once the dust has settled, but for now, it's a problem to keep her away from her computer for five minutes. I suppose it will benefit you in the long run.

- Speaking of that, she still hasn't come up with anything concrete regarding the relationship between the blackouts of the viewers and your experiences when you and KF go supernova together. There's a hunch she's following, and she might have found some evidence of what's causing the AI to blip out. I'll keep you posted on that one.

For now, keep doing what you're doing. You're taking the Obsidian world by storm, Chloe. A little longer, and I predict you'll be ranked the #1 player. From what I've heard, that brings with it its own rewards.

Peace out

Doc

Chloe laughed, then composed a quick reply and blinked away the message. The doc had informed her of the situation during their showdown with Fukmos and his aide, and how the static had found its way onto the screens of thousands of viewers once again when Chloe had allowed KieraFreya to control her body, the pair working in unison to take down the enemy.

The whole thing seemed bizarre. For Chloe, the experience was seamless. She entered into a near-perfect alignment with the goddess and felt her power grow.

The viewers had missed all the action, their feeds showing nothing but a blizzard on their screen.

This was a problem to be fixed if Chloe was to take the #1 spot in the Obsidian player ranks. Every time it occurred, the doc informed her that her viewership had dropped.

Although it was a small drop, due mostly to frustrated players wanting to see all the action and feeling cheated of the excitement, it was a drop all the same, and viewership grew slower after each occasion.

"Do we really think she can handle this?" Gideon asked, breaking Chloe from her thoughts.

Chloe looked ahead, to where Therese was leading the procession. She already had her shield in hand and her hammer drawn as the tree line drew ever closer.

"Undoubtedly," Chloe replied. "She's a tank dwarf. It's what they're made for."

Gideon looked doubtful. "That's what I'm worried about. If the Wrangler was smart enough to know that we didn't need help with the ghouls, who's to say he won't sense what's going on here?"

Chloe thought about this, then asked, "What's the alternative, Gid? Hang around for days or weeks on end until another god decides to try to stop our quest? I don't know how many of them there are, but we know they're out there now. They're actively trying to break our mission. Any day lost is a day gained for them."

"She speaks wisely," KieraFreya added. "Fukmos is but one of the dark gods. Who knows who might have their eyes trained on us, now that he has failed?"

Gideon fell silent.

Ben led them all into the forest, taking the trail he had taken yesterday with the rangers. To the others, it seemed impossible that he could navigate through the trees with such confidence; every square inch looked the same to them.

Just trees. All they could see was green.

"Here. This is the spot," Ben said, pointing to a piece of flattened earth where the bulk of the warg had lain.

Therese took her place, crouched to one knee on the ground. She held her shield in front of her with her left hand, her hammer ready in her right.

Chloe and the rest of the KieraSlayers found nearby trees to shinny up and take residence in. Even Blueballs demonstrated an impressive ability to climb, shouldering Huk and pawing his way up a thick, knotted branch a few meters away from where Therese waited.

And waited.

And waited.

They waited in near-enough silence, listening for any sign or sound of the wargs. They could hear creatures scurrying around the undergrowth, the flapping wings of birds taking flights, and the chirruping of some winged insect, but nothing close to a warg.

Chloe began to grow impatient. A few times, Therese looked up and shrugged. Chloe caught Ben's eye in a neighboring tree and signaled the ranger to check his messages.

FROM: Chloe

Dude, how do we know when they'll arrive?

FROM: Benjamin Summers

I don't know. Yesterday they were just here, so I assumed this would be their hunting territory.

FROM: Talbot

I *knew* you wouldn't be patient and sit it out [laughing emoji]

FROM: Therese

So, what do you want me to do here? I'm literally a sitting duck right now. My knees and back hurt and I'm bored.

FROM: Gideon Fleetwood

Anyone got any meat ?

FROM: Chloe

How can you be thinking about food at a time like this?

FROM: Gideon Fleetwood

Not for me. To attract the wargs. Maybe some raw meat will draw them closer to us?

FROM: Huk

Nothing from me.

FROM: Leonie

Nor me
FROM: Veronica
Me neither

Chloe's attention was drawn back out of her messages when she heard the whistle and *thunk* of an arrow speeding through the air.

"There," Ben mouthed smugly, nodding at the small fox that now lay pinned to the soft ground by the arrow. "Food."

Their attention returned to the spot where Therese waited, but still nothing came. Five minutes passed, then twenty. Therese grumbled as she stood up and cracked her back, stretching from the discomfort of her long-held defensive position.

She turned to the party in the trees. "Guys, I don't think this is working. I'm getting achy and tired, and I can smell is decomposing fox…"

Her words trailed off. Therese was staring into the undergrowth, where a large figure waited in reverent silence.

From where Chloe perched, however, she couldn't see the figure. All she saw was the terrified look come over Therese's face as she flopped into position near the ground and hid behind her shield.

Why has she gone quiet? Chloe wondered. She shimmied around on the bough to get a better look, but she needn't have bothered, for the next thing she knew, the clearing was filled with the thunderous roars of a gigantic bear.

Chloe's body reared up for action, her muscles coiled. She was ready to jump down to help her friend.

If it hadn't had been for KieraFreya, she would have been down on the ground with Therese. *No, Chloe. Remember, this is the plan. She needs to do this alone if we want it to work.*

Chloe nodded, realizing what she had been about to do. She couldn't help it. It was instinctual. If a friend was in danger, she wanted to help. *Had* to help. It took every ounce of effort now to remain in position as the bear strode toward Therese. Even lumbering on all fours, it towered above her, and it walked over her toward where the fox lay dead.

Therese pivoted, facing the back end of the bear as he sniffed (for it was clearly male) and chomped into the fox. Only once or twice did he turn his attention to Therese, not bothered in the least by her presence.

What's it doing? Chloe asked.

Feeding, KieraFreya replied. *Contrary to popular belief, even the largest predators will often go for the easy prey if they don't feel threatened by what's around them.*

Interesting, Chloe thought.

The bear made short work of the fox. Therese waited patiently, eyes peeking over the top of her shield. A few moments later, the bear grumbled, licked his lips, and began moving away and back into the forest.

Therese looked at the others for help.

"Oh, for goodness sake," Chloe murmured, creating an ice shard and throwing it at the bear.

The shard sped through the air toward one of the bear's massive paws. The tip grazed its skin as it passed, finally half-embedding itself in the forest floor.

The bear growled and looked back, his eyes dark. In the tree above, Talbot stripped several pinecones from the branches and pelted the bear with them. The pinecones bounced off his hard skull, and his nostrils flared.

Unaware of where the projectiles were coming from, the bear focused his attention on the girl in front of him. He stood on his hind legs and roared to the sky, the sound shaking the trees. The next thing she knew, the massive bulk of the bear was sprinting toward her.

That's more like it, KieraFreya said.

Chloe was alarmed by the hint of pleasure she detected in Kiera-Freya's words.

Therese ducked behind the shield as the bear smacked into her, sending her tiny form flying several feet backward.

"Therese!" Chloe couldn't help yelling.

The bear seemed not to notice, his eyes now locked on the dwarf. Therese took her position again, her hammer raised. As the bear neared, she smacked him on the nose. The beast growled and swiped at her.

The sound of claws on steel rang out and Therese was swept sideways, rolling several times before regaining her footing. Chloe had a brief flashback to her first moments in Obsidian, when players could feel everything because their pain receptors hadn't been properly adjusted.

She reminded herself that that wasn't the case now and Therese would be fine. Even the deepest of scratches would feel like little more than a paper cut.

Chloe hated paper cuts.

Therese, her pride unable to cope with not attacking back, let out a scream as she sprinted toward the bear. His eyes widened and he snapped at the dwarf, who dropped onto her knees and skidded beneath him.

What's she doing? KieraFreya asked.

Chloe didn't respond.

Therese slashed at the bear's stomach, the thick hide absorbing the majority of the blow. She crawled out from the under the bear and swung her hammer like a baseball bat, audibly impacting on the bear's knee.

The bear's leg folded and he cried out in pain.

"Therese, remember, you *have* to let it get you," Chloe called through cupped hands. "If there's no danger, he won't come."

"That's certainly how *I* like it," Veronica called back, tongue poking out the side of her mouth.

Chloe couldn't help snorting.

"How about one of *you* volunteers to come down and get smashed around by a bear? I don't see anyone else offering to step in and help."

"You're doing great, buddy," Huk shouted. "Keep it up."

Therese cursed, the game covering the words with its grating censorship beep. Even the bear was momentarily jarred by the sound, limping toward Therese with saliva dribbling out of his mouth.

"Let it bite you!" Ben shouted.

"You guys are crazy," Therese said. "Let him bite me? Do you realize how demeaning that would be?"

"Take one for the team," Talbot encouraged.

"Yeah, you got this!" Leonie shouted.

Therese rolled her eyes, letting her shield drop to the ground. Her eyes narrowed, fixing on the bear's, seeing the bloodlust within. The bear growled as he hobbled toward her. When he was only a few inches away, he sniffed at Therese, clearly taken aback by the dwarf's sudden change in stance.

Therese froze, feeling the bear's wet tongue on her face. His breath was rank and thick, his snarls finding their way into the marrow of her bones.

The whole party watched on tenterhooks. Talbot leaned so far forward it looked as though he were going to fall out of the tree.

The bear snorted a blast of warm air in Therese's face and growled. His eyes were black as coal.

"C'mon…" Chloe urged under her breath, more than aware of the lunacy of the situation.

And then came more pinecones, the last kick into action. Talbot rained the objects on the bear's head.

Unfortunately, the bear looked up, seeing Talbot leaning from the boughs above. Once again, the bear moved over Therese, this time thrusting his large claws into the tree and dragging himself up. His broken leg hung limply as the others worked to compensate.

Talbot's eyes widened. He called to the others for help.

Ben shrugged from the opposite tree. "I suppose it doesn't matter *who* it is, buddy. Someone has to make the sacrifice."

The blood drained from Talbot's face. He tried to kick the animal away, but the bear was already on him, dragging him down to the ground. He landed with a large exhalation of air, the bear turning around and going for him now.

It bounded toward him as best it could, dragging its leg. Talbot retreated on his hands and knees, crawling as fast as he could, but soon the bear's teeth gripped his leg.

The bear pulled him back, throwing him across the forest until he slammed into a tree. Talbot coughed and scrambled to get to his feet.

"Great work!" KieraFreya shouted. "Keep it up."

"Keep *what* up? He's not doing anything! He's just getting pummeled."

"Yeah, like we wanted him to. Well, actually, the dwarf, but I'm okay with either."

Therese simply watched from the sidelines, mouth agape. The bear picked Talbot up in his mouth, shaking his head furiously before tossing him once again.

"How are you doing, Tal?" Veronica called down, her face pained.

Talbot, to his credit, stared up at them with keen eyes. He gave them a thumbs-up, a fire apparently lit in his belly by the chance to help the group.

Chloe didn't know how much the warrior could take. Although he had picked warrior for his class, Talbot was hardly a fighter. He'd proven himself in wits and smarts, but he was no more than average when it came to a blade.

The bear roared loudly once more and made a final charge. The KieraSlayers closed their eyes, not wanting to see what came next. Chloe hoped the Wrangler was nearby and their plan would work, but there was no sign of him. The forest seemed to have cleared for their battle.

Or so she thought.

The bear was almost on Talbot when a blur of brown fur sped toward them. The black bear was huge in comparison to the other bears they'd met, but this latest addition was even bigger. Its skull was the size of a boulder, and it smashed into the side of the black bear.

Talbot yelled in a mixture of relief and shock.

The brown bear reared, its maw gaping. The black bear rolled twice over, then slowly turned around, his eyes flashing.

The two locked eyes for what felt like an eternity. The black bear rose to his feet, looking as if he was about to coil for the strike, then snorted and turned away, limping back into the undergrowth.

The brown bear watched the black bear hobble away. It was enormous, standing on its two legs. Chloe realized their perches in the trees couldn't have been more than five feet above the bear's head.

The bear turned its attention to Talbot, who had begun to crawl backward. His foot caught on a twig, which snapped with a loud crack. Talbot gasped. The bear lowered to all fours, the ground shaking slightly at its weight.

What's it doing? Chloe asked.

I have no idea, KieraFreya replied.

As if it could hear them, the bear craned its neck toward the trees and locked eyes with Chloe.

Chloe's body stilled and her breath caught. There was intelligence in those eyes. A thousand years of memories and thoughts processed in the galactic pools of darkness that were the bear's eyes.

Chloe gasped.

"It's him."

Quick as a flash, the bear whirled, grabbed Talbot in his powerful jaws, and lifted him off the ground. Without turning back, the bear ran into the forest, the injured warrior dangling helplessly from his mouth.

CHAPTER SEVEN

Talbot dared not open his eyes.

Hidden under a blanket, he felt safe. Not safe like away-from-danger-safe, but it felt comforting to have something else—anything else—separate him from the terrifying bear.

He could hear it now, somewhere around him. Great thumping footsteps stomping around the space. He imagined he was in a cave or a den or wherever it was that bears lived. He hadn't seen where the bear had taken him, which might have been a mistake, in hindsight.

But he knew he was under a blanket, at least. The thin, soft material covered him and was keeping him warm, his body shivering from the attack as the adrenaline began to slowly wear off.

How could a bear have a blanket?

That was something he couldn't understand. He was a man of logic, after all. Even in his in-game persona, Talbot (or Daryl Weaver, in real life), was something of a book nerd. He'd spend hours reading through the small print of games before first signing in, probably the only man in the world to read the Terms & Conditions of every game before he checked the small box and dived into play.

So, the notion of a *bear* covering Talbot with a *blanket* was absolutely absurd.

A *bear*.

A *blanket*.

Sometimes along their journey, Talbot would close his eyes and pretend he was someone else. Pretend he had the valor and bravery of someone like Veronica, Therese, or Chloe. If they were here right now, they'd probably leap up, sword in hand, and take on the bear one-on-one.

The bear would put up a damn good fight, but with the skills they'd honed over the course of the game, they'd ultimately win. It wouldn't be like any of the others to fall out of a tree and make a fool of themselves, luring the bear away from the bait and instead replacing it for the Wrangler.

And the bastard hadn't even shown up. No one had come to save Talbot.

He imagined the others would be on their way—well, he hoped they would—but he had no idea where they were.

How fast had the bear run?

Had it zigzagged and confused its trail? Left them clueless in its wake?

What velocity could a bear such as this one achieve in the forest? Could it move faster than the average earth bear? How did it grow so large? Its internal skeleton must be powerful indeed to hold its weight up and keep it from collapsing in on itself.

If only he could catch the bear and examine it. That would be amazing. To study the beast and feed the information back, potentially utilize it somehow in future battles.

Not that Talbot had much chance of that. While he loved accompanying the KieraSlayers, there was a part of him that thirsted for knowledge. Loved the cities, and reveled in the libraries and the study of culture.

But for right now he was stuck under a blanket in a cave with a bear.

A *bear*.

A *blanket*.

Talbot sighed, not realizing that, although he could hear the heavy footsteps of the bear, the growls had stopped ages ago.

"Well, that has to be a good sign."

Chloe nodded. The large wooden shack ahead would have been all but invisible had they not watched the bear enter the front door a few minutes before.

The wood was covered with ivy and other vines, the browns and greens blending perfectly with the rest of the forest. There were trees growing out of the roof and twisting into the canopy above.

"Why would a bear live in a shack?" Therese asked, her voice chipper since she had avoided becoming the ragdoll for the bear to play with. "And how the hell did he open the door?"

Chloe agreed it had been a strange sight, the bear had stood on his back feet, raised the front ones, and pushed on the door. He had ducked his massive head and wandered inside as if he weren't a bear.

"There aren't any hinges out here, Therese," Veronica scoffed. "Didn't you see it shove the door open? Damn beast. We have to rescue Talbot."

"Don't you get it?" Ben asked. "This is the Wrangler's shack. I'm sure of it. The bear must be some kind of guardian or something. We wanted to catch the man, but we caught his guard dog."

"You know you're using the word 'caught' rather loosely, right?" Gideon asked.

Ben shrugged. "Yeah, I guess."

They remained crouched for some time, studying the entrance and listening to the sounds of movement inside. Soon a small ribbon of smoke curled up into the trees.

"He's inside," Leonie announced.

Therese frowned. "How do you know?"

"Fire. Look. No bear could light a fire."

"Not intentionally, anyway," Huk added.

Blueballs growled behind them, his eyes fixed on the shack.

Something rustled behind them. They all turned, breathing a sigh of relief when Huk appeared through the bushes, back from his reconnaissance mission.

"Well?" Chloe asked.

"Only one other entrance, a door at the back of the shack. No windows that I could see into the shack through, but I'm sure they're still both in there. You can hear that bear's paws thumping from miles away."

"Okay, then," Chloe said, her resolve hardening as she stared at the shack. "Here's the plan…"

A few minutes later, they were in place. Chloe and Ben each led a team, taking positions on either side of the shack. As one, they were to smash the doors down and take the Wrangler and the bear by surprise.

"What are we waiting for?" KieraFreya hissed. "Let's do this already."

"We wait for the signal," Chloe said. A bird call rang from afar.

"Was that it?" Huk asked, face full of confusion. "It sounded like a bird. It was the bird call, right?"

Chloe had no idea. Ben had demonstrated the bird call, describing the distinctive characteristics of the warbler's cry and how it was differentiated from other birds, but to Chloe's ears, it sounded just like any other bird.

"Right," she said uncertainly. "Of course, it was. I'm sure it was."

The door on the other side of the house was kicked down.

"It definitely was."

They marched up to the door, Chloe, Huk, Therese, and Blueballs booting the door until it fell out of its frame and smashed to the floor inside.

Chloe ran in first. Plumes of dust kicked up from where the door had connected with floorboards, creating a thick haze. She could just about make out Ben coughing and shielding his eyes on the other side of the large room.

"Keep your guard up," Chloe shouted. "Find them both. Restrain them."

They ran around blindly for a few seconds, knocking into each other, listening intently for the bear or for any kind of enemy. After Gideon caught his foot and heard an *"Ooof"* before he fell to the floor, they all gathered around a small bundle wrapped in a blanket on the floor.

"Talbot?" Chloe asked. "Is that you?"

"Er...yes?"

The party calmed down. Chloe ripped away the blanket, their eyes now focused on Talbot.

"Oh," Talbot whined. "That was warm."

"So's the fire," a deep voice behind them said.

They turned as one, eyes widening at the sight of the giant sitting in a large chair in the corner of the room. There was an open hearth beside him, the fire crackling merrily.

The man smiled. "Might I inquire as to who you all are?"

There was a pregnant pause before Chloe took a step toward the man. "First tell us who you are, and then we shall tell you our names."

The man's smile grew. It was warm. Homey. There was something reassuring in that smile.

"I am known by many names across the world. I am Retoran in the south, Drestara in the west, in the east, I am known as Klerongaria, and in the north, I am known as simply 'the Wrangler.'"

The others stirred at the sound of the name.

"Even though my birth name is far from any of these whimsical titles," he continued, "these are the names by which common folk identify me."

"You don't want people to know your real name?" Therese asked before she could stop herself. "Sounds a bit sketchy to me. Surely it would be easier to go by the name you were given at birth?"

The Wrangler grinned. "You'd think so. But eight hundred years of travel has fractured my identity, and it is only in legends that they now speak my true name."

"You had a bear," Chloe said, enjoying the history lesson but remembering the danger that the large brown bear had inflicted upon them. "Where is it?"

The Wrangler gave a curt nod and, for a moment, just stared. Chloe was about to lose her patience and ask again when she noticed that the Wrangler's pupils had bled into the rest of his eyes, the whites turning black.

His brown hair grew thick and coarse, spreading across his body as his muzzle lengthened and his ears grew pointed.

Blueballs' fur stood on end and he bared his teeth at the creature before them.

The chair groaned under the bear now sitting nonchalantly before them. The KieraSlayers stared with mouths open, unable to believe what they'd just seen.

"He's a…" Gideon started.

Ben finished for him, "…werebear."

The Wrangler laughed in his bear form, the sound sharp roars. He closed his eyes and concentrated and the bear form began to revert, his body shrinking as the fur receded and his features returned to normal.

"'Werebear' is not a term I've heard before," the Wrangler said. "What is this…werebear?"

"It's…well…it's kind of hard to explain," Gideon stuttered. "It's kind of like a person who…when the moon is full…can…"

"It's a person who can turn into a bear," Therese snapped, glaring at Gideon. "See, that was easy."

Huk sniggered behind his hand.

"Interesting," the Wrangler said, stroking his chin. "I like this term, although I could not adopt it for myself. I am not limited to bears."

"What do you mean?" Leonie asked.

The Wrangler closed his eyes and spent the next few minutes going through a series of transformations. One minute he was a black bear, the next he had shrunk into the form of a fox. He became a badger, a warg, and an eagle, finishing by transforming into a perfect replica of Gideon.

The KieraSlayers burst into laughter at that last. Although the imitation was flawless, the Wrangler couldn't conjure clothing. The only saving grace for Gideon, who was staring at his naked double, was the pixelated blur in the region of his crotch.

"Okay, okay, we get it," Gideon said, taking Talbot's blanket and wrapping around his doppelgänger. The Wrangler laughed, transformed back to his human form, and fixed the blanket around himself, gathering up the clothing that had fallen from his body.

"So, you're a shapeshifter?" Chloe said. "You can adopt the form of anyone and anything you see?"

"Not everything," the Wrangler said, pulling his t-shirt over an impressive set of abs. "I can't imitate inanimate objects."

"You managed to imitate Gideon," Ben quipped.

Even Gideon joined in their laughter this time, seemingly more comfortable now that his double wasn't staring into his face.

"And now you have me at a disadvantage, for you have yet to live up to your end of the bargain," the Wrangler said.

Chloe and the KieraSlayers went around the room and introduced themselves. When they were done, the Wrangler impressively repeated all of their names back to them without missing one.

"Amazing memory," Chloe said.

"After several centuries of roaming the world, it helps to keep it sharp."

Chloe couldn't comprehend how someone could live for so long. She wondered what the average life expectancy of people in this game was; she'd seen elderly folks in the towns and cities but had never even thought of asking their ages.

"How is it that you've lived so long?" Ben asked, sitting cross-legged on the floor. The others followed, and the room soon looked like a bedtime story scene. "Are you some kind of god?"

The Wrangler chuckled. "I am no god. I am just as mortal as you all are. My organs and body parts are vulnerable to damage and aging, and I certainly don't compare myself to the gods in their heavenly thrones."

Chloe saw his eyes glance at hers, then flicker to her armor before returning to look at Ben.

"Then what are you?"

"I believe many used to call us 'ancients.' Beings born from the earth in years past, mortal beings with specific talents to benefit the world and guard those who need protection."

"I think I've heard of those." Talbot sat up straight. "Yeah, it was in a book back in Gallen Hollows. The ancients…there were ten of them. Ten beings who guarded the forests, seas, and mountains. Shapeshifters who were placed upon the earth by the gods as sentinels and conduits for their mighty power."

"So, you *can* communicate with the gods?" Chloe smirked.

The Wrangler shook his head. "Don't believe everything you read in books, young warrior. Remember that even the most revered of books could have been authored and penned by the greatest liars of the world. History truly is written by the victors."

Talbot's head sank. He looked hurt by the comments, as if The Wrangler had told him that Christmas no longer existed.

The Wrangler took a deep breath, turning his attention to the roaring fire. The flames cast a homey glow over his features and washed over the room, making them all slightly drowsy.

"I sense that this questioning relates to why you decided to track me down?" the Wrangler asked. "I have to admit, many have tried to lure me out of hiding, but none have been so bold as to go about injuring their own kin in the process. You are all blessed, aren't you? I've heard a lot about the blessed appearing in these regions, though I've yet to meet one."

"Well, now you've met seven!" Therese exclaimed.

Chloe chuckled, pushing down Therese's arms, which she had punched into the air.

"You're right, and we wouldn't have put ourselves in danger if it would hurt or we wouldn't come back to life within a few hours. We've been trying to track you down for a while now but didn't know where to start. I guess the only way to say this is we need your help."

"They get bolder and bolder." The Wrangler laughed. "To break into my house and ask me for a favor. Would *you* offer help to someone who did that?"

Chloe shuffled awkwardly, cheeks flushing. "I suppose not."

The Wrangler silently studied them. "It takes a lot to be truthful, and truth is something I respect. Tell me what you desire help with, and I'll see what I can do. I make no promises to get involved in matters beyond my jurisdiction. My life is simple, and will remain so."

Chloe nodded, took a deep breath, and told the Wrangler as much as she could about herself, the armor, and her hunt for the horse.

"And they told you I'd be able to help?" the Wrangler asked when Chloe had finished her tale. The sky had turned dark outside, and moths and other insects had begun to swarm through the open door toward the fire.

"Can you?" Chloe asked.

The Wrangler scratched his chin. During her telling of her story, his naked face had sprouted a fresh, thick beard.

"I might know of a place where such a beast exists. It is beyond the capabilities of the average mortal to reach, and is only accessible by… aggressive means."

"What does that mean?" Huk asked Leonie.

"It means, shut up and listen," she scolded.

"Can you take us there?" Chloe asked hopefully.

The Wrangler laughed, his belly shaking with the motion. "You blessed really have no sense of danger, do you? I warn you about it, and you leap at the chance. You really are a curious breed."

"So, you'll take us?"

The Wrangler shook his head. "I didn't say that."

Chloe raised an eyebrow in confusion. "Then you'll show us the way?"

The Wrangler shook his head. "If I am to perform a favor for a bunch of miscreants who lure me out of hiding and trespass on my property, I must have something in return. A token to send you on your way."

"And what might that be?" Ben asked.

The Wrangler turned his eyes to Chloe. "Oh, I think you already know…"

CHAPTER EIGHT

"He *can't* be serious," Veronica said as the walls of Hammersworth came into view.

They had been marching all night. Thanks to Ben's keen sense of direction and Chloe's **Dark Vision**, they were eventually able to navigate their way through the forest and back to the city.

Chloe shook off the irritation she felt at the onslaught of insects that had gravitated toward the tiny areas of exposed skin beneath her armor, drawn by sweat as the party trundled through the cloying heat.

"Well, apparently, he is," Huk said, standing straight and doing his best impression of the Wrangler. "If you want *my* help, then this is *my* request."

Chloe checked out the quest notification, not quite believing what they'd been asked to do but somehow having known this would be the end result all along.

"Look, guys, I know it's a tad insane, *but* if it gets us closer to our goal, then that's what we have to do."

"It won't work," Leonie said, shaking her head. "We'll never get it."

"We don't know that," Chloe shot back.

Ben glanced toward the forest. "We could always…steal it?"

"*Ben!*" Gideon and Chloe exclaimed together.

"What? It was just an idea. It's dark, it's quiet, she'll never know."

"*We'll* know," Gideon told him.

"We'll just wait until morning, okay? That way, we can do this properly. Wait until daylight and then…maybe…we'll be able to get what he wants. There's a chance she'll just hand it over."

"Yeah," Therese grumbled. "I can see *that* happening."

Chloe rolled her eyes, marched through the gates, and led them toward the inn.

Soon they were all tucked into bed, waiting quietly in anticipation of sunrise.

Cockerels signaled the morning's arrival.

They were large creatures, dotted in several locations around the city. It was the only way to ensure the workers began at the same time every day. Heads arched to the sky, they belted out their morning tune.

Chloe awoke with a start at the sound. She couldn't remember the last time she had let herself sleep properly and enjoyed waking up to find that a buff of **+10% stamina regen** had been added to her character after a good, deep rest.

The others were more difficult to wake up, considering they had all logged off during the night. Having had no idea what time it had been when their heads had hit the pillow, Chloe imagined that they wouldn't be awake for another hour or two, at least.

All, that is, except Gideon and Blueballs.

"Morning, sunshine." Chloe smiled, struggling to hold back a laugh as Gideon rose from his bed, hair sticking out in all directions.

"Huh? What time is it?"

"Morning time."

Blueballs gave a small growl as if to say his own good morning.

"Come on," Chloe said, swinging her legs off her bed and crossing to the other side of the room. "We've got some time before they wake up. Let's get ahead of the game, shall we?"

Gideon agreed, and soon they were waving goodbye to Blueballs at the door. The toffet looked downtrodden, but after a quick word of reassurance from Chloe that they would be back soon, he settled down and went back to sleep.

The streets were alive with activity. Clearly, morning was one of the busiest times to be out and about. Chloe and Gideon snaked along the cobblestone streets, avoiding caravan carts packed with wooden boxes, weaving through crowds of makers and sellers, and dodging excited customers.

The atmosphere was completely different today, and Chloe caught her first hints of the festivities. They tried to navigate to the gate but kept finding the streets choked with people wearing home-made gowns and tiaras. Ribbons and banners decorated everything, and at nearly every intersection, musicians were playing festive tunes.

Chloe asked a dwarven street merchant what was going on.

"It's decision day!" The dwarf beamed. "King Abaxis has met with each of the suitors, and today the queen-to-be will be chosen!" He clapped his hands and indicated his wares, a table overburdened with royalty-themed merchandise. "You see?"

Chloe and Gideon nodded, determined to move away from the merchant before he started extolling his items.

When they were out of sight of the merchant, Chloe said, "I can't believe how excited they are. It's a guy marrying a girl."

"That's because you're American," Gideon replied, leading Chloe down yet another street after a bunch of people barred their way. "If you went across the pond to England, you'd see how much *they* cele-brate the monarchy even in this day and age, when the royals have less sway than they did in the Middle Ages."

Chloe squeezed through a group of teenage girls clapping and discussing the choice animatedly.

"You seem to know a lot about the royals and the UK."

Gideon shrugged. "It's interesting, y'know? A family so powerful and influential that people from around the world flock to see them, yet it's the British government that oversees the majority of the decisions. I mean, why are kings and queens special? Who dictated that they were anything other than 'normal?'"

Chloe considered his point, agreeing with a small nod. There were some people in the world who were born with all the gifts life had to give, her included.

And then there were others like Gideon, who were born into troubles and had had to work their asses off to make anything of themselves. Yet, who said Chloe was in any way better than Gideon? She had been lucky, she supposed. Born to rich, successful parents and given everything she asked for.

She felt a frisson of shame. She hadn't ever considered her life through the lens of someone like Gideon, and the worst part was that he had no idea of her true identity. To him, she was just a regular person.

"Where the hell are we?" Gideon asked, stopping after a while and trying to figure out their location.

"Beats me," Chloe replied. "I was following you."

Gideon furrowed his brow, took a swift walk down a narrow alley, and found himself climbing a set of stairs that looked to have hardly ever been used. When they reached the top, they discovered they were on an outcrop of rock that looked out over the whole city.

"Woah…" Gideon breathed.

It was throbbing with life. They could see thousands of people on the streets and the rain of confetti. They could hear the music as if it were coming from a tinny AM radio.

"This view is killer," Chloe said. "If only we had cameras here."

Gideon gave Chloe a weird look.

"What?"

"You didn't know you could screenshot?" Gideon asked.

"I…*no!*" She rifled through her menus and found the camera button, then looked out over the city and confirmed the picture, hearing the click of a camera shutter before a still image appeared in the bottom right of her vision.

"You can save them in albums and share them when you're not in-game," Gideon told her. "My wallpaper on my computer at home is the nine of us at the table in the Twisted Spire in Killink View."

Chloe gave him a small smile. "One of the last times we were all together."

Gideon nodded.

Chloe fell into her thoughts, remembering the moment well. The gang had been laughing and having a great time. Blueballs sat in the corner, wondering what the fuss was about.

The nine...

Veronica's words came back to her: *As long as you believe in the nine, your mission will be successful.*

Was that what Veronica had meant? That the nine—the Kiera-Slayers—were what was needed to complete her quest? All of them? Tag and Jessie included?

It can't be, Chloe, KieraFreya chipped in. *You know it can't.*

But what if it is? Chloe mused. *What if I can resurrect her again?*

You know you can't. Besides, she's gone now, and Tag is out of action. Maybe another two will come. Maybe many nines will form before the journey's through.

Chloe tried to digest this, wracking her brain to understand the meaning of Veronica's words.

It wasn't until she heard the Gideon gasping and felt his hand on her shoulder that she was pulled back to the present.

"What is it?"

For the first time since they had ascended the stairs, Chloe noticed a second flight of stairs leading down into another part of the city, this part a lot less busy than the rest.

But it wasn't the stairs that drew her focus. It was the dwarf who stood frozen at the top of the stairs, a terrified expression on his face.

"Er..." he managed.

"Hello?" Chloe said.

The dwarf's mouth opened and closed, eyes shifting as if he had just been caught under spotlights. There was something about him that looked slightly out of place.

His beard was incredibly groomed, as opposed to all the other dwarves she had met in her time. He wore a dark gray cloak that he held tightly around his person. His cheeks were rosy on his flawless skin, and his boots looked brand-new, barely a trace of mud or dirt on them.

"Are you okay?" Gideon asked. "You don't look so great."

"Yes. I mean, no. I mean…" the dwarf stuttered. "I guess I'm just…lost."

"Ha!" Chloe burst out. "You and us both, brother. We have no idea how we even got here. Have you looked down there, though? It's a nightmare. I wouldn't go that way unless you want to get stuck in the crowds."

"Actually, that's exactly where I want to go."

"It is?" Gideon asked.

The dwarf nodded. "Of course. I actually want to get out of the city and away from the crowds. It's been a nightmare since the festivities began."

Chloe felt sorry for the dwarf. "I can see how that could happen. Well, how about this? We're looking to get out the front gates too. How about you show us the way back to our friends and we'll all head out of this city together?"

The dwarf's face lit up. "Really? You'd help me?"

Gideon chuckled. "It'd really be you helping us."

"Chloe." Chloe offered her hand.

"Gideon," the mage added.

The dwarf took their hands in turn. "I'm…" he paused, eyes shifting once again, "Abe. Call me 'Abe.'"

"Abe, it is," Chloe said jovially.

Before they knew it, they were back on the streets again. Abe kept his cloak wrapped tightly around him, his face in shadow as he expertly led them through the streets, turning down tight alleys that Chloe and Gideon had to shimmy sideways to get through.

"He doesn't look very lost," Gideon commented as they squeezed out of an alley. Abe looked left, sighed at the number of people standing and waiting in the streets, and took a right instead.

Chloe agreed but decided not to say anything. He moved swiftly, and if they dawdled for too long, they might lose him.

At one point along the journey, the dwarf *did* disappear from sight. They reached a wide street with its edges choked with spectators. Several carts were trundling down it, led by impressively muscular horses.

As the carts passed by, Abe took a deep breath, lowered his head, and sprinted across the street. Chloe and Gideon tried to follow, but one of the horses had been disturbed by the traveler and paused, whinnying excitedly.

By the time Chloe and Gideon had calmed the screaming lady dwarf-suitor and reached the other side, he was gone.

"Crap," Chloe hissed. "Do you have any idea where we are?"

Gideon looked up at the morning sky. "Judging by the sun, east of where we were earlier."

"That's really helpful."

"I'm sorry, Chloe. I don't have a GPS in my head."

Chloe laughed, spying a dark shape at the end of the street a second later. The figure waved them over.

"Come on," Abe hissed.

Chloe and Gideon sprinted to catch up, impressed by the dwarf's speed.

When the inn came into sight, Chloe breathed a sigh of relief. The KieraSlayers were all seated outside on their favorite bench, waiting patiently in the sunlight.

Blueballs was the first to spot them, excitedly bounding over and pulling Chloe into a tight hug. She was thankful for the metal armor that covered her body.

"I missed you too, pal." She laughed.

"We *knew* you'd already be off on some crazy adventures," Veronica said, her face annoyed although her eyes betrayed she was more pleased to see them than mad. "What, we can't even log off for a short break anymore without you guys off canoodling in some tiny hollow of the city?"

"Did you get it?" Huk asked. "Did you find her?"

"What?" Chloe asked, forgetting all about the Wrangler's task for a minute. "Oh, no. We got waylaid. The city is manic today. Everyone is out in the streets to celebrate the king choosing a suitor."

"And let me guess: this is the king?" Leonie smirked.

Abe's head came up, his eyes wide.

Chloe laughed. "Don't be silly. This is Abe. We met him on our travels. It's because of his expert guidance that we were able to make it back here."

"Pleased to meet you all," Abe said, a weak smile on his face. He refused to let go of the front of his cloak. "If it's not too rude of me, I really do have to go. Duty calls beyond the walls."

He turned to leave, but Therese placed a firm hand on his shoulder.

"Not so fast. You can show us the way. We've got business beyond the walls too."

Abe tensed, slowly turning to meet Therese's eye. When he did, his whole demeanor changed. He took a step back and studied her.

"Of…of course," he said goofily. "Absolutely, yes. I'll show you the way. Yes, of course."

Ben rolled his eyes. "Well, that didn't take long."

"What?" Gideon asked.

"He's in *luuurve*," Ben whispered.

Veronica appeared beside them. "Did you say what I think you said?"

Ben chuckled, not that Therese or Abe heard. Therese was already following the eager Abe as he walked on, continually turning around and smiling at Therese.

Chloe giggled, shaking her head at the ridiculousness of it all.

"Come on," Veronica said. "Before the lovebirds leave us behind."

"Speaking of lovebirds, we better go find ours," Chloe added, walking side by side with Blueballs as Abe led them through the streets and out toward the fields beyond the city walls.

CHAPTER NINE

"Wow! She really is a beauty, isn't she?"

Veronica stared in hypnotic admiration at Fernando, the peacock strutting around the pen with gentle nods of his head. Behind him trailed his feathers in a dazzling display of rainbow colors.

"Fernando is a 'he,'" Doris said rather sharply.

"Really?" Veronica replied. "I'd have thought the girl birds would be the pretty ones."

Chloe raised an eyebrow. "Have you never seen a peacock before?"

Veronica shook her head. "Not down our way, no. You don't get peacocks in the inner cities. I can tell you what pigeons and rats look like. I used to be able to shoot pigeons from fifty yards away with a slingshot."

"Not even at a zoo or a petting farm?" Ben asked. "They're always at those."

"Nope," Veronica replied. "Never. Not once. To be honest, I thought they only existed in fairytales. It makes sense when you think about it. What other brightly colored birds do you see flying around on US soil?"

"Parrots?" Huk suggested.

"They're not American." Veronica scoffed. "They're tropical."

"I've still seen them in the US."

"And they don't fly." Doris raised a finger, as if teaching a class a very important point she was rather proud of. "Well, not really. They flap a lot and can sort of hover, but you won't see them trailing through the sky."

"Then what's the point of them?" Veronica asked.

Talbot shrugged. "I hear they make a great dinner."

Doris gasped.

Chloe, quick to try to recover, flapped her hands and said, "But that's not why we're here, is it, guys?"

No one replied.

"*Is it, guys?*"

Realizing what Chloe was trying to do, the rest of the group very quickly shook their heads.

Doris looked at them with a trace of suspicion. "Look, I appreciate what you're asking, and it's a very generous offer, but I'm sorry. Fernando is not for sale. He was a gift from my late husband. He's all I have left of him. I can't give him up that easily."

Chloe's heart sank. The task had seemed so simple, but now that she looked into Doris' eyes, she knew it would be a lot harder than she thought to separate the two.

"We have gold," Chloe said, scanning her menu and feeling herself deflate when she saw the meager number of coins left in her inventory. It seemed the cost of living in Hammersworth over the last week or so had taken its toll on her pockets. "We have *some* gold."

"I'm sorry," Doris said, turning to head back inside. "If you have any questions about them or any of my other livestock, let me know. But I really should be getting on with preparations for the big feast tonight. The king's palace has asked me for two hundred chickens to feed the table at the after-service dinner."

"Two hundred chickens?" Ben said incredulously. "Seems a bit extravagant, even for a dwarven wedding."

"Nah," Veronica chipped in. "Dwarves can stomach anything. They're like cows or goats. Everything in sight goes into their mouths and down into their bellies. Ain't that right, Therese?"

"I wouldn't know." She glared at Veronica. "I can't speak for my race, seeing as I'm not a real dwarf."

"What about you, new blood?" Veronica asked Abe. "Wouldn't you say dwarves can eat *anything* until their stomachs are fit to burst?"

Abe, who had remained relatively quiet up until this point, studying the others intensely, suddenly gave an awkward laugh. "Ha! Yeah, anything, those dwarves. I mean, us dwarves. It's too many chickens, really. I should ask…I mean, the king should ask for fewer. Or maybe some variety, y'know? A cow, or a pig, or a…" his eyes hunted the paddock again, "a peacock!"

Doris glared at Abe. "*No.* The peacocks are off-limits."

With that, she stormed into her house and shut the door firmly behind her.

"You know," Huk said, eyeing Fernando greedily, "she's not the smartest farmer in the land. We could just…"

Leonie shook her head. "Don't even think about it."

"What? We've just told her we want her peacock, and she said no before leaving us *outside with the peacock* while she stomps indoors? I'm just saying, I think she *wants* us to take it."

Chloe shook her head. "No." Her words were firm. She glanced at the cabin, where they heard pots and pans clattering. "I'll go talk to her myself. See if I can somehow change her mind."

To her surprise, Abe added, "I'll go with you."

Doris was at the sink, looking out the window toward the group when Chloe poked her head through the door. "Hello?" she called.

"In here," Doris replied, furiously scrubbing her pots.

Chloe and Abe joined her. "We really meant no offense," Chloe began. "It's just… To be completely honest, we really need Fernando to make a deal with the man who visited you the other day."

"The big man?" Doris replied.

Chloe nodded. Abe cocked an eyebrow, his interest piqued.

"Tell me," Doris said, taking a step away from the sink and placing a hand on her hip, "why is this so important to you? I mean, it must be something big for you to want to take one of my prized possessions and bother me so."

Chloe paused for a moment, deliberating whether or not she should tell the truth, the whole truth, and nothing but the truth. She had seen her parents and siblings over the years bend and twist the truth to manipulate people to submit to their will and take what they wanted. It seemed to be a fair business technique that worked in the cutthroat environment of high-stakes investment.

But that wasn't what Chloe was about.

If she'd learned anything over her time in Obsidian, it was that honesty was the best course of action. Many had responded well to being told the truth.

No matter how ludicrous it could sometimes be.

So, Chloe told Doris the story of their meeting with the Wrangler. How they had put Therese forward as bait, and how Talbot had accidentally replaced her. The battle of the bears, and the journey to the hidden cabin in the woods. The task that the Wrangler had set and the promise he had made.

"You're telling me that a magical bear-man...shapeshifter...*thing* asked *you* to fetch *my* peacock, and in exchange, he would show you the way to collect your magical goddess horse? I'm sorry. I've been spun some tales in my time, but this is one of the most preposterous I've heard in my life."

"It's all true," Abe said sternly. "Every last word is true."

Chloe looked at the dwarf with appreciative curiosity.

"I mean, just think," he continued. "Surely she could come up with a better story than the one she just has, right? Why would anyone paint such an absurd picture *just to get a damned peacock?*"

Doris nodded softly, still unconvinced. "Well, my answer's still no." She flapped her hands, glancing at the sun out of the window and seeing it high in the sky. "Oh, my. Is that the time? I need to get a move on if I'm going to finish getting my stock ready for the king's chefs. The delivery wagons will be here in an hour."

"Why don't we help?" Chloe offered, desperate to find any way to gain favor with Doris.

Chloe, we don't have time to help collect chickens. We've got a horse to find. Just grab the peacock and run, KieraFreya said.

No, Chloe hissed back. *I have such a thing as integrity. We'll find another way.*

Oh, sure, KieraFreya replied. *Why don't we just paint one of the brown ones?*

You know what? That's not such a bad idea.

You're kidding? KieraFreya scoffed.

Of course, I'm kidding, Chloe thought as Doris accepted her offer and led her around the back of the house to the chicken coops.

Quest unlocked: Get the chick in the wagon

Doris is running out of time before the king's delivery men arrive, expecting 200 chickens to be ready for their wagons. Help Doris round up the chickens and deliver them on time before you feel the wrath of the king for delaying his celebrations.

Difficulty: 1/10

Rewards: 400 exp

Accept quest: Y/N

***

Ben closed his eyes and basked in the warm sun.

"It's never going to happen," Huk complained. "She's as stubborn as an old mule. If we want to get the prize, we need to take it by force."

Leonie clicked her tongue. "Will you relax? There'll be a way we can make this work for everyone. Just give Chloe a chance. She'll come through."

"She always does," Ben replied.

"It's that new guy I'm not sure of." Therese narrowed her eyes. "He appears from nowhere, joins the group, and now he's helping Chloe with negotiations? I mean, who is he?"

Gideon, who had been busy studying the peacock pen, a look of confusion on his face, half-turned and said, "We met him in the upper levels. Me and Chloe got lost in the crowds, and he helped us find our way back. Nice guy. Said he wanted to head out of the city. A little shady, perhaps, but anyone who helps us is a good guy in my eyes."

Gideon returned his attention to the pen, confusion on his face as he counted the peacocks with his fingers.

"And no one's asking why he was running away from the city? Why he kept himself covered with that shroud the entire way out of the city gates?"

Veronica, who was resting with her back to the pen's fence, elbows propped on the wood as she also bathed in the sun, said, "What does it matter? He helped us. End of story."

"There's something about him," Therese said, stroking her chin. "He looks…*different*."

"Wow." Leonie laughed.

"What?"

"I didn't know discrimination had crossed the barriers into the digital world. You're telling me you don't like him because he's… different? You know he's one of you, right?"

"That's not what I mean," Therese protested. "For a dwarf, he's very…clean."

"So, perhaps he cares about his appearance?" Ben suggested. He could see Chloe and Doris through the kitchen window, but he couldn't see Abe. The dwarf was so short that his head didn't reach the lower sill. "Not every dwarf is as filthy as you and Tag."

A small ripple of giggles worked its way around the group.

Leonie asked, "Do you think he's coming back?"

"I honestly don't know," Ben said. "He's thrown some rage-quits in his time, but never for this long. When he's gone silent before, it's only ever been for a day or two."

"Or until the next *Relic Hunter* was released," Gideon added.

Ben smiled. "Yeah."

Therese, who seemed to want to talk about anything but Tag, said, "Can we focus on one dwarf problem at a time? I don't trust him."

Veronica laughed.

"What?" Therese said.

"Nothing. It's just funny to see the color jealousy paints on you."

Therese's mouth flapped open, then shut, like a fish out of water. Color rose to her cheeks.

"Hey, guys?" Gideon suddenly said, cutting in before Therese could get anything out. He scanned the paddock, counting once more just to be sure of what he was seeing. "How many peacocks did Doris say she had?"

Ben opened his eyes, turning toward Gideon. "Ten. Nine ladies and Fernando."

"Great name, by the way," Huk added.

Blueballs grunted in agreement.

"Then is it just me?" Gideon asked, pointing toward the end of the pen, where not one but *two* brightly colored peacocks strutted. "I'm counting eleven."

The group turned, confusion on all of their faces.

Huk opened his mouth to speak, but before he could, Chloe's head popped out of the door.

"Hey! Guys! We've got a small quest, and we need your help. All hands on deck."

The party looked at each other. Huk gave a curt nod, slipping away from the group as they all headed toward the back of the cabin, the sounds of clucking chickens rising as they approached the large coops.

No one even noticed he was gone.

CHAPTER TEN

They had gathered the majority of the chickens before the clatter of wagon wheels sounded from the stony road.

Dozens and dozens of chickens, flapping their wings and shedding feathers, were placed into large crates that comfortably fit twenty-five apiece. Even though the chickens were headed for dinner plates, it was of utmost importance to Doris that they lived their last day in the best possible conditions.

The party was exhausted. Sprinting after chickens turned out to be a lot harder than they had imagined. Gideon's arm was covered in red spots from the chickens' beaks, and Therese's armor was so covered in bird feces that she was anticipating a good few hours of scrubbing it all down.

Blueballs was a natural, scooping the birds up in his large paws and dumping them in the boxes. By the time the wagon pulled up to the coops, they had only a handful left to gather.

Despite their efforts, however, the sullen dwarven guard riding shotgun in the wagon hopped down and said, "You're late."

Doris looked abashed. "Excuse me, young man. Your chickens are ready to go." She glanced over her shoulder. "Give or take one or two."

The guard wrinkled his nose, a cruel smile on his face. "You're not finished. That'll come out of your pay."

Doris' face dropped. "You can't be serious. I *need* that money. It's all that'll get me through the next few weeks until the next order. You know you're taking nearly all of my chickens, right?"

The dwarf chuckled darkly. "Twenty-five percent less. That's the pay. No arguments. Orders of the king." He glanced at Therese, then Abe, pausing for a second on the dwarf's features.

Doris screwed up her face, looking as if she were ready to give the guard a good tongue-lashing, then thought better of it. "Very well."

Chloe watched with helpless pity. She wanted to say something—do something—but what could she do?

The guard collected the chickens, not even bothering to count them all, and drove back to the city. They watched him until he was out of sight.

Quest complete: Get the chick in the wagon

Don't get cocky, kid. Even my grandmother could have completed this one, and in less time. With more skill. I mean... they're chickens, not basilisks.

Rewards: 400 exp

Chloe grinned at the small increase in experience gained.

"I don't know what I'm supposed to do," Doris said. "That money was supposed to last me for weeks. That was almost all my stock. Do you know how long it takes to raise chickens?"

Before anyone could answer, there came a high-pitched screech from the other side of the cabin.

"And knowing my luck, that'll be someone trying to steal my Fernando." Doris sighed.

Chloe's eyes widened as she realized who was missing from their group. "Huk!"

Doris hiked up her dress and sprinted around the front of the cabin, the others following her.

The sight that met them was beyond comical. As they rounded the house and the pen came into sight, they could all see the small goblin wrestling with the peacock. His hands were on the bird's neck, and he was trying to drag it through a gap in the fence. The peacock stood firm, plumage fanned in a brilliant display as he stubbornly held his ground, occasionally pecking Huk's face.

"Huk! What are you doing?" Chloe shouted, running over to the goblin.

"It's…fine." Huk struggled. "There are two of them. She'll never —*ow!*—notice."

The peacock gave a strange strangled gurgle, his eyes flashing as he pecked Huk's nose.

"*Ow!*"

Doris approached, arm held high as if ready to give him a beating. It wasn't until she saw that Huk was telling the truth—there actually *were* two male peacocks—that she deflated, trying to work out exactly what was going on.

"There are two of them?"

"That's what I said." Another peck to the face and Huk let go of the peacock. It staggered backward, sprinting into the center of the pen, watching them carefully.

"How is that even possible?" Doris asked.

"Maybe a wild peacock was attracted by the other females?" Ben suggested.

Doris shook her head. "I haven't seen another male in over a decade. I've even tried to breed them and only ever gotten females. This is…" Her smile grew wide. "This is a *miracle*."

"So, we can buy one?" Chloe asked eagerly.

Doris' face straightened. "I, erm, I suppose. Maybe."

"Great!" Chloe said, leaping the fence in one bound and dropping into a crouch. She stalked the peacock, moving gently, each step measured and slow.

When she was close, she coiled, was about to spring when—

"Hold on a minute!" Doris shouted, scaring the peacock, which fled from Chloe's clutches.

Chloe landed with a thud on the ground, particles of dirt and peacock poop flying into her mouth.

"What?" she growled irritably.

"Are you expecting me to just overlook the fact that your goblin friend was trying to *steal* one of my peacocks?"

"How do you know it's *your* peacock?" Ben asked. "They look identical."

Doris glanced at the two males, the second one at the far right of the pen, watching the hunting game with great interest.

"Well, I just—" Doris stuck her nose in the air. "A mother knows these things. *My* Fernando has a scar on his right foot, right across the third toe. And anyway, it doesn't matter. The important part was that your friend was going to steal my bird."

Huk tugged on his long ears. "That one's *not* your bird!"

"My paddock, my birds," Doris shouted, her voice rising an octave. "You are *thieves*."

"Oh, give it a rest!" Abe boomed, breaking his quiet and storming to the fence. His voice was authoritative, instantly quieting everyone. "Enough of this horseplay. Let's first establish which peacock is which, and then you *will* grant one of them to the party, okay?"

Doris blubbered, clearly ready to protest.

"Okay?" Abe repeated.

A shadow passed over Doris' face. "Okay."

"Good."

Abe ducked beneath the fence and strode across the pen. The peacock didn't flinch at his arrival, despite his heavy steps. With one confident arm, Abe tucked the peacock in the crook of his arm and carried it across the paddock. He then grabbed the second peacock and brought them both back to the fence for examination.

"Here," he said, holding them both against the fence.

Doris and the KieraSlayers watched, impressed. Doris lifted her dress and dropped to her knees, taking each of the incredibly calm peacocks' feet in her hands in turn.

She smiled, staring into the right peacock's dark eyes, stroked his head, and said, "Fernando!"

"Good," Abe said, passing the left peacock to Huk. "It's settled."

The goblin clutched the peacock tightly, his small body overwhelmed by the large bird. He looked at the others for help. Ben crossed to him, took the peacock in his arms, and began stroking its head.

"How did you do that?" Huk asked the new dwarf in amazement. "Those birds were riled up before I even got near them."

Abe shrugged. "One of my skills, I suppose."

Therese eyed Abe suspiciously.

Doris, who seemed a lot happier now that she had Fernando in her arms, smiled and said, "I suppose, since there are two of them, you can have the other one. I honestly can't think where it would have come from. It is a gift to see two so close to each other. Not only are they rare, but they're very territorial."

"There are no issues here," Chloe said, leaning against the fence and eyeing the peacock clutched in Ben's arms. If she didn't know better, she would swear it was staring at her with a knowing look, its beak impossibly smiling.

Before they left Doris' house, they stopped to have a drink in the mid-afternoon sun.

They were all in good spirits after the mess with the peacocks, and even Doris seemed to have lightened up despite her encounter with the king's guard.

"I'll be okay," Doris said. "I've always found a way to get by. Even after my husband passed, I managed to make ends meet. You guys should count yourselves lucky. You never realize how blessed you are to have good companions until the day that the world takes them away from you."

The KieraSlayers looked at each other and smiled.

Ben raised his glass. "Hear, hear."

They all joined in, except for Abe, who sat there nursing his own drink and looking troubled.

"What's wrong?" Chloe asked quietly as the others chatted among themselves. "You'd think you'd be happy. You're out of the city like you wanted, *and* your superpower helped solve the great—" *beep* "—debate" She nudged him gently, laughing as she did so. "Wait, damn. That was meant to rhyme with 'sock.'"

"It's not fair," Abe said. "This lady has so little, yet she is being given less by the city for, what, not packing the chickens quickly enough?"

"Sounded like the king's decision," Gideon said, eavesdropping and leaning closer to them both. "It's the same in most monarchies. The ones at the top don't see the daily struggles of the average Joe. They don't see the impact just a little bit more gold could have on the people they govern. It's a sad but inevitable truth."

"Well, it doesn't have to be this lady's truth," Abe said, standing up suddenly. "Doris, I'm sorry for the wrongs that have befallen you on this day."

Doris waved a hand. "Forget about it. It's not your fault, and there's nothing you can do about it."

Abe's cheeks flushed. He seemed to consider his words before saying, "Actually, there is. I can do *everything* about it. By tomorrow morning, I will ensure that you are given your missing twenty-five percent, plus an additional fifty percent from the royal treasury."

Doris looked at Abe as though she were speaking to a madman.

"Oh, yeah? Under whose authority are you going to do that?" She laughed.

Abe unfastened his cloak, whipping away the ragged, dark material. The party gasped as he revealed what lay beneath it. It was some of the finest armor they'd ever seen.

"Is that…the royal crest?" Talbot asked, pointing at the emblem with two crossed hammers, their handles decorated with diamonds and other jewels.

"How can you tell?" Huk asked.

"It's printed on everything in the city," Talbot said with awe. "The flags, the currency, and the palace doors."

Abe nodded. "I grant you your riches under the authority of King Abaxis. On my honor as king of Hammersworth."

A horn blew, a great booming drone. It was immediately followed by another blast, then another. Before long, the drone echoed across the city and out toward the farmlands beyond.

"What was that?" Leonie murmured.

Abe's face grew serious. "They've just realized I'm missing."

CHAPTER ELEVEN

"Let me get this straight," Chloe said, her breath catching as they hurried out of Doris' door, Ben still with the peacock beneath his arm. "We're running away from the city because…"

"Because I'll be damned if I'm getting married to any of those tramps." He grunted, pulling his cloak back across him. "Have you *seen* those women? They've got zero personality, and even less in the way of looks. Marrying one of them and being stuck with her for the rest of my life would be like sleeping with an armoire. Heavy, wooden, and lifeless. I don't want that…"

They paused near the paddock, the drone of the horns still going. The KieraSlayers glanced at the city walls, minuscule from where they stood.

Ben shielded his eyes, his elven vision enabling him to see farther than the others.

"Dwarves on horses heading this way. At least a dozen of them."

"Damn," Abe hissed. "We need to go."

"*We?*" Therese replied. "I don't see how 'we' are a part of this. Your problems are your own." She caught Chloe glaring at her and gave a mocking curtsy. "Your Majesty."

"Well, considering I own this kingdom, I think it might be in your best interests to help me," Abe replied with a smirk on his face. "Trust me, I can make your passage through my lands considerably easier than it will be without my aid."

Chloe's eyes went glassy as he spoke. She brought up her menu and selected her horse. A moment later, she heard galloping hooves as her beautiful black Ewing stallion sprinted toward her.

"Bolt," she said affectionately, stroking his muzzle. "Missed you, buddy."

She hopped onto the horse's back and stretched out a hand for Abe to take.

Abe took it, his heavy weight no problem for Chloe's strength. One by one, the other players' horses came into view, each member of the party mounting rapidly as the sound of the guards' horses' approaching hooves grew louder.

Chloe urged Bolt forward, the others falling into line. Behind them, Doris waved goodbye, shouting after Abe that he should hold true to his promise.

"So, I've got to ask," Chloe called back, wind streaming through her hair as Bolt tore toward the forest. "Surely, if you're the king, you can change the rules? Why aren't you just dictating what happens rather than running away from your problems?"

Abe clung tightly to Chloe, his hands fumbling for purchase on her smooth armor.

"At first, it was a rash decision," Abe said. "Fear, mostly. I saw the girls, and my hopes just dropped. Do you know how boring princesses can be?"

"I'm afraid I don't," Chloe replied. "We don't have kings and queens where I come from."

"Anyway," Abe continued, "I panicked, running out the moment I was alone. I found myself sprinting through the city and, well, you know the rest. I bumped into you, and now we're here."

He gasped as Bolt jumped over a shallow ditch. Chloe glanced behind and saw the other riders determinedly following. Beyond them, the city guards were past Doris' house and were now doubled over their horse's backs, trying to catch the party.

"I never gave it much thought," Abe added. "The laws have been in place for hundreds of years, from my father to his father, and many fathers before them. I can't just change the laws on a whim because of a sudden fancy to not marry some dull, snooty toad from Brackenhurst or Witherwinter."

"But you can run away from your kingdom and hide?"

"I didn't say it was a perfect plan," Abe replied. "Though I have to admit that, chicken-gathering aside, this is the most fun I've had in years."

"Well, welcome to the party," Chloe said, eyes narrowing as the tree line approached. They were still ahead of the king's men, but Chloe knew that if they didn't find a way to hide soon, they would be in a lot of danger.

"Let's just hope the wargs and ghouls are fast asleep," Chloe muttered.

Abe's ears perked. "I beg your pardon?"

"Do you think we lost them?" Gideon said quietly as the trees closed around them.

"I guess so," Chloe said. "Blueballs, can you smell them?"

Blueballs stared blankly at Chloe, his frame ridiculous behind the uncomfortable Gideon.

They had been riding for some time, their pace slowing increasingly the farther into the forest they went. Having rushed into the trees, Ben's sense of direction was off, and he now took the front of the procession, trying to get his bearings on where exactly they were.

When they reached an area with trees so close together and undergrowth so thick that it was actually slower for them to ride than walk, they hopped off their horses, thanking them for their help as each galloped off into the shadows and disappeared back the way they had come.

"I love the steeds." Huk beamed. "So handy for someone with short legs."

"You're telling me," Therese said, jogging to catch up with Abe and Chloe. "So, King Short Legs, you going to tell us what the hell is going on?"

Abe told Therese and the others exactly what he had told Chloe on the ride into the woods.

"Couldn't you just find a better girl?" Veronica asked incredulously.

Abe's eyes lingered on Therese a moment longer than was comfortable. "That's not how it works. It's royalty or nothing. That's the law."

"Screw the law!" Gideon exclaimed, to everyone's surprise.

"Woah, what's got you so fired up?" Chloe asked.

"Sorry, I've just always wanted to say that." Gideon blushed.

Everyone laughed. Veronica patted Gideon on the shoulder.

"It's nice to see the fire within you, mage," Veronica said.

Gideon grew even redder.

"The laws are in place for protection," Abe continued. "They're in place for a reason. Without the law, the world would be in anarchy."

"Then what do you propose?" Therese asked. "If the law is the law, you'll have to go back eventually and marry one of those bimbos, right?"

Abe looked at her questioningly. "'Bimbos?'"

"You know, idiots? Empty-heads? Girls who are all boobs and no brains?"

Abe sighed.

"They didn't even have boobs, did they?" Ben asked.

Abe shook his head.

"I guess maybe I can just stay hidden. Travel the world. Without me, the city will keep on turning. They'll find a new king eventually. All will be right again."

"Who's next in line for the throne?" Talbot asked.

Abe chewed his cheek. "Tarinto. My cousin."

"Oh," Talbot said, eyes going to the floor.

"What?"

"It's nothing," Talbot said. "Only, I took the time to speak to some of the locals this week, and most of the reason they're excited for you to marry is so Tarinto doesn't become king should anything happen to you. According to people—or at least the few I've spoken to—he's a bit of an...well, you know..."

"No," Abe said, face suddenly stern. "Tell me."

Talbot looked at the others for help. Realizing he wasn't going to get any, he said, "An..." He mouthed the word "asshole."

"My cousin is *not* an asshole," Abe retorted, voice echoing through the forest. "I mean, sure, he's a bit abrasive. Very rough around the edges, and..." He slowed down as if remembering something. "There *was* that time when he...but that was an accident, and he was cleared. The whole thing passed." He flapped his hands. "Oh, let's just forget about it, okay? Where the hell is this wood house we're looking for?"

Abe stormed off, catching up with Ben in the foliage ahead.

Ben looked in either direction, uncertainty on his face. The peacock began to fidget beneath his arm.

"You okay?" Chloe asked.

"We might need your map, Chloe, to see where we've been. This part of the forest holds no memory for me."

Chloe nodded, opened her menu, and selected her map. The map worked by illuminating only the places they had already traveled, so the majority of the wood was shaded. She could see a lightened path of where they had entered into the woods. A few inches across was the path they had trodden the other day, although there was no symbol or legend that showed where the house was.

"We need to go east...I think," Chloe said.

"Okay." Ben raised his head to the leafy canopy. "Which way is east? I can't see the sun."

"That way?" Chloe said, pointing to their right.

"No," Veronica chipped in. "It feels like that way should be east."

"What do you mean, 'it feels?'" Talbot asked. "How does direction 'feel?'"

"It feels right," Veronica retorted.

"Okay, let's stop bickering," Leonie said. "This is getting us nowhere."

"Ouch!" Ben suddenly cried, dropping the peacock onto the ground. In a sudden dash, it sped off to their right and lost itself in the undergrowth.

"Quick!" Chloe said, running after the bird. "We can't lose that thing now!"

Ben matched Chloe's speed as they tore through the forest after the peacock. It was nimble and swift, darting through brambles and tangles and weaving around trees. If it wasn't for its bright plumage, they would have lost it many times along the way.

The rest of the party scrambled after them, managing to just about keep Chloe and Ben in their sights.

Chloe jumped over a fallen log, feeling herself begin to sweat beneath her armor. KieraFreya and Ben encouraged her to keep running, the pair of them closing the gap on the bird.

Ben broke ahead of Chloe slightly as the peacock bore left. He swung from a low-hanging branch, flying through the air for a few seconds before landing, his fingers outstretched in anticipation of the catch.

"Almost!" Ben exclaimed, his greedy eyes focused on the bird.

He didn't hear Chloe cry, "Watch out!" as the bird made a small hop and went through the window of the house. Ben's momentum carried him forward until his face smashed into the side of the camouflaged building.

"Ow!" he complained, sitting up and rubbing his head. "There wasn't a window there before…" Chloe doubled over in a fit of laughter, the other KieraSlayers catching up one by one and joining in, realizing what had just happened.

Ben turned his head suddenly, the speed dizzying him after his crash. "The peacock!" he cried.

He needn't have bothered worrying, for the peacock stood in the doorway, its form slowly morphing into a man they instantly recognized.

Chloe shook her head, unable to believe what she was seeing. "You've got to be kidding me."

The Wrangler chuckled, his massive form jiggling. "Great job, mortals. You've passed my test."

Chloe wanted to scowl, but she couldn't help but join in the laughter. The only person who wasn't laughing was Abe, who stood transfixed by the sight that he had just seen.

"Come, come," the Wrangler managed at last, ushering them into his house. "You've proven yourselves worthy, KieraSlayers. Let us drink and laugh and eat, and I will grant you your reward."

When Huk reached the doorway, the Wrangler put out a hand to stop him. "Except for you."

Huk looked shocked. "Me? What did I do?"

"There is a grain of darkness in your heart. Thievery of a lady's most treasured possession is no way to take on this world."

"I…I didn't," Huk blubbered.

"Before there were two, you wanted to steal the one. Don't think I didn't see it. There is too much darkness in the world. Don't let yours take you, too."

Huk nodded wordlessly. The Wrangler stepped aside and let him in. He clapped his hands, adding, "Okay, the task is complete, and the guests are here. Tonight, we feast!"

CHAPTER TWELVE

They hadn't had a meal so merry in as long as any of the KieraSlayers could remember.

The Wrangler was a master of food. Somehow, miraculously, a long table had appeared in the house, with small carved logs for chairs lining the edges. There was the perfect number, including a seat for Abe, and each place at the table already had a goblet full of wine and plates with meat and vegetables.

Chloe had no idea what the meat was, but she didn't care. She hungrily tore into the food, the amount seeming never to diminish despite how much she shoveled into her mouth.

The Wrangler took the head of the table, a large deer skull with antlers pinned to the wall behind him. When viewed at the right angle, it looked as though the horns were his own, which, she supposed, they could have been. The man could apparently trans-figure into any animal that suited his fancy.

The wine loosened their tongues, and soon they began to talk of the real world. Of life beyond Obsidian, and their own trials on Earth. Chloe grew quiet, listening to the tales of the others, yet somehow knowing that soon the questions, as always, would turn to her.

Luckily, that was not the case tonight. Abe kept the others busy with many a question about the realm of the blessed and their adventures and life in the real world. He clapped and whooped at talk of electricity and the independence of their real-world selves, and took a rather hungry interest in the makeup of the political system and the idea of democracy.

"That sounds highly inefficient," he said, the only dwarf Chloe had seen dab his beard and chin to remove the wine stains. "How does anything get done if everyone has a vote? It can't be quick?"

"Oh, it's not," Therese replied. "Once a motion gets carried, it can take weeks, or sometimes months or years for anything to happen."

Abe laughed, shaking his head. "Stupid. If I want something to change, I snap my fingers and it happens in seconds."

"Except for changing the laws of marriage," Talbot muttered under his breath.

"I *told* you…" Abe started, the booming voice returning.

"Now, now," the Wrangler said calmly. Despite his relaxed demeanor, his voice was even more authoritative than Abe's. "Let's keep this merry. Politics and sex are two subjects never to discuss at the dinner table, or so I've learned."

"Damn, there goes my next topic." Veronica snorted.

They navigated away from troublesome topics, eventually asking many questions of the Wrangler. Even Abe, who had some knowledge of a mythical man living in the forests but had never quite believed in him, joined in.

The Wrangler answered as many questions as he felt he could, before snapping his fingers and laughing at the expression on the party's faces as a dozen brilliant blue and green peacocks jumped through the window and collected their plates and cutlery in their beaks, darting quickly through a small door that Chloe swore wasn't there before.

Another snap and foxes came through the door with plates of sweet fruits piled high.

"You guys must have a lot in common," Talbot said, mouth full of berries. "You both have a way with animals."

Abe waved a hand. "I'm sure my skills are nothing compared to this gentleman's. I am but an apprentice in your presence."

"Don't do yourself a disservice," the Wrangler said. "The talents of the king's line are legendary in this region, your affinity with animals second to none."

"Second to yours," Abe said, raising a glass.

"Hear, hear!" they chorused.

The Wrangler cast his eyes down. "A compliment well put," he said, thanking the animal servants as they fled back out of the door and left the party in peace.

After the food was finally finished and the table had been cleared, the party found themselves sleepily sitting on the floor, nestled with blankets and cushions in front of the fire.

The Wrangler had taken his seat again, while Abe sat in a chair that had appeared across from him. The pair of them looked like statues from the old world, great kings from a time before time had been recorded.

At last, as the fire crackled and night fell upon the forest, the Wrangler broke the silence that they hadn't been aware had fallen.

"Now comes the time to give you your reward," he said.

"You mean that food wasn't our reward?" Therese hiccupped, her eyes misty from the wine. Abe chuckled, his eyes fixed on the female dwarf.

The Wrangler continued as if nothing had been said. "You are on the hunt for a beast of legend. A foal of fable. There are a great many beasts in this world, and those which are valuable know places to hide where mortal man cannot tread without guidance.

"Shikora, the fabled horse of the Goddess of Divine Retribution is on another plane, one that is not within the boundaries of this world but rather is caught in a world twisted with unreality and trickery. She is safe but she is lost, and only reuniting with her mistress will allow her to make her way back to the surface world."

"Sounds dark," Huk said.

Leonie agreed. "Sounds tricky."

"How do we get there?" Chloe asked.

The Wrangler sighed. "With a great deal of magic, young one. The Nether Realm is a place that requires immense mana and a focused will to access. Think of it as a prison between worlds. A place where reality must fracture, where the etheric must bleed. Shikora was cast into this eternal prison, trotting in the cursed realm until such time as a mage strong enough to harness the etheric can open it."

Chloe considered this. The power that was required sounded far too immense. Greater than anything she'd ever conjured.

"And this must be completed by a single mage?" Chloe asked, eyes finding Gideon's.

The Wrangler's face creased into that warm smile. "I never said that."

"Chloe and Gideon can do it," Veronica said excitedly. "And I've got magic too. Can't we all work together to do this?"

"I'm afraid it'll take even more than the three of you," the Wrangler said. "The last time access to the Nether Realm was attempted was three hundred years ago, and the effort did not end well."

"What happened?" Talbot asked, his curiosity about the history of the land piquing his interest.

"A great gathering of mages," Abe answered before the Wrangler could continue. "It was legendary." He took a deep breath, closed his eyes, and began to sing.

> *"When two dozen mages doth gather below*
> *The clouds and the rain and the sleet and the snow*
> *A harrowing tale will soon come to pass*
> *Of mages who tried, and they failed in their task.*
>
> *But two dozen mages was not what it took*
> *Another two dozen it would take to shook*
> *The land when they broke into realms that had passed*
> *Four dozen mages now failed in their task.*
>
> *But hearken o'er there on the hills far ahead*
> *Another two dozen gallop in stead*

They raise horses high and hold up their staffs
Another two dozen to fail in their task.

Now eighty young mages, well, some young, some old
They grasp the etheric, a task oh so bold
To break into that where they want to bask
A realm they can't reach when they fail in their task.

And so it's the rub, the next dozen do come,
They make up near hundred in heads with the sum
And there it now comes, a true test of cast
A hundred now fail in the mages' grand task.

The Nether Realm's broken, it's guarded and true
And never grant access for me or for you
The horrors are hidden, though one crack remains
That fateful day filled with the dragons that came.

They snuck through the doorway and into the air
And hovered and flew and breathed flames in
    their hair
The dragon which birthed from the Nether Realm
    cracks
Flew over the forests and never came back.

So there lies the story of brave and of true
A horror now passed when the dragons did flew
The mages all burned and reduced to ash
Though a hundred did try, they still failed in their
    task."

"That's haunting," Therese said, her eyes shimmering in the fire-
light. "And it's true?"

"To a large extent," the Wrangler replied. "The truth is that dragons
existed on this plane long before the Nether Realm was breached. It

just so happened that on that day, the disturbance in the etheric drew them close. There's something about great amounts of power that draws them from hiding."

"Dragons…they're real?" Chloe asked.

Abe sat forward in his chair. "Oh, they're real. Particularly this far north in the world. Their nests can be found in the mountains, but it is rare we glimpse them these days. Their breed is ancient."

Chloe tried to imagine them. Dragons. *Real* dragons flying overhead. Great winged lizards with breath of flame soaring above them all and raining hellfire. It seemed almost impossible.

More impossible than a hundred mages trying to open the portal to Nether Realm? KieraFreya thought.

Have you heard of this realm? Chloe asked.

I have. A prison for the gods. A place of banishment and reprimand. Used rarely, and all but lost to the general knowledge of most. I wonder why they threw Shikora in there?

A desperate move from a desperate god trying to keep you in pieces? Chloe wondered.

KieraFreya agreed.

"So, in order to free KF's horse, we have to break open a portal to another realm?" Veronica asked, trying to get her head around it all. "If a hundred mages failed, what hope do we have?"

The Wrangler sat up in his chair, taking a slow sip of his drink. The house was warm now, the sweet smell of ale and leftover food filling their senses and making them drowsy. If not for the realization of what they had to do, they would all have hit the floor by now.

"Each generation learns from the mistakes of the last," he said. "If a hundred mages fail, you try two hundred. The task is not impossible. The door opened, just not enough."

"And when it does open?" Chloe asked. "How do we know that no other dangers will come forth? It sounds like this has never actually been achieved before. If the rumor of dragons coming forth from the portal holds any kind of truth, who's to say other worse things won't follow?"

The Wrangler shrugged. "These are the risks we take in the search for knowledge and hope. The world has been unbalanced since the fracturing of KieraFreya. For thousands of years, the balance has been disturbed, and darkness has been leaking ever more into the zeitgeist of our times. Without the restoration of the fallen, the world will never be at peace."

"He's right, y'know," Ben said. "On every step of our journey, we've encountered darkness. Black mages, skeletons, trolls, thieves, assassins, and more. Every single step. With the world shaken by the arrival of the blessed, it'll only get worse. If we can't restore balance, how will the world survive?"

"But we can't do it," Huk chipped in. "We don't know two hundred mages. How are we going to find them all?"

Chloe looked at the Wrangler and Abe, a smirk on her face. "We're currently in a room with an ancient guardian of the forest and the king of the largest city in Obsidian. I think we'll be able to find two hundred mages. Maybe even a few other classes with a useful pool of mana, using the right communication channels."

Abe stared at the Wrangler, clearly caught by Chloe's mention of the man being ancient, a goofy smile on his face. Then he seemed to realize what Chloe had said, and his mouth dropped open.

"I beg your pardon?"

CHAPTER THIRTEEN

"Something's wrong," Mia said to the darkness.

The lines of code went rogue. An inspection sheet on her laptop created line after line of its own script before her eyes.

Not an unusual occurrence, given that Praxis Ltd. had sourced the best artificial intelligence technology to drive their game to new heights of realism.

This was a technology that swallowed knowledge and intelligence into its code before taking what it had learned and generating its own instructions to grow the game larger and more realistic than anything the world had ever seen.

But this was somehow different.

Rather than a steady stream of letters and symbols drifting lazily across the screen, this was a burst of digits. Letters and numbers hurled into the code lines as though somebody had hired a room full of monkeys to smash the keys.

Mia tried to read it all, but it moved faster than her eyes could process. She picked out small lines of the code, the words doing nothing to calm her beating heart.

LAUNCH: (GOD.PROGRAMME.EXE)

#ERROR404

```
#ERROR404
#ERROR404
SEQUENCE_FOUND
LAUNCH_LOCATION=(X.REALM.3.4)
LAUNCH_CHARACTER=MYARIS
LAUNCH_CHARACTER=DRYANA
LAUNCH_CHARACTER=FUKMOS
*FAILED*
REBOOT_POPUP
MISSING_SEQ
LAUNCH_CHARACTER=FUKMOS
ALIGNMENT=(NEGATIVE.6)
```

And on it went.

"Honey?" Demetri mumbled, blinding himself by turning on his bedside lamp.

Mia started at the disturbance.

"Mia, it's 3:30 in the morning. What're you still doing up?"

He sat up in bed, face turning sour when he saw the laptop whirring away on her lap.

"You promised," he said.

"I know," she replied, a pleading expression on her face. "But I've been so close for a few days now, and I just needed a little more time to get this figured out."

"And have you?" he asked, resigning himself to another disturbed evening, despite the fact he had to work in the morning.

Mia nodded. "Look."

She pointed at the screen. Demetri stared blankly.

"Code."

"Right," she said, eyes bright. "It's writing itself. More code than I've ever seen in such a short window of time." She fought against the code, scrolling to a few key spots in the dialog. "There. See? It's them. It's the gods. They're taking over."

Demetri grunted, rolled over, and put on his glasses. He squinted at the screen, seeing the gods' names written in red. "Fukmos 2.0? What does that mean?"

"I don't know," Mia replied. "But they're talking. Now. To us…well, sort of. They're alive in the system, and they're up to something."

Demetri stared at the screen, eyes going blurry from the light attacking them and the speed of the scrolling text. "You think we should warn Chloe?"

Mia nodded. "I think we *have* to."

"It's not safe to play with the etheric boundaries," Dryana crooned, her voice hollow and wispy. "The disturbances can be detected. Our homes unbind."

"She's right," Myaris agreed. "Only the naughty know the way."

Why do you think I'm known as the God of Mischief? Fukmos thought, his eyes narrowed.

They had been grating on his patience for days. The two sisters jabbered like schoolgirls and agreed with each other on every point.

It had been like this all their lives. Ever since Fukmos had first breathed the fetid air of the underworld. Ever since he had performed his first prank and cackled with glee.

Myaris and Dryana had been perfect targets to begin with. The perfect recipients for his wicked ways. Fukmos would lure them into lost recesses, turn them against each other, find ways to make them hurt…

For a while.

Once the girls came of age and grew into their powers, it was nearly impossible to catch them. Myaris would conjure her magic, inflicting disease and illness upon Fukmos to keep him bound in darkness for days on end. Dryana would bring the spirits to her aid, summoning her tricks and driving Fukmos mad.

When it came time to practice again, Fukmos turned to the mortals. It was easy at first, raining down mischief and delighting in the chaos it wrought. Kingdoms turned against each other, families were torn apart, best friends were at each other's throats…

The good old days.

The days before Oella, the almighty Goddess of Love, discovered the mischief and clamped down on his visits to the mortal realm. Security was tightened, and the curtains of the etheric drew shut. KieraFreya was destroyed and left below. Life moved on.

It had taken Fukmos years to figure out the lost and forgotten paths. It was through these paths that he discovered the blessed. On them, he had discovered the girl he manipulated, and he found a way back to the mortal realm.

It was these paths he now trod with his sisters, the new guardians of his trickery assigned by his no-good father.

The portal rippled before them, all life a blur through a migraine's lens. The very air shone, a pulse of rainbow colors accompanied by the heat of energy and etheric power.

"It's beautiful…" Myaris breathed.

Dryana merely nodded.

"Does it hurt?" Myaris asked.

Fukmos looked at her, surprised. "Not scared of a little pain, are we?"

She shook her head. "No. I rather enjoy it. You can't feel life without feeling even a little bit of pain."

"So true," Dryana agreed.

"How do we activate it?" Myaris asked.

Fukmos dragged a dark hand over his face. "You cut your wrists and bleed your way through. Didn't anybody tell you that's how you cross the etheric?"

Dryana shook her head, her expression passive. "If it must be so."

She shook her pale wrist free from her dark garb and dragged a fingernail across the skin. Dark blood rose in lazy globules to the surface.

"There. Am I granted access?"

Fukmos couldn't believe it. Had the sisters gone back to believing his trickery once more? After all the years that had passed, did his father's quest for the three of them mean he once again had their trust?

He grinned wickedly. "Of course. After you."

Dryana stepped forward, momentarily going completely white. Her body faded into the immaterial substance of the ghosts she ruled as she unfolded her arms and fell through the portal. A hideous shriek trailed after her, then shut off as suddenly as it began.

Myaris copied her sister, dragging a fingernail across her poxed skin, catching scabs and boils. She coughed into the ring of her fist, felt the blood swell, and walked forward, disappearing a second later through the portal. Another shriek accompanied her vanishing.

Fukmos couldn't help but laugh out loud, trying and failing to mute himself with the back of his hand. His tremendous glee at his mischief spread to his cheeks as he slapped his leg, furrowed his brow, pictured the mortal girl in golden armor, and dove through the portal.

CHAPTER FOURTEEN

When morning came around, Abe was nowhere to be found.

"Abe? Abe!" Chloe called, startling the others into wakefulness as she searched the house. The doors that had appeared the night before had miraculously vanished, as had their host and Therese.

"Relax, they'll be somewhere nearby," Ben said. "Maybe they're just out chopping wood, or they're on a walk? They can't have gone far."

But they were nowhere to be found. By late morning, Chloe had searched as far from the house as she dared. With little confidence in her own directions within the forest, she would travel as far as she could while keeping the tiniest fragment of the house in sight.

"Anything?" Gideon asked on her fifth return to the house.

"Nothing." Chloe was getting worried now. Not only did the majority of their plan rest on having the king of Hammersworth in their company, but she was also pretty sure the king's guards had gotten a good enough look at the KieraSlayers' faces to be able to recognize them if they all turned back up in the city empty-handed.

"They'll arrest us on sight," Chloe said, hand on her forehead as panic sank in.

"Calm down, Chloe," Veronica said, still clearly slightly hungover from the night before. "Even if he doesn't make it back, we can still make this happen."

"Do you think they're together?" Chloe asked. "Therese and Abe? You think they're somewhere with the Wrangler?"

Ben shrugged. "They're probably off talking about something dwarvish."

By lunchtime, there was still no sign of any of them. Even Gideon began to worry about where they'd gotten to.

"Surely they would've left some kind of note if they were leaving?"

"With what, genius?" Huk replied. "Do you see any paper or pens in that house?"

Gideon blushed.

"We *need* to find them," Chloe repeated. "What if people think we killed the king? If we go back without him, we've got no hope of getting the mages together. We'll end up in prison for years, and I've served my time in prison. I don't need to go back to the slammer."

Veronica, Leonie, and Huk looked at Gideon and Ben as if to say, "She *what?*"

Ben shook his head, indicating that it was better that they didn't ask.

"What about those extra rooms in the house? Maybe they're in there?" Huk suggested.

"What rooms?" Chloe replied. "I looked this morning, and they'd vanished. I swear this house has some kind of magic in it. There's no way that table from last night could suddenly just disappear without a trace."

"Just try, Chloe. What harm is there in looking again?"

Resigned, Chloe followed Huk's lead. She felt foolish running her hands along the walls and looking for hidden crevices or doorways. She tried the place where she'd seen the animals disappear and found nothing. She placed her ears against the wood and only heard the forest noises outside.

The whole thing made no sense.

It wasn't until she heard Gideon calling from outside that she felt hope return.

"They're here!" Gideon called out excitedly. "They're here!"

Chloe ran to the door and saw the two dwarves walking back through the trees. They were talking loudly, laughing and joking. Not only that, but they were also holding hands.

Chloe ran out to meet them, shoving Therese firmly. "Where the *hell* have you been? What is this?"

Therese looked down at her hands and blushed. "We've been out for a walk, okay? It's beautiful out there. So much lush undergrowth in the forest. You should see the flowers and animals! It's like another world."

"We've been worried sick," Ben said, hands on his hips. "You could've told us you were leaving."

"Sorry, *Mom*." Therese giggled, Abe laughing beside her. "I didn't realize I couldn't go out unaccompanied. No one was awake when we woke up, so we figured we'd go for a walk." She said to Abe, "Come on, baby."

They passed the stunned onlookers and headed into the house. The others watched with mouths agape. A moment later, something crashed through the trees. The lumbering shape of a brown bear appeared, slowly morphing back into the form of the Wrangler.

He strode past the others too, smiling at their dumbstruck faces. "Don't ask," he said, tapping his nose with one finger and following the pair inside.

Chloe looked incredulously at Ben and Gideon. A second later, they all ran inside.

The large table had somehow returned, the plates once again piled high, goblets full. Therese and Abe sat side by side, already munching their food.

"Can someone tell us what the hell is going on?" Chloe exclaimed, taking a seat beside the pair. "What is this? What are you doing? What happened?"

Therese blushed, then swallowed. "What does it look like? Abe and I are...well, an item."

"An item?" Abe asked.

"Intending to be married," Therese clarified.

"Hold on," Chloe said, hands outstretched, trying to get her head around this. "You're getting married?"

"Yep," Abe said gleefully, bread spilling out of his mouth. "You guys were right. I'm the damn king. I can make my own rules, and I rule that I want to marry this beautiful woman."

Veronica poked two fingers into her mouth, feigning throwing up. Leonie and Huk snorted behind their hands.

"But you two seemed so…" Gideon mulled his words, "friction-y before."

Ben nodded. "I didn't have you down for the marrying type."

Therese shoved another forkful of food into her mouth, talking without concern for the bits she sprayed into the air. "Me neither. But after we got to talking, I realized something. I've never had much power in any game I've played. I've always been the tank who just got bashed around by the enemies and protected everyone by taking a beating, and I figured, you know what? What would it be like to sit beside a king, ruling a kingdom? Now *that's* power you can't buy."

"Unless you get the expanded edition with the DLC and pay the monthly subscription for the premium package," Huk noted, doing his best impression of the adverts they'd all seen for various other MMORPGs. The others laughed.

"Is that what you want from me, pookey-bear?" Abe asked, hurt in his eyes.

"Of course not," Therese replied, placing a hand on his cheek. "You're a kind, loving, generous, funny, man. I'd be honored to sit by your side."

Chloe, who was still wrestling with this latest revelation, watched the pair with fascination. She tried to picture their wedding, the streets filled with hundreds of citizens screaming Therese's name. *Would* the city accept her? She supposed they would. Anything for royal festivities.

"So, you're going to leave us?" Veronica asked, realization dawning. "You're…what? Out of the party now? You're going to spend the rest of your days as arm candy for the king while we continue the rest of the adventure without you?"

"Nope," Therese said. "Of course not. We had a long talk about that out by the lily pond… Oh, you *have* to see it, it's absolutely beautiful! White flowers in bloom in a small pond surrounded by the most colorful moss you've ever seen—"

"Who are you?" Veronica exclaimed as she knelt by Therese and stared deep into her eyes. "What spell have they put you under?"

Therese shook her off. "I'm under no spell or illusion, okay? I like Abe. He likes me. For once in my life, I was able to spend a morning within a game without being under the threat of impending death, and I realized how beautiful the world was. Abe has never been this far into the forest. He rarely leaves the palace walls."

"It's true," he confirmed. "I've been stuck in something of a rut, lately, but this lady is snapping me out of it."

"I think it's cute," Leonie remarked. "They deserve happiness."

Chloe eyed them both suspiciously. "You'll still be in the party?"

Therese nodded emphatically. "Oh, hell, yes. If anything, think of what this'll do for our reputation. You'll have the queen of Hammersworth with you on your journey and the royal guards by your side. It's a win-win for everyone."

"And think of all that dwarvish sex," Ben added.

"Ben!" Chloe laughed.

Therese and Abe blushed, unable to meet each other's eyes.

"You should bless the union," the Wrangler said, breaking his silence. "It's rare that such an act of change comes about on the levels of royalty. This union will give every little girl born in the city the hope of one day achieving greatness. No longer will the monarchy be an exclusive club for kings, queens, princes, and princesses; it will be a step toward a fairer future for the whole of Obsidian."

After a small pause, Chloe chuckled and shook her head. She reached for a goblet on the table and raised it in the air. "To King Abaxis and Queen Therese, I suppose."

The others picked up their goblets and lifted them high. "To the king and queen."

They started back through the forest a little after noon. The day was bright, small rays of sunlight bursting through the gaps in the leafy canopy. Around them, birdsong was in full swing, a chorus of tweets and whistles from a variety of avians.

Led by the Wrangler, they managed to make great time, the journey seeming far shorter going out of the forest than it had going in. Whether this was by some illusion of the Wrangler, Chloe had no idea, but the trees soon began to thin and the light grew brighter.

The Wrangler bade them farewell as the fields came into view, laughing as a few of the party came forward and placed their arms around his mammoth waist.

"Be careful, young folk." The Wrangler smiled. "The way might be rocky. Remember, the kingdom may believe you have stolen the king. Although this will be remedied quickly upon your return, remember that there are many who shoot first and ask questions later."

Chloe nodded solemnly. "Thank you for everything."

"This is not goodbye," the Wrangler said. "I have a feeling we will meet again before too long. The Nether Realm takes a great deal of power to open. Don't turn down help from strangers. Remember that union in light is the only way to destroy union in darkness." He leaned forward and whispered to Chloe, "And I have a feeling that darkness is gathering."

With that, the Wrangler transformed into his bear form and trundled back through the forest. They stared after him until he was gone, sadness falling over the group.

As the Wrangler predicted, the group was met halfway to the city gates. They had chosen to continue their travels on foot, enjoying the gentle breeze and the sun on their faces. Before too long, they heard the sound of galloping hooves.

A few moments later, they were surrounded by a phalanx of the king's horsemen—a dozen dwarves on stubby steeds pointing their spears at the KieraSlayers.

"By the king's command, we order you to stop. Declare yourselves," the lead guard thundered. His helmet had patches of gold among the silver plating.

King Abaxis lowered his hood, revealing his stern face. "By the *king's* command, I order you to lower your spears, lest I have you imprisoned for threatening the king."

The lead guard's face dropped. "Your Majesty, I-I…"

"Less blubbering and more protecting the realm, Captain. Now, on your way, and inform the kingdom of my arrival. We've got a union to celebrate."

The captain looked abashed. He nodded and darted away with his men, the dust from the dried mud kicking up a cloud behind them.

"That was impressive," Huk said in admiration.

Abe grinned. "Being the king has its perks."

Compared to the last few days, the streets were a lot easier to navigate after they passed through the gates. The swell of the crowds had died down following the king's disappearance and a solemn atmosphere had fallen upon Hammersworth.

"You can really feel the shift," Chloe whispered. "It's almost like someone died." She poked out her tongue at the dwarf.

A blast from a horn sounded, a different tone from the day before when the city had discovered the king had fled. Chloe wondered how many horns there were, and for what occasions they were used. Abe explained that this horn sounded to note the arrival of royalty.

"Just watch," Abe said, pausing in the street with the KieraSlayers behind him. His cloak was back on now since he wanted to remain hidden until he had at least reached his quarters.

At the sound of the horn, there was an excited buzz from the houses around them. Heads poked out of windows, doors opened, and people stepped into the street. A feverish chatter began to rise, the people of Hammersworth not having seen this much excitement since the death of Abe's father and his subsequent coronation.

They heard the word "scandal" thrown around. Women gossiped and trod slowly into the streets, heads close together as they whispered animatedly.

"Told you!" Abe said. "Come on. We've got to move fast if we don't want to get choked by the bodies again."

By the time they made it to the palace gates, there was a crowd waiting for them. Women and men alike rose on tiptoe to look at the gates, as if expecting someone to pop out and say hi at any minute. Children were lifted onto shoulders. The horn continued to sound, louder than ever now.

"I suppose it's time to put on a show," Abe said, making his way to the large carved-stone gates.

At his presence, the crowd parted, confused at first by the dwarf staring up at the gate guard. Abe called up and commanded that the gate be opened.

The gate guard, in a similar fashion to the captain of the troops in the field, gave Abe a look of disbelief.

"On whose orders?" he called, quiet washing over the crowd.

"On the order of the king," Abe called, once more lowering his hood.

A ripple of shock and excitement worked its way through the masses.

"That never gets old." Veronica grinned.

The guard's eyes widened in shock. He nodded and immediately began issuing instructions for guards on the lower level to open the gates for the king.

When they were wide open, Abe began to walk through. He stopped when he heard a woman shriek, "We thought you dead!"

Another cried, "Has he chosen?"

Abe turned, his warm smile reaching the crowd. "It takes more than a day of disappearance to kill a king, and it takes more than a stranger to make a wife."

He took a deep breath and then sighed. "Friends, brothers, Hammersworthians, a new day is upon us. A day of celebration and rejoicing. A day of change, and the introduction of a new order. It would be easy to soothe you with a lie, but that is not the tack I wish to take. Honesty is the greatest ally any man can have.

"The truth is that I have been soul-searching. The princesses and brides-to-be who graced these halls were not a suitable match for your king. Despite the arrangements of the past and the history and traditions of this land, it would have been impossible to have formed a strong union that would be worthy of your adoration. Though they have their desirable qualities, no princess was deemed worthy."

An audible gasp came from the crowd. "Impossible."

"Unheard of."

"This'll never do."

"But fear not," Abe boomed, hands outstretched. "For you shall not be left without your day of celebration. A union has been decided upon. Not within the confines of our laws, but from a new order. An amendment will be made that will enhance our great city and bring hope and joy to *every* citizen who remains. The union of the king with his queen will be with whomever he chooses to marry."

Men's eyebrows raised and a few fists clenched. Women, however, swooned, hands clapping to their mouths.

A sudden rush of chatter arose. Women began to reach forward, raising their hands. Cries of "Pick me," and "I'm the one! It's got to be me!" echoed around the palace gates.

Once more, Abe hushed the crowd with his hands. He let out a laugh. "There is no need to squabble. The match has already been decided."

At this, Chloe saw a young dwarf appear by the back doors of the palace a small distance beyond the gate. His eyes were dark, his ears cocked and ready.

"Therese?" Abe smiled. "Will you please step forward and make yourself known?"

Heads turned in every direction to look for the woman Abe was summoning. Therese's ears flushed and her eyes darted around awkwardly as Huk shoved her forward, setting her numb legs in motion. The quiet returned. She emerged into the cleared space and stood by Abe's side.

"Ladies and gentlemen, I present to you your future queen, Therese the blessed!"

There was a mixed reaction from the crowd. The majority of those gathered cheered and whooped, a few whistling between their fingers. Several women exploded into unhappy tears, their dreams of becoming the next bride shattered in a matter of minutes. A few heads turned and mumbled harsh words of disgust at having one of the blessed lead their city.

Face clouded with anger, the young dwarf stood on the steps, fists shaking with rage before he turned back into the palace and slammed the doors behind him.

"To the queen," the KieraSlayers exclaimed.

A chorus from the crowd echoed them.

"To King Abaxis and Queen Therese," Ben called.

This time the crowd made a heartier effort. Abe and Therese waved the KieraSlayers over. The group followed them inside the palace as the gates closed behind, leaving a fever of gossip and excitement to sweep through the city.

CHAPTER FIFTEEN

Doc (and Mia),

Great to hear that you're doing so well in the new place. Well, old place, really. It'll be nice to finally see you guys again when I get out of here, although I don't see that happening for some time.

Hopefully you're taking care of me and looking after my body. It's going to be surreal stepping back into the real world and feeling everything at full capacity again.

Things in here are pretty bizarre. I know you've been watching on the screens (well, I hope you've been watching!), but it feels as if the world has just been blown wide open. We're on track for a quest that will swamp any other I've completed. I mean, opening a portal into the Nether Realm? Can you say "bat-shit crazy?"

I'm not forgetting that we've got to somehow unite hundreds of mages and magic-users to help the cause. I'm thinking that might be a bit more difficult than anticipated, given the somewhat frosty reception to Therese's union with Abe.

Seriously, can't these NPCs see that the blessed are only trying to help? We're making their world wider. Defeating darkness.

All that crap.

I don't know how it's all going to play out. It's hard to make the city folk here see the enormity of what we're doing. It almost reminds me of those "Perfect Work Culture" seminars Father and Mother used to send us on when we were teens.

At the time, I fell asleep a lot in those, but from what I remember, there might be some useful information to unravel. I remember the main message being "make your employees feel like a part of your cause."

But how to do that on such a grand scale?

Anyway, I suppose that's a problem for me to figure out. KF is as impatient as ever. She just wants her friggin' horse. I don't blame her. I want my body back to myself, and to explore parts of this land that don't have us attacked by revenge-seeking gods.

C'est la vie.

Thanks again for the updates on Praxis. Great to see that, even in this fully-immersed state, I can have an impact on the wider world. I feel like I'm finally getting a glance into my parents' life, juggling several businesses and splitting my attention among them all. It's kinda fun.

Shudder

Did I really just say that?

If you could just keep an eye on the figures for me and let me know what exactly the #1-viewed guy is doing in Obsidian, that'd be great. I'd love to make it to #1 and rub my snooty siblings' faces in the success.

Obviously when I'm out of here, of course.

Speaking of, has there been any news about Henry or Henrietta? They seem to have gone silent. It's making me nervous.

Thanks for the warning about the AI, too. If anyone can figure out exactly what's going on, it's Mia. I still can't believe she met my parents and didn't freak out! Most people burn under their laser vision.

I'll be keeping an eye out for any sign of Fukmos. I hoped we'd seen the last of him, but these new additions don't bode well. I suppose that, once more, I'm running against the clock...

Fun.

Anyhow, I better get back to my digital life. I've got a rift to open to create a portal to a realm that hasn't been accessed in three centuries and could release untold horrors on the world.

Wish me luck...

Chloe.

Chloe

I'd hardly say this place is old for either of us. After spending weeks at Mia's place, I appreciate this place a whole lot more. I'm viewing it like a whole new pad now that Mia is sharing it, too.

Don't you worry about your earthly body (insert alien reference here—laughing face emoji). We're taking as good care of you as we possibly can. You might be shaky for a few days when you return, but Mia has told me that Praxis is constantly updating their care sequences based on the latest research. You'll have nothing to worry about, trust us.

I can't believe the latest direction of your mission either. You know, I thought that when you took on the Volcanic Titan you might have peaked in badassery, but then you meet a shapeshifter bear-man who tells you about the Nether Realm.

The chat *exploded* at that.

Seriously, it's almost impossible to keep up with your fans out here. You know that there are now Facebook groups, Discord chats, and entire Twitch streams dedicated to following your journey and advertising Obsidian? The fans go nuts for it! It's incredible!

One person even got KieraFreya's armor tattooed on their bicep!

It's nuts to think how far you've come since starting off as a weak human who could barely take on a goblin. Now look at you. I have to say, I definitely think this game is doing you a world of good. Who'd have known you'd need a break from your family, huh? (Winking face).

As for the blessed, I don't think you'll have much to worry about. Just bring them around to your way of thinking. Show them why they need this. People don't like to leave their comfy bubbles unless they know there's no other choice. Help them see the light. If anyone can do it, it's you.

And never underestimate what you've learned from your mother and father. They might be cold and emotionless, but they've learned a lot on their journey. Some of it has already found its way into you. Just guard and protect what makes you Chloe and you'll be fine.

No problem on the figures and stats. You know I've got your back. Everything is on the up and up, so there are no concerns right now. I'll do some digging and see what I can get on the leading player.

I don't understand how *anyone's* journey could be more exciting than yours.

And, of course, with the twins. I'll do some more digging when I get the chance. Silence isn't always a bad thing.

I hope.

Just keep an eye out for Fukmos and the others. I don't know much about them, but a recent Wiki article says that the two girls mentioned in the code with Fukmos are the goddesses of ghosts and disease. I might be going out on a limb here, but I'm going to say that's not good.

Wish me luck as I try to keep Mia's head above water, and go and kick some Obsidian ass.

Doc

CHAPTER SIXTEEN

Several days after the excitement of returning to the city and announcing the king's union, the city was still abuzz.

The date had been set, and the arrangements were being made. By the end of the week, under the burning glow of the sunset, Therese was due to wed King Abaxis.

While the king's servants ran around the palace getting things in order and the town prepared to sell merchandise and set up the streets for the big day, Chloe was busy watching a burly man in a stained shirt hammer a nail into a length of wood.

The man turned back over his shoulder. "There?"

Chloe deliberated. "A little higher."

The man gripped the large board and raised it higher.

"Perfect!" Chloe said.

A second man moved into place and held the board at the right height while the first man finished hammering and making his adjustments.

"Nice one," he grumbled. He wiped the sweat from his forehead and stepped back to admire his handiwork. "And you're going to do what with this, exactly?"

The first man raised an eyebrow as he examined the board.

Located at an intersection, the board was long and stuck out like a sore thumb.

Chloe tapped her nose, paid the men from her ever-shrinking pocketful of change, and watched them disappear down the street. When they were gone, she folded her arms and smiled at the board.

"It looks good," Gideon said, appearing from behind her, arms laden with small sheets of paper and charcoal to write with. "You really can't miss it."

"That was the intention." Chloe beamed.

A notification popped up in Chloe's vision.

You've unlocked a new skill: Entrepreneur (Lv 1)

You've set up your first business! There are many ways to make money in Obsidian, but only a few learn the glorious benefits of letting the money make you. The more passive income you make, the higher this skill will increase.

Requirements: Start your first business

Bonuses: +5 intelligence

"Remind me again how this is going to help us?" Gideon asked, handing over the items.

Chloe knelt and began to get to work, sketching letters and pictures on various pieces of paper and sticking them up as she went along.

"It's a Heroes-for-Hire board," Chloe explained. "Anyone who has any issues or problems can come along and post their requests on the board, stating what their issue is, what they need, and how much they're willing to pay for it. Anyone willing to help can read the board, take the paper, complete the quest, and earn some money."

Chloe tried to pin a piece of paper to the board but stuck her thumb instead.

Gideon rolled his eyes, moving to help her. "I know what a Heroes-for-Hire board is, but I don't see how this is going to help *us*. I mean, it's an admirable thing to get started, fixing people up to help each other more, but haven't we got mages to gather?"

"This is one step toward that plan. You see, for every quest that gets completed, I've configured the board so our party gets ten percent of the profit. That way, we're making money that'll help our cause without having to constantly look for monsters or needing to complete quests."

"But we *will* keep completing quests, right? I mean, that's the point of the game."

"Oh, absolutely," Chloe agreed. "This way, while we gather the mages and earn the trust of the city, we're making enough money to cover our rent. I don't know if you've noticed, but we're on our last pennies, and we can't afford to get thrown out of the inn."

Gideon nodded. "Y'know, I'm still not sure why we can't just stay with Therese and Abe. Surely, they could just give us a bedroom. We are part of the queen-to-be's party, after all."

"That's exactly it," Chloe replied. "'Queen-to-be.' She's not queen yet. It's not decent for us to stay in the palace while she's unofficial. It's bad enough that a few groups of NPCs are riling people up against the blessed."

"Good point."

Chloe stuck her tongue out as she attached another piece of paper to the board, ignoring the strange looks she was getting from passersby. "Secondly, by creating a central location where heroes have to come to complete these quests, we've created a meeting place for all types of altruists. We can even pin our own news on here, and with any luck, we'll be able to lure talent to help our cause."

Gideon nodded, impressed. "It certainly can't be any worse than our visit to the Mages' School."

Chloe's face soured. Compared to the Mages' Academy in Killink View with its large, ornate rooms and passionate academic staff, the Mages' School in Hammersworth was a veritable pile of dung.

The School had been their first port of call the day following their return to the city. If mages were what they needed, a school full of them should certainly bolster their numbers and help them make a start toward their quest.

What they quickly discovered, however, was that the mages in Hammersworth were a different breed than any others Chloe had met. Not only were they extremely xenophobic, viewing anyone outside of their circle as nothing more than dirty scum, but the academic staff wasn't inclined to listen to Chloe's plea.

Chloe and Gideon had been fuming when they'd exited the School, Chloe's fists clenched so tightly that her knuckles had turned white.

"It's no great loss," Gideon said, trying to calm down and see the positive side of their experience. "That school could only house… what? Fifty students or so?"

"Still…" Chloe complained. "We would be a quarter of the way there." She grunted and threw down her arms. "Irrational, bigoted, no-good…*wizards.*"

Gideon had clapped a hand to his mouth and strode in Chloe's furious wake toward the inn, where it took a great effort for the others to calm her down.

Gideon was glad that in comparison to that Chloe, this Chloe was a lot brighter and optimistic.

They finished up the board and took a seat on the opposite corner, nonchalantly keeping an eye on any activity that might happen to occur. She had to admit the sign looked fantastic. Big and bold, with the legend Heroes-for-Hire in large letters across the top.

Several people stopped to take a look, reading the long scroll Chloe had written that detailed the purpose of the board and how it worked. After an hour or so, however, no one had added anything to the board.

"Come on," Gideon said. "Let's leave it and come back. It'll take time before anyone puts anything on there. It *is* brand-new, after all."

Chloe agreed, reluctantly allowing herself to be led away.

As they left, they passed a small table with mini figurines, dried fruits, and drawings for sale. Chloe picked up one of the figures and showed it to Gideon.

"Hey, Gid. It's Therese." She laughed.

Gideon examined the doll, a crude replica of their dwarf friend.

The two started laughing, put the ornament back, and disappeared down the street.

Therese wasn't sure which was worse, the fancy gown she found herself in or the constant interruptions and attention from the maids and servants.

There was a knock on the door.

Therese took a sharp breath and glared at the sound. "What. Is. It?"

"It's me," came the syrupy sweet voice of Beverley Crocker, the chief handmaid of the palace.

Ever since Abe had introduced Therese to Beverley, she had been nothing but lovely and attentive. At every meal, she had ensured that Therese had all the napkins she needed.

In the mornings, she was the first thing Therese saw, fussing at the end of her bed and tucking in the sheets before she'd even risen.

Down every corridor.

Through every door.

In every room.

There she was...

"I'm fine!" Therese snapped, finally reaching her wits' end. "For goodness sake, leave me alone!"

"Very well," Beverley replied, no hint of annoyance or anger in her voice. Even her footsteps made Therese shake with rage, soft and perfectly gentle on the stone floors.

What did it take to get a moment's peace around here? Did she have to shout and order the help to leave her alone? It seemed so simple. Why hadn't she thought of it before?

And then she heard the sound of scrubbing from her lavatory. She rose from her seated position at the end of her bed and stormed across the room. She poked her head inside to see a young dwarf maiden on her knees, scrubbing around the edges of the room.

She froze with the brush in her hand.

"W-would you like me to leave?" she stuttered.

Therese felt herself overheating. Without a word, she stormed out of the room and tramped down the corridor.

Abe wasn't prepared for someone to hammer on his door. It was early morning, and the king was famously a late sleeper. He jackknifed in bed at the sound of her knocks, and before he could even throw off his duvet, the door opened.

Therese stood in the doorway, her face beet-red. Behind her was a handmaiden, trying her best to calm the situation and apologize to the king at the same time.

"Therese? Whatever is the matter?" Abe asked, his face concerned.

Therese turned sharply, scaring the handmaiden, who scampered down the corridor. She stepped inside and slammed the door.

"I'm really sorry. I know that it must be lovely for you to be waited on hand and foot by servants, but if you don't tell them to leave me alone, I swear you're going to need to hire new help to replace the ones I've killed."

Abe looked taken aback. In his groggy state, it took him longer to digest the words than usual. Eventually, his expression turned into a smile. "What is this about?"

"What do you mean? Ever since I arrived here, I haven't had a second to myself. I mean, I'm super excited to become the queen and everything, but I didn't sign up to have obnoxious shadows follow me around everywhere I go."

"Obnoxious… Sweetie, you're thinking about this all wrong. The servants aren't here to get in the way; they just want to make sure that you have everything you need. Think of them as the wi-fi from your homeland."

"Nice try." Therese smirked, the wind leaving her sails. "Look, I need to be honest with you, Abe. I love the idea of becoming the queen of Hammersworth, and I can't wait for our wedding day and to see what the future can bring with us two side by side. But I can't live like this." She gripped the hem of her dress and held it up. "This isn't who I am. I'm an adventurer. A tank. I need my armor, and I need my friends. Without them, I am nothing."

Abe thought about that for a long time, his internal conflict written all over his face. Eventually, he took Therese's hand and looked at her.

"If that is what you wish, that is what you shall have."

"You mean it?" Therese said.

Abe nodded. "I'd rather have you happy than have the shadow of what you were living here. The reason I like you is that you are so different from everyone I have ever known. And, although I know this is not yet love, I feel as though every day that passes in which you are happy brings me one step closer to the love my forefathers shared with their cherished wives."

Therese smiled.

"Besides." Abe nodded. "It's not like we haven't already broken plenty of rules already. What are several more along the way?"

They kissed for a long moment before Therese began to list the things she'd like to change. After Abe had noted them all down and promised to speak to the relevant people that day, their attention turned to the windows, where a great black bird had appeared on the sill.

"Hello?" Abe said, crossing the room and holding out his arm.

The raven hopped onto his forearm, flapping his wings gently to balance as the king brought him back to the bed. He detached the small scroll attached to the bird's leg.

King Abaxis,

It is with honor that I receive your summons of my men to your keep. Your mission and need do indeed sound great.

However, every kingdom has its problems, and I am loath to lend help at a time when our own city is in need. Therefore, I offer you a counterproposal.

A great plague has been scourging our town. Men and women are dying like flies, and we are in dire need of assistance. I can rally mages to your cause if you would be able to lend clerics to help ours. While the healing abilities of mages are useful, it is with the clerics that the true power remains. We need the grace of the gods on our side.

Send us your response with haste.

Your loyal subject,

Erendal III

Abe read the letter out loud to Therese, face dark and shadowed.

"This is the second instance of this plague I have heard of," Abe said. "It seems that darkness really is falling upon the land."

"What kind of plague is it?" Therese asked.

Abe shook his head. "I don't know. I don't know. What I do know is that Erendal is one of the most loyal among all my subjects. He rules a small town beyond the forest, a fishing village that provides us great amounts of fish each year. He wouldn't reject my invitation without a dire reason. He needs help."

"How many clerics do you have here?"

"Enough," he replied. He stumbled over to a chest of drawers and took out a paper and pen, scribbling a quick response before attaching it to the raven's leg and sending him on his way. "It's a fair exchange of services," he said, watching the raven grow smaller in the sky. "A good king should always prioritize the health of his subjects."

He thought for a minute, then returned his attention to Therese. "Now, where were we? Ah! Yes. Let's get you out of that dress."

CHAPTER SEVENTEEN

Chloe heard the sound of coin against coin, a notification tone she had set up to inform her when a quest had been completed on her hire board and money had found its way into her pocket.

Another winner for Chloe, she thought, smiling.

I have to give it to you, KieraFreya said. *Not a bad idea. Let the others do the work for you while you reap the spoils. Bravo, girly. Bravo.*

It's not like that, Chloe retorted. *It's a fair finder's fee for helping get people together. We've already made enough to cover the costs for the final night at the inn before the big wedding, so I must be doing something right.*

KieraFreya accepted this, congratulating Chloe again on her venture.

The board had taken a while to get going, but like any boulder that is pushed for long enough, momentum had begun to build, and now it was rolling.

The notice board was almost filled with quests, everything from helping an elderly lady clear the rats out of her basement to sightings of wargs near the borders of the forest. An extermination team was brought together to tackle the warg problem.

Since the reward amounts were set by the NPCs, not all of them were fair. Chloe saw a quest put up just that morning by a sinister-looking character who offered five bronze pieces to help him re-roof the entirety of his house.

The good news was that offers had been accepted by people wanting to partake in Chloe's quest to open the Nether Realm. Not that she had stated that explicitly, of course. She figured not many people would be open to the idea of tearing a hole in the fabric of the etheric for someone they had never met.

Still, the meeting was to take place after sundown that night. It was to be held in one of the abandoned barns just outside the city gates.

Chloe hadn't been happy with the choice of location at first, but after Gideon had reassured her, stating they'd need a big space if they got the numbers they anticipated, she had calmed down and gone with the flow.

The invitations had been accepted in dribs and drabs. The option was there for the blessed to accept the quest on the spot in front of the board. For every player who accepted, Chloe got a notification.

Congratulations, a player has accepted your invitation to join your quest: Mage after Sundown

However, just because a player didn't accept right away, it didn't mean that she wasn't prepared for those who had been indecisive to just turn up, or for NPCs to tag along as well, drawn by their curiosity and sense of adventure.

Another sound of coins tinkling.

Chloe brought up her inventory, enjoying the increase in her wealth. She grinned. "I'll never get tired of that sound."

When nightfall came, Chloe collected the rest of the KieraSlayers (minus Therese, who was otherwise occupied before her big day), and headed outside the city walls.

To her surprise, she could already see several people strolling ahead, lit torches in their hands. The flames floated like wisps toward the barn.

"Looks like the party's getting started," Ben said excitedly.

He was in high spirits after a good few days of grinding his skills with the city rangers and slowly trying to convert them to join their cause. Although the rangers weren't great users of magic, Ben and

Chloe figured it wouldn't be the worst thing in the world to have a set of powerful archers on their side when the time came.

The others in their party had been pursuing similar efforts, affiliating more strongly with their classes and trying to harvest as much knowledge as possible in the city.

Talbot, Huk, and Leonie had made fair strides with the warriors' guild, befriending some of the key groups and joining them on their quests.

Veronica had been working with the clerics, although she had recently informed Chloe that a great many of the clerics were being sent out to cure the ailments of towns within the king's reach who had come under the shadow of sickness.

Blueballs, on the other hand, had been drawing the affections of the local ladies. Hammersworth took a very different approach to Killink View in that the guards had come to know the bright blue fluff and felt no qualms about having him stroll around the city.

Chloe's only instruction to Blueballs was that he stay near the inn, and to his credit, he did. The ladies came to him, and he loved the adoration, purring affectionately as a great many hands stroked his fluff and cooed over just how cute he was.

Sure, Chloe had thought, arriving late one night to find three teenage girls who had taken a certain shine to the toffet. *He's cute now, but you haven't seen him in battle. I know what those claws and teeth can do.*

When they made it to the barn, Chloe was more than amazed to see at least three dozen people patiently waiting for her. They had arranged hay bales into raised platform seating, centered around a small clear area that would act as a stage.

And there was still time before they were due to start.

"This is good," Gideon whispered.

Chloe nodded. Even if only a handful of those in attendance were magic users, it was definitely a start.

The KieraSlayers waited a little longer as more people dribbled through the door. There was a mix of races and statuses. A few grubby-looking humans, a group of clean-looking dwarf women, and,

Chloe was surprised to see, the two gentlemen who had helped her build the Heroes-for-Hire board.

By the time they were ready to start, they must have collected almost a hundred city folk, eager and ready to listen.

Chloe began to speak, introducing herself to the room. She informed them of the party's past and how they had found their way to Hammersworth. She cut no corners, telling the congregation exactly what had happened with KieraFreya and her armor, and how she had come to be wearing the entire armor now.

She held nothing back, wanting to keep no secrets. If these people were going to fight alongside her, she needed them to know the whole truth. Although part of her feared she was making a target of herself— she remembered the hungry lust in Tohken's eye when he had seen her bracers—she knew this was the right path to take.

Tell the truth, and the rest will follow.

She continued speaking, telling them about the next phase of her plan—her desire to rescue Shikora and fully restore KieraFreya to her true form. For that, she needed help.

When she was done, the room was in stunned silence.

"Well?" Chloe asked softly. "Who's with me?"

A few people shuffled uncomfortably on their seats. A stocky dwarf with dark leather armor rested his hands on the top of an axe and said, "That's a very nice story, wee lass. But do you really expect us to believe a word of that nonsense?"

Beside him, three more dwarves sniggered.

"It's not a tale," Chloe replied. "On my honor, it's all true."

The dwarf snorted, turning to the others. "C'mon, lads. Let's get out of this nuthouse. I could've seen my kids to bed tonight rather than listen to this pile of horse crap."

The dwarves rose with a chuckle and sidled out of the barn. A moment later and several more decided to follow, shaking their heads and uttering similar words.

"You're losing them," Ben said out of the side of his mouth. "Pull them back, Chloe."

"How?" Chloe asked. She couldn't understand it; everyone she had met along the way had believed her. She had never had much difficulty bringing them around to the truth, no matter how ludicrous it sounded.

You've got this, Chloe, KieraFreya encouraged. *Just make them see that it's real.*

It hit her; the obvious answer had been inside her all along. These people didn't know her from Adam. They'd lived lives far from real adventure, so of course they struggled to believe the truth.

Because they hadn't seen the evidence.

"Say that again, KF," Chloe said aloud. A few heads turned her way skeptically.

What do you mean?

"Talk out loud, b—" *beep!*

"Don't you call me a bitch!" KieraFreya exclaimed, the words booming from the armor.

Chloe beamed as all heads turned back to the center. Even those who were on their way to the barn door stopped and looked on with interest.

"Ladies and gentlemen, I'd like to introduce you to the Divine Goddess of Retribution, KieraFreya."

"Erm, hello…" KieraFreya said, suddenly nervous beneath the spotlight.

"You're not shy, are you?" Chloe laughed.

"You caught me off-guard," KF replied. "What can I say?"

"Trickery!" one of the more skeptical attendees shouted back, pointing a finger. "I've seen ventriloquism before. Don't be fooled by her cheap tricks."

"Cheap tricks?" KieraFreya said through the armor. "Shall we show you what cheap tricks look like?"

KieraFreya took control of Chloe's body, Chloe's eyes turning white as she hovered several feet above the ground. She pointed a metal-clad hand at the man, and the next thing he knew, he had joined her in the air.

His body floated over the crowd and hovered next to Chloe's. His own eyes turned white as KieraFreya manipulated the etheric to enter his mind and show him a series of vivid pictures, pictures of her and Chloe during their adventures.

When she was done, she gently lowered the man to the floor. His knees buckled, and he landed on all fours. He was suddenly breathless, unable to comprehend what he'd just seen.

"Well?" KieraFreya said. "What do we think now?"

The man nodded emphatically. "True, it's all true. The… The friggin' goddess is in the armor!"

Chloe grinned, her eyes returning to normal.

"Thanks, KF. Stellar job."

"Anytime," KieraFreya replied.

Chloe cast her eyes around the rest of the attendees, many of whom had now returned to their seats and leaned forward with great interest.

"I know this quest is a lot to ask, and I know that for many of you, this might be your first real foray into something big. But we need all the help we can get to make this happen. Work alongside us, and we can do something great together. We can return a goddess to her home and help her take her place back in the stars before darkness takes the realm and claims it for its own."

A pause, then, "I ask again…who's with me?"

This time there wasn't any hesitation. The majority of the room stood up, holding their fists in the air. One or two shook their heads and exited, clearly overwhelmed by the enormity of the venture.

Chloe beamed, instructing everyone to meet here again in two nights, bringing along anyone and everyone they could to join their cause. There she would divide them into groups and begin their training.

The atmosphere was electric. Chloe couldn't believe the change in attitudes in such a short time. However, the attitudes would change again all too soon.

As Chloe stepped out of the barn and into the night sky, she heard the first wild calls of animals growling in frenzy and saw the silhouettes frantically sprinting toward them from the forest.

CHAPTER EIGHTEEN

"What the…"

At first, Chloe couldn't make out what she was seeing. None of them could. They all stood frozen, squinting into the darkness.

The creatures were tall. Two arms, two legs. They moved quickly. For a half-second, Chloe thought they might be human—a group of terrified humans sprinting toward them from the depths of the forest, chased by some mighty beast.

That is, until they were within an uncomfortably close distance and they began to shriek again.

"Chloe?" Gideon urged.

Chloe used **Creature Identification** and sighed.

She had been right in some respect. These creatures were humans…of a sort.

Creature: Infected (Lv 5)

HP: 312

Resistances: Dark, Water, Earth, Poison

Weaknesses: Fire, Close-range attacks

"They're infected?" Chloe uttered, drawing KieraFreya's sword and preparing herself for combat. "Infected with what?"

She felt something pass her ear, then heard the arrow's whistle as it found its first victim. "Who cares?" Ben said. "They don't look friendly, now, do they?"

Chloe raised her voice, her tone commanding, powerful. "Prepare for battle, everyone. This can be our first test."

The majority of the group looked at each other uncertainly before drawing their weapons.

They hadn't been armed for battle when they'd come out to find out more about Chloe's quest, so all they had were a few low-level warriors with basic swords, a couple of rogues with knives, a ranger with a bow, and a handful of mages who looked like they'd rather be anywhere in the world right now than out in the dark under attack by infected.

Chloe didn't mind. All great leaders were able to work with what they had. She hadn't lost a battle yet, and she was determined that this one would be no different.

The KieraSlayers flanked Chloe, the rest of their mini-army behind them. The infected ran closer. They were low-level threats, but with the numbers they had, it still made quite the challenge. She could see around fifty of them now.

"They're weak against fire and close-range attacks," Chloe called to her troops. "Any magic users with flames, I suggest you get yourselves ready."

Gideon prepared **Purple Blaze**. Chloe closed her eyes, connected to the etheric, and summoned her own.

"Hey!" she called to the nearest infected, now just twenty yards away. "Catch!"

Her free hand flung a monstrous orb of purple fire. She propelled the orb forward, the magic speeding through the air and swallowing the infected whole. A second orb followed, the light illuminating the horror of the creatures coming for them as they doubled their pace.

She heard gasps of surprise behind her as she imbued her blade with flame and ran into the throng, her sword whistling and leaving afterburns in their vision as she attacked.

The other members of her party wasted no time getting involved.

Blueballs fell to all fours and bounded into the crowd, his large paws swiping and sending infected flying.

Ben took a step back, finding a space next to the shaky ranger. He spoke words of confidence, teaching and encouraging as he used his **Double Shot** to slow down the onslaught of attackers. The ranger beside him fired several shots, his aim off at first, but growing ever more accurate as he got bolder.

Huk and Leonie broke free of the formation and worked as a synchronized pair. Although short, Huk's strength stat was high, meaning that even a glancing blow to an infected's leg did enough damage to cripple them. When they were down, Leonie would deliver the killing stroke, sending heads flying across the field.

Talbot watched the other two, his sword clutched in his sweaty palms. He took his own steadying breaths, and when an infected spotted him and came straight for him, he managed to find his courage, driving the blade into the infected's lower hip before withdrawing it and slicing across its stomach.

"Keep up your strength!" Chloe shouted. "Find your courage! We cannot fail as long as we fight!"

Chloe's sword seemed to draw the attention of most of the infected. In the light from her flame, she watched their monstrous forms.

They might once have been people. Many of them had the same features as anyone Chloe had ever met, the main differences being the pallid, waxen look of their skin, the dark veins that stood out, and the blank expressions in their eyes as they tried to scratch and bite the fighters.

What the hell were they infected with?

"There are too many zombies," Gideon cried. He was fighting near Chloe, his display of purple fireworks keeping the infected from getting too close to him. "We can't hold them off."

Chloe raised an eyebrow as she launched a fireball into the air. It arced twenty feet high before crashing down into what she had thought was the tail end of the horde.

She turned full-circle with her sword, slicing flaming violet trails across the infecteds' stomachs. When she was finished, she glanced over to see where her orb had landed…

And saw even more infected coming from the trees. Another fifty or so, at least.

"Crap," she hissed.

"We need to get out of here, Chloe. I mean, your guys are strong, but we'll be overrun."

Chloe heard a clang and felt a bony finger bounce off her armor. She raised an elbow and knocked an infected—which had gotten too close for comfort—unconscious.

She blasted another fireball, staving off those nearby, and turned to see how the others were getting on.

The few warriors, clerics, and mages they had seemed to be in great spirits, taking down any enemies that made it past the Kiera-Slayers, but it seemed as though they hadn't taken into account the other infected coming to join the battle.

Chloe assessed their situation. There were at least fifty fighters on their team. More infected were now coming from the forest, taking the total up to several hundred at an estimate. She and her band were around half a kilometer from the city gates, and she guessed they could run faster than the infected, although that theory was yet to be tested.

"Retreat!" Chloe shouted, sheathing her sword and conjuring two enormous fireballs. She tossed them one after the other, illuminating the terrifying expressions on the infecteds' faces. "Fall back to the city!"

The fighters who had met at the barn looked up, surprised at the number of infected coming at them in the dark. Without needing to be told twice, they turned on their heels and began to run.

Chloe called to the KieraSlayers, who nodded and shepherded the new additions to their teams. Ben ran and occasionally turned to fire an arrow into the crowd.

"Gid, any chance you want to try something new?" Chloe asked as she sprinted behind the lot of them.

Gideon nodded. "Always."

"Try this."

Chloe wasn't sure if it would work, but she had yet to turn down a challenge.

She paused very briefly, summoning **Purple Blaze**, only this time, instead of focusing on creating fireballs, she straightened her arms and turned her palms to the ground. She parted her arms slowly, feeling elated as the flames took to the grass, following where her palms pointed until a thick line of purple fire a good twenty feet in length scorched the ground.

Spell power increased: Purple Blaze (Lv 4)

You're on FIRE! You've found a new way to manipulate your spell. Your spells-dex will keep a record of any and all manipulations you discover. Continue with your experiments to unlock bigger and better forms of your Purple Blaze spell, Hot Stuff.

Manipulations:

- **Fireball: Summon a fireball to throw at your enemies. Size varies dependent on focus and mana invested in the spell.**
- **Scorching trail: Mark your territory, create barriers, or just draw pretty pictures with the purple flame. Size and duration dependent on focus and mana invested in the spell.**

Bonuses: +1 etheric potential, reduced cast cost (n x 18MP)

Skill increased: Experimental (Lv 2)

You've discovered a new way to manipulate a spell! Keep pushing the boundaries of common thought to discover bigger, better, and more efficient ways to enhance your abilities and further your knowledge of Obsidian.

Bonuses: +2 intelligence, +1 dexterity, +1 endurance, +2 etheric potential

(NOTE: Increases in skill override any previous bonuses gained from the skill).

Gideon nodded, impressed. He copied Chloe, and soon they'd created a flaming barrier. The infected paused, momentarily confused by the flames. Chloe and Gideon were able to retreat a good distance before several infected realized they could go around the flames.

Chloe ran on, growing breathless. The gap between the city and their group closed, but there was still some way to go. Despite her initial observations, she was perturbed to discover that the infected were gaining on them. They were faster than she had thought.

"Keep going!" Chloe called, not that the others needed encouragement. Blindly, she summoned fireballs and tossed them behind her as she ran, hearing the infected falling but knowing it wouldn't be enough.

When they were within shouting distance of the gate, those at the front of the procession cried out to the gate guards. Torches lit, indicating that they had caught their attention, but the gates didn't open.

"Please! Open the gates!" a man at the front shouted, taking a deep breath between each word.

"They're coming! They're coming!" another shouted.

It wasn't until they were a stone's throw away that the guards' eyes lit up, suddenly taking in the swarming mass that was coming for them. They called down orders and the gates began to slowly open, their bulk taking some effort to move.

Chloe chanced a look behind her, heart sinking as she saw them on her heels. If she didn't do something now, they wouldn't have time to filter through the gates *and* close them in time to stop infected from making their way into the city.

She turned on her heel. She had no time to channel the etheric and preserve mana, so she threw her palms at the ground and created a **Scorching Trail** with her **Purple Blaze** spell.

She was just quick enough to stop an infected that had dived straight at her, its body now melting in the fire. She saw the flames rise and smiled as she spotted Gideon channeling his own trail, thinner and weaker than hers but still a useful deterrent.

A few infected managed to sneak past, but they were picked off by the gate guards' spears and arrows. Chloe and Gideon focused their power, making the trail ever wider until it reached in an arc from wall to wall, protecting them from the infected.

The infected screeched in anger. A few jumped through the flames in frustration, only to burn and die on the ground on the other side. Chloe turned and leaped through Gideon's flames, praying that her armor would protect her from their heat.

It did.

"Come on," she said, tugging at his sleeve. "They won't hold forever."

She ran toward the gate, realizing in a sudden panic that they were already closing it.

"Hey! Wait!" she called. She could see the KieraSlayers through the gap. Could hear their calls begging the guards to stop.

She was almost at the gate doors when someone called, "Heather! Just leave it!"

Chloe turned to see a young woman doubled over and struggling to walk. In her hands, she gripped the frayed shirt of an infected as she dragged it toward the gate with great effort.

"Gideon, would you do the honors?" Chloe requested.

Gideon hesitated, then nodded.

The cackling glee of the infected got louder as the fire barrier began to dwindle. Chloe's heart rose into her throat as the gap in the gates shrank.

She closed her eyes and took a second to channel the etheric before casting **Telekinesis** on the gates. They paused, the guards on the other side audibly struggling, confused as to why the gate had suddenly frozen.

Gideon, meanwhile, tore over to the woman named Heather and

grabbed her clothes. "Leave them alone. What are you doing? Now's not the time to play hero. They're beyond healing."

She turned to him, face earnest and raw emotion in her eyes. "How do you know? I'm a cleric. We heal. That's what we do. I need to know what caused this."

Gideon ran a hand through his hair, exasperated. His attention was caught by the infected now breaking free.

"We need to go."

"No."

"Why?"

"Because he's my brother," Heather said sharply.

Gideon froze.

"He's a cleric too. He was trying to heal these people."

Gideon looked from the infected to her, then over to the creatures sprinting toward them.

He found his resolve and made a decision. Without a word, he picked the infected up and threw him over his shoulder in a fireman's carry.

Heather pulled herself to her feet and they ran for the gate, the gap growing ever smaller between them and the infected.

Gideon sprinted past Chloe, Heather taking the lead. Chloe kept her power focused and made her way through to the other side. When she was there, she focused on moving the gates, snapping them shut as the first infected dived through, the gate's closure trapping and squishing him in the middle.

Chloe sat down, struggling for breath. She swallowed and said, "Man, he sure ended up in a jam."

Gideon dumped the body on the ground and rolled his eyes. "Really? That's what you're going with?"

Before Chloe could answer, she was bathed in a golden glow. Finally, she had made it to level 15.

Chloe held her breath, waited to see the notification telling her of what grand steps awaited her now that she'd gained another level.

Nothing came.

CHAPTER NINETEEN

The call to arms rang out almost immediately after the gates closed. A signal was sent from the gate guards all the way through the levels of the city until it reached the ears of the king.

King Abaxis was sitting on his balcony enjoying the night air when the summons came—a series of sharp horn blasts, growing louder as they worked up the chain.

There was a knock on his door.

"Who is it?"

"Therese."

"Come in."

Therese joined him on the balcony to stare out over the city. "What is it?"

"Danger," Abe said, simply, staring toward the gate, where he could see the dying purple fire. For a brief second, he saw the darkened silhouettes of dozens of bodies in the light. "We're under attack."

Therese's eyes widened. "My party is down there. They need me."

"How do you know?"

Therese was already halfway out the door. She paused only to say, "Because I know them."

Abe grinned, loving the ferocity and fire in his bride-to-be. He walked over to the other side of the room to where a mouthpiece was hidden in the wall, a security measure for kings to keep themselves safe should danger ever find its way into their keep.

He placed his lips on the mouth of the horn and blew, initiating the **Royal Quest** sequence that would alert all NPCs and blessed alike that the kingdom needed protecting.

Chloe took up a position on the top of the gates with Ben beside her, shooting projectiles down into the fray as the infected swarmed before the gate.

"I can't believe it. Nothing. I got nothing for that."

Ben aimed his bow at the infected. "What made you think there would be something?"

"I don't know. It was a hunch, okay? I thought, well, increments of five."

Ben shrugged. "Fair enough." He tracked his arrow as it arced down into the mass of bodies.

There were several hundred of them now. A great writhing mass of the creatures pushed at the gate, climbing on top of each other in an attempt to make it inside.

Ben loosed arrow after arrow, putting the accuracy of the gate guards to shame. While their arrows inevitably hit *something* in the crowd—it would be harder to miss than it would be to hit the mass of bodies—Ben's found the weak spots, taking out infected by piercing their hearts, eyes, and heads.

"They're really falling head over heels for you." Chloe smirked as she watched an arrow hit an infected that had climbed on the shoulders of two others. It tumbled to the ground, rotating several times before landing in a clumsy heap.

"What can I say? I've got a certain charm."

Laughter sounded nearby as a blessed Chloe had never seen before took a position along the gate's perimeter. A mixture of men and elves mingled with the dwarves. There were now axe-throwers, rangers, and even a few spellcasters.

These Chloe looked at with disdain, still remembering the reception she had received at the Mages' School.

Sure, get involved when the damn king asks, but when I need you to help the whole damn world...

The rest of her new party arrayed themselves near the gate, bracing against the stone to stop the pressure from the countless bodies from forcing it open.

Blueballs led the charge, his fur matted with blood. Though he was the strongest of the lot by far, he was worn out. His eyes were hazy, and he took deep, heavy breaths.

"Are you okay, buddy?" Leonie asked, stroking his fur.

She saw several small scratches on his skin.

"Oh, no," she said quietly, realization dawning. She called to the others, "Move. We need to get Blueballs out of here. He needs help."

The others were hesitant until they saw the scratches. Their minds all reached the same conclusion: *If Blueballs has been hurt by infected, what does that mean for him? Imagine* him *rabid and infected...*

Leonie led the toffet away from the crowd, moving through more and more bodies as new players migrated to the gates, ready to partake in the king's party quest and mine some experience. They didn't realize until they saw the enemies beyond the gate what they were up against.

They were pouring in now. Chloe could see them coming down the streets behind her, hundreds of active players ready to protect the city. She couldn't believe the sheer numbers. Soon enough, the walls were overcrowded, filled with players fighting to get involved and get experience.

Even Therese had come down from her castle on high, hammer in hand, ready to join the battle.

Arrows flew, rocks tumbled down, and fires blazed and roared. The infected screeched and cried, desperate to try to make it through the gate as the night wore on.

A few times the infected managed to stack high enough on top of each other to grab the collars of fighters on the gate, but the casualties were few and far between, and immediately countered as all projectiles targeted the stacks and brought them back down.

Slowly the mass of infected began to dwindle. Stragglers arrived from the forest, mindlessly joining the fray in a constant trickle, but the bulk of them were dead.

Chloe spotted a few at the back of the crowds peel off and begin to work their way toward the houses and farmhouses in the rural land beyond.

"Doris and Burdock. We have to help them," she called to Ben.

"What do you expect them to do?" Ben asked. "There are too many people up here and at the gates to get down and chase after them. Besides, they're not going to open the gates while they're under attack."

Chloe searched frantically for a solution. She pictured the sweet, lovely lady and her peacocks. She imagined Burdock and his wife at home, hiding in fear of the passing horde.

She couldn't allow them to end up like these creatures.

Glancing below, she saw that there were small gaps that opened and closed like the lungs of some living thing, and when she spied a gap large enough to land without fear of instant attack, Chloe leaped.

It might have been considered a reckless move by some. However, Chloe had faith in her skills.

Her **Acrobatics** skill kicked in, helping her leap in a long arc.

Impressive stuff, KieraFreya said.

You haven't seen anything yet.

KieraFreya chuckled. *What have you got in mind?*

Chloe grinned. *Don't hate me for this.*

She landed softly on her feet, standing up and noticing something odd.

The infected were still moving, but they were moving at half speed around her. When she investigated further, she was surprised to see that the fire was moving in slow motion too.

"What's going on?" Chloe asked.

KieraFreya brought up her notifications. Chloe scanned them, seeing a few very nice bonuses.

Skill increased: Reckless (Lv 7)

Okay, okay. We get it. You're *craaazy!* Since you're determined to risk your neck and go down unwise routes, you have gained an exclusive "time-slow" buff anytime you do something considered reckless.

Bonuses: +17 strength, +12 endurance

(NOTE: Increases in skill override any previous bonuses gained from the skill).

Woah! Time has slowed.

Thanks to your Reckless skill, you've received the Time Slow buff.

Effects: Time has slowed by 25%

Duration: 2 minutes

"Well, isn't that just—"

"Chloe! Watch out!"

Chloe flicked away her menu in time to see an arm slowly swiping toward her. She banged it to the side with her forearm and ducked out of the way.

The infected was knocked off-balance and fell slowly, as if underwater.

"Nice," Chloe said aloud, impressed. "Now for phase two."

"What's phase two?" KieraFreya asked.

"The bit you might not like."

Though KieraFreya babbled, Chloe didn't listen. She fell into her thoughts, focusing on the etheric and finding her familiar. She was surprised to see that the rabbit's horns had evolved from stumps to what she could only describe as spikes. The creature obeyed her command, connecting her with the magic she needed.

All of a sudden, Chloe burst into flames.

"Woah! Chloe! What have you done?" KieraFreya called. "Put it out. Put it out!"

But Chloe wasn't listening. This was exactly what she had planned.

Every inch of her metallic armor was now imbued with **Purple Blaze**. She was an effigy of purple flame, a bonfire in human form.

She gritted her teeth and screwed her eyes shut. Out of all the risks she had taken in her gaming career, this one felt the most stupid. She had seen what **Purple Blaze** did to her enemies, and now she was casting it on herself.

She half-expected to feel the intensity of heat. She was trapped in metal, a known conductor of heat, so she waited for the moment when her skin started to bubble so she could turn off the magic and try another method.

But she didn't feel the heat.

She could barely even hear the crackling of the flames.

Skill increased: Etheric Manipulation (Lv 4)

With every level increase in Etheric Manipulation, the worlds open up to you. Not just your world, but that of the etheric.

There are many bonuses to this. Accuracy of casting and reduced spell cost, but most importantly, you are now immune to your own spells.

No longer will you have to live under the threat of friendly fire. Accidentally shoot lightning at your own foot? Don't worry about it.

Accidentally cast a spell of aging into your nostril? Forget about it.

The possibilities are endless. See what you can do.

Bonuses: +10 etheric potential, spell cast cost dramatically reduced, immunity to friendly fire

(NOTE: Increases in spells override any previous bonuses gained from the spell).

"Nice!" Chloe beamed as she strode through the horde, feeling more powerful than ever as the infected stepped back and gave her clearance to pass.

She drew her sword, imbued the blade once more with flame, and took down any and all that dared to get within her reach before spotting the shadows disappearing into the darkness ahead and giving chase.

Her sights were fixed on a band of five infected that tore off toward Burdock's house. She frowned and sprinted after them.

Gideon and Heather secured the final leather straps on either side of the large wooden table and stepped back.

Gideon shuddered. He hated the idea of being dirty, much less having touched the naked skin of an infected who had, until very recently, been fully conscious and ready to attack and bite them.

What if the disease made its way into *him?*

Heather stared down at her brother with a solemn expression on her face. His breath was coming in short gasps and his eyes were firmly closed.

Gideon shuddered again.

At first, Gideon thought that he had been flogging a dead horse. That Heather had managed to convince him to bring back a corpse on which she could do her experimentation in order to find a cure.

It wasn't until he had carried him to the small room located within the guard's sentry post that he realized that his chest was rising and falling. Her brother was somehow still very much among the living.

"He looks so peaceful," she whispered.

Gideon looked at Heather incredulously. He hadn't realized it at the time, them both being under the threat of death, and all, but she was a very pretty girl. Freckled cheeks and red hair. Plump lips, perfect for kissing.

She realized he was staring at her.

"Sure, sure…" Gideon recovered.

Heather tottered around the room, pulling various ingredients out of a small satchel she wore belted around her waist. Gideon saw various leaves and liquids, as well as a book with illustrations of various ailments and infections and instructions on best methods to heal and aid.

"What do you think it is?" Gideon asked, taking a seat beside the table. They could hear the onslaught of battle outside, the din of raised voices and battle cries. Part of him wanted to go out and help, but he knew there were enough people out there to cover the field. He had received the same quest as everyone else.

Heather shook her head. "I don't know. It's like nothing I've ever seen before. Illnesses can take from people. Can drain them dry and keep them in bed, believing they will never get better. But it's rare to see an illness that drives a host into a frenzied state such as this."

"So, zombies?" Gideon said, rather bluntly.

Heather glanced up from under her eyelids. "Excuse me?"

"You know, zombies? The undead." He turned his fingers into claws and pretended to chomp the air. "Zombies."

Despite herself, Heather laughed, the sound a tinkling of bells juxtaposed against the battle outside.

"What?" he asked.

"You're stupid," she replied, the words not intended to hurt, judging from her smile.

Their eyes met briefly. Gideon smiled goofily back.

Heather returned her focus to her brother, her hand gently touching the dark veins on his body. "It looks like a darkness in the blood. Something that has worked its way into his body and seized control. See here? Where the pupils are dilated? That's an overabundance of adrenaline. An overload of a stimulus meant to drive survival. For all we know, their minds are in there, but they're telling them we're the enemy."

Her hand slid down his body as she continued. "His heart rate is fast. Too fast. Even unconscious, their bodies are working overtime. We need something to slow down the blood flow around his body. Something to calm down his frenzied state and try to bring back a semblance of recognition."

"You think he's forgotten who you are?"

"Maybe," Heather said. "At least, for now. I don't think it'll be gone forever."

"How do you know so much about medicine?" Gideon asked.

Heather blushed. "I was a trainee nurse in real life. Well, at one point, anyway. I spent several years practicing and studying medicine, delving deep into the anatomy of the human body."

"Sounds fascinating."

"It was," she said sadly. There was memory deep in her eyes, and some sadness. "An endless search down the rabbit hole of knowledge for the betterment of people. Who could ask for more?"

"So, what happened?" Gideon asked softly.

Heather's eyes met his. For a moment it looked as though she was about to tell him, but the next thing he knew, she had closed up. "Life. Life happened."

Gideon didn't know what to say to that. He still considered himself far too young to have anything close to what anyone would call "life experience." He had no idea how old Heather was in real life, but he could tell her roots were deep.

They stood for a moment in awkward silence before Gideon nodded toward her satchel. "So, do you have anything that slows the heart rate?"

Heather chewed her lip. "I think so. I have some things we can try, at least."

She pulled out a jar half full of a thick, brown substance that flowed like molasses.

"Eurgh," Gideon said, sniffing the contents. "What is that?"

"Probably best not to ask," Heather replied, giggling as she got out a bowl and started making her concoction.

Gideon watched her in fascination, all the while keeping an eye on the man on the table and praying to the heavens that the straps would be enough to hold him.

In the room beside theirs, he heard the pained cry of a toffet.

CHAPTER TWENTY

By the time Chloe reached Burdock's house, she couldn't see the infected anymore.

But she could *hear* them.

She had withdrawn her flame from the armor, using only the light from her sword to lead her onward. Above, the sky was clouded, not even a sparkle of a star in sight.

Banging on wood. The sound of beams splintering.

Chloe raced around to the back of the house, seeing the legs of the infected trailing inside as they climbed through the broken doorway, their instincts somehow drawing them toward the residents of the property.

"Not on my watch," Chloe muttered, picking up a rock and hurling it through the upstairs window.

There was no response.

She picked up another and threw it.

No response again.

This time she rolled her eyes. She channeled her mana and pointed her fingertips, sending two bolts of her **Volt Shock** through the window, the static lighting up the room and eliciting several distressed cries.

"What in the name of…" came Burdock's voice in a higher register than usual.

A moment later, his head meekly poked out of the window as he looked around for the source of the invasion.

"Chloe? Is that you?" he called down, a hand on his chest as he breathed a sigh of relief. "What are you doing at this time of night?"

Crockery clattered downstairs and furniture was knocked over.

"Who's that?"

Chloe shouted up to him, explaining the situation as quickly as possible. "Block your doors. I don't know how strong they are."

"Block my… Dear, don't you know that I'm the *man* of this house? I can defend my keep from intruders, no sweat. Just let me find my axe…"

He disappeared from view. A moment later, he could be heard rooting around his room, his wife shouting angrily at him as he hunted for his weapon.

Chloe, deciding she couldn't really afford to wait much longer, took the stairs into the house and went after the infected.

It wasn't hard to find them. They were hardly expert burglars. She found them in Burdock's living room, crashing and bumping into objects as if drunk.

Chloe, terrified of setting the whole house alight, extinguished the flames from her sword and began her attack.

The infected closest to her launched itself at her. Chloe twisted out of the way just in time, and it smashed through a table and landed face-first on the floor.

"Ouch!" KieraFreya said.

Before Chloe could respond, two more came for her. She navigated behind a large chair, putting it between her and them. Then, with one well-timed kick, she sent the chair into one of the infected and knocked it backward, taking advantage of the space she'd given herself as she stepped forward and drove the blade into the next infected's shoulder.

She drew her sword back and shouted as she drove the blade into the infected's skull, relieved when it folded to its knees and went down.

But the first infected was now back up, splinters of wood stapled to its chest, making it look like a human pincushion.

Turning to Chloe with malice in its eyes, it reached out for her. Its nails were blackened and sharp.

Chloe swiped away the infected's arms with her free hand and head-butted it, causing it to stumble backward. She kicked in the center of its chest and it crashed into the wall behind it. Once it was down, she took her blade in both hands and spiked it through its chest.

There was movement on the stairs, and heavy footsteps. Chloe counted the infected, only finding three in the living room. She was sure there had been more…

A shadowy figure appeared from the doorway to the hall, arms flailing. It came at her fast, and Chloe was caught off-guard at its sudden appearance. She moved to raise her sword and attack, but the creature suddenly stopped mid-movement.

"Has the reckless buff been added again?" Chloe asked.

KieraFreya replied. "I doubt it. That buff slows things down, it doesn't freeze them."

The infected's mouth hung open in horror. Only its eyes twitched.

Chloe prodded the creature with her finger as a strange sound came from behind.

The infected flopped to the floor, eyes blank. Standing behind it was Burdock, his axe now stained with blackened blood.

"I told you I can protect my abode." He smirked.

Chloe nodded, a smile on her own face. "I never doubted you for a second."

"Hey! Hey!" Reyner called from upstairs. "There are more of them. They're running!"

Chloe and Burdock lunged to the window, seeing the silhouetted shapes sprinting across the fields outside.

"Crap," Chloe said, turning on her heel, about to run.

She paused, looked back at Burdock. "You coming?"

Burdock's face went from confusion to excitement. "Hell, yeah, I'm coming. This is more excitement than I've seen in years!"

***

Once Heather's concoction was complete, Gideon couldn't keep himself from poking his head outside to get some fresh air.

The damn stuff stunk. Not only did it look like recycled feces and smell worse than anything he could imagine, but after watching Heather tease the mixture into her brother's mouth, he found himself feeling very unsteady on his feet.

"Lightweight." She laughed, watching Gideon stumble away.

He gripped the doorjamb, staring out into the street. The battle was winding down, with quite a few players already calling it quits and heading back to wherever they had come from.

He was surprised to see a number of people making their way through the gates, considering how desperate they had been to close them not that long ago.

Amazing how quickly problems can be solved when everyone comes together, Gideon mused, smiling as a fond memory took him.

He had been a few years younger, making his first foray into the world of online gaming. Until then, he had only ever enjoyed single-player games with immersive campaigns, but he figured that since his friends were into it, he might as well give it a go.

The *Relic Hunter* series had been all the rage back then. Gideon dived straight in, choosing the heroic warrior—Gambon the Great—and went in search of missions and quests.

One thing he learned very quickly was that in MMORPGs, it was very easy to get caught up in missions far beyond your levels. Take one wrong turn, and your Level 2 warrior would be facing a Level 24 Hydra.

This was something he had never experienced before. Until that point, all missions undertaken were a result of the missions completed. They were sequential. Guided. Only by completing

Mission 1 could you move on to Mission 2, and so on. Progression was gradual. Inevitable.

In the world of *Relic Hunter*, Gideon found himself quickly swept away on a mission with fellow warriors, the online chats alive with conversation and feverish excitement as they encouraged and cheered Gideon on, driving the young warrior and his Level 2 companions ever deeper into the dragon's dungeon to fight the great Attarik.

It was only after fire had consumed his screen that he realized the obvious. The higher levels had used the lower ones as dragon fodder. Gideon was nothing more than a number. Dispensable. Disposable.

He learned quickly from then on that friendships were important in games. Creating parties was a quick way to level up and attack the stronger dungeons. People you trusted. People you admired and looked up to. It had been a few hours later, as he had been perusing the taverns for possible party talent, that he had found Tag.

Another couple of days and, in a chance encounter in the forest, he had found Ben.

The three of them had been inseparable ever since, creating parties, making friends, and losing some along the way. The lesson had stuck, though: safety in numbers.

Which was why he wasn't surprised that the battle was over. The blessed players had come out in droves, a stark contrast to a few weeks ago when they had been hard-pressed to meet any blessed. Now, he could see the evidence of the growing popularity of the game. They were everywhere now. Obsidian was *alive*.

From where Gideon stood at the house's window, he could just make out the faces of the people by the gates. He wondered where the KieraSlayers were. He could hear Blueballs somewhere nearby, still moaning in pain. Maybe they were with him?

Yeah, that'll be it. They're nearby, I'm sure.

He shrugged, remembering something Tag had once told him after chasing several goblins into the woods mid-combat.

You should never get mad at what happens in the heat of battle. Survival is the priority. Sometimes people split, but as long as you can keep in touch with messages, you'll find everyone again.

Gideon took one last breath of fresh air and turned back toward Heather.

He was glad to find that the smell of the putrid mix had faded somewhat. Heather waited patiently as he made his way across the room. She held a potted plant in her hands.

"What's that?"

"Lavender," she said. "I figured you needed a break from the aroma of my potions."

"Thank you." He grinned and took his seat once more. "Is it working?"

"Hard to tell," she mused. She reached over and picked up his eyelids one by one. "His breathing has slowed, but it's hard to say. This might require more work than just my combined concoctions."

"What work do you mean?"

Heather tucked a lock of hair behind her ear. Gideon couldn't help but stare at the smooth skin of her neck.

She reached down to her neckline and pulled out an ornament on a silver chain, a small vial that looked as though someone had melted starlight and placed several drops inside.

"The aid of the cleric class," Heather said. She unscrewed the vial and tipped a drop onto the end of her finger. "Here." She offered her finger to Gideon.

Gideon raised an eyebrow, uncertain of what to do for a moment. She nodded encouragement, her finger inches from Gideon's face. He nodded back, placed her finger between his lips, and licked the droplet off.

Heather retreated sharply. "What are you doing?"

"What?" Gideon exclaimed, alarmed. "Was that not what you're meant to do?"

"*Taste* the tears of Holistis, the holy God of Healing?"

"Those were *God's* tears?"

"*A* god. Not *the* God," Heather snapped back. "And yes!"

"Oh, my God, oh, my God," Gideon said, hands flapping. His head whirled, looking for somewhere to spit.

"No! Don't spit it out!" Heather said. "You can't *waste* them. Do you know the lengths I had to go through to acquire those? Just swallow."

"What?"

"Swallow!"

"What will happen? What's going to happen to me?"

Heather shrugged, sudden curiosity in her expression. "I guess we'll find out."

Gideon stared at Heather, his mouth fixed in an upside-down smile. He sighed, then closed his eyes and swallowed, feeling the warmth from the droplet as it traveled down his throat.

Heather waited patiently.

"Anything?"

Gideon shook his head. Heather sighed.

"Ah, well." She took another droplet. "Okay, let's try this again."

This time, she guided Gideon through the process. He tentatively leaned forward, and she smeared the droplet in an arc across his forehead. She then took a droplet for herself, replicating the smear on her own head.

When that was done, she dished a final drop—Gideon surprised to see that the vial was already two-thirds empty—and smeared it across her brother's forehead.

"What now?" Gideon whispered. He felt a warmth growing inside his stomach, a slightly unsettled feeling he normally associated with indigestion.

"We wait," Heather replied, shaking her head and laughing. "I can't believe you drank it."

"Well, how was I to know?"

Between giggles, she said, "You're an idiot."

The laughter left Gideon's face.

"What is it? What did I say?"

His eyes met hers. "That's twice you've said something like that now. I'm stupid. I'm an idiot."

Her face straightened, a slight flush to her cheeks. "I don't mean it in a negative way. It's just…I don't know. I think you're pretty cool."

Gideon raised an eyebrow. "Well, why don't you say *that*, then?"

She hesitated, then said, "Because you're an idiot."

They both laughed, the sound filling the room.

The time ticked by, as time does. The pair of them talked in the quiet privacy of the room, next door having fallen quiet, their thoughts far from their troubles as they lost themselves in tales, each taking an incredibly keen interest in the other's stories. Gideon felt light, immaterial, nothing troubling him. He could see the same state of bliss reflected on Heather's face.

She reached over her brother and took Gideon's hands. The room fell away, the walls turning white as they floated through an endless sky together. Her eyes were the color of the brightest sapphires he had ever seen.

Her laugh echoed as if caught in a chamber and an ecstasy he had never felt before drowned him. Only once did she check that her brother was okay, and then the worry was gone, replaced instead by boundless, endless laughter and joy.

When he looked at their hands, he discovered that they were no longer there. His arms had fused with Heather's. They were one in an endless cycle of life. No "him" or "her." Just "what is," and nothing more.

Only the lightness of being. He became mildly aware of someone above them. A pair of giant eyes that sparkled like diamonds. An enormous smile that spanned the cosmos and filled him with the nostalgic warmth of home.

The mouth opened.

Words in a language that he shouldn't have understood came out.

The language of emotion.

"Expunge the poison. The gods know so…"

Gideon chuckled goofily, his whole face creasing. Heather laughed as well, her hair falling over her face as their heads came closer together. The figure on the bench between them rested, his breathing steady, unaware of the mystical dance happening around him.

Heather's face hovered a few inches before Gideon's. He could taste her aura, sense it in the air. He hesitated, remembering the last time she had teased him with a substance and how he had ingested it incorrectly.

"Kiss me," she whispered.

He needed no more encouragement. He felt her tongue on his, felt the warmth of her lips. Their eyes closed, and they lost themselves in it, an eternity of holy darkness claiming them. Their bodies subjected to the tears of the gods.

It wasn't until they heard a cockerel crowing that they realized morning had come.

And her brother was awake.

CHAPTER TWENTY-ONE

Chloe and Burdock stopped a small distance away from Doris' house. The sounds of the battle at the gates had died out, and all was deathly still.

"Are you sure they went this way?" Burdock whispered.

"Of course, I'm sure," Chloe replied, relying heavily on her **Dark Vision** to see ahead to where the house stood. "Trust me. I followed the others to *you*, didn't I? You don't think I can track these?"

Burdock stood on tiptoes, craning his neck to see better. "It doesn't look like they're here."

Chloe resisted the urge to glare. She snuck forward until they were touching the outer walls of the house.

"The lights are off," Burdock said.

Chloe rolled her eyes. "I can see that. Now, will you shut up? They'll hear us."

"They're not here."

"You don't know that!" Chloe hissed.

Burdock folded his arms, his foot tapping impatiently. When he couldn't remain quiet any longer, he said, "I'm just saying, they could have gone *past* this house and stopped somewhere beyond. We might already have lost them."

Chloe took a steadying breath, eyes closed as she strained her ears for any indication of the infected.

She heard the tell-tale thump of footsteps on wood.

"Aha!" Chloe hushed. "Did you hear that?"

"Hear what?"

She was already gone.

Chloe skirted the building at speed, once more imagining the haunting scenario of someone she knew getting mauled by infected. Doris was clearly still asleep, the lights off and the upstairs soundless.

Strange, she thought. *The infected hadn't bothered being quiet at Burdock's house.*

She reached the corner of the house and listened carefully. Several sets of footsteps now, accompanied by hissing voices.

"She *did* come this way, I swear."

"Why would she come all the way out here?"

"To protect the others."

"Was she really aflame?"

Chloe let out a breath, her body relaxing at the sound of their voices.

Burdock caught up with her. "What is it?"

"Check this out," Chloe winked before stepping out from behind the corner of the house with her sword drawn. "Have at thee, cowards!"

Ben, Talbot, Huk, Veronica, and Therese turned as one, eyes wide in surprise. Their hands were on their weapons.

"You son of a…" Ben breathed, a smile growing on his face. "You scared the crap out of us."

"I'll say," Huk agreed, looking down at the floor behind him.

"Me? What about you guys? Sneaking around in the night like a bunch of—"

"Infected?" Veronica interrupted. "That's what we thought we were stopping. Ben said you mentioned something about Doris' house, so we headed straight here to find you. We thought you might need some help."

"She had all the help she needed," Burdock said smugly, stepping out from behind Chloe. "If it wasn't for me, Chloe would be dead by now. Nearly mauled by an infected, she was, until I hit it square in the spine with my axe."

"Nearly killed?" Ben said, making a mocking face at Chloe. "Really? Who is this guy?"

Chloe subtly shook her head, mouthing, "A friend. Just give him this one."

"And hello to you, princess." Chloe smirked at Therese. "Nice to see even royalty doesn't mind getting her hands bloody."

"I'm not royalty yet," Therese said. "And besides, who says I will do this after I'm crowned? Do you see my husband-to-be out here?"

They all laughed.

"Well, we're glad we found you," Veronica said. "Have we cleared all the infected out of the fields?"

Chloe shrugged. "I don't know. We managed to kill the ones at Burdock's house, but there's no way to track any of the others that peeled away from the horde. For all we know, there could still be dozens out there. Is everyone in the city okay?"

Ben nodded. "Looks like it. One or two casualties, but they're mostly blessed who should return, good as new." He paused, face growing pained. "All, that is, except Blueballs. He's not doing well. Leonie took him away from the gates after seeing he'd been scratched by the infected at the barn. She took him somewhere to get him fixed up."

Chloe's frowned. "You don't suppose the infection is…catching?"

They looked at each other, but no one wanted to say that that was exactly what they were thinking.

"We'd better get back," Chloe said.

Ben nodded. "Agreed."

"Particularly if we want to get the princess back to her fancy-pants life in her palace." She smirked.

They summoned their steeds and rode toward the city.

Leonie watched over Blueballs as he slept, taking a moment to relax in the peace and quiet his rest brought.

He was healing, which was great. After spending a good deal of time trying to get the toffet to calm down and sit still, she was able to clean his wounds, to a certain extent.

Dark marks now stained the skin the infected had scratched. She marveled at how quickly the skin knitted itself back together, but she didn't feel settled. How would the infection work on a toffet? Would it be the same as it was on those that attacked?

She leaned against the wall and rested her eyes. Somehow it was already morning, which meant she had been up all night. She found it impossible to believe how tired she got inside a video game but applauded Praxis on their efforts to create realism within Obsidian.

At the sound of hooves on stone, she sat up and made her way over to the outpost window. Blueballs stirred gently in his sleep, purring with every exhale. She saw Chloe and the others and beckoned them over.

"How is he?" Veronica asked the minute she stepped through the door.

"Okay, I think," Leonie said. "He was difficult to settle, but the wounds are healing. I'm just not sure the infection has gone."

Chloe strode over and leaned on the edge of the table to try to see any patches of exposed skin. For her, the tell-tale signs were the blackened veins, but she couldn't see any. Maybe that was a good thing. Maybe the toffet's skin was too thick for the disease to take root?

"How do we know when we're out of the woods?"

Leonie shrugged. "I guess we'll know when he wakes up. If he tries to maul us, he's infected."

"That's one way to do it, I suppose," Ben replied.

Chloe ran a hand across Blueballs' forehead, the movement instinctual. His temperature was steady. That must be good, right?

"How'd it go?" Leonie asked, breaking the silence that had fallen.

They told her about their chase across the fields. How there might still be some infected out there somewhere. Therese told them she'd inform the king and send out soldiers to monitor the situation.

"Especially today." Ben grinned. "Wouldn't want anything to ruin your big day, would you?"

Therese smacked her forehead. "I almost forgot! I should be at the palace getting ready!"

"'Getting ready?'" Talbot mocked. "We're in a fantasy realm. There are no makeup or hairdryers or fancy lotions to put on. How long is it really going to take you?"

Therese shrugged. "I honestly don't know. I guess we'll find out." She ran to the door and paused. "I'll see you all later, yes? I want you front and center to witness my radiant beauty."

Chloe turned up her nose. "Who the hell are you?"

The party chuckled as Therese waved and disappeared. They could hear her heavy footsteps trailing away and resume in the street outside.

Chloe turned her attention back to Blueballs, hand stroking the fluff on his head. She stared at the peaceful expression on his face, unable to quell the mild discomfort in her stomach. Something niggled in the back of her mind, telling her she should have somehow expected this attack. She should have known it was going to happen.

She just couldn't place how.

The murmuring of desperate voices was suddenly audible from next door. Chloe recognized Gideon's, realizing only then that he wasn't with their party. She strode over to the thick wooden door and gently knocked.

Gideon couldn't believe his luck. Somehow this beautiful woman was kissing him—voluntarily!

He had never had much success with ladies, either inside or outside of video games, and had convinced himself he wasn't really interested in affection and romance. That somehow, he would just be alone in life, and that would be okay.

But now this incredible cleric was kissing him, he realized how hungry he had been for company. How he had yearned for something like this to happen for years.

Sure, he would have *preferred* for it to happen in real life, but what with being in full immersion as he was now, this was certainly a great consolation prize.

They locked lips for what felt like hours. He was aware that she must have given him some kind of drug. What else would explain their total isolation in a cloudless sky? The great god watching over them as they united saliva and tongues?

And the funny part was that he didn't mind. He guessed that the god's tears he had drunk were not in any way like the drugs on Earth. For one, he couldn't believe that Heather would provide something that would damage his system, but also, the comedown was gentle. The comedown was kind.

They broke apart, hearing the sound of hooves on stone outside. It acted like a pin in their bubble of romance. Heather's head remained near Gideon's, her eyes staring into his.

"It's amazing, isn't it?" Her voice was low and raspy. She clutched the vial in one hand. "A god's tears. Even a small amount soaked into the skin can somehow make you feel closer to them."

Gideon nodded. "I could see him. Holistis. He was there. He…he was watching. The clouds…they were everywhere."

Heather looked at Gideon strangely and giggled. "I think maybe you had a little too much. Tell me, what did you see?"

Gideon told her.

"Wow!" She looked down at her vial with newfound appreciation. "Good to know. If I ever want to be closer to the gods, I just need to drink this…and kiss you." She blushed.

Gideon let out a small laugh, looking at his feet. "What's the real purpose of it? Were we just getting high?"

Heather shook her head. "It increases your connection to the gods. For clerics, this can bolster your abilities, providing a healing buff for twenty-four hours. Anyone affected by liquid from the same vials automatically gets bonded to the cleric, and their well-being is enhanced for the same duration. Check it out."

Gideon pulled up his notifications, smiling as he saw the buff granting him increased stamina and faster healing for a twenty-four-hour period.

He closed his menu, suddenly taking in what Heather had said. "Does that mean...well, being affected by the tears, does that mean that...all of what just happened...with us...was the effect of the liquid?"

Heather gave a crooked smile and simply said, "No."

"When you two lovebirds are done making googly eyes at each other, I'd really appreciate some help here."

Heather broke Gideon's gaze and looked down at her brother.

He was smiling, but it was certainly pained. His eyes were puffy and red, and although his veins had lost some of their darkness, they still did not look healthy. His skin was covered with sweat, and he seemed to have trouble swallowing.

"Tyrene!" Heather exclaimed, leaning forward and hugging her brother.

The minute Heather's skin came close to Tyrene's face, his disposition changed. His eyes darkened, and he gnashed his teeth at his sister.

Gideon pulled her back quickly. Heather hadn't noticed until the last minute.

Tyrene moaned.

"Brother," Heather said, relief setting in as his eyes returned to their usual color once more. "What happened to you?"

Before he could reply, there was a knock at the door. Gideon was surprised and relieved to see the door open and Chloe's head poke through.

"Hey! We heard noises. Are you two okay in here?"

Gideon moved to the side to reveal Tyrene strapped to the bed.

A smile reached Chloe's face. "Well, I didn't mean to interrupt whatever freaky bondage games you're into..."

"No. No, it's not like that." Gideon blushed. "He's her brother. It's the guy we pulled through the gates last night. One of the infected."

"Wasn't he just talking, though?" Veronica asked, her face appearing behind Chloe's. "I could've sworn I just heard him talking."

"Infected don't talk," Ben said, adding his head to the mix. "Not the ones we've seen, anyway."

Gideon rolled his eyes. "Instead of just standing out there, why don't you all come in?" A thought suddenly occurred to him. "Veronica, you're a cleric, right?"

"Nice to see you're paying attention, mage-pants."

"Heather, Veronica is a cleric too. She's been our healer in the group in many a combat."

Veronica strode across the room and shook Heather's hand. "Pleased to meet you."

"Likewise," Heather replied, slightly perturbed by the number of people who had just entered the room. "I figured I knew your class from the seminar Chloe gave last night. It was honestly impressive, what you showed us with your armor. Imagine a goddess living alongside you!"

"More like *she's* living alongside *me*," KieraFreya quipped.

"Who's living inside who?" Chloe snapped.

Tyrene groaned once more, head rolling back on the table. "When you're done with your family reunion, can you *please* help me?"

"Of course, brother," Heather said, her cheeks flushing. "Anything you need. Tell us what happened, and maybe we can set about fixing it."

Tyrene grimaced, adjusting against his bonds. He took a breath and began his tale.

He told them that he had been visiting a small village on the outskirts of the forest to the east. Sent on the errand by the king himself, Tyrene and a handful of clerics had traveled out together, their sole intention to discover more about the plague that had been spreading among the villages and find a cure.

After two days of journeying, they had found the village in question. The group had split up, their intention to visit the ill and congregate each evening to discuss their findings and work on a cure.

"The first thing I noticed was that there was something unholy about this plague," Tyrene croaked. "I sensed it when I walked into the room. A woman, middle-aged, was writhing in her bed and sweating. But it wasn't just her coughing and groans that caught my attention. I could feel something in the room. Some presence watching over her."

It had been the same everywhere he went, he said. After visiting a dozen patients across the village, he had collected enough data on the illness to meet with the other clerics and discuss possible solutions.

Only, out of the handful of clerics who had accompanied him, only two others were able to join the conversation. The other two were now infected and bedridden.

"We came up with possible solutions. The usual tricks. Potions and remedies from handbooks that have been staples for clerics for millenniums. Nothing seemed to work."

For several days they were out there, the constant feeling of being watched looming over them. Each day took another cleric, and before he knew it, he was alone.

"I struggled to sleep. At night, although the evenings turned cold, I'd feel heat washing over me. I'd sweat in bed and hear voices and see people standing at the bottom of my bed, three figures cloaked in darkness. Once, when I sat up suddenly in bed and snapped my eyes open, I thought I'd catch them. But there was nothing, only echoing giggles, as if some small girl had played a trick and vanished into the night."

"You should have come back, brother," Heather said. "At the first signs of delusion, you should have returned."

Tyrene shook his head. "It is not our way. You know this. Clerics do not leave people to suffer. We help at all costs. I suppose this cost was just too great."

He told them that the following day, the illness had taken him. He couldn't remember a lot of what had happened thereafter, just a sense of being guided by some invisible hand through the forest.

"No creature touched us, nor bothered us. It was as though we were under a bubble of protection, and our guide knew the way."

It was later that night that the darkness took them all over and they ran for the city.

"It makes no sense," Heather said, brow creased in thought. "What kind of illness takes over a person's faculties and sends them on a frenzied mission?"

Chloe shook her head gently. As Tyrene was talking, the pieces had begun to fall into place. It was at the mention of the three that she finally remembered the words the doc had shared in their message. Then the penny dropped.

"It's not like any illness you'd normally encounter," Chloe said dryly. "It's a plague, put forth by evil gods."

"What are you talking about?" Veronica asked.

Chloe sighed. "Fukmos is back, and he's brought his friends, Dryana and Myaris."

"Who the hell are they?" Ben asked.

"Fukmos' sisters," Veronica said. "The Goddess of Ghosts and the Goddess of Disease."

"Well, that makes sense," Huk grumbled, his tiny form barely able to see the man on the bench.

"An unholy illness?" Heather said, cast deep into thought. She touched her chin and chewed her lip. "Which means only the holy can purge it from the bodies of the afflicted?"

"I suppose," Chloe said.

Veronica moved over to the table and rolled up her sleeves. "Okay, explain everything. You've made this guy—"

"Tyrene," Gideon interjected.

"*Tyrene*, well enough to be able to talk. What did you do? How did you push back the illness?"

Heather detailed her use of Holistis' tears and the effect the solution had had in bolstering healing.

"So, power from the gods might be enough to heal? We're going to have to purge the darkness from your brother entirely. The illness within him is not biological. It's spiritual and etheric. With the right amount of power, we might be able to eject it from his body and bring him back to normal."

Heather looked down at her brother, face resolute. "It's worth a shot."

They took their places on either side of the table, the rest of the KieraSlayers moving back to give the clerics room. Leonie ducked out to keep an eye on Blueballs as they worked, his grumbles audible through the walls.

They passed their hands over Tyrene's body like ancient women blessing the water before they washed their hands. Their hands glowed in a faint white light which seemed to ring gently.

Chloe had seen Veronica work, but she had never seen her perform true miracles. Sure, casting **Healing Hands** and keeping the party restored during battle was incredibly useful—the spell had countless benefits and it was easy to learn—but she had never seen a cleric operate.

Without making eye contact, words spilled from their mouths like water from the lip of a waterfall. The aura around them grew. Their eyes turned pure white, light shining from beneath their lids.

"It's beautiful," Ben muttered.

Gideon nodded, unable to take his eyes off Heather.

The faint ringing grew louder, and each placed a hand on Tyrene's chest. The minute their hands made contact, his eyes turned dark and he began to thrash, his body shaking violently beneath the straps. The darkness rose to the surface of his skin, his veins looking like ink spills on white canvas.

Talbot took an unconscious step forward, held back only by Chloe's arm. "Let them work."

Tyrene began to shout, his mouth wide open. His muscles tensed like knotted rope. The women kept their cool, their hands now so blindingly bright that they were impossible to see.

"It's working." Chloe grinned.

The darkness trailed out of Tyrene's mouth in gaseous ribbons. It coagulated in the air, forming a dense, dark shadow that hovered for a moment. The shadow let out a soft girlish chuckle before darting at the KieraSlayers and smashing through the stone wall, leaving a powdery hole behind.

They watched as the shadow flew into the sky, disappearing out of sight in a flash.

"Holy…" Ben uttered, mouth agape.

"No," came Tyrene's voice from the table, his head held up by Heather. "There's nothing holy going on here."

CHAPTER TWENTY-TWO

Purging the darkness from Blueballs took a little more effort but was far less messy than Tyrene's healing.

Whether it was because of the biological makeup of the toffet, the creature being notoriously tougher than many creatures they'd met before, or because the darkness had had less time to take hold, they didn't know.

What they did know was that after the darkness had been purged and the small cloud of shadow had emerged and disappeared into the atmosphere, the whole party needed rest. The wedding of their friend and the king was to take place at sunset, and they were all exhausted.

Luckily for the party, the inn wasn't too far from the outpost. Gideon hung back for a few moments longer to say goodbye to Heather in private before they took to the streets. They were shortly in the warm glow of the public house.

"I've got to hand it to you, I didn't think you had it in you," Ben said as they took the stairs and headed to their rooms.

"It was nothing," Veronica said. "It's actually one of the innate skills clerics have. Some call it exorcism. I call it purging."

"I wasn't talking about you." Ben chuckled. "I was talking about Romeo there."

Gideon's ears burned and he looked up meekly. "I don't know what you're talking about."

"Sure you don't, stud." Ben winked. "All I'm saying is that it's okay to have a digital girlfriend. Just be careful you don't get too attached, okay? Those kinds of relationships don't always last."

They all fell silent, no one needing to say what the others were thinking. Their minds had gone to their comrade, still lying at the inn at Killink View.

The party split into their respective rooms. Chloe helped Blueballs through the door, the great beast ducking to gain entry. He was visibly exhausted from the fight and his battle with the darkness. All too soon, he was curled up and snoring in the corner.

"I suppose I best log out for a bit, too," Gideon said. "It's been some time since my mom has heard from me. She'll likely be going nuts, wondering how to reset the pod."

Chloe laughed. "Really? She'd do that?"

"Nah." Gideon grinned. "She's a pure technophobe. She can't even turn her phone on without help."

He said his goodbyes and laid down on his bed. Chloe rested on hers, checking her stats and seeing that her stamina had taken a beating as the night had progressed. Maybe a little sleep wouldn't be a bad thing, after all.

As she lay in bed, she couldn't help but think about all that had happened in the last few hours. She had found several dozen city folk willing to help her in her quest to open the Nether Realm, the party and city had been attacked by infected, and the news that the doc's warning was right and Fukmos was back and had brought company was unsettling.

She couldn't help but begin to think this was personal. Before, she had been more than aware that she was completing a quest. She had been following instructions and piecing the puzzle together in order to unite KieraFreya.

But ever since she had defeated Fukmos and his host in the mountains and acquired the last of the goddess' body armor, she had somehow known that it would come to this. You couldn't upset a god without expecting some form of retribution.

She wondered about these two new additions to the game, Myaris and Dryana. If the illness was but a taste of their power, she feared what was to come. The infection was clearly the product of the Goddess of Disease, but what monsters might the Goddess of Ghosts bring forth?

Chloe rolled over in bed, watching Gideon. Blueballs' snoring was a welcome sound in the otherwise empty room.

She had made a start. That was good. Although those who had shown up at the barn were of…questionable ability, at least she had people already willing to fight for her cause. If the battle against the infected hadn't put them off, she'd be interested to see how they got on tomorrow night, when they met once again and began their training.

Would they bring more people with them?

That remained to be seen.

Loose change rattled, the sound caressing Chloe's ears. She smiled.

The Heroes-for-Hire board was working. That was something, at least. That also meant people were reading her notices about her cause, and maybe more people *would* come tomorrow.

As she closed her eyes once more, she thought ahead to Therese's wedding, picturing the ludicrousness of what a dwarfish marital cere-mony might look like.

Who'd have believed I'd be here just a few months ago? Chloe thought. *When life was partying and shallow gossip. Who'd have thought I'd be recruiting an army in a medieval realm and celebrating the marriage of one of my dwarvish best friends?*

She chuckled and closed her eyes. With that, she slept.

To anyone arriving in the city that afternoon, it would have looked as if nothing had happened the night before.

No one seemed worried or stressed, and there were no signs that a battle had taken place. The guards had cleaned up the remains of the infected, and the city gate had been cleaned. By early afternoon, the streets were filled with spectators, ready for the wedding.

Children darted between their parents' legs. The merchants were back on the street, peddling their wares. Flags flew, horns blew, bunting decorated every street, and spirits were higher than ever before.

This wasn't just any wedding. This was a wedding that signaled change. A wedding that would supersede all weddings which had come before. The king had changed the laws and chosen a commoner. A nobody, someone with no royal standing.

And that had given the little girls and women of the city hope for the future. Given them the dream that any girl could be a princess.

The wedding was to take place on an outcrop of rock that towered over the city, on a platform hewn from the stone. The location could be viewed from nearly every street. The bride and groom would take their place at its edge, their tiny figures bringing tears to the eyes of thousands as they took their vows and became one.

The afternoon wore on, and the streets grew more choked. People could barely move. The temperature rose, and on a few occasions, a punch was thrown by an irritated, dehydrated bystander who had lost his patience.

There was nothing the guards could do. They had taken their places at the front gates of the city and at their posts around the palace. They couldn't get involved in the squabbles of the peasants, not on this day.

Yet, while the atmosphere was alive and electric for the many thousands waiting for the union, for the dwarf still sleeping in her chambers, the excitement was lost.

"Miss Therese!" Beverley's voice snapped.

Therese jumped up and a trail of drool stuck to the sheets. "Hmmm?"

Beverley stood in the doorway with a pile of folded laundry in her hands. She marched over to Therese, laid the laundry down carefully, and grabbed her by the ear.

"Hey! You can't do that. I'm your queen."

"Not yet, you're not," Beverley scolded. "And since you're in no way prepared for today's ceremony, there's a good chance you won't be queen. I left you to get ready. Why were you asleep *again*?"

She released Therese's ear.

"I had a long night, okay? I couldn't help it."

"Well, the king personally instructed me to ensure you're as ready and prepared as you can be, so here." She snatched the wedding dress from the door and passed it to Therese. "Wash yourself, put this on, and meet me in my quarters in twenty minutes. I'm not having my reputation as a server put at risk because *you* can't keep your eyes open."

Despite herself, Therese smiled.

"What is it?" Beverley said.

"Thank you."

Caught off-guard by the comment, Beverley nodded and said, "Yes, well, chop-chop, now, Miss Therese."

Therese obeyed Beverley, standing up, stretching and getting herself prepared. She joined the handmaiden in her chambers a short while later and groaned and moaned as she was examined from every angle and made as presentable as possible.

When she was done, she looked in the mirror and couldn't believe what she was seeing. She had never imagined a dwarf could look so beautiful. Even in her dress—which had been a compromise with Abe, that she could wear whatever she wanted the rest of the time, as long as she obeyed custom during their wedding day—she found she actually liked the frills and laces.

"You're almost ready," Beverley said, standing behind Therese and appreciating her handiwork.

"What's missing?"

Beverley reached around Therese and gently nudged her cheeks into a smile. "There. Perfect."

Therese laughed, fanning her dress around her in appreciation. "Do you think he'll like it?"

"He'll love it."

Therese imagined it, standing atop the precipice and looking down at her future subjects. The wind blowing around her as she towered above the city that she would soon rule. It was status and power she'd never experienced in a game before, and she knew she wouldn't ever get the chance to experience in real life.

"And the people?" Therese asked, her smile slipping. "Will *they* like me?"

"A queen's duty is not to be liked. It is to be respected and loved. If you can make them respect you, you'll make a perfect queen."

Although Beverley said the words, Therese wasn't convinced. She knew that Beverley was having trouble with the king's decision not to marry royalty. As a handmaiden who had served the city for years, Beverley had made it clear in a hissed conversation with Abe, which Therese had overheard one night, that she thought it was a mistake.

"Come," Beverley said with a wry smile on her face.

She led Therese into another room with a wide balcony at the far end. She guided her to the open air, and they looked out upon the kingdom.

Therese's breath caught; she couldn't believe the number of bodies in the streets. A few in the streets below her looked up and pointed, the action creating a wave of pointing fingers and smiling faces. A moment later, the crowd was cheering for her.

Therese's eyes pricked with tears. She was overwhelmed by what she was seeing and hearing.

"You see?" Beverley said. "I don't think you've got anything to worry about."

Therese nodded, her heart filling with joy.

"Okay," she agreed, finding her resolve. "Let's rule a kingdom."

CHAPTER TWENTY-THREE

It had taken so long to squeeze their way through the crowds that Chloe thought they'd never make it in time. Therese had arranged it so the KieraSlayers could watch the ceremony from the outcrop, and it was only a few moments before the sun first kissed the horizon that they emerged at the top.

After identifying themselves, they were hurried through the palace by the guards and eventually emerged onto the platform.

They lined up neatly beside a row of guards, taking positions on either side of a long, flower-strewn aisle.

"Talk about a wedding with a view," Ben said out of the side of his mouth to Chloe. "And I thought *my* friends were showing off when they wanted to get hitched in Ibiza."

"Shhh." Chloe giggled.

They waited patiently, each party member as scrubbed and neat as they had ever been. Chloe's armor shone dazzling gold and emerald, catching the eye of many of the spectators down below, who began to ask questions as to who this mystery figure could be.

Blueballs had been the only member of the party to stay behind, his deep recovering slumber not yet over. The party had decided it would be hard enough to get themselves through the crowd without dragging the lumbering toffet behind them.

Still, Chloe thought. *He would've made a great usher.*

The air was chilly but calm. The sun slowly sank beyond the forest, fracturing the azure sky into a hypnotic array of fiery hues. When the time was right, a series of horned instruments blew to declare the arrival of the king.

King Abaxis appeared in the stone archway, adorned in his finest clothes. Around his shoulders, he wore a long, trailing cape made of rich black material and studded with jewels. He had a crown upon his head and held a scepter in his hand.

Chloe could barely recognize him as the scruffy runaway they had met just a few days ago. He looked ethereal, glorious, beyond any dwarf she had previously met.

As he passed the KieraSlayers, he turned his head and gave a curt nod. Chloe couldn't resist the urge to curtsey and lowered herself, head bowed.

Ben shook his head and laughed.

"Any excuse to drop to your knees."

Chloe blushed. "Shut up. Is that not what you do in the presence of a king?"

"Look around," Ben whispered. "No one else is. Maybe that bit comes later."

King Abaxis made his way to the end of the platform. A short wall, about two feet in height was the only barrier to prevent the king from falling a hundred feet to his death, yet he showed no fear.

He spread his arms wide, eliciting an enormous eruption of cheers from the spectators. When he spoke, his voice was impossibly loud. Chloe realized that this platform had been built for optimum acoustics, an anomaly where the sound traveled around the city without resistance.

"My lords, ladies, gentlemen, and *gentlewomen...*"

There was a ripple of laughter.

"I thank you for your attendance on this wonderful occasion. The union of the king and his bride and the coronation of a new member of our royal family are traditions that date back generations.

"Although the manner in which my bride was selected was a little...unorthodox..."

More laughter. Some groans and cries of protest.

"The ceremony will remain much the same as our forebears. I am more than happy that you have joined me on this occasion, under this glorious sunset, and I wish you all health, vitality, and strength as our kingdom proceeds into its next generation and faces whatever challenges are to come."

With that, he bowed and turned toward the stone archway.

"Send her forth," he said to his waiting guards with an enormous smile on his face.

Chloe's breath caught with excitement. She hadn't been aware that she was looking forward to this moment, but now her eyes were locked on the stone archway.

Jeesh, girl. Relax. It's only a wedding, KieraFreya said.

Chloe chose to ignore her, all thoughts of KF pushed aside when she saw an impossibly beautiful dwarf appear.

At first, Chloe didn't recognize her. She had never seen Therese in anything other than her armor. What she realized now was that the armor had widened the figure beneath and added weight to her body that wasn't there. As she began to walk down the aisle, Chloe's jaw dropped at her figure. The train of her dress flowed behind her like ripples in a stream. Without a helmet on, Chloe could see the fire of her hair, braided tightly to her scalp.

Therese struggled to meet their eyes as she passed. Ben, Talbot, and Gideon wolf-whistled, ignoring the odd looks they received from the guards. Leonie and Veronica laughed and smiled.

Throwing caution to the winds, Chloe broke rank and stepped into the aisle, wrapping her arms around Therese.

The guards reacted instantly, aiming their pikes at Chloe. The king laughed, calming them with a wave of his hand while the women had their moment. Veronica joining in shortly after the disturbance died down.

"You look so beautiful," Chloe said, fighting the tears in her eyes. She never knew she could care this much for someone, let alone an entire party. "I'm so proud of you."

Veronica echoed the sentiment, and soon they wiped their tears and stepped back into the ranks of the guests.

Therese continued toward Abe, pausing at the end and taking his hands.

The ceremony was short but sweet. The crowds cheered at the right moments. The officiator was an elder cleric with much experience in marital unions, and he flowed through the wedding without any issues. When the service was complete, Therese tossed several bouquets of flowers behind her and watched them rain down into the hands of the squealing women below.

Chloe took screenshot after screenshot, determined to remember this moment. A moment in which she had her friends surrounding her, all troubles had been put aside for one day, and she had allowed herself to be swallowed by happiness and joy.

The semi-regular *cha-ching* of coins on coins only enhanced her enjoyment of the day.

When the officiator had finished his sermon, Abe offered his arm to his new wife. Therese smiled thoughtfully, but before she obliged, she turned and looked over the crowd.

There was an immediate explosion of applause and adulation.

Therese raised her arms, then lowered them, a technique she'd picked up from primary schools to hush children.

It worked. The crowd instantly fell silent.

"People of Hammersworth," she began, surprised by her booming voice echoing back at her. She cleared her throat. "I thank you all for your adoration and celebration on this happy day. It is with great pride that I am blessed with the role of your queen, a role that would not have been available to anyone had our gracious king not found his courage and been true to his heart.

"It is a time of great change, not just for Hammersworth, but for every city across Obsidian. Though many do not know, I have traveled from afar with mighty adventurers who have seen many corners of this realm.

"It is because of these experiences that I can tell you the darkness is coming."

A murmur of voices made its way through the crowd, caused by those who weren't quite sure they'd heard their queen correctly, and those who couldn't believe what she'd said.

Even Chloe raised an eyebrow, wondering what Therese was doing.

"Although a wedding is a happy occasion, I would be remiss in my role as your new queen if I were not to offer a warning of tougher times ahead. Many of you saw the darkness that attacked the city last night, and I fear that it was only the beginning of what is to come. Should the right people not unite and help bring the world together for the benefit of the greater good, we will all suffer."

Therese took a deep breath and turned toward the KieraSlayers. She motioned to Chloe.

"Chloe of the KieraSlayers, will you please step forth?"

Chloe did so, slowly breaking ranks once more. She made her way to the end of the platform and stood between Abe and Therese.

Another wave of murmurs issued from below them as Chloe came into view and a few of those who had pointed and made guesses about the warrior clad in gold and emerald armor wondered whether their theories were about to be confirmed.

"This is Chloe, a battle mage, and one of the bravest fighters this realm has ever seen. Together, we have been fighting the darkness that has been growing across the realm, but we cannot do it alone. We need your help."

"What are you doing?" Chloe hissed.

Therese ignored her.

"In order to combat this darkness, and as one my first duties as your queen, I invite any and all fighters with abilities to draw on the etheric to make themselves known by joining us in the abandoned barn on the eastern front of the city tomorrow night. There we may configure a plan to push back the darkness and ensure that light reigns supreme.

"Those who are able but choose not to join will not be reprimanded, but neither will they find great reward for their efforts when the darkness eventually takes us all and the world ends."

Ben shuffled uncomfortably, whispering to Gideon, "Well, that's cheery. Has she ever been to a wedding before?"

Gideon didn't reply.

"For my second act as your queen, I wish to thank Chloe for all the contributions she has made to our protection thus far by assigning her the role of Chief Guardian of the Queen. Separate from the king's guard, the queen's guard will consist of the KieraSlayers party, and will spread the word of the queen across this city, protecting my legacy and aiding in the distribution of tasks and civility."

A notification popped up in Chloe's vision.

New title acquired: Chief Guardian of the Queen

As the queen's chief guardian, the duties and responsibilities of ultimate protection will fall upon you. You will rank as equal to the king's guards, and your word will hold weight among the people of Hammersworth.

New locations unlocked

You now have access to more locations in Hammersworth, namely, the palace. While there are still some rooms and floors that will remain a well-guarded secret kept by the city's royalty, you will no longer have to wait while guards check your identity before entering the palace.

A word of caution: while your new title might unlock many doors and opportunities, it will also expose you to more threats within the city. Remember that there will always be someone else vying for your spot and rank.

Bonuses: new areas of the city unlocked, For the Queen! skill granted, permanent residence within the palace available

(NOTE: bonuses and effects only remain while title is held. Should player lose title, they will also lose all granted effects and boons)

You've unlocked a new (unique) skill: For the Queen!

Unite and inspire any and all allied fighters surrounding you in battle with a war cry, backed by the queen herself.

Fighters will rally around you, finding courage in their hearts to fight longer and with increased strength for a limited time.

Bonuses: +5% strength, +5% stamina, +5% endurance, +5% mana regeneration, +5% health regeneration.

Duration: 3 minutes

Chloe was stunned and her mouth fell open. She looked at Abe for help, but he merely laughed and shook his head. "Didn't I tell you? She'll make a great queen."

Therese grinned and poked her tongue out of the corner of her mouth.

"Chloe, do you accept this charge?"

Chloe didn't know what to do. She turned to her friends for help and found Ben miming a curtsy and nodding his head emphatically. When she still didn't respond, he cupped his hands and called, "*Now* would be the time to curtsy."

Chloe fell to one knee before the queen, to a reverent silence across the city.

"Chloe, I dub thee Chief Guardian of the Queen. Arise and fulfill your duties."

When Chloe stood up, the silence remained. Below them came the single clap of an excited old matron, then another from the woman beside her. Slowly, one by one, a large majority of the town began to whoop and cheer. Never had they seen such excitement at a royal wedding.

As the cheering and applause continued to swell, Therese ushered Chloe back to her place in the ranks. Chloe tried to hide the tears of joy beneath her helmet, not wanting anyone to see her cry.

Not that it made a difference. Everyone saw it. No one said a word.

After the public ceremony was complete, the newly-crowned queen and her husband made their way into the dining hall of the palace, where their staff had outdone themselves. Tables fifty seats long were decorated in silver, gold, and white. Plates and trays were piled high with food, and servers were on hand to keep the cups filled.

Chloe had never seen so many people dining together. She sat toward the head of the table with Gideon, Ben, and Talbot on one side and Veronica, Leonie, and Huk on the other.

They ate until their stomachs hurt and drank until the room swam. They clapped and whooped and celebrated all the excitement that had gone on during the ceremony.

"You know what we really need?" Ben said, arm looped around Gideon's neck. On an average day, even this simple gesture might have made Gideon uncomfortable, but it seemed the mage was more than happy to engage, thanks to copious amounts of mead. "A song."

"You know who sang great songs?" Veronica asked, her words slurring.

"Tag," Therese finished. "He had a song for every occasion. Had a way with the words, that one."

Chloe nodded. "Only in song, though. If he opened his mouth to speak, you'd be better off running for the hills."

"You're goddamn right." Ben laughed, raising his drink. "I miss that scamp."

"Scamp?" Talbot chuckled.

"Hey, I'm in a game that doesn't let you swear without blowing your ears off. Excuse me if my vocabulary is limited."

"Try saying *that* three times fast," Leonie remarked, the quietest of the group now that the alcohol had hit her system. She smiled goofily and her eyelids softly closed.

"Vocabluraly is limited, vocebaculary ish limided, vocabsuwary..." Ben stopped, unable to control his laughter.

After the food was finished, they took to their feet and went to the next room, larger than even the dining hall.

The ceiling was at least three stories tall; a large fireplace took up the majority of one wall, where a miniature bonfire crackled and sent heat forth. At the far end of the room, an open wall dotted with pillars led out onto another balcony that looked across the city, where lights twinkled down below. The people of Hammersworth indulging in their own celebrations.

In the corner of the room, a ten-piece band produced beautiful music. Accompanied by strings and horns, a singer with a rotund stomach and an impressive voice provided the tunes while the guests set about dancing.

Dresses whirled, men bowed, laughter rang. Chloe couldn't help but feel slightly out of place, clad in her armor.

"Forget about it, Chloe," Gideon said, sensing her discomfort. "You can still dance in that, right?"

Chloe shrugged. "If I can, it's a miracle suit. I've never been able to dance out of armor. Not like these people dance, anyway."

Gideon grinned, emboldened by his mead. He offered a hand. "Come, let me show you."

Chloe had never had so much fun in her life. Gideon was a confident instructor, taking her in his arms and guiding her effortlessly around the room. Despite her reservations, she found herself falling into step, enjoying the ebb and flow of the music and the dance.

Other dancers whirled around them, their smiles sincere and broad. When the song ended, Chloe lingered a moment longer in Gideon's arms.

"You're a fast learner," he said.

"You're a great teacher." She smirked.

Their gazes held for a moment longer before the next song started to kick in.

"Care for another spin?" Gideon asked.

Before Chloe could answer, someone called Gideon's name.

"Heather?" Gideon said, his smile broadening. "How... Why are you here?"

Heather coyly grinned. "After all that happened with my brother, we reported to the cleric elders. Turns out that a few of them had invites, and after hearing how we helped identify the source of the illness and possible healing measures, they managed to get me invited along for the evening celebrations."

"Well, it's great to see you." Gideon beamed.

"I'll leave you to it," Chloe said, taking a shy step backward. "Good to see you, Heather."

"You don't have to go," Gideon protested.

"It's fine," Chloe said. "Turns out this armor chafes when I dance. You'll be better off dancing with Heather."

Heather raised her eyebrows, impressed. "You dance?"

"I dabble."

"He's an expert." Chloe winked. "Now, go on, you two. Have fun."

Without looking back, Chloe worked her way to the edge of the room, stopping by a table filled with bowls of punch. There she found Ben and Talbot deep in a heated debate over whether either of them could beat Blueballs in a fight.

They broke apart when Chloe approached.

"All okay, Chloe?" Ben asked.

Chloe nodded, turning back to face the room. At that moment, she had everything she needed. Good friends, good company, and an upgraded standing among the people of Hammersworth.

Even though a tiny part of her felt a little odd at watching Gideon lock eyes with Heather, she was truly happy he had someone to give him everything he needed.

CHAPTER TWENTY-FOUR

Unlike the previous morning, when the rising sun kissed the stone walls of Hammersmith, the streets were nearly empty.

Trash littered the roads, rolling around lazily in the breeze.

The streets, which would usually already be slowly filling with morning traffic, were empty. Only a few residents were out and journeying to their daily chores, regretting their decisions to celebrate well into the early hours with copious amounts of mead and ale.

Jobs still needed to be done, livestock taken care of, food prepared, and fields tended to. The few who were up dragged their feet and staggered a bit as they made their way to their respective jobs, scolding themselves and believing a good night's sleep would fix everything.

Even the palace was quiet that morning. The festivities hadn't finished until the first signs of dawn had approached. Starlings had sung on the balcony, causing the few who remained to finally find places to rest their heads and sleep.

Bodies littered the floor. Chests rose and fell as snores and whistles created a symphony that echoed around the chambers. A few servants began cleaning, tiptoeing over the unconscious, mopping up spills, and working to set the palace to rights again.

"It's like an episode of a teen drama," Chloe mused, scanning the chamber that had only hours ago been alive with dance and song. Not for the first time, she was incredibly grateful that the pain gauge on the blessed players had been all but removed, so hangovers really didn't have much effect.

Not only that, but with a quick jolt of her **Healing Hands** spell, she felt right as rain.

"You'd never think such a thing would happen in a palace, would you?" Gideon commented, sipping a mug of something hot and sweet-smelling a handmaiden had offered him. The liquid thick and green.

"Maybe that's why they keep everything so secret. The celebrations of high society behind locked doors. That way, the lower classes won't get jealous."

"Maybe." Gideon nodded, enjoying the warmth of the sun on the back of his neck.

The morning wore on, and the palace began to find itself back in order. Like dandelions, the nobles rose one-by-one, soon disappearing and floating off back to the reality of their own lives.

By midday, the remaining KieraSlayers showed no signs of waking.

"Maybe they've logged off?" Gideon suggested.

Chloe agreed, stating that they all needed the rest after the last couple of days. She and Gideon headed outside into the sun and worked their way down the city streets, finding it incredibly refreshing how easy it was to walk through the city now that the celebrations were over.

They passed a flower shop on the corner, where a woman with a tangle of dark hair hunched over as she arranged her vases. She caught Chloe's eye as she passed and executed a crude bow.

A woman on the other side of the street who had been busy brushing the knots out of her son's hair saw the florist, looked around in alarm, and bowed low too, nudging her son to do so as well.

"What are they doing?" Chloe asked.

"Showing respect." Gideon grinned. "You're the new Chief

Guardian of the Queen, remember? I suppose you'd better get used to people not being sure how to react to you. Fear does that to people."

"Fear?" Chloe whispered. "I don't want them to be scared of me."

"It doesn't matter what you want; you can't control an entire population. I suppose you'll just have to get used to it."

It was easier said than done. The farther down the levels of the city they got, the more reactions she received. A few bowed. Some curtsied. Several dark-looking gentlemen hanging around outside a nearby tavern narrowed their eyes and saluted mockingly.

Chloe shook her head and focused ahead, not sure how to feel about the attention she was receiving. When she rounded a corner and came to the intersection where her Heroes-for-Hire board hung, she was surprised and excited to notice several figures standing in front of it, fingers tracing the words on the notices as they read the various quests.

"It's being used," Chloe squealed.

"That's nothing new. You told me you've been making money for a few days."

"But I haven't *seen* anyone using it," Chloe replied.

Which was certainly true. After all the excitement of the last few days, she hadn't had time to visit the site of her first in-game business venture. The view filled her with glee.

Not least because the board was doing exactly what she wanted it to do. The figures standing in front certainly *looked* the part of heroes.

Maybe I can put up more boards. Grow the business. Expand across Obsidian...

One step at a time. KieraFreya chuckled.

There were three of them standing there, two mages and a warrior by the looks of them. The warrior was in the middle, taller than the other two by a good couple of feet. His shoulders were broad, and his biceps bulging beneath his plate armor. A broadsword that stretched from his head to his ass was strapped to his back.

The mages on either side were arrayed in cloaks. The one on the left wore purple, while the one on the right wore red. Their hoods were pulled over their heads, but she could make out the narrow frames beneath the folds of the material.

The mage wearing red held a long gold staff with some kind of crystal on the end.

"Magic-users," Gideon breathed, only then realizing that Chloe had already peeled off and was approaching the trio.

"Good morning, gentlemen," Chloe said brightly. "How does thee fare on this fine golden morning?"

How does thee fare? KieraFreya mocked. *The Dark Ages have long since passed.*

Shut up.

"Gentlemen?" inquired a soft, sweet voice.

The mage in purple turned around and proved to be a slender elven woman. Her cheeks were pinched, and her eyes were ice blue.

"Who's she calling 'gentlemen?'" the mage in red asked. She was a tall elven woman of much the same appearance as the first. The two were almost identical. "You know it's rude to assume a person's gender."

Chloe backpedaled. "I'm sorry. I meant no offense. It's just, I saw your friend there, and…"

"Assumed I was a man?" the warrior asked in a gruff voice that did *not* match her gender. Chloe couldn't place her race. Her skin looked as though it was partly stone. Her features were rough and looked carved. Her jaw was wide, and she had two stumpy fangs jutting from her lower gums.

"To be honest, yes," Chloe said, unable to think of what else to say. "It was my mistake."

The mage in purple looked at Gideon. "What's your friend's problem? She's never seen a troll before?"

"*Half*-troll," the giant corrected.

"How can you be half troll?" Chloe asked.

"Simple," the mage in red replied. "When a mommy troll and a daddy human love each other very much—"

Chloe waved her hands and screwed her eyes shut, trying not to picture it in her head. "Enough. I get it. Science, or some pseudo strain of it. Fine."

The troll chuckled. "She's a gullible one, isn't she?

"What do you mean?" Gideon asked.

"I'm not an NPC," the troll said. "I'm one of the blessed. I got to choose this character."

"You *chose* a half-troll?"

"Yeah, why not?" The troll smiled. "Seemed a lot more interesting than some of the other races offered to me. Elves, men, and dwarves have been done to death."

"No offense taken," the elves said in unison.

The troll beamed and offered a hand. "Name's Gelda."

"Chloe," Chloe replied. "And this is Gideon."

"Pleased to meet you," Gelda said, almost crushing their hands in her grip.

"Holly," the mage in purple said, offering her own hand. "And my sister Molly."

"Holly and Molly?" Gideon spluttered before he could help himself. He wilted under their raised eyebrows. "Doesn't that get confusing?"

"Not for us." They giggled.

"For other people, maybe," Holly agreed.

Molly nodded. "But that's not our problem."

Gelda rolled her eyes.

"So, what exactly are you two doing spying on us, anyway?" Molly continued. "We can share the board, you know? Just wait your turn. We're almost done."

"Oh, yeah?" Chloe smiled. "Anything in particular catch your eyes?"

"Well, we were giving quite a lot of consideration to this one here," Gelda said, indicating the notice with a thick finger. "Assistant needed to shovel horse manure. A mountain of horse manure has accrued following the absence of my husband. Looking for strong, powerful man to clear the pile for a special reward."

"I bet I know what special reward *she* has in mind." Holly laughed.

Molly hunched, acting like a distressed old lady, "Oh, help me. My man is gone, and I need some hunky chunk of muscle to use his big, strong arms to fix my problems."

Holly snorted. Gelda chuckled and shook her head.

"Or what about this one?" Molly said, straightening to her full height and prodding another notice. She cleared her throat. "Night-time companion required to ward off evil. Must be slender, chesty, and fine with night-time tumbles."

"Are those really written on those posts?" Chloe moved closer, unable to believe what she was hearing.

"Yep." Gelda nodded. "Every single word."

Chloe couldn't help but give a disbelieving laugh. She hadn't intended the board to be a place for Hammersworth's residents to fulfill their sick desires. She had genuinely wanted to help people and provide a place for quests to be offered.

"Wait, what about that one?" Gideon said, reading from a scrappy bit of paper detailing a man who required assistance from anyone willing to help dig a trench. His voice trailed away when he realized that the trenches required were detailed as being seven feet by four feet, the approximate size of a dead body.

Chloe threw her hands into the air. "Oh, for God's sake."

"Don't get yourself tied in knots," Holly said, finally able to talk again. "There's this one we were looking at. Something about mages and help required to do some kind of city mission."

"Sounds interesting," Molly added.

Chloe and Gideon looked at each other.

"What was that look for?" Molly asked.

"You've made a good choice," Chloe said smugly. "That notice would be mine."

"Yours?" Molly said, looking her up and down. "Nope. Not possible."

"Why not?" Chloe asked.

"You look like a slightly more fashionable C-3PO." Holly chuckled. "And your friend hardly looks able to perform any magic. Are we supposed to believe you're the great Chloe we heard about on our way into the city?"

Chloe couldn't prevent a small smile from appearing on her face. "From who?"

"*Everyone*," Holly replied. "Apparently, you're the talk of the town right now. Which is strange, because didn't the king and queen get married last night?"

"Yep," Gideon said. "The queen is actually a member of our party."

"Shut the front door!" Holly exclaimed. She realized she might have betrayed her excitement and immediately restored her passive face. "Well, prove it, then."

"Prove what?" Gideon asked.

Molly sneered. "Prove your magic is greater than our magic."

"Not this again," Gelda said, exasperated. "Can't we come into a city without you two making fireworks? Y'know, we *could* just bunk down in a tavern and quietly integrate with the locals."

"Where's the fun in that?" Molly replied.

Chloe felt a rumble of excitement in her stomach. She had never dueled with another mage before. Well, not since her experience in the Mages' Academy, and even then, it had been one-sided.

She and Gideon agreed, finding themselves a short distance from the pair. Chloe stood in line with Molly, with Gideon opposite Holly.

Molly explained the rules. No fatal attacks, nothing that could lacerate or destroy. When Gelda called it, the mages were to stop.

"Ready to do this?" Holly asked, excitement clear on her face.

Chloe steeled herself, already channeling the etheric in her mind, finding her rabbit familiar and using it as a conduit to summon the power of the mystical realm.

"Go!" Gelda called.

Gideon and Chloe paused, waiting for the attack from Holly and Molly, wanting to see what they were up against.

Holly's hands began drawing circles in the air. A golden ring was drawn, and it started sparking as though it were generating electricity. The inside of the circle grew dark, and from its depths jumped several large toad-like creatures that were roughly the size of dogs.

Their skin was black and rippled like liquid. After the fifth had left the hole, they bounded toward Chloe and Gideon, tongues darting out of their mouths, aiming straight at their faces.

Reacting fast, Gideon ducked and splayed his hands. Small beams of light erupted from the tips of his fingers. He pointed them at the first frog and was pleased to see that the light broke the darkness and caused the frog to bubble and explode.

"Light against darkness," Chloe mused, keeping her eye on Molly, who had tapped her staff on the ground. Sparks exploded where the staff met stone.

Chloe felt a rumble beneath her feet and wasn't fast enough to move as the ground suddenly spiked into the air, the force of it sending her several feet skyward before she landed on the resulting stone pillar on the flat of her stomach.

The force of it knocked the wind from her.

Chloe closed her eyes and began conjuring a spell, her focus on Molly.

Meanwhile, Gideon had destroyed several of the frogs and now battled with the final two. Using both hands, he sent light at the creatures and was happy to see them erupt into black goo, melting into the crevices between the cobbles beneath their feet.

Holly was already conjuring her next trick. Gideon could see the power flowing behind her eyes.

Thinking fast, Gideon summoned **Aqua Orb**, determined to shield and allow himself time to think about his next move. The orb appeared in a liquid shimmer around him, the mage having just enough time to smile and appreciate the mastery of his work, remembering how difficult the spell had been the first time he'd cast it, before hearing the sound of something smashing into the side of the orb.

Wolves, now. Dark, shadowy wolves, their bodies made of stars trapped in tar. They bit and chomped and drove their fangs at the orb, blocking his sight on all sides.

Gideon took a deep breath and steadied himself. As his fingers glowed blue with power, he muttered, "Nothing beats the classics." He crouched and placed his hands on the wall of the orb, imbuing the water with **Volt Shock**.

The orb exploded in crackling light. The unfortunate wolves who had parts of their body touching the orb at the time the spell was triggered were sent flying backward in a spray of sparks, their health greatly diminished.

Gideon took the opportunity to look through the spark spray to where Holly was watching, impressed. He leered, lowered his head, and began to run forward. The **Aqua Orb** rolled with him as he closed the distance.

Chloe was aware of all this from twenty feet off the ground. Several citizens gathered around them now, watching the mage duel with fascination, their eyes sleepy and tired from their late-night celebrations.

Chloe did her best to maintain her focus, her mind now exiting her body in thin dark strands and flying through the ether toward Molly. With creeping fingers, she used her **Mind Manipulation** and entered into the mage's head, seeing the world through Molly's eyes for a few seconds.

How about we play with your gray matter and make something dreadful appear? A great distraction from the battle, Chloe mused. She summoned the image of a terrible dragon, skin orange, scales thick and sharp, spikes trailing down its spine. In Molly's mind, the city square was dark under the shadow of the giant lizard, its mouth agape as it roared and belched a column of flame into the air.

Chloe exited Molly's mind, leaving the image with her. The stone pillar receded back into the ground as Molly's eyes opened in horror. Her mouth was wide as she cried out, begging everyone to run from the danger of the dragon that wasn't truly there.

I might have to use that one more often, Chloe thought.

Evil, KieraFreya commented. *I like it.*

Chloe spread her arms wide, fingers tensing as if pulling on invisible ropes. Shadows began to slither out from underneath buildings in long tendrils as she used **Shadow Tweak** to create coils that solidified and sprang from the ground, wrapping themselves around Molly's body and tightening around her wrists and waist.

She was almost bound when she screamed and called for help. Holly looked at her near-identical comrade, confusion on her face as she wondered why shadow binding would be so terrifying, not realizing that the simple spell was coupled with the dragon Molly was still seeing.

She sent several of her wolves over to bite through the shadows and they obeyed immediately, their sharp fangs tearing the coils apart. As the ropes broke, Chloe's focus flickered, and at that moment, Molly's inner perception returned to normal.

"A dragon! I saw a…"

"No, you didn't," Holly said simply.

It took Molly a moment to realize what had happened. Her eyes went wide. She pointed at Chloe. "You?"

Chloe gave a coy shrug.

"That's *it*!" Molly shouted, her hands exploding with light.

"You want in?" Gideon called, nodding toward his orb.

Chloe held steady. "I'm good, thanks. Just watch out for those wolves."

There was a flash of energy as the wolves returned, doing their best to destroy the orb.

Molly crouched and touched the ground, which began to shake. Those watching the group backed away, unnerved.

The stones in front of Chloe began to crack and crumble. There were pops and bangs as fractures grew, a lump now rising from the ground. Not unlike the platform, it grew to an amazing height, reaching about ten feet.

Chloe stared at the stone giant, a small laugh escaping her lips as she noticed the resemblance to Gelda.

"Really? You couldn't have picked any other likeness?" Gelda called.

Molly grinned. "You're my muse."

"Aww…"

The stone giant reared back, moving to use its massive fists on Chloe.

Chloe jumped backward, leaning around the stone to yell, "Hey, I thought we were going easy on each other?"

"We were until you stuck your fingers in my brain matter and made me see dragons."

Chloe suddenly remembered the description of the **Mind Manipulation** spell she had read when she first acquired it. *There are many who frown upon the manipulation of people's minds. Use with caution to maintain good standing among those in Obsidian.*

Oops, she thought.

I liked it, KieraFreya said.

"Okay, then. If we're going full bore, let's get this over with."

Gideon was on his knees now, his energy slowly depleting. His protective bubble still crackled with electricity, but he was able to watch Chloe as her fingers began to glow and her eyes seemed to roll back into her head.

Just like in rehearsal, Chloe said to KieraFreya.

Which rehearsal?

You remember the cave where we found your armor, right? The day we defeated Fukmos?

KieraFreya gave a grunt of understanding before Chloe felt the goddess take some of the control of her body.

The stone giant reared back, ready for another strike. Its boulder-like fist drove down at Chloe, freezing in place an inch away from her helmet.

The stone giant's face was a mask of confusion. Chloe heard Molly urging it to strike.

But the giant was shaking now, micro-vibrations that grew more violent. It lifted off the ground, its body slowly pulling apart. Chloe clapped her hands and the creature disintegrated into its core components, a shower of rocks left hovering in the air.

Chloe and KieraFreya concentrated as they brought the stones back to the ground, configuring the shape in increments until their sculpture was complete. When all the pieces of rock were finished, Chloe's eyes returned to normal and she nodded at her craftsmanship.

"Not bad." She smiled.

Holly withdrew her wolves, bursting into laughter. Gelda doubled over and slapped her legs, howling too. Gideon, realizing the threat was now gone, lowered his shields and moved to the front of the structure to get a better look.

"Classy." He chuckled.

Where the stone giant had been, now stood a rock statue of a hand, with a giant pixelated middle finger pointed directly at Molly.

Molly stared in disbelief before bursting into laughter. "I'll be honest, that's impressive."

Gelda walked between Gideon and Chloe, taking one of their wrists in each of her muscular hands. "I declare Chloe and Gideon the winners!"

The spectators gathered around the square gave them a mild round of applause.

Chloe grinned at the others. "You know what that means, right? We get to claim our prize."

"We didn't discuss prizes," Molly retorted rather sharply.

"It's only fair, sis," Holly said. "What do you want?"

Chloe's grin grew. "As we were saying before, I'm in need of a few good mages for a project I'm working on. I think you have exactly what it takes to help."

CHAPTER TWENTY-FIVE

Chloe took a steadying breath as people slowly began to file into the barn.

It had taken them a while to set up the space inside. The mess from a small scrap with some infected that had taken up residence inside the old building was tough to clean up, but with a little elbow grease and some strategic placing of hay bales and straw, they were able to get the place ready for their meeting.

Now the barn had at least two dozen fighters sitting talking among themselves. Chloe was glad to see a few mages she hadn't seen before.

That's good, she thought. *It means word is spreading.*

Either that or your royal buddy's plan worked, and now people are afraid not *to get involved*, KieraFreya said.

Chloe chewed on that. Sure, she wanted more fighters to join her cause since opening a rift in the etheric was not going to be an easy task without them, but she wanted people to be with her because they wanted to be, not because they *had* to be.

She recognized some familiar faces coming through the door: their ranger friend and a few warriors from their previous meeting.

Behind them was Heather, who gave Gideon a coy wave that sent his blood rushing to his cheeks.

"Am I missing something here?" Therese grumbled, leaning closer to Chloe.

Chloe chuckled, just happy to have Therese back among them, even if it did come with the pressure of needing to keep the queen alive.

Heather took a seat in the front row alongside Holly, Molly, and Gelda, who had been intrigued to hear what Chloe and her team were up to. Chloe gave a brief overview of their situation for the newcomers, happy to see that their total was nearing a hundred, and finally clapped her hands, ready to start training the group.

Before she could start, however, a few people raised their hands to ask questions.

"Yes," Chloe said, pointing to a frail-looking warrior in the third row.

"Before we begin, I, well…I wanted to ask…are we expecting another attack from the infected? My brother—he was here the other night—he's been taken by the illness and has been bed-bound ever since." He played with his fingers, looking at the floor. "I heard you had a cure?"

Chloe's eyes found Heather's, who nodded. "We do. It's part of the reason I've returned today. I was going to tell you, Chloe, there have been a few cases of the disease in Hammersworth. I was hoping we could use your command to summon clerics to help expunge the infection. There are still those in the outlying towns as well who need our help, and we can't do it alone."

"What about the other clerics? Can't they help?" Therese asked.

Heather shook her head. "Many of the clerics who went to help have turned, and most of the remaining clerics are frightened. We need fighters to go with us for protection, people who can guard us while we work our magic and try to revive those who have fallen."

Chloe sighed. "You're asking to borrow some of the few fighters we have here?"

Heather again shook her head. "A lot of your plan relies on the powers of the magic users, which a few gathered here cannot help with, and I was hoping that perhaps the queen might be able to use her status to create a party mission? A royal quest for chaperones and protectors to restore peace in the villages and towns. Every moment we delay is more time for the disease to spread and for a repeat of the night before to occur."

"She's right, you know," Ben stated. "If Fukmos is rallying the darkness to his side, we need to have people out there fighting to keep it back."

"It's too dangerous," Chloe said, her mind filled with the image of the small imp leering and manipulating the infected like tiny marionettes in his cause, his sisters beside him. "We need safety in numbers."

"And you'll have it," Therese said, her eyes glassy. "It says here on my new menus that party missions can affect everyone within a radius I set, up to a limit of five miles. I can trigger it, and even those who are traveling nearby will have the option to get involved."

"She's right, Chloe," Gideon chimed in. "To open the rift, we will need mages and magic users. The fighters can be put to better use, surely?"

Chloe's face grew stern. "And what happens if we open the rift and monsters fly out? What then? The last time this happened, it's rumored that dragons came out, too. Will magic alone be able to defeat whatever scum pours out of that tear? I agree that we need to keep Fukmos in check, but splitting the party might not be our friend, here. As long as we're together, we'll be able to fix this whole mess."

Therese took a step toward Chloe and placed a hand on her arm. Even she could sense that something was bugging Chloe that she was unable to verbalize. "It's not your fault, Chloe."

Chloe looked down at the dwarf.

"Jessie. Tag. It's not your fault. Nothing could have changed the outcome."

Ben gave her a sympathetic nod. "It's true, Chloe. We can't keep everyone alive and happy just by sticking together. This mission is bigger than the KieraSlayers. Hell, it's why we have all these people here. If we're to defeat the darkness, we need to work on strategy, and you can't stop the tide from rising by planting your roots, being stubborn, and building a wall around yourself. Eventually, it'll find a way inside."

Chloe's breath caught. She hadn't even realized what she was feeling. Fear of separation. Fear of what might happen if they weren't all together. She had come so far in Obsidian, found friends who she would—and had—given her life for, and now she had to admit that she was afraid.

But it made sense when she thought about it. She, Gideon, Molly, and Holly could train the magic users and prepare them for what was to come. She wasn't sure how long the mission would take, and in that time, what would happen?

The disease was spreading. They hadn't been able to catch all the infected. Even since they had left the Heroes-for-Hire board that morning, they had heard of encounters with infected, and it looked as though there were still cases across the city that needed healing.

Not to mention that the kingdom of Hammersworth stretched far beyond the limits of its walls. Although the onslaught of infected the other night had seen large numbers of farmers and rural workers turned into frenzied beasts, did that account for a quarter of the residents out in the wilds who had the capacity to turn?

Chloe had no idea.

"Very well," Chloe said, addressing the KieraSlayers. "Veronica, Leonie, Huk, and Talbot, you go with Heather and the band of clerics and find out more about what's going on. Ben, you're to lead the party in my absence."

Ben nodded, his chest puffing out as his face grew resolute.

"Blueballs?" Chloe said, seeing the toffet at the back of the room, sitting on his butt with his back against the wall. "You'll be with me, pal. I'm not risking you turning again; you'd destroy us all." She winked.

Chloe turned to the others. "Any willing and able fighters, rangers, tanks, or clerics who wish to travel beyond the city and provide aid, make yourselves known. You'll be in the safest of hands with my team, I assure you."

There was a moment's hesitation before a couple of hands found their way into the air. Before long, several dozen had volunteered to join.

"It is settled, then," Chloe said. "Therese, can you provide aid for the clerics, calling specifically for healers and protectors?"

"Already on it," Therese said, eyes glassy once more.

"As for the rest of you, I think we've lingered long enough. We've had our fun and games; we've battled infected and celebrated a wedding." She shot a quick glance at a smiling Therese. "Now it's time for the big leagues. Follow me outside, and we'll begin your training. We've got some work to do."

Half the crowd began to file outside, while the other half came toward Ben and the others. Before Chloe left with Gideon, Therese, and Blueballs, she grabbed Ben by the arm and leaned in.

"Keep them safe. Don't take risks."

Ben smiled. "I know."

Before she knew it, her arms were wrapped around his neck. They would be fine. With them under Ben's leadership, she didn't have anything to fear.

Then why was she so sad to part with them all?

When Ben pulled away, he held Chloe's shoulders and grinned. "I'm going to need a party name for my guys now?"

"Excuse me?" She laughed.

"You know, because they're *my* party now," he mocked, stroking his chin. "You can keep the KieraSlayers. I'll call mine...the *Destructicons*."

Chloe laughed, instantly taken back to their first conversations about party names for their group. Tag's suggestion of a group named after a bunch of world-destroying robots had not been one she took too kindly to.

"You are KieraSlayers. We are KieraSlayers. End of."

"Ah, man..."

They hugged once more before Chloe ducked out the door and found her mages waiting patiently outside.

She took a deep breath. The clear sky above allowed the moon and stars to illuminate the world in a ghostly glow.

Chloe channeled power through her hands and summoned an enormous ball of purple flame.

Several mages stared wide-eyed, gasping.

"Okay, team. Let's start powering up that magic."

CHAPTER TWENTY-SIX

The drive to the Praxis offices was a lot more straightforward than Demetri was expecting.

The sun shone brightly, and the daily traffic was moving at a gentle pace. Although he hadn't anticipated following Mia into work on his day off, there was something about it that set the bees in his stomach to buzzing.

The offices were modest, just several rooms spanning one floor of a fifteen-story tower on the outskirts of the city. It was not one of the sparkling new offices in the city center, but more like an old 1980s tower, with dusty windows and rusted doors.

Despite its outward appearance, Demetri felt the modern vibe of the energy running through the Praxis staff. Most of them were under twenty-five years of age, a few stretching to thirty.

There were dozens of desks around the room. Large double monitors sat on each, with flickering fluorescents above. The corners were stuffed with colorful beanbags.

Mia explained that Praxis existed very much on a "manage your own schedule" regime. There weren't strict work hours; as long as employees got their work completed on time, it didn't matter all that much.

So it surprised Demetri to see that the office was nearly full. Only one or two desks were empty.

A man with his hair permed tightly to his scalp walked briskly past the pair, a mug of coffee in his hand. He almost bumped into them, only realizing at the last second that someone was standing in the walkway.

"Oh, sorry, Mia. I didn't see you there."

"No worries, Charles. Keep that head up. Big day today."

That must be the understatement of this company's career, Demetri thought, following Mia to a glassed-in corner office with her own computer and chair, a plant wilting in the corner of the room.

When Demetri had woken up this morning, he had foreseen a lazy morning, followed by breakfast at Marko's diner on the next street down and maybe a brisk walk with Mia. Despite his various attempts at trying to help her with her work/life balance, Mia had become hungrier and hungrier to find out what exactly was going on with Praxis' artificial intelligence.

She hadn't even needed to say the words when he rolled over and saw her checking her emails on her phone. A simple flicker of her eyes was enough for Demetri to sigh and say, "Where to, then?"

And now, as they entered Mia's personal office—a space she had yet to visit, having preferred to work remotely until that point—she took her former boss Devlin's name plaque out of its door holder and shut the door behind her.

"Still feeling okay?" Demetri asked, looking out of the glass and seeing a few pairs of eyes glancing their way.

This was Mia's first foray into her new office. Since she had taken over from Devlin, she had kept working remotely, since someone who had been in her position would never have gotten promoted to run the development department without a nudge from the Lagardes.

Not only would a junior developer have to spend several years working their way up the ladder, she also had gender working against her. She knew she was more skilled than all these tech-monkeys combined, but that didn't change a system constructed to hold her back.

Mia nodded. She took a steadying breath and booted up a laptop she'd brought with her, loading Chloe's feed for Demetri to keep an eye on.

"It'll be fine," she whispered.

"It'll be fine," Demetri agreed, giving her his best reassuring smile. "Be confident, bring them together, and lead them. That's all they need—a strong hand to get them moving."

Mia glanced at the clock. Thirty seconds until the agreed 11am team meeting. She took another breath, smoothed her clothes, and strode out into the office.

The meeting started off better than Mia could have imagined. She replayed the projects they had been working on over the last few weeks, getting updates from the various groups on developments and offering solutions for support.

She caught up with all the latest patches and upgrades, making sure the team was on track to deliver and improve the gaming experience.

When the discussion segued to AI, Mia turned to the three sitting nearest to her, two guys and a woman. They were her personal AI team, who had been working tirelessly with her to understand what was going on in the game.

They fed their updates to the team. Jonathon was a stocky guy with dark hair and a patch of fuzz on his chin, who looked like he needed more time in the sun. He told Mia and the room how he'd been spending hours trying to find patterns in the code to see if there were ways to slow down what was happening long enough to decipher how the AI was learning.

This elicited a few questions from the rest of the team. Some asked if it was wise to slow it down since they had a functioning AI within the game, which was something that had never been achieved to this level before.

"It's a fantastic thing," Mia stated. "Just as long as we know we have a kill switch if we need it. The last thing we want is a lawsuit on our hands if something goes out of balance and causes real-world harm."

"Are you thinking the pods and headsets are going to come alive?"

Damien, a man with dark eyes and a chiseled jaw, chuckled. He had caused Mia problems in the past and was reluctant to accept her leadership now.

The woman on Mia's team, Lucy, adjusted her glasses. "Yes, very much so." Her frank response caused Damien's laughter to cease. "Although it's a very faint possibility, it's something that has to be treated with caution. If the program begins to run away from us, who's to say it won't suddenly cause mass seizures? That it couldn't affect the machinery keeping our fully-immersed players alive? It's all electronics, after all, linked together by wires and cables. We've got to keep it in check."

"We've already seen examples of NPCs reacting badly to the blessed," Jonathon continued. "A member of the KieraSlayers was kidnapped by NPCs only a few weeks ago, and they were just low-grade NPCs." Jonathon moved around in his chair, leaning forward and resting his elbows on his knees. "Remember that the gods are NPCs, and we've already seen examples of what can happen when they get involved in the game."

Lucy clicked a button on a remote and a projector turned on. Video footage of Chloe and KieraFreya in battle played, the immense white power taking over before the screen turned to static. This was footage the team had seen a few times, but some of them still didn't understand its importance.

"If the gods can affect the AV outputs, we need to know what else they can do," Mia said. "So far, we've got four gods actively participating in the game, and we've only seen the real power of one of them —KieraFreya."

"Woo!" someone shouted from the back. Mia craned her neck and saw a large man she knew as Phil sporting a KieraSlayers t-shirt. The desk behind him was littered with tiny statues of Blueballs, Chloe, and the others. "Sorry, big fan."

"And are we getting anywhere?" Damien asked. "You're telling us all this stuff, but I don't see solutions. Didn't people think of this when the damn thing launched?"

"AI can be unruly," Mia snapped back. "We still don't know everything it has to offer. We had a great launch, and this is just a bug in the system. A bug we can squash. We just need to identify it and flush it out. Any more questions?"

Damien didn't reply.

Mia nodded to Lucy. She stood up, played with the computer connected to the projector, and displayed a screenful of code.

"We've created something we're calling 'the Muter.' It's a program that essentially feasts on the code and pulls it back when it starts to spike or get out of control. Think of how audio software can keep sound from becoming distorted by intelligently adjusting the gain, or how particular weed killers can take out problem plants without damaging the harvest."

"It's a really cool piece of code," the third in Mia's party, Charlie, said, eyes wide with admiration of their work. "Essentially, it's programmed with an understanding of the basic functionality and the limits that already exist within modern gaming. We've fed it every piece of code we can find from previous MMORPGs and stuck in lines that create the safety restrictions that will 'mute' the advancement of the original AI."

"So, basically it's AI cancer?" Damien said, face screwed up in disgust. "You're telling me we've pushed the boundaries of technology and created something the world is praising, and now we're going to cull it? Do we want this or not?"

"It's not a killer," Mia replied. "Think of it as a chaperone—a second AI to keep the initial AI in check. The original AI can keep doing what it's doing, but if it begins to step out of line and does anything that might be deemed dangerous to a player or the environment, it shuts it off."

"Like an electric switch." Jonathon smiled.

"Exactly."

Lucy continued, showing footage of the code in action. "It's surpassed any and all tests we've given it so far. Today it's ready for implementation."

Damien nodded as he came to a sudden realization. "Which is why you've graced us with your presence, right, *boss*?"

Mia clenched her teeth, not liking the way he spoke.

"Exactly. Today we need all hands on deck. You have permission to suspend any non-urgent requests for the next eight hours. Please attend to anything pressing, but we need every possible eye on the code. This is your critical project for today."

Within half an hour, they were all in place. The sequence to launch the code rested on Mia's computer, and now she sat with Demetri, cursor hovering over the "Execute" icon.

"Ready?" Demetri asked, his attention on Chloe and the others as they trained their magicians and sent magic flying in the dark.

Mia took a breath, nodded, and clicked the icon.

"All systems go," she said, giving a thumbs-up to Lucy outside her office.

Lucy called out the instruction and the team got to work.

All, that is, except for Damien, who leaned back in his chair and checked messages on his phone, wondering how stupid Mia was to believe he'd help after she had gotten his best buddy fired from the company.

CHAPTER TWENTY-SEVEN

Over the course of the next few days, Chloe and Gideon did nothing but eat, sleep, and train with the others.

Their training went without much incident, aside from a few friendly-fire shots of magic. The majority of the mages who had joined them were newbie players, going fresh-faced into Obsidian, looking for ways to level their skills, which meant that Chloe and Gideon had a lot to provide in the ways of sharing their knowledge on etheric manipulation.

They taught them a variety of spells, happy to pass on what they'd learned. They also kept an eye on the Heroes-for-Hire board, looking for any quests that might be beneficial for mages to complete to level up some of their greener fighters.

One useful thing that came out of the training for Chloe happened after she divided the fighters into groups. As they'd trained more and more, it pleased Chloe to find that new mages were joining every day. Their numbers were now close to the one hundred mark, which meant the group had to be divided into teams for closer instruction.

It was after the groups had been divided and Chloe had assigned Molly and Holly to impart wisdom to their teams that she discovered something strange. The students being taught under the two mages were leveling faster than the other groups, despite Chloe and Gideon being higher levels than the sisters.

Chloe checked her stats, looking specifically at the **Tutor** skill she had acquired after her first pupil had managed to conjure a weak **Purple Blaze** spell, wondering if she was missing something.

You've unlocked a new skill: Tutor (Lv 1)

You've taken that dangerous first step to imparting your wisdom to others. Whether you're correct or accurate doesn't matter! People are listening, and you can use this power how you desire.

Remember, though, that every student who learns from you becomes your reflection. Choose wisely how you want to share your knowledge with the world.

Requirements: Impart wisdom to your first student.

Bonuses: +2 intelligence

Nice. I'm an influencer. I must remember to add that to my dating profile.

During the lunch break on the fourth day, Chloe found herself sitting with Gideon, Molly, Holly, and Gelda. Blueballs lay on the grass beside them, eyes closed, basking in the sun. Groups of magic-users milled around them, taking a well-earned break.

"How are you doing it?" Chloe asked, unable to hold back. "How are they learning so fast under you?"

"What do you mean?" Holly asked smugly.

"Don't get me wrong, I'm impressed with my group, but I watched your guys learn shadow and stone magic so quickly, it was like they'd been doing it all their lives."

Molly gave Holly a knowing look.

"What?" Chloe exclaimed.

"Someone clearly didn't learn about specializations," Holly said, finishing the last of the bread she had packed for her lunch. "I mean, don't get me wrong, your magic is incredibly impressive, and the variety of tricks you've got is second to none, but…"

"But if you were to specialize, you'd have grown your spells' power much more quickly."

Chloe thought about that, remembering the battle she'd had with Holly and Molly. She couldn't believe it had only just sunk in that Holly had only used shadow magic and Molly had stuck with stone.

"The more you use the same strain of magic, the more powerful it becomes. It's something we learned pretty early on by playing with a few different spells." Molly leaned back on her elbows, face turned to the sun. "I connected with stone, so that's what I went with. There's normally stone around to play with."

"Same with shadow," Holly said. "Even if it's bright, there's always enough power in our own shadows to manipulate. It's lots of fun. Maybe you two should specialize as well?"

Chloe looked at Gideon and they both immediately shook their heads. "If it's a choice between power and diversity, I know what I'll pick any day," Chloe stated.

"Me too," Gideon added, although his face showed that he was deep in thought.

Holly and Molly shrugged. "Still, maybe it's worth giving your students the option. It could benefit them mightily."

And that was exactly what they did. Although Chloe hadn't hesitated in making her choice, when the groups regathered, she gave them all the choice and informed them of the progression benefits specialization had. That afternoon she saw better results than anything she had seen thus far, causing yet another increase in her skill levels.

Skill increased: Tutor (Lv 2)

Although you prefer your own methods, you've left the path open for your students to choose their own way. The key to being a solid instructor is to nourish your students, not push them in one direction. Keep this up and the benefits will continue to grow.

Bonuses: +4 intelligence

(NOTE: Increases in skill override any previous bonuses gained from the skill).

Samsun, who had up until that point been a level 3 mage who had struggled to form even the most basic of spells, immediately found his formerly hidden confidence.

The poor guy had spent days trying to master all of the elements but had found that there was one missing from Chloe's repertoire that he was dying to try.

When Chloe came over to check on their progress, she had been distressed to find that Samsun was doubled over, his back heaving, with strange bubbling sounds coming from his shadowed face.

"Samsun?" Chloe pulled his shoulder and helped him upright.

Samsun had the biggest smile on his face, his hands throbbing with a grim purple energy that leaked dark liquid onto the ground. Small acidic bubbles rose and popped above his hands.

"I did it." He beamed. "A new spell, **Toxic Injection**."

He told Chloe that the spell could be imbued into weapons or could be combined with ingredients when preparing food to be eaten by enemies, creating an undetectable poison. She raised her eyebrows, happy to see his progress but disturbed by his chosen direction.

Still, progress was progress, and Chloe had been concerned about Samsun up until that point. A few hours later, his level and spell ranks had grown by 2.

Each night, they gathered for a debriefing with Chloe. After day six, she was so impressed by their progress that she told them all it wouldn't be long before they were ready. Still, mages were slowly making their way forward, and when they reached the hundred and twenty mark, Chloe began to get excited.

"I really think we can do this," she said to Gideon one night as they were on their way back to the castle. They had had a particularly good day of training, their students were advancing beyond expectation, and their numbers were swelling. "I think we'll find Shikora soon."

"Finally," KieraFreya exclaimed. "And then I'll be free of you."

Chloe chuckled. KieraFreya's words were not laced with the venom they had once been. When they had started on their journey, part of her had genuinely feared what would happen when the armor had been collected and the task was complete. But over the months since that time, she felt they were finally at peace. They might actually end it all as friends.

They approached the gates, passed the guards, and began to make their way to the palace.

"Chloe," Gideon asked, his voice trailing off into nothing as they walked.

"Mmm?"

"Do we know how we're going to open the rift? I mean, we've got mages, and we're bonding as a team, but how are we going to, you know, *do* it?"

Chloe arched an eyebrow. It was a question she'd been pondering ever since they had split into groups and begun their training, which had made the whole thing seem more real.

"I don't know," she said simply. "I have my theories, but I don't think we'll know until it's time. We'll likely have to hack into the etheric, that's for sure, and I'm guessing KF will provide some kind of boost."

"That's your plan?" Gideon confirmed, unimpressed. "You might as well just fire your magic into the sky and hope for the best."

Chloe nodded. Truth was that she spent time each night riding into the forest on Bolt, looking for the Wrangler. The ancient guardian obviously knew a lot about the process, having given them the knowledge to follow the path they were now pursuing. If anyone had the answers, it was him.

Only he was impossible to find. Chloe followed the paths she had taken with the others, but the location where his house had been was now vacant.

Just last night, Chloe had employed Sir Wingsalot in her cause, flying the terror-daxil over the canopy of trees, hoping the creature would be able to pick out the giant with its sharp eyes.

But her search had been fruitless.

I have a feeling we will meet again before too long.

The Wrangler's words echoed in her head, words she felt like she knew the meaning of. She had to trust her gut to access their intent.

They made it to the palace a little before nightfall and supped with Therese and Abe, catching up on all the latest gossip from across the kingdom. Chloe and Therese caught the king up on the clerics' quest by reading the messages they received from Ben throughout the day, and soon they finally found themselves back in their rooms preparing for bed.

As Chloe lay on the soft linens, she stared at the blank ceiling, listening to the soft murmur of voices from the city below. She imagined the swirls and patterns were the portal to the Nether Realm, seeing the dark shape of a horse leaping out of the rift and galloping toward her.

"What's going to happen at the end?" she asked the darkness.

She felt KieraFreya contemplating this. "I honestly don't know. This whole process is unprecedented. Nothing like this has happened to a god or goddess before."

Chloe opened her mouth to speak, then closed it. When she remembered that KieraFreya could read her thoughts and being silent wouldn't work, she said, "What will happen to me? What will I become?"

The question would have no answer until the end, but there were infinite possibilities. On the one hand, Chloe considered that she might keep all her powers and abilities. She might also keep her strength, her spells, and her attributes.

On the other hand, there was the very real possibility that by uniting KieraFreya with her horse and freeing her to return to the gods, Chloe would be stripped of everything. That she would revert to her first hours in Obsidian, naked, defenseless, and alone.

"You'll never be alone," KieraFreya comforted her. "You've got people who love you. People who will ride with you until the end. That's more than I ever had."

"How do you know?" Chloe asked. "Your memory was nearly wiped. Maybe you've got a whole fleet of friends up there."

KieraFreya shook Chloe's head. "If that were true, they would've come for me ages ago. I've seen neither hide nor hair of anyone except that little shit Fukmos in the last thousand or so years. Count yourself lucky, kid. You've got more than friends, you've got a family. That's a hell of a lot more than I've got."

Chloe contemplated her words. Maybe KieraFreya was right.

"Part of me thinks I'd be better off in your shoes at the end of all this," KieraFreya told her softly. "At least you know you'll be okay. I have no idea what's waiting for me up there."

Chloe continued to stare into the darkness, her mind on the gods, a subject she still knew very little about. She closed her eyes and drifted into an uneasy sleep.

CHAPTER TWENTY-EIGHT

Ben wondered if he had somehow drawn the short straw.

He was several days into his journey with the clerics, and the whole thing had been jam-packed with excitement—but not the good kind.

He and Heather had led the clerics and the willing warriors and rangers through the forest and out toward the villages, with no more bother than a handful of ghouls and a sentient tree that had trapped several warriors in its roots until Ben had had the genius idea of threatening it with a torch.

The tree had relinquished its hold, allowing them passage, but Ben was almost certain he could hear its whispers following them the rest of the way.

Arriving at the first village, Hidesdown, had been an eye-opener. The infected were everywhere, but they acted differently than those that had attacked several nights ago.

These infected strolled around lazily, only going into a frenzy when they detected healthy people nearby. When they attacked, they were quickly dispatched by the fighters, which caused a strained relationship with the clerics. Those worthies were beside themselves, wanting to try to heal *everyone* they saw.

"We're going to have to compromise," Ben said, taking control of the situation as a teary-eyed cleric batted at an unbothered warrior clad top to tail in armor. "We'll save everyone we can, but we can't allow them to attack us. We have to take this threat seriously. Try not to kill whenever possible, but don't let your compassion cloud your sense."

On their exploration through Hidesdown, they discovered several healthy citizens cowering around the village. They were malnourished and terrified, unable to believe that soldiers had come to rescue them and give them food. Some were hiding in bins and basements, others on roofs and in pantries.

It took them a good few hours to round up everyone in the village and secure the area. There was a large hall in the center of the village where they brought infected who had been tied and bound to allow the clerics to do their work.

Heather took the lead, demonstrating with Veronica how they had expunged the darkness. The clerics who were lower levels teamed up in larger groups, while the more experienced were able to manage in pairs.

Soon ghostly trails of darkness filled the air, each thread of the disease drifting up through the gaps in the roof and disappearing into the atmosphere.

"Where do they all go?" a young cleric with flaming red hair asked Heather and Veronica.

"We don't know," they replied, wondering if they were really helping the situation or if all the pieces of darkness were re-gathering for a second attack.

Ben oversaw the warriors who guarded the hall. Occasionally more infected would lazily stroll out of the trees, spot the healthy fighters, and whip themselves into a frenzy as they mindlessly began running toward them. These would be shot in the leg at first to try to keep them alive long enough to save them, but this couldn't be achieved in every case.

When they were finished with their cleansing and those who had been infected were left to heal, Ben, Veronica, and Heather set about bringing everyone inside. Night had already fallen, and rest was needed by all.

They set up a guard watch to rotate every few hours and, aside from a pair of stubborn infected that the guards managed to wrestle inside and hand to the clerics to heal, they passed the night quietly.

When they'd reached the next village the following day, Ben had expected to have it go much the same. What he hadn't expected, however, was for a united force to aim their weapons and try to attack them upon arrival.

They had just crested the hill and seen the small collection of buildings a short distance ahead when they had heard the *thunk* of an axe embedding in wood.

Ben had called everyone back, ducking behind the hill and using his skills to look ahead.

There was a line of dwarves, their faces muddy, some of them bruised and bloody. Their axes were held high, ready to attack whoever came at them.

"Who goes there?" a gruff voice shouted.

Ben glanced at some of the warriors, thinking it would be better for a dwarf to talk to the dwarves. He hadn't yet experienced it in Obsidian yet, but he knew that many MMORPGs fostered old resentments between elves and dwarves, and he didn't want to take that risk.

A young dwarf with a beard only to his chest volunteered, cautiously waving a white handkerchief and proceeding forward. Though the dwarves were on their guard, they allowed him to move forward, and soon he managed to get them into the town.

"Our village was full of the scum," Beldro, the dwarf who had thrown his axe, said as he guided them into the village and took them to their local tavern, a place that looked like it had seen better days. The tables and chairs had been upturned and were covered in blood.

"What happened to them?" Ben asked. The group set about righting the chairs and tidying up as they took their seats, the other dwarves explaining that they hadn't used the inn since it had all happened, but it was the only space big enough to accommodate everyone.

"No idea. One minute they were upon us, our guys fighting for our lives, and the next thing we knew, they'd all turned and fled in the direction you all came. Can't say we were sad to see them go."

Ben looked at Veronica, both thinking the same thing. The gods had somehow intervened, guiding them away and toward the city.

"Well, not *all* of them," a smaller dwarf with a scar across his lip said.

"Aye, not all. Some of them are still here. We've got them chained up and locked away. Couldn't bring ourselves to kill them once we caught them. They're family, after all."

He showed them down to the tavern cellar, where growls and screeches could be heard. When they opened the door, half a dozen infected strained against their chains to reach them. Barrels of ale and mead had been knocked over and spilled all over the floor.

"Nothing's going to bring them back," Beldro said sadly.

It wasn't until Veronica followed his eyes that she realized he meant the alcohol.

"Well, Jesus did once turn water into wine. Maybe we clerics can do something for your precious booze."

"Oh, thank you!" Beldro clapped. He paused suddenly, eyebrow arching. "Who's Jesus?"

"Never mind." Veronica giggled. "I think we should prioritize the infected, don't you?"

They bent to their work, several clerics crammed into the cellar. When the first of the shadowy demons was released, Beldro and several of his men threw themselves to the floor.

The ceiling was thick concrete, meaning that the darkness couldn't pass. It thrashed around wildly until it found the exit up the stairs behind them. They heard it screeching out of the building, cries of alarm coming from the other dwarves as it exited.

"Four more to go." Heather laughed. Veronica joined her, and soon they had cleared yet another town, instilling enough confidence in the dwarves of the village that they elected to follow Ben and the others on their mission to rid the land of shadow.

And so the pattern went for several days. They visited nine villages in total, bringing a good number of infected back to the side of the light. Along the way, they only lost a few of their number, and by the fifth day, they had gathered an army of almost four hundred dwarves.

This did, however, bring problems of its own.

"How can we accommodate them all?" a shrill-sounding dwarf they had recently brought back to health asked. Her hands fondled the tangles in her hair. "There're too many. I can only sleep twenty!"

Ben looked around, exasperated. As their numbers had grown, their mission had gotten easier. In each town, they'd brought around more clerics and taught them how to cure the infected. However, now that they had found themselves in a small hamlet at night, it seemed that there wouldn't be enough room for everyone to sleep inside.

Ben turned to Heather, Veronica, Talbot, Huk, and Leonie. "Any ideas?"

"Send some back," Leonie suggested. "Our numbers are beyond what we need to do what we're doing. I'm sure Chloe would be happy with the help."

Ben pondered this. He sighed, coming to a conclusion. "We've got no choice. Make it so."

"What about the forest? Won't it be dangerous at night?" Huk asked.

"No more dangerous than any other time," Heather said. "Besides, these dwarves have lived here all their lives. You think they won't be able to survive the woods?"

Ben was pleasantly surprised by the number of people who volunteered to go to the city when asked. The village dwarves, it seemed, were big fans of the city, and a few had never been there. They jumped at the chance to head toward the tall stone walls and see the city they spent their lives providing for.

Ben watched them go with a fond smile, sending his prayers along with them. He knew Chloe would be pleased to have the additional numbers in the city if what was to come was to be as dangerous as they suspected.

When morning came around, Ben and the KieraSlayers rallied the others and continued their trek west. Heather warned them that the town they were headed to, Rivermere, was one of the largest outside Hammersworth and had the biggest potential for things to be awry.

"Rivermere is where my brother was sent to heal the infected. He says it was overrun, infected in every cranny and corner."

Ben tried to imagine it, the scene more like something out of a zombie series than the MMORPGs he was used to. Infected stumbling aimlessly around as the winds blew and the days passed.

"Better bring our A-games, then, eh?" he replied, following the bank of a river that chuckled along beside them.

By the time the outskirts of Rivermere came into sight, it was long past noon. They passed grain silos, small farmhouses, and paddocks for livestock. They saw signs of where the infected had attacked, the fences broken and signposts knocked to the ground.

Soon enough, Rivermere appeared ahead, a town crowning a large hill, ringed almost in its entirety by a river that created a natural moat that funneled traffic into the town.

Ben paused, preparing himself for whatever was to come. He could see movement on the crown of the hill and small silhouettes stumbling around.

Then the first screeches of the infected floated to them on the wind.

Or so they thought.

CHAPTER TWENTY-NINE

"The challenge for today is to sustain your magic."

Chloe looked over the heads of the mages she and her friends had been training. The group who, almost a week ago, had been nothing more than amateur magicians, fresh into the game or not confident in their skills.

Now, staring back at her were mages who had progressed by leaps and bounds. Magic-users who had worked on their skills day and night, put in the effort and energy to progress and increase their mana pools, manipulate the etheric to work *for* them instead of *with* them, and learned a ton of useful spells along the way.

"That's easy," one of them called. "We've done that a thousand times."

"Not like this." Chloe smiled. "Today we're going to compete against each other."

A ripple of excitement went through the crowd. Faces under hoods of red, blue, yellow, and purple stared up with eager eyes.

"Today I want each group to start at the same time and cast a spell. You must hold that spell for as long as possible in order to win the competition. Our efforts to open the rift will depend on exactly this—

being able to maintain our focus and keep our spells working for as long as possible."

"What's the prize?" another mage called.

"Yeah! We're not doing this for free."

There was a swell of giggles.

"The prize will be this," Chloe said, reaching into Gideon's pack and pulling out a long gold staff as if from thin air. "A mage's staff, decorated with topaz and emeralds and imbued with the power to enhance mana efficiency and increase your etheric attribute."

An awed murmur made its way around the crowd. It was the exact effect Chloe had been going for when she had gone to the ancient shops in the back alleys of Hammersworth's commercial quarters, looking for something to inspire and incentivize her mages.

It had cost her an arm and a leg, but thanks to her Heroes-for-Hire board and not having to pay to sleep in the palace, her coins had been stockpiling over the last few days. She had gladly handed the money over to the withered old crone and now held the item aloft for all to see.

The only person not impressed by the item was Molly, who looked at her own staff as though she had somehow been given a raw deal.

"Copycat," she whispered.

Chloe stuck out her tongue, eliciting laughs from Holly and Gideon.

The competition was stiff. The mage cohort divided into groups of ten, each competing against the other. Anytime someone failed to sustain their magic, they were dropped from the competition and the remaining mages were given a few minutes of rest.

By noon, a hundred and thirty or so had been filtered down to just over forty mages. Those who had been the first to go now watched and cheered on their friends. The competing mages did whatever they could to block out external disturbances and focus on the task at hand.

"Impressive," Chloe said, fingers laced behind her back as she wove between the remaining groups.

She watched a mage holding an ice shard suspended in his hand, his fingers turned blue from cold. A bit farther on, she watched a woman who had gentle electrical sparks jumping between her fingers, racing like flies in the hot summer air. Beyond her were two mages who were in the midst of using the same spell to create droplets of rain that fell into the cups of their hands.

"Chloe?"

Chloe heard but did not turn, her attention caught by a sweating mage with an impressive illusion of a bird flapping between his hands. "Yes, Gid?"

"You've got a visitor."

Chloe tore her eyes away to find Gideon standing behind her. "A visitor? Is Ben back?"

"Not exactly," Gideon said his voice trembling. He jerked his thumb toward the castle gate, where Gelda, Holly, and Molly stood chatting with a woman who stood at least seven feet tall and was draped in shimmering clothing.

"Who is she?"

"She's from the Mages' School," Gideon told her. "She doesn't sound happy."

As Chloe approached, the woman turned her attention to her. "Am I to guess that *you're* Chloe?"

"In the flesh," Chloe said, offering a hand to shake.

The woman looked at Chloe's hand as though it were covered in dung. She ripped back her hood and revealed a face so aged and withered it was impossible to believe it belonged to a person.

Her eyes were dark, shadowed by purple eyelids. Her nose was angled and sharp, her lips tight and thin.

"What right do you think you have to be imparting lessons on magic within our city?" the woman snapped.

"I'm sorry," Chloe replied, unfazed. "Who are you?"

"*I'm* the headmistress of the Mages' School. Tabitha Ludlow, if you must know." Her voice was shrill. Chloe found herself wincing as the sound scraped her ears. "Do you have *any* idea what damage you are doing?"

Chloe raised an eyebrow and stood up straight. She imagined that

Tabitha was used to people wilting beneath her stare, but Chloe refused to yield.

"I'm sorry," Chloe said sarcastically, "but all I'm doing is gearing up these mages for a quest of great importance and teaching them how to harness their powers."

"And you didn't think to consider that the Mages' School would offer this assistance, or that we'd even provide a good spot for practicing? My dear, the Mages' School has been around for *hundreds* of years—"

"Oh, we tried," Gideon interrupted, finding his voice. Chloe was oddly proud of the pause he forced from Tabitha. "We went to your precious school. We wanted nothing more than to learn and increase our skills. We wanted to get better, but all your mages were useless. No one helped us. I don't see a mage among us now who came from your school, and that's *after* Queen Therese gave the townsfolk a command to help Chloe."

Tabitha flushed, taken aback. Clearly, she wasn't used to being spoken to this way.

"I... My school is... For hundreds of years, we've been..."

She looked pained.

"It's true, Tabitha. When we came to this city, we visited your school, thinking we'd find a home like we did at the Academy in Killink View. What we found was dusty tomes and a load of mages so dated and stuck in their ways that they weren't of any help."

Tabitha mulled this over, her eyes flicking back and forth as she thought. A few of Chloe's mages were staring in her direction, curious as to what the commotion was about.

When she eventually managed to compose herself, she said, "Regardless of your experience of my school, this needs to stop. Magic is a gift that must be taught and nurtured in the correct way. It cannot just be handed from person to person like some common weapon. It is an unpredictable mistress that needs to be harnessed properly.

"When the city was first constructed, the Mages' School was the first stepping stone for hundreds of mages. For years, we've strived to provide the best education for potential magic-users. It's because of this that under the King's treaty of 346, we were promised total control over the use and education of magic in the city."

She smirked, enjoying the expression she'd put on Chloe's face.

"A legal document." She sneered. "Dictating that I have complete magical control, and you must stop what you're doing."

Tabitha felt a tap on her hip. She turned to look beside her, and her smile melted.

"Well, many things are changing around here, aren't they?" Therese grinned through the visor of the gold armor she had been given by Abe. "As your queen, I'd say that maybe we should revisit this treaty of 346 and have a word with the king to see what we can do about it."

Tabitha let out a sound that did not seem human, and her pale skin turned dark red. "I… No! It's not…" she blubbered.

Therese clapped her hands and several gold-clad guards flanked Tabitha and led her back to the castle.

Before Therese left, she turned back to the others and said, "I think this new treaty will mean you guys get some brand-new mages to join your cause."

Chloe beamed. Behind them, a round of applause broke out as the next round of winners was determined. Of the forty remaining mages, ten more had now dropped out of the competition.

"Great stuff." Chloe beamed. "Break for lunch, then we'll make it interesting. On to the final round!"

When the mages came back together for the final round of competition, the remaining thirty stood back to back. The rest of the group formed a circle around them and watched their comrades eagerly.

Chloe counted down to the final leg of the competition. "Remember, the last person left standing wins this!" She held the staff aloft once more.

The mages stared at the staff with hungry eyes. They knew what they were playing for now.

"Ready, set, *go!*"

The mages cast their spells—mixtures of elements, their faces creased in concentration. The final round wouldn't last as long as the others, the mages having spent a lot of their mana on the previous rounds.

Chloe circled them, watching them carefully, testing their mettle. She was more impressed than she'd thought she'd be. She looked at Danny Tucker and admired the impressive orb of light hovering between his hands. Just a few days ago, he had struggled to hold it longer than a few seconds. Now they were nearing fifteen minutes.

In the group was Lindsay Croy, a mage who had been a recent addition but had proven she could stand with the best of them.

One by one they began to drop, sweat pouring off their heads as their shoulders slumped and they joined the large group. Before long, only three competitors remained.

Aron Elrod, a mage who had chosen fire as his specialty, balanced a vivid green flame between his fingers. Lindsay Croy, whose butterfly illusion flapped in slow motion, and Peter Loopin, a mage who grew plants between his fingers, and now trailed and looped a vine around his hands as though it were a small snake.

The sun beat down on them. Their hands began to shake. Aron's flame flickered. Lindsay's butterfly image faded in and out. Peter's vine began to turn brown and wilt.

As the competition neared its end, the crowd were on their feet. They clapped and cheered as the three mages struggled on, shouting and chanting for their favorites.

Peter was the first to fall, his vine withering into nothingness and crumbling to the floor. It looked as though Lindsay would be the second to go, her butterfly almost invisible to the naked eye.

"Come on, Lindsay!" a woman who Chloe had seen hanging out with Lindsay a lot over the last few days shouted. "You've got this!"

A fire seemed to build in Lindsay then. She let out a strained shout and the butterfly reappeared in its full glory. She raised her hands and sent it into the air, where it swirled and flew above the heads of the others, growing until it was as big as an eagle.

Aron looked up in awe, losing his focus long enough for his flame to flicker and die.

"Aron's out!" someone shouted, pointing to his hands.

"Lindsay's the winner!" Chloe exclaimed. "Congratulations, Lindsay!"

Lindsay's face was a mask of shock as she turned to the crowd. Distracted, her butterfly faded into a shower of sparkles. She was rushed by dozens of bodies as people hugged her and lifted her up and cheered.

Chloe and the tutors laughed with glee, happy to see the students bonding. They really had come a long way over the last few days, and a small part of Chloe thought that they might be ready for the challenge.

This feeling was confirmed when, unnoticed by the mages who shouted and focused on Lindsay, a group of dwarves emerged from the woods and found their way to the group.

"Ben sent us," the lead dwarf said in his gravelly voice. "Reinforcements for your cause."

Chloe caught Gideon's eye and couldn't stop herself from smiling.

CHAPTER THIRTY

The cry for help grew clearer the closer they got to Rivermere.

"You can hear that, right?" Ben asked. Where before he had seen an infected limping around and screeching, he now saw the silhouette of someone waving. The call for help carried on the wind.

Veronica nodded, urging the unit of dwarves onward.

They funneled across a bridge that led over the natural moat and drew their weapons. A wooden fence around six feet tall ringed the town. Ben, Leonie, Huk, and Veronica led the way, easing themselves through the open front gate, alert for any danger.

The moment Ben crossed the threshold, an infected launched itself at him.

It came from his left, all arms and gnashing teeth. Ben was ready, firing an arrow that drove straight through the creature's skull. It flopped to the ground in front of him.

"Arm yourselves!" Ben called back, running forward with his knives drawn and taking down the next infected to come his way. Beside him, Leonie and Huk had engaged with several infected, the creatures now pouring out of every nearby crevice.

Ben felt hands grip his body. He pulled back, twisting and maneuvering away, slipping from their hungry grasp. They were less than twenty feet into the town, and already they were being overwhelmed. It was like a holding pen for the infected.

"Retreat!" Ben cried. He ducked his head and rushed backward, only to find the gate choked with dwarves. The fighters moved faster than the message and it was a few moments before there was enough breathing room to duck out of the town.

The KieraSlayers and any dwarves remaining created a barrier, then stepped slowly back and took down any infected that came their way. Veronica and Heather set about healing at a frantic pace, purging any darkness that found its way into the cuts and grazes on their comrades' skin, until finally they were out of the village.

Ben had expected the infected to funnel through and attack them, but the minute they were clear of the fence, the infected stopped, watching them idly from the open gate.

"What the hell?" Ben muttered, unable to make sense of it.

"It's them," Veronica said. "It has to be. They have control over the infected."

"Who?" Heather said. "The dark gods? How is that possible?"

"They sent them after us at the city in the first place, and they are controlling them here. I don't want to make people nervous, but I think they might be nearby."

Ben shuffled uneasily, disturbed by the horde of infected milling around the town's entrance. "So what do we do?"

"We need to come up with a plan. Either draw them out or find a way for us to get in there and rescue any survivors," Veronica said. "We can't just leave them to die, can we?"

"I think I might know a way," Heather interjected. "But it's risky. I've only ever tried it once, but it might just work."

Ben's battalion receded from the town, finding places to settle on the other side of the bridge. The dwarves washed and drank from the river while Veronica and Heather collected all the available clerics for their cause, finding space in the grass nearby to communicate their plan and practice.

The solution was a spell, something Heather had picked up in a clergy book early in her Obsidian adventures. The spell had the ability to cloak clerics in a protective aura of holy light, the same kind of magic used to expel the darkness from the infected.

Heather explained to the group its uses and how to cast the spell, many of whom looked afraid of the consequences that might occur should the spell not achieve its desired effect. It was a moderate-level spell that might be beyond many of the clerics, who until recently had wandered along with the rest of the infected in their own villages.

"Any questions?" Heather eventually asked. She had just given a demonstration of the spell, her whole figure emitting a powerful white glow that they could sense from several yards away.

"Just one," a timid cleric with layers of fat spilling over his trousers said. "What do we do if this doesn't work?"

"Simple," Veronica snapped. "We shut you in the pen with the other animals until we can work out a plan B."

When she saw the fear on the cleric's face, she added, "We can't think negatively about this. Negative thoughts will weaken us and our spells. We have to believe we can do this for it to work."

Heather nodded in agreement, and soon they were back on the bridge, facing the town.

If the infected noticed them, they showed no signs. They milled and stumbled around the town, visible through the open gate as the clerics prepared their march.

Ben shuffled uneasily nearby, hating the fact he could not be of more help.

"Don't fret." Veronica grinned. "Leave it to the pros."

Ben snorted. "We'll see."

"Okay, clerics, are you ready?" Heather called.

A grumble was her response.

"I said, *are you ready?*"

The grumble turned into an awkward mix of enthusiasm and terror.

"It'll do." Heather rolled her eyes. "Okay, auras up!"

Most of the clerics began to glow with a faint pulse of white light. A few of them looked at their hands and bodies as if impressed that they were able to make the spell work.

A handful of clerics, however, failed, and were sent to wait with the other fighters.

Heather gave an encouraging nod to Veronica and the two led the way into the town.

The minute they crossed the threshold, the infected rushed them. They tore through the streets to meet them, arms pinwheeling. They jumped and bashed into the clerics but were thrown back by the power of the light.

Veronica and Heather grimaced in the first instances, prepared for the worst. The relief was clear on their faces when the protection of their spells proved out.

"Hurry," Heather said. "Let's find the others and work out what's going on here."

Veronica had never found anything more distracting than she found the infected. Navigating the streets was nearly impossible with body after body throwing itself at her. Although her aura kept the infected at bay, each assault was a distraction.

They ran through streets, shouting for the ones who had called for help. They could hear nothing above the growls and cries of the infected, so they continued blindly, turning at junctions and finding themselves swallowed by the streets.

They'd pause at the odd house where someone detected movement, staring through the window only to find a room upturned and emptied. It soon became apparent that they were lost.

"Which way?" Heather asked at yet another T junction.

"This way?" Veronica shrugged, knowing it didn't really matter. They only had a limited window before the clerics behind them began to run out of mana for their spells.

It was as the streets rose upwards that the call came from behind. One of the clerics at the back had stopped glowing and now stared ahead with a terrified expression.

"Protect her," Heather shouted. "Put her in the middle of the group."

The group readjusted, protecting the cleric in a glowing cocoon, and ran onward, sure they were going in the right direction. More and more clerics ran out of power, and soon the center of the group was filled with terrified clerics.

And yet they could not stop. Surrounded and bombarded by infected, they had to run, had to keep moving. Heather occasionally tried to lighten the mood for Veronica and the others around her.

"Now might be a good time to invest in real estate, you know? Snap up one of these houses while they're cheap. Sell them once the infected are gone and boom, you've got yourself a profit."

Veronica snorted, taking a sharp left and reaching the crest of the hill.

They paused momentarily, Veronica's head whirling around. "They were here, right? We saw them here?"

"What if it was an illusion. Like a mirage?" an exhausted cleric offered.

"No." Veronica shook her head. "It couldn't have been. We heard them."

The back of the pack was dealing with the worst of the infected. No matter how many times they were shoved back by the aura, they didn't give up. They began to swarm around them again.

"Quick! This way!"

Veronica looked around for the source of the voice. A head was sticking out of the ground, a flap of square grass raised on a hinge. A man with a grubby face stared out, urgently waving a hand.

"Come down quick," he said.

Veronica and Heather wasted no time in obeying. They called back to readjust the formation, letting those whose power was depleted file into the hole first. Those with more power followed, their bodies lighting the way as the door snapped shut behind them and encased them in the dank dark of the underground bunker.

***

Ben had begun to grow anxious. He had watched the clerics disappear through the gate and could hear the onslaught of the infected as they had attacked, but he could do nothing but watch and wait.

He kept an eye on his inbox, hoping Veronica would find a safe space to update them on their progress. He knew they had no option but to wait it out until the clerics had done their thing.

It wasn't worth risking so many lives to force their way through.

Ben had read all about the Battle of Thermopylae in online forums several years ago when he had taken an interest in battle strategies and tactics that might help him out in-game. Thermopylae was a battle fought between the Greek forces and the Persians, in which 7,000 Greek troops managed to fend off 150,000 Persians by funneling the Persian army through a thin canyon where only a few could pass at a time.

Although the Greeks put up a good fight, they eventually lost, but that didn't mean they didn't have an impact, and that their lesson couldn't be applied and improved upon.

The infected were the Greeks.

Ben and his battalion were the Persians.

Numbers didn't count in this game. Short of scaling the walls and throwing themselves at the town, there was little they could do but wait it out until the clerics had performed their duty.

Twenty minutes passed. Thirty. Forty. Ben tapped his foot, pacing around Huk and Leonie. They could still hear the infected, but the sounds gave no indication as to what they were dealing with.

Ben kept an eye on his messages, waiting for any sign that the others were safe.

The stone stairs spiraled down into the center of the hill. The walls were damp, packed earth, with small roots sticking out of the ceiling and moss clinging to the pillar the stairs revolved around.

They must have gone down at least four stories before they came through a stone door into a room that sent a chill down their spines.

They filed in, two dozen clerics, breathless and alarmed. The room was large enough to contain them with some space left over. Barrels and wooden crates had been piled around the walls, half-opened, foodstuffs spilling out the sides.

They shut off their auras as a torch was lit and placed in a sconce at the side of the room by the grubby man. He reached the far end of the room and knocked three times on the door.

"Looks just like the one-star I booked for my holiday last year." Veronica chuckled. "Only nicer."

Another knock from the other side. Three of them.

"Who's in there?" Heather asked quietly.

Questions in a similar vein were whispered from behind.

The door creaked open. Several wary-looking dwarves poked their heads out of the darkness. They looked pale and ghostly in the glowing light of the torch.

"You've come for us?" a female dwarf choked out, her hair standing out in all directions. "Someone's finally come to save us?"

"It's a miracle!" a small girl celebrated, hands in the air as she collapsed to her knees.

Veronica gave them a warm smile, encouragement for the dwarves now waving them through the second door. She looked at Heather, whose eyes were brimming with tears.

The second room was triple the size of the first, which was lucky, considering that there were close to twenty dwarves hiding in the bunker.

"How long have you all been here?" Veronica asked.

"We don't know," the grubby man replied. On the wall were scratches making a tally, "Four days since we started keeping count. Feels like longer than that, though."

"We just can't get out," the female dwarf added. "The minute we open the trap, they come flocking toward us. We've tried taking them down one at a time, but…"

"But they're family," the man continued. "They're people we knew and loved. Not only that, but we can't risk the infection spreading down here. If just one of us gets a good enough scratch or cut, it jeopardizes us all."

Heather nodded grimly. "So, you're trapped?"

"In a word, yes," a dwarf with a deep voice grumbled.

"At least you've got provisions," said a cleric from farther back in the group, someone Veronica recognized as Tomas. "That's something, right? You're not starving."

"For now," the grubby man replied. "This bunker was built for the lord of this town and his wife. There's enough here for two people to last in the event of an attack of some kind. This place wasn't built for ten times that. And if you guys are going to join us down here, well, we're screwed."

"We're not staying down here," Veronica said resolutely. "We've got a way to get you out. It's just going to take a bit of time to get to it."

"Impossible," a young dwarf said. "There's no way you can pull us out of here."

Veronica grinned. "That's what you think."

They waited a few hours for the clerics' mana to regenerate. In that time, they were given a tour around the rest of the bunker and were offered food from the stores. Dried fruit and nuts mostly, things that would last for a while without fear of spoiling.

Veronica messaged Ben to give him the update that they should be expected soon. She also put out a 'hi' to Chloe and the others, letting them know she was thinking of them and hoping their training was going to plan.

Once they were all ready, Veronica checked that everyone was in position, with the weakest clerics taking the outer ring of their formation until their power depleted. They would be replaced by the stronger clerics.

Dwarves from the bunker would be placed in the center of the formation in groups of five and would shout directions to lead the group back to the outer perimeter, where Ben and the others would be waiting.

There they would drop off the clerics who had used their mana, head back in with a fresh group, and go through the process all over again.

Veronica stood near the doorway, counting the dwarves behind her. The grubby-faced man waited behind, wanting to be the last to leave.

"Are we all ready?" she asked.

The clerics nodded a little less enthusiastically than she'd hoped.

They trailed up the spiral, the stairs taking their breath away. When they reached the top, Veronica placed a hand on the trap and counted down from three.

At zero, she shoved the trap, only to find that it wouldn't budge.

"What?" she asked, shoving more aggressively with her shoulder now.

"Let me try," Heather said.

"Oh, because you're *so* much stronger than me."

"Maybe it's technique," Heather replied, but when she tried, it was the same.

Veronica looked down at the five dwarves huddled in the middle of the procession. "Any tips?"

That was when Veronica realized that something was wrong. Rather than reply, the dwarves stared up at her with wicked grins on their faces. Their bodies turned translucent, and they began to glow with a sickly pallor.

"What's going on?" Veronica asked. "Why're you…"

Before she could finish her sentence, she heard wicked cackling traveling up from the bunker.

"Who's that?" Heather asked, panic in her voice.

"It's them," Veronica replied, resignation in her voice. "The dark gods. They've got us trapped."

CHAPTER THIRTY-ONE

Chloe could feel the butterflies in her stomach, every inch of her body thrumming with excited energy for the task ahead.

They had celebrated last night, Chloe allowing the cohort of mages to let their hair down and bask in their progress over the last week. They had all leveled up in their skills and spells—a few leveling up their characters, too—and after the competition was over, Chloe brought the mages to the king's palace for a meal and some revelry.

They were ecstatic, most of them never having been in the palace before. Therese sweet-talked Abe to join them and kept him in check as he sat at the head of the table. He watched with a strange kind of curiosity over the table of mages, NPC and blessed alike.

The night ran long, but all too soon, the mages headed back to their homes. Their instructions from Chloe were clear: meet outside the city walls at noon and prepare for their first attempt at opening the rift.

"You really think they're ready?" Gideon asked, watching the group slowly swell as mages passed through the gate and joined them outside.

Abe had forewarned the city guards, ensuring that those watching from the walls were prepared to help if need be. He was also watching from the balcony in his palace, ready to call in a party quest should the time come.

"I do," Chloe said. "We've amassed more mages than the last group to try this had. We've trained them well and honed their skills, and I believe we can do this."

Whatever it is, Chloe thought, staring into the cloudy gray sky and wondering what would happen next.

"Well, as long as you believe in them, you've got me," Gideon assured her.

"Aw, how cute," Molly cooed as the two mages approached with Gelda in tow. "Always knew you two had a thing for each other."

Chloe and Gideon looked awkwardly at each other, laughing nervously.

"Me?" Gideon said. "And her? Behave."

"Nah," Chloe said. "Gideon's got a thing for clerics. Ain't that right?"

"Oh, jealous, are we?" Holly crooned.

"Not," Chloe said, genuinely okay with the situation. "Whatever makes Gid happy is all I care about."

"Thanks, Chloe." Gideon blushed.

"Don't mention it."

As it neared noon, the space outside the city began to fill. A hundred and fifty mages were ready and waiting for their commands. They chattered apprehensively, occasionally glancing at Chloe as they stood talking. When Chloe was certain those who were attending had arrived, she nodded at Blueballs and was lifted into the air by his powerful paws.

"Brothers and sisters of mage-hood," Chloe called, straining her voice to be heard by the horde. "Thank you all for joining us here, on the verge of what promises to be the most triumphant display of magic ever seen in Obsidian."

There was an immediate uproar of cheers and claps. Chloe paused, her breath taken away by the sight of them.

"We are on the cusp of a magical revolution. What we will attempt today has been tried once before but did not end in success. We have taken every measure to ensure that our success is certain, and you are all part of that."

Another chorus of cheers.

"When the time comes and the signal is given, it will be up to each of you to concentrate your power on the rift. I will set off the reaction in the same way a key unlocks a door, and then I will need your aid."

The cheers settled down.

"What we are asking is dangerous. There are risks involved. You have stuck by us this past week and proved you are worthy; now show the universe you are worthy, too.

"I will be sharing this task with you all. As promised, a large amount of experience will be awarded to anyone who helps us complete this quest. Accept the quest, face front, and we'll begin."

Chloe waited as the cohort of mages grew glassy-eyed and accepted the mission. There were audible gasps from players across the field when they saw the fifty-thousand-point experience prize. A few mutters and mumbles came from people wondering how Chloe had come across such a mine of experience.

Chloe nodded, pleased to be able to share her opportunity with as many players as possible and knowing that she was leading the next generation of Obsidian players.

When most of the eyes were back up front, Blueballs lowered Chloe back down and she turned her attention to the sky once more.

She closed her eyes and took a deep breath, focusing on her **Etheric Manipulation**. She was elated when the skill leveled up before her eyes.

Skill increased: Etheric Manipulation (Lv 5)

Congratulations on reaching level 5 in this skill. You are surely

working your way down the path of magedom, and with that, you can reap a host of rewards.

You will now be able to learn basic spells by observation. Simply watch another mage use a spell, and you will be able to absorb that spell's knowledge and set yourself on the path to taking that spell further. Not only that, but specialization bonuses are now in play. Should you choose to narrow your skills to a specific elemental path, you will progress in these spells twice as fast. You will also have the option to change your title to reflect your specialty and reward yourself with bonus tuition from the academies and schools across Obsidian to further your skill set.

Should you wish not to specialize, you will find that combining spells and playing with experimental magic will have its rewards. Bonus buffs will be available any time spells are combined, and any new spells unseen before in Obsidian will be labeled with your name as the founder and creator.

Bonuses: +12 etheric potential, spell cast cost dramatically reduced, immunity to friendly fire

(NOTE: Increases in spells override any previous bonuses gained from the spell).

Chloe gave a broad smile, happy to see the bonuses that either path she chose might bring. She made a note to look at specializations more in-depth when she had the chance and returned to the etheric.

The rabbit was waiting for her like an obedient pet. She noticed that the rabbit now had a perfect pair of horns protruding from its head.

She remembered something she had seen in a book once about a mythical creature that looked incredibly similar. A "jackalope," she thought it was called.

Chloe grinned, about to set the jackalope into action when she became suddenly aware of horns blowing. Three short, sharp blasts were followed by the clopping of horses' hooves on stone.

Chloe opened her eyes, watching with interest as a group of around forty horses came out of the palace to meet them, led by a face she had thought she wouldn't see again.

Tabitha pulled her horse to a stop a short distance from Chloe.

"May we help you?" Chloe asked when it became clear that Tabitha was not going to say the first word.

Tabitha looked down her nose and spoke as though every syllable hurt. "The king has requested our attendance at your attempt," she said reluctantly.

Chloe studied Tabitha for a moment, the angles on her face looking sharper than ever. Behind her, the other mages on their horses stared out grimly from under their hoods—ancient, miserable mages whose last choice would have been to join forces with fresh-faced magic-users who had been trained outside the rules of the school.

"The king requested this himself?" Chloe asked.

Tabitha gave a small nod. "Not my preference, but when the very foundation of your school and its future is called into question, what else can you do?"

Chloe and Tabitha stared for a long time into each other's eyes, a thousand words unspoken. Chloe advanced toward Tabitha and offered a hand.

"Your help is most welcome."

Tabitha, looking unsettled, gripped the tips of the battle mage's fingers and gave a half-shake. "Well, I must admit that your words the other day unsettled me. If we at the school can reinforce our worth with the wider public, it can only be advantageous for us in the long run."

"Thank you," Chloe said.

Tabitha made a half-attempt at a crooked smile, then reached into the folds of her cloak. "There is also this. Something I found in the library that might aid you in your quest."

She handed Chloe a small piece of aged parchment covered in scrawled script and the diagrams of motions for an incantation. In the corner of the page was a sketch of a rippling rift with figures emerging from its depths.

"The tale of the Nether Realm is legendary," Tabitha explained.

"For the school to play a part in the second chapter of the tale is something few will live to bear witness to."

Chloe smiled and gave her thanks, studying the document carefully and absorbing as much of it as possible.

When she finished, she set about readjusting the positions of the mages. She placed the younger mages in the center, with the mages on horseback on either side and in a thin line in front. She positioned Tabitha alongside her, Gideon, Molly, Holly, and Lindsay, who had proven her worth and now looked fit for the part with her gold staff in hand.

"Okay," Chloe murmured, satisfied that everything was ready. "Here goes."

Chloe closed her eyes and found her jackalope familiar. The etheric barrier around them seemed to bend and warp, swimming into amorphous shapes as the jackalope guided it toward Chloe. She felt the power of the etheric coursing through her, every fiber of her body tingling.

She concentrated fully on her task, remembering the scribbles and instructions on the corner of the ancient scroll. She opened her eyes and pointed her hands at the clear space in the sky, imagining a rift opening, moving her hands in the sequence she had seen on the parchment.

Sparks shot from her fingers, and her hands and arms glowed with power. She sent the sparks away from her body, raining into the air as though she were grinding steel across metal.

She waited for something to happen. She waited for the tear to appear, the first sign of a rip in the fabric of reality. A crosshair that might indicate where the world ended and the etheric began.

But nothing happened. After several minutes of trying, she stopped, realizing suddenly that she was out of breath.

"I don't understand," Chloe said, withdrawing the piece of scroll and scanning it again. She had followed every instruction, and nothing had happened.

What was she missing?

Try again, KieraFreya said. *Sometimes when a door is rusted, it just needs a little extra push.*

Gideon offered Chloe a mana regeneration potion and she drank it greedily, nervous about having close to two hundred bodies waiting for her to act, including the forty or so from the school who intensely disliked her.

"Come on..." Chloe muttered, focusing once more. The jackalope returned, swiftly pulling the etheric toward her. She stared at the sky, begging KieraFreya to get involved. She felt the goddess trying to do what she could, but it seemed impossible. Sparks flew, but nothing happened.

It was just as Chloe was about to give up again that an eagle cried out. The call was loud enough to echo around them, drawing the eyes of the mages to it.

The bird was easily double the size of any eagle she had ever seen. It sped across the sky from over the canopy of trees, moving like one of Ben's arrows loosed from a bow. Its streamlined shape tore through the sky toward the party.

"What the..." Gideon muttered.

Before anyone could respond, gigantic wings started beating. The very air around them pulsed with a sudden change in temperature as the winds grew warm. Following the trajectory of the eagle was a creature so big that Chloe had to take a second look.

The dragon appeared as if from nowhere, materializing over the trees. Each beat of its wings sent waves of air that squashed the canopy as it raced after the eagle, smoke billowing from its mouth and trailing behind.

The eagle darted low, coming so close to the crowd of mages that many of them ducked in fear. As it passed near Chloe, she saw a familiar glint in its eye.

"The Wrangler," she breathed.

Gideon's mouth fell open.

The shapeshifter pulled up at the last minute and sped into the sky. He climbed ever higher, finding the space in the clouds and vanishing from sight. The dragon followed the eagle.

All around them, Chloe heard cries of fear. The mages had signed up to open a rift, but a dragon? That hadn't been a part of the deal.

"Stand steady," Chloe called, her voice authoritative. It boomed around them, drawing the attention of the mages as the dragon disappeared into the clouds. "We do not cower from our enemies. Stand steady and wait. The rift is near."

They waited in tense silence. They could hear the dragon somewhere above them. The clouds swirled and blackened, the smoke from the dragon's throat darkening their hue. Occasionally they could see the two creatures through breaks in the clouds.

And then the eagle was diving. It plummeted from an immeasurable height, dropping so fast that Chloe thought she could see the air rippling behind it. The dragon was on its tail, mouth swelling with flame as it readied for the blow.

A split second after the dragon belched its flame, the eagle made a ninety-degree turn, speeding back toward the group. The dragon used its momentum to tear after it, the air behind now wobbling like tarmac during a heatwave.

"This is it!" Chloe exclaimed, realizing suddenly what was happening. "Prepare yourselves!"

The dragon was a dark blur now, and a sound like a speeding plane thundered around them. The eagle slowed, hovering in the air in front of the dragon's path. The dragon grinned excitedly, summoned its flame, and shot a column of fire from its throat.

For a heart-rending second, Chloe thought the flames had consumed the bird, but then she saw him diving toward the ground, finding his way toward her. He flew at an impossible speed, stopping just as he reached Chloe and transforming in mid-air into the Wrangler.

"Now, Chloe!" the Wrangler wheezed, pointing at where the air wobbled around the dragon. It hovered in the air, its wings beating loudly as it confusedly scanned for the bird it had been chasing.

Chloe aimed her power at the air around the dragon, the start of a tear that would become a rift—as long as Chloe's power worked.

Chloe closed her eyes, sparks once again raining from her fingertips. She shot them forward, the power making its way into the sky, irritating and blinding the dragon, who screeched and roared in frustration.

But something had started to happen. The sparks found their way into the rippling air. A small slit began to form, opening like a blinking eyelid. She called to the mages, requesting their power to help. The next thing she knew, dozens upon dozens of beams of power found their way into the air, each line connecting with the rift as it slowly began to open.

Chloe grimaced as she focused every ounce of energy on keeping the doorway open, her mana bar slowly dropping as the dragon finally abandoned its post in front of the rift and flew up into the air, its eyes trained on the mages below.

CHAPTER THIRTY-TWO

The rift slowly began to part, and impossible folds of air widened to reveal something beyond. Chloe could hear strange noises coming from the rift.

The very air around them changed as it inched apart as if fingers were clawing open a broken elevator door.

The dragon rose higher, hovering above them all now, its mouth alive with flame.

"Tabitha! Can you do something?" Chloe roared above the din of magic bolts and the beating of wings.

Tabitha called a sharp command. Immediately the mages from the Mage's School turned their attentions to the dragon. Without uttering a word, they focused, their spells turning to the crystal blue of water.

A net began to appear above the heads of the gathered mages, the strands made from cool water that dripped and soothed those sweating beneath. When the dragon loosed its flame, it was met with nothing but the hissing roar of steam rising and clouding the air above them.

But Chloe could see none of this. She could hear it all, but her focus was on the rift which, once the school mages had turned their attentions away, had begun to slowly close.

"Change of plan," Chloe shouted. "Mages back to the rift, please."

Tabitha rolled her eyes. "If she could make up her mind, it would be great."

"Oh, I'm sorry," Chloe said. "The next time I want to prevent my comrades from being roasted by dragon fire, I guess I'll ask someone else."

The mages directed their spells back at the rift, and it began to ease open again.

Gideon let out a cry of effort from beside her. His face was pained from the energy spent holding the rift. "What's the plan for the dragon? We can't keep getting distracted like this. We barely have enough energy to hold it."

Chloe heard the colossal steps of Gelda from behind her. "Leave it to me," she said.

Gelda wove between the lines of mages, finding a clear space where she could operate. The dragon in its rage and fury had swooped back into the air and now plunged toward the mages.

"Blueballs!" Gelda called, summoning the toffet to her. He ripped his eyes from the dragon and sprinted over on all fours. "I've got a job for you, kitty."

Blueballs looked at her curiously.

"Here, climb."

Gelda laced her fingers together, bent her legs, and created a launchpad. Her stony muscles glistened in the dazzle of the surrounding magic.

"One…"

Blueballs placed a foot in the makeshift stirrup.

"Two…"

They both coiled.

"Three!"

Blueballs jumped at the exact moment Gelda threw her hands into the air. The toffet arced high into the air just as the dragon swooped by, its jaws snapping.

Blueballs grabbed the beast's thick neck, gripping tightly and adjusting himself until he was safely straddling it.

Shifting to compensate for the added weight, the dragon roared and beat its wings harder, the wings' membranes almost knocking several mages off their feet.

And then it was back in the air, twisting and writhing furiously, distracted and determined to rid itself of the toffet now slashing his claws into the dragon's tough flesh.

"I think it's working!" Lindsay called, surprised laughter decorating her voice. "I think it's opening!"

"It is!" Holly shouted.

Gideon laughed between grunts of effort.

Chloe saw that they were right. The tear in the sky fissured its way toward the ground, cracking like ice down the side of an iceberg. The air moved in waves and the door parted. Mouths dropped open in awe as they saw what lay beyond the rift.

"The Nether Realm," KieraFreya gasped.

"Almost there!" Chloe called, doing her best to ignore the cries of the toffet and dragon locked in deadly battle. "Just a bit farther!"

A sudden screeching cry filled the air around them. Chloe looked away from the rift to where the dragon had landed. It was doing its best to shake Blueballs from its back, its enormous tail whipping around and smashing their barn to shards.

The dragon snapped at the toffet, its dagger-like teeth missing the creature by inches. Chloe could see a gash at Blueballs' side, though he fought like nothing had happened.

There was a blur of movement from beside her. Before Chloe realized it, the Wrangler had transformed into a warg twice as large as any she'd seen. Its furry back was striped with black and brown, a great hunch across its spine from which its powerful front legs extended and pawed at the ground. It bounded toward the dragon.

"No! The rift!"

In the split-second Chloe's attention had been diverted, her energy hadn't been on the doorway. Her eyes widened in alarm when she saw it slowly begin to stitch back together. She narrowed her eyes, focused on the doorway again, and shot her magic forward.

"Not on my watch," she muttered, sweat falling from her in buckets. She was dimly aware of shouts from behind, coming from mages who had depleted all their energy and were now worried that there wasn't enough power to make it happen.

"KF? A little boost, perhaps? Anything?"

"I'm doing all I can," KieraFreya replied. "It's nearly there. I can feel it."

"Pass the mana potions!" Chloe cried. "Restock! This is it! Just a bit more!"

Although her words spurred on her battalion, she had no idea if they were true. When would this end? Would magic be needed to hold the rift open forever?

And what exactly were those shadowy figures within the rift that were coming toward them?

The mages who were depleted refueled, the magic was boosted. The doorway inched open, melting reality around it. Before too long, Chloe clearly saw the Nether Realm beyond, only the shimmer of heat distorting what was coming toward them.

Two things happened at once, sending several of the mages to the ground in fear.

The first was a colossal boom like a thunderclap, the sound reverberating around them and echoing in waves. The very walls of the city shook, and the ground wobbled beneath them. An explosion of light surged from the edges of the rift, and Chloe was at last certain they'd completed their task. The doorway now stood open before them.

The second was the dragon's dying cry. Heads turned to see Blueballs and the Wrangler, their bodies dripping with the dragon's blood as it breathed its last and stilled.

There was a moment's silence as the mages processed what had happened. The flows of magic began to cut off one by one until there were only the rift and the battalion, a faceoff of power against power.

"We did it," Gideon whispered. "We really did it."

The battalion fell silent. All eyes were fixed on the rift.

One by one, mages began to glow gold. People all across the field leveled up, cheering and whooping as the notification of their quest being complete hit their menus.

Quest complete: The Rift to Nether Realm

You have unlocked the entrance to the Nether Realm—congratulations!

This was deemed an impossible task by those who came before, but you managed to unite more magic-users than the city has seen together. You have found the tear in the fabric of reality and can now access the Nether Realm.

Celebrate your victory but tread carefully. Explore the unexplored. Strange paths lie ahead, but for now, rest up a bit...

If you can.

Rewards: 50,000 exp

Chloe beamed, elated. They had done it. *They had actually done it.* She laughed as she was lifted into the air with the rest, her level jumping to 16, her health, stamina, and mana replenishing instantly.

All around her were cheers. People high-fived, clapped, and hugged each other. A few individuals walked over to the dragon to get a closer look at the fallen creature. Horn blasts from the city gates signaled their victory.

"Good work, Chloe." Gideon grinned.

Chloe waved a hand. "It wasn't all me. Nothing would have been accomplished without you and all of these people here—"

When a second horn blast came, Chloe's attention was drawn back to the rift. The sound was rough and shrill, not made by the finely-crafted brass of the horns of the city heralds.

Her eyes widened as she focused on the shapes moving toward them on the other side of the rift. They were hundreds of yards inside of the impossible realm but were getting closer, of that she was sure.

There were more than one hundred from what she could see. Tiny figures dotted the horizon, shapes littering the sky, they moved fast, dark figures growing larger as they drew closer to the rift. Before too long, Chloe could see that they were on horseback. Several figures rode on the back of large birds. Another horn blast rang from the rift and a sudden thought struck Chloe.

Now that we've opened it, but should we need to, how the hell do we close it?

The first arrow fired from the rift, a black thing with dark feathers trailing behind it. The arrow struck the ground near Chloe's feet, missing by a few inches.

"Prepare!" Chloe cried, going into battle mode.

The mages around her, who had been celebrating seconds ago, now craned their heads to see the danger, alarm on their faces as they heard the hoofbeats and saw the stream of figures pounding toward them.

Each mage tapped into the etheric, spreading their feet apart and taking a battle stance. Their hands glowed with power, determination on their faces.

"Defensive maneuvers," Chloe called.

Gideon powered his **Aqua Orb**, allowing Holly, Molly, and Chloe to step inside. Several other mages who had learned similar protective spells encapsulated their comrades until the majority of the mages were encircled by protective spells.

Animalistic whooping and jeers came from the enemy as they neared the rift. Finally Chloe could see them clearly—a great wave of orcs and other foul creatures riding beasts, the likes of which she had never seen. They moved at an alarming pace, one minute racing through the darkened purple rocks that littered the Nether Realm, the next breaking through the etheric and charging toward the mages.

Chloe clapped her hands as the first wave filed through. When she pulled them apart, an ice shard stretched between her palms. She rocked back, and when she cast the shard, it shot through several enemies before stopping.

Spell after spell now fired. Chloe could *feel* the etheric energy around them as mage after mage cast spells to fend off the enemy. She had no idea exactly what these creatures were and had no time to cast **Creature Identification** to find out.

"Gideon, how we doing, buddy?" Chloe asked the mage, who had once again imbued his orb with **Volt Shock**. Enemies crashed against the bubble, causing the power to glitch and explode in blinding light. Chloe was aware of Holly and Molly utilizing the shadows and rocks around them to knock enemies off their steeds and finish them off.

"There're too many of them." Gideon grimaced, his hands splayed as he poured his power into maintaining the bubble. "I can feel every attack."

They were surrounded on all sides. Everywhere Chloe looked, she saw dark beasts, jaws snapping as riders threw spears, fired arrows, and slashed with their swords.

Chloe was dimly aware of Blueballs behind them, the toffet's massive bulk swimming through the enemies and causing a great deal of damage. He managed to make his way behind Chloe, who paused for a few seconds in her attacks to send **Healing Hands** his way. Where the Wrangler was, she had no idea, although she could hear the roar of some animal she hoped was him.

Great winged beasts circled overhead, and the foul army kept coming. Chloe turned her attention back, sending columns of **Deic Light** in front of her and sapping the health of a large number of the enemies.

As she managed to take down a particularly scarred and fierce-looking rider and his beast, Chloe took a deep breath, wondering what the hell they'd unleashed and how were they going to defeat it when half their party was on the other side of the forest.

It had all been going so well, or so Abe had thought.

On the palace's balcony, he had one of the best seats in the house to watch a tear in the fabric of reality right outside his city. This would go down in legend. His *name* would go down in legend as the king who oversaw it all. The one who granted access to the Nether Realm.

The idea gave him chills.

At first, it had seemed like everything was going well. Chloe and the mages were in position. Magic was being concentrated. The miserable old crone from the Mages' School had arrived with her reanimated sacks of dust and were lending a hand. It had all seemed positive.

But then Abe had wondered whether something was wrong. The battalion of mages had been still for a good few minutes with no result. Sparks had flown from Chloe, but they had achieved little.

What Abe had not expected was for massive winged creatures to race across the canopy of the forest. In all of his years of life, he had never seen a dragon. He'd had to blink to make sure he wasn't seeing things. And when the eagle had turned out to be the Wrangler, he couldn't believe it.

And what a plan, too! For a dragon to create the first ripple, the first pebble tossed into a still lake. Only the dragon's speed, power, and etheric pulses could cause the initial tear to occur. It was like a speeding bullet plowing through a thin sheet of paper. Now all that was left was to pull and pull until the whole thing tore.

Abe had clapped when the rift opened. After the blinding flash and the cheers of the mages, he had joined in. Had even held Therese nearby to watch with a wide grin. From where they stood, everything was fine. They couldn't see through the rift, but it didn't matter. They had won. They had accomplished the impossible.

That moment already felt like a lifetime ago. On the turn of a dime, the situation had changed. He could sense it in the air, in the silence that had fallen over the mages, and now they were overrun. Hundreds upon hundreds of the creatures spilled out of the tear.

They came like waves trying to swallow a sandcastle. The initial force gunned straight for the frontrunners. As each wave came, more creatures circled the group, surrounding them on all sides. They were surrounded now. They needed help.

And help was coming.

Abe urged Therese and the dwarf battalion onward as they neared the gate and took their positions. Several hundred dwarves who had been rescued from the surrounding villages were ready to defend their kingdom. He had sent word to the rangers, the warriors, the rogues, anyone who would listen and come to their aid.

The gates opened. Therese shone in her gold armor, leading the charge, taking out the stragglers from the waves who split off and took their chances, firing at his gate guards.

From his vantage point, he could see hundreds of creatures peeling off from the main horde and gunning for the forests, driving with such clear determination that he wondered what exactly their dark purpose was.

Footsteps approached from behind. Beverley. Her voice soft was laced with concern. "Are you ready, sir?"

Abe turned and saw the helmet in her hands. It had been years since he'd worn full armor, but he would be damned if he was going to let his army be led by their queen.

He nodded, ducked his head, and aligned himself with his head-gear. Satisfied, he ordered the command to be sent out, an urgent party quest to jump to the king's aid.

Whatever was coming through that rift wouldn't stand a chance.

CHAPTER THIRTY-THREE

Ben began to grow impatient. She should have messaged by now. Should have been in contact some time ago, surely? The sounds of the infected had died down, and the town seemed still.

Then where were they?

No one was replying to messages. He had left several in the group chat, but there was simply no response. Not from Veronica, not from Chloe and Gideon, not from anyone. The only sign they'd had of any progress was that Ben, Talbot, Huk, and Leonie had risen from the ground and leveled up.

They had whooped and cheered for Chloe, glad to see that progress was being made. It didn't help in their current situation, particularly when all around them, the dwarves were questioning why they'd gained a level without doing any work.

Ben explained his ties to the KieraSlayers and the quest he was part of.

Now they stared at the gate, a helpless feeling in their stomachs.

"We have to try again," Huk said, eyes narrowed at the gate. "I don't like this."

"Me neither," Ben replied. He paused a moment longer, chewing his lip and trying to figure out what Chloe might do.

Chloe would run in there, all guns blazing, and take them down. Especially if it meant the difference between life and death for a comrade.

Ben took a step toward the gate. Already he could see infected stirring, slowly congregating near the entrance as if to say, "Try it, bud. See what happens."

But they couldn't just stand around and wait, could they?

"Gentlemen! On your feet," Ben called, catching the attention of the dwarves.

"Oi!" a female voice called.

"And women," Ben corrected. "Stand up. Weapons ready. We're storming the town."

"What about the infected? They'll swarm us instantly. We'll never get to the others."

Ben sighed. "That's a risk we're going to have to take. Keep together. Don't let them scratch you. If you get hurt… Well, we're just going to have to pray that our clerics are waiting for us on the other side."

Veronica sat down helplessly, her back against the wall.

They had put up a good fight. The minute the ghostly versions of the dwarves made themselves known, they had attacked with their cleric auras, doing their best to use their holy powers to defeat the ghosts…

But it had not been enough.

Every attack went straight through the ghosts, yet they could materialize enough to drag the clerics back into the bunker.

Veronica and Heather had struggled against them, impressed by the strength of their grasps. They had been close to slipping free a couple of times, too, until they heard the cackling giggles and noticed the three bodies lined up against the far wall.

Veronica had recognized them instantly, having seen their images carved into shrines around Obsidian. Dryana had the same ghostly sheen as the dwarves, pulsing with a translucent glow.

Beside her, Fukmos leered at them from yellow eyes, his presence enough to make her feel sick.

Completing the trio was Myaris, the Goddess of Disease. Her body was shrouded in the living presence of a dark shadow Veronica recognized instantly as the substance she had expelled from the sick.

"You know your friend can't keep fighting forever," Fukmos crowed, his words laced with malice. That sickening grin on his face never quite faded. "Divide the group and you diminish its strength. It's basic math."

"This was your plan all along?" Veronica snapped.

A few heads turned toward her. Everyone else was too frightened and awed to stand in the presence of the gods, but Veronica had been here before. She had seen the pitiful little cretin in the caves with Chloe and had witnessed his downfall.

Fukmos cocked his head to the side. "In a sense. Of course, I had rather hoped my old friend KieraFreya would have come and joined us, but I'll take what I can get. Without her party working alongside her, neither she nor Chloe will be able to do much to stop us." He nodded at the girls on either side of him. "I've brought some friends. Do you know them? Myaris…"

Myaris put a fist to her lips and giggled. She dipped a slight curtsy. "Pleasure."

"And Dryana," Fukmos continued.

Dryana said nothing but gave a slight nod of her head. She had the air of someone who wasn't quite present. Someone whose head was in a whole other place entirely.

"See? I'm one to always learn from my mistakes. The problem before was that I fell into the trap of KieraFreya. I relied on a damn human to aid me in my task, whereas now I have my sisters with me. Beings of incredible power, in case you didn't know."

Dryana raised her arms slowly, her eyes turning white. From the ground beneath them came a rumbling.

Fukmos howled with laughter at the look of concern on their faces. "Did you know that this hill is manmade? A mound of dirt on the top of an ancient burial ground? No? Well, let's meet some of the old residents."

Spirits appeared around them, rising from the ground in a ghostly blue haze.

"And, of course, the reason you're all here today," Fukmos cackled. "The Goddess of Disease herself, creating a wonderful concoction for you mortals."

Myaris took a few slow steps forward, kneeling in front of a cleric who couldn't turn away, eyes transfixed. She tapped his forehead and immediately his eyes went dark, those repulsive dark veins appearing over his body as he turned into an infected before their eyes.

Fukmos stood proudly in front of them. "With us three together, we are unstoppable. Your friend will be no match for us, and, even if she unleashes that stupid horse, she doesn't realize the monstrosities she will encounter when she tears the Nether Realm open."

That caught their attention.

"What are you talking about?" Heather asked. She had been one of the first to come around to Chloe's quest and her way of thinking. "The Nether Realm contains Shikora. Once she reunites with the horse, the darkness will be defeated."

Fukmos stroked his chin in mock thought. "Maybe, although that, of course, doesn't account for the legion of darkness that lies in wait." He paused, head cocked as if listening to something none of them could hear. "Oh, scratch that. It has been released. An army of creatures was once banished to the Nether Realm to serve an eternity of punishment. They have now been freed and set loose upon the world."

"And they're on their way here," Dryana said dryly.

Fukmos' nostrils flared. "*I* was going to call them here…" He took a breath and closed his eyes. "No matter. They are coming."

"It doesn't matter," Veronica said, doggedly shaking her head. "No matter what you throw at us, we'll never turn. We've got light on our side, and once KieraFreya is reunited and this whole thing unravels, you'll be cowering in the corner, wishing you *could* die."

Fukmos' face straightened and he nodded appreciatively. "I admire your balls. Really, I do. Only, how are you going to do that when you're stuck down here and your friends are up there? I'll be honest; I don't like your chances. A small enclosed space and a handful of infected? I give you half an hour before you're all slaves to the darkness."

"A handful?" Heather said. "You've only infected one…"

Myaris jumped forward with such rapidity that it startled the group. She poked four more heads and let out a howling shriek of laughter.

Fukmos leered. "Best of luck, all. Oh, and Dryana, bring your friends, please?"

The three of them melted into shadows and slithered away from the group, disappearing up the stairs with the ghosts of the dead floating behind them.

Silence fell over the group, broken only by the hungry snarls of those who had been infected. Veronica pushed herself to her feet and let her hands pulse with healing energy.

It was nearly impossible to make anything out. With the frantic energies of the creatures around them and the constant crackle and buzz of electricity and water, Chloe could hardly see a thing.

"Are we even making a dent in these things?" she asked.

"I've lost count of how many there are," Holly called, blasting energy out of the orb. The shadows created massive hands from the ground that gripped and battered the orcs. "Maybe?"

They had been battling in a nearly blind state for what felt like hours. The only indication of time passing was the horns blaring from the city gates. Gelda was behind them, flinging her colossal arms around and pummelling enemies, and she managed to see over the heads of the crowd.

"Reinforcements," she cried. "The city is coming."

Chloe jumped, trying to see over the crowd, but it was impossible.

"Oh, screw this," she said, opening her menu and doing something she should have done some time ago. When she heard the screech, she yelled, "Gelda, throw me like you did Blueballs."

Gelda looked incredibly pleased. "Twice in one day. That almost never happens."

She counted down and tossed Chloe high into the air, keeping her arms outstretched for the catch while elbowing the creatures out of the way. She needn't have bothered since Sir Wingsalot swooped in and Chloe landed on his back.

"Long time, no see, old friend." Chloe beamed, then let out a cry as a winged creature came for her. She couldn't see it at first; it was all wings and claws.

When she adjusted, she saw the strange bat-like wraiths all around her. There were creatures similar to orcs but with narrower faces and leering eyes riding atop each one.

She guided Sir Wingsalot past the attackers, diving and spinning until she was able to steal a few seconds.

There they were, hundreds of reinforcements piling out of the gate. A mixture of dwarves, elves, men, and other races held their weapons high. She was elated to see them, to see the city unite to help one cause. At the head of the charge were Abe and Therese, powerful and proud in their royal armor.

I wonder what kind of defensive stats that armor gives them? Chloe mused before a pang of guilt hit her. The orcs hadn't stopped coming. The landscape below was littered with mages and their enemies locked in battle. They were everywhere, like ants at a picnic. Even with the additional reinforcements, it would be tough to take them all out.

Rather than speculate on their odds, Chloe nudged Sir Wingsalot into action and swooped down among them. The terror-daxil obeyed her every command, flying fast enough that the arrows and projectiles missed and low enough that she could reach the enemy.

With outstretched fingers, she blasted her **Volt Shock**, clearing a path down the middle where the creatures had begun to break through. She looked for groups of them and blasted them every time she could, doing whatever she could think of to thin their numbers.

"What a *shocking* number of bad guys." Chloe laughed, her humor returning now that she was above it all and actually in a position to help.

"Nope. Nope, stop," KieraFreya scolded. "No more jokes from you."

Chloe laughed, taking out a cluster of orcs and setting their wargs aflame. She guided Sir Wingsalot to the gathering near the city and waved down at Therese, who looked beyond regal in her gold armor. Her hammer was decorated with jewels and had already sampled its first taste of blood.

Over there, she could see Blueballs swimming through bodies. Across the way, she could make out Tabitha, face creased in rage as she shot magic across the field and blasted swathes of enemies.

Chloe continued her flight, helping and shooting spells wherever she could, the whole time keeping an eye on the portal, curious to know when it would end.

"Watch out!" KieraFreya said, ducking Chloe's body for her as a spear flew by.

"Thanks."

"Don't mention it," KieraFreya replied. "What were you doing?"

Chloe nodded ahead. "We need to know what's in there. If we can find Shikora, we'll be one step ahead of the enemies. You can unite with your beast, then maybe call the gods and end this damned nightmare."

KieraFreya nodded Chloe's head.

"Well, what are we waiting for?"

Chloe grinned. Sir Wingsalot headed for the giant rift, the split in reality at least fifty feet long. They hovered in front of the tear, anxious to cross the threshold.

"Has this ever been done before?" Chloe asked.

"Of course," KieraFreya said. "People are always going through portals into alternate realms."

"Really?"

"Well, maybe not mortals."

Chloe took a breath and reached a hand to where the air rippled before her. It looked like the clearest liquid she'd ever seen. She half-expected her skin to turn cold at its touch, but to her surprise, her hand just slipped through to the other side.

"Onward and upward," Chloe said, looking down at the army still filing out of the Nether Realm. "Sir Wingsalot, forward!"

The terror-daxil briefly looked as if he wasn't going to obey, then flapped his wings and soared into the Nether Realm.

CHAPTER THIRTY-FOUR

The air around her felt different.

Despite the chaos and mania of the battle outside Hammersworth, it was deadly silent in the Nether Realm.

Below her, the lines of orcs and their steeds filed out steadily. Chloe was relieved to see that there was indeed an end to the line. There were some four hundred or so left to make it through, at a guess.

"We can't let them go through," she mused, looking around her as if expecting something to shoot her way to knock her off Sir Wingsalot.

But nothing came. The army below didn't even notice she was there.

The quiet was unsettling. Chloe tried to put her brain in gear but found it was reacting slower than usual.

"The effects of the Nether Realm," KieraFreya said. "If it was meant to be a place of luxury and fun, it wouldn't be used as the prison of the gods. Keep your wits about you. Your mind might melt inside here."

Chloe raised her head and scanned the landscape.

The world was a strange mix of burnt orange and purple. It was like a scene from another planet, a landscape devoid of plant life or water. Only the dark army passing through was alive.

The place reminded her of the plains of the Wild West, the strange rock formations and the barren earth. There wasn't anything in the way of a sky above them, just a painted canvas of darker shades of purple.

And no sign of Shikora.

"Damn!" Chloe said. "Where is she?"

"I don't know," KieraFreya replied.

The army moved steadily beneath her. Soon they would all be out and loosed on Obsidian. Chloe felt that pang of guilt again, knowing she had done this. She had released this evil. No matter how unintentional, this was her fault.

She wondered, not for the first time, how she had ended up on this quest. Her mind flashed back to the journey she had undertaken. The friends she had made. The cowladites and their kin, the sandworm, the sherikans. The tribal people of the forest and their village, the minotaurs, the city of Killink. Her battle against the dreads, rescuing Lady Gwent from danger. All of it had led up to this moment.

And still she could not complete her task.

"Chloe, look," KieraFreya said, pointing to a strange rock formation that towered over the remaining battalion.

Chloe grinned, understanding exactly what KieraFreya was suggesting. "Wingsalot, take us closer."

When they were near enough, Chloe channeled the etheric and sent a blast of fire at the rocks. Great chunks and boulders fell off and rained on the army, causing those who weren't squashed to scatter. The canyon around them collapsed, and although they fled, many were flattened beneath the rubble.

"At least that's something." Chloe nodded smugly. She was about to turn back and look once again over the landscape for Shikora when something caught her eye.

Gideon, Holly, and Molly. Their protective bubble had failed and they were being overrun.

Ben ran through the town, arrows singing from his bow.

Thanks to their dash, the group had worked their way inside. There weren't as many infected as there had been before, and Ben wondered if the others were somewhere near Veronica, Heather, and the clerics.

Which provided the perfect breathing space for the hundred or so dwarves to file in and attack.

They took no prisoners, wanting nothing more than to live and realizing they were working against the clock. The longer they waited, the more likely it was that the clerics would be lost to infection, nothing more than shells wandering around aimlessly. If that happened, who would be left to heal others?

Ben followed his instincts, leading the group up the slope. He remembered seeing the figure on the crown of the hill. If he could make it there, maybe he'd be able to find the others.

Three infected to his right, three shots in quick succession. Not quite death blows, but enough to cripple them and leave them for the army behind him.

This is SO much more epic than Relic Hunter, Ben thought.

At the crest of the hill, he paused and looked around. He was standing on a wide patch of grass that looked from afar like the bald head of a green giant.

There was no one in sight.

Ben checked his messages once more, still seeing nothing from the others.

"Where are they?" Leonie asked.

Huk shaded his eyes and sniffed the air.

"What? Are you, like, Lassie now? Can you smell them?" Leonie rolled her eyes.

They heard muffled screams.

"Wait, what was that?"

They cocked their ears, the dwarves around them taking care of any infected that came their way.

"It came from down there," Huk said.

"Are you sure?"

"Of course, I'm sure. Look how low I am to the ground compared to you people."

He fell to his knees, ear to the grass.

"Definitely something inside—"

Huk flew several feet into the air as the trap door was slammed open, a large flap peeling from the grass.

Ben took a step back, relief flooding his face when he saw Veronica's face sticking out of the hole.

"Oh, hey, buddy," she said, breathless but casual. "How've you been? We could've used you down here."

Gideon felt drained. Every ounce of his energy was spent. Even with the reduced cost in mana **Etheric Manipulation** granted, casting two spells at once and holding back the tide had taken its toll.

Every attack and every collision with the enemy took a chunk from his mana, and his protection was about to fail.

"Hope you've all brought your umbrellas. It's about to get rainy out," Gideon breathed.

Before Holly and Molly could open their mouths, the bubble was down and they were exposed to the elements. In one way it was refreshing, given that their spells had mostly been cast through a buzzing haze of electricity and water, but now they were able to see everything. They were out in the fresh air with nothing between them and the enemy.

Nothing.

"Crap," Gideon said. He had not trained for this. Didn't know how to fight with his bare hands.

"We've got you," Holly said, realizing the problem. She pulled Molly closer and summoned Gelda over, and the three of them formed a protective shelter with their bodies for the mage.

"Focus on re-gen," Molly shouted.

Gideon did. He closed his eyes and tried to pretend the enemies weren't there. He fought with his mind to relax and let his body regenerate its vital stats.

The only problem with that was that the enemy *was* all around, and it was nearly impossible to relax when every bump or scream sounded like death was approaching and you were counting the seconds until your number was called.

Then Gideon heard the roars of some giant beast. He opened his eyes and saw a warg twice the size of the others coming for them. He smiled, elated to see the Wrangler nearby, jumping into action to help them again.

The warg roared and charged toward them, his head knocking creatures out of the way despite their size. When it reached Gideon and the others, it raised a paw and slashed Holly and Molly out of the way.

"Wait, what?" Gideon muttered. The realization dawned on him as he looked over his shoulder and saw a second warg of the same stature fighting the bad and avoiding hurting the good.

Gideon deflated. "Oh, crap."

Gelda, seeing the danger, jumped to Gideon's aid. With her stone muscles and shape, she matched the warg in height, at least. The beast snapped at her, trying to wrap its teeth around her thick waist.

Gelda roared and punched the warg's muzzle. It twisted sideways, snapping at her again. She took a jaw in each hand and pulled in opposite directions, stopping the mouth from closing.

"Gelda!" Gideon shouted.

Holly and Molly rose, dazed, from the ground. Before they could work out what was happening, the warg nudged Gelda forward with a powerful surge and sent her tumbling onto her back.

The teeth came once again. Gideon stood there, helpless, not knowing what to do without any mana to aid him. It was regenerating, sure, but so slowly it was still no use.

Gelda grunted with the effort of holding the warg back. Having regained her feet, she once again held its muzzle at bay, her muscles taut like knotted rope. The warg was gaining ground, inching closer to her body.

It was about to make contact, about to bite her, when the dazzling light appeared and a strange hush fell over the field.

***

"Is it working?" Mia asked, her face so close to the screen that she was nearly cross-eyed. "Is it?"

They were watching the action on the small monitors, which showed a cross-section of players they'd found involved in the battle outside of Hammersworth City. Right in the center was a screen that had just turned to static.

"I don't know," Lucy said. "There's nothing yet. Nothing…"

Mia stared at the screen, not even wanting to blink. For several days, they had waited for a moment like this. The moment KieraFreya and Chloe synchronized and the static blockages came.

The moment the gods were up against the AI.

"Still nothing…" Lucy muttered. "Nothing…"

"Wait, what was that?" Jonathon said suddenly. "There. *Look.*"

In the small rectangle of static, they could just make out a shape. A fuzzy outline of a figure as if someone was approaching through a hailstorm.

A jolt of excitement shot through them all. Even Demetri, who had been forced to take a backseat, was now on his feet, crowded around them all and watching.

"Can you see her?" Mia grinned, finger tracing features on the screen. "The hair, the arms. She's still there."

"Hmmm. Needs a tune-up," Lucy said, tapping some lines of additional code into a second monitor. She peered through her glasses and hit Enter.

Jonathon laughed. "It's like tuning an old satellite TV." He cupped his hands to his mouth and called to an imaginary man on the roof, "Hey! A little more to the left."

The image suddenly came into focus.

"Yes!" Mia shouted, pumping her fist. "It worked!"

They could see Chloe clearly now, her whole body emitting a white glow. She was hurtling through the air atop Sir Wingsalot, leaving the Nether Realm and speeding toward the battlefield.

"Damn, that's cool." Jonathon nodded.

Lucy couldn't keep her own smile from growing. She sat back and laced her fingers behind her head. "Well, there we go. A successful secondary artificial intelligence, now able to prevent the gods from shutting down the main images to our feed."

"Just look at those comments," Charlie pointed out. "From Hard-on for the Bard-on—damn, that's a choice name—'Wahoo! *Finally*, able to see Chloe go Super Saiyan. Woo!' From *Little_Leia72*: 'YES PRAXIS! Fixed the most annoying bug EVER!' Oh! And get this one, from *Herbil_Da_Gerbil*, 'Upvoting the shit out of this bitch right now!'

Lucy, Jonathan, and Charlie burst out laughing. When they saw that Mia was still straight-faced and staring at the screens, Lucy said, "Come on, boss. We've done it. We've created a good thing. It works, look!"

Mia shook her head, her attention diverted by the small image in the top-right of the monitor. The place where she could still see Ben, Veronica, and the others battling past infected in a place surrounded by trees.

"No, we haven't. We've taken one step, and that's amazing, but something's still not right. We haven't controlled the other gods, Fukmos, Dryana, and Myaris. They're still wandering around like nothing can stop them."

"Isn't that a part of the experience?" Charlie offered. "We can't mute them entirely."

"You haven't seen them as much as I have. I don't trust them. They're still working beyond the borders of what the game should allow. They shouldn't be directly involved in the game, making their presence known."

"What are you saying? Someone has neglected a line of code? Something has slipped through the cracks? Mia, we have our whole team at it. We've been working tirelessly for days. How could we have missed something?"

Mia leaned against the glass walls of her office and stared out at her team. Her eyes caught the loafer who currently sat in his corner cubie with his feet on the table.

Damien, she thought.

CHAPTER THIRTY-FIVE

Chloe felt etheric power pulsing through her as Sir Wingsalot lowered her to the ground and she dismounted.

The whole battlefield seemed to have paused, all eyes on this shining light amidst the group. Chloe straightened her back, adjusted her grip on the sword in her hand, and gave a wry smirk.

"Okay, you sons-of-words-I-cannot-say, let's see what you've really got." She looked over the battlefield at the countless heads of mages and fighters and remembered her new title, then took a deep breath and shouted, "For the queen!!"

"For the queen!" came the rallying cry as fighters all across the battlefield suddenly gained the +5% strength, +5% stamina, +5% endurance, +5% mana regeneration, and +5% health regeneration bonuses granted by Chloe's unique skill.

Then Chloe was back in the fray, her sword leaving an afterburn on the retinas of her enemies. The blade sang. She took out the large warg with one clean slash, freeing Gelda and setting her loose once more on the battlefield.

The whole thing felt like a dance she had known all her life. With KieraFreya offering her power and Chloe guiding the sword, they were unstoppable. Her body moved fluidly, and her attacks were measured and pure. Pretty soon, the last of the enemies had filed out of the rift, and finally, they could see the numbers being reduced.

She cleared a space around Gideon, Holly, Molly, Lindsay, Gelda, and Blueballs, giving them their first moment to breathe since the battle had begun. Chloe shouted encouragement to the others, trying to bring everyone back together and get them moving toward the gate.

If we can pile everyone back up, we'll be able to take the rest down, she said to KieraFreya.

Sounds good to me. United we stand and all that.

Hold on. Chloe chuckled internally, grunting as she took down another warg with a single blow. *I thought you guys had no access to the outside world? How did you know that's an American phrase?*

KieraFreya shrugged Chloe's shoulders. *I didn't. It's an Obsidian phrase too. Not everything is about your world, girly.*

Chloe continued to call to her comrades, rallying them to gather around the city gate. The message spread quickly, and Chloe and her team made their way around the field, taking down stragglers and helping those who were unable to work their way out of their own engagements.

There were casualties, of course. Several bodies littered the field behind them, which she knew would clear itself only a short time later when the game decomposed the figures and respawned the blessed.

The wargs and the orcs continued to give chase, but finally, guided by the blinding light of Chloe and KieraFreya and flanked by Blueballs, Holly, Molly, Gelda, and Gideon, everyone managed to regroup.

Even Therese had come forth to help them. They were now a much stronger unit, and the orcs, wargs and other creatures who kept up the attack broke against them like water against rock.

Doubt started to become visible in their eyes as their numbers shrank, and when Chloe blasted a thick column of **Deic Light** and took out their frontrunners, the creatures turned as one and fled toward the forest.

Chloe, buzzing with rage and excitement, summoned Sir

Wingsalot to her and was about to chase after the remaining few hundred sprinting across the grass when a hand grasped her shoulder and held her back.

"Chloe, leave it. We've won. They're running."

Chloe looked from the rift to the creatures and shook her head. "We may have won the battle, but we definitely haven't won the war. In case you haven't noticed, they're running in the direction of Ben, Veronica, and the clerics."

Gideon's face fell when he realized she was right.

"Ben's out there? Away from you? Maybe it wasn't just me who needed a break from this whole damn mess."

When she heard his voice, Chloe froze. She was sure she was imagining things.

"What? Not going to turn around and give your old buddy a hug?"

Chloe slowly turned, looking across the sea of dwarves for the originator of the sound. He stuck out like a sore thumb, clad in armor much grubbier than the rest, and with a shield that was not of Hammersworth.

Chloe couldn't believe it.

"Tag?" Her face broke into a smile. "What the hell? When did you… What?" She ran over and embraced him tightly.

"I came looking for you all. You know how hard it is to find your way across this world when you're a solo dwarf on a mission? Little did I know that I'd be walking into a friggin' battle zone. Good thing you had me, too. These dwarves don't know a thing about fighting."

Chloe hid a laugh behind her hand at the evil glares Tag got from the surrounding dwarves.

"We thought you'd gone forever," Gideon said. "I thought you'd never come back."

"Don't be silly," Tag said, patting Gideon's arm. "And leave you lot to create havoc without me? I just needed a bit of space, was all. I went back out into the world. Tried a few new games. Do you know that there is *nothing* out there as good as this? I'm telling you. Once you're out of here, you'll see. All you'll want to do is come back."

Chloe beamed, unable to hold back the happiness welling in her heart. Even KieraFreya said a few kind words to Tag.

"I hate to break up this reunion," King Abe said, appearing at their side, "but we need a game plan. We've got wounded and tired fighters waiting for their next orders."

"Who's this?" Tag jerked his thumb at Abe.

Gideon laughed. "The king of Hammersworth."

"*And* my husband," Therese said.

Tag's jaw nearly hit the ground. "How much did I miss?"

"A lot," Chloe said, putting her arm around Tag's shoulders. "But it's okay. We can fill you in. You know, after we've gone to the Nether Realm and found Shikora, of course."

"The Nether... Shikor... What?"

"Tell the troops to head back inside and deal with their wounded," Chloe said. "They might be gone, but we know for damn near certain that they're going to be back. Everyone, rest up and get yourselves back together, but set up a guard around the rift using any able-bodied and willing fighters. I have a funny feeling a war is coming."

"Without a doubt," Gideon said. "Come, let's clear up this battlefield, then go find our cleric friends."

To Chloe's great surprise, they were only a short distance into the forest when they became aware of people marching toward them.

At first, they took cover and prepared for a fight, then she saw Ben emerge from behind the trees, followed by a hundred or so clerics and dwarves.

"You've lost your touch." Chloe winked, breaking from the group and stopping near Ben. "I thought you were stealthy."

"You try blending in when you're followed by a hundred dwarves." He sighed, clearly exhausted from his trip. "You going to mock us or help us along?"

"Probably just mock you," Tag said.

Ben's tiredness vanished in an instant at the sound of Tag's voice. "What! How did you… When did you… What?"

Chloe nodded. "That's exactly what I said."

"I'll tell you about it on the way." Tag beamed. "Let's get out of these freaky woods before something comes out and attacks us."

As they walked back, Tag spoke of his return journey to the group and his time out from the game. He asked why Ben and Veronica had split from the group, and they shared their story of what had happened on their journey to the towns and villages, everything from healing the infected to being trapped by Fukmos and his sisters.

Chloe's ears pricked up at this, unable to believe what she was hearing.

"You saw him?"

"Oh, yes," Ben said. "And his reinforcements."

"It's because of them that the infection came around in the first place," Veronica said. "His sister Myaris is the Goddess of Disease."

"And they have ghosts, too," Heather said. "They're amassing an army, I'm sure of it. We need to find a way to end this all, and soon."

"Speaking of…" Chloe said. "You didn't happen to see any wargs or orcish creatures heading this way, did you?"

They shook their heads.

"Why?" Ben said.

Chloe looked at Gideon and Tag. "It's kind of a long story."

"We've got time," Ben said, blinking at the light as they emerged from the trees and the city came into view.

"Oh, I don't think we do…" Chloe pointed to the rift.

Ben, Veronica, Heather, and a hundred dwarves' jaws dropped as one.

EPILOGUE

Compared to the chaos of the previous day's battle, all was calm in Hammersworth. Quiet had fallen over the city, as if the very stonework was in awe of the rippling rift hovering outside their gates.

Chloe could see it now: the guards in a circle around the tear, the great cluster of dwarves obediently standing in their gleaming armor, likely sweating under the heat of the sun.

"She's in there somewhere," Chloe whispered. The comment was intended for herself, but as usual, it had been intercepted by the goddess living in her armor.

"Has to be. I don't know where else to look if she's not."

Chloe nodded. Since opening the rift, purging the foul creatures that had emerged from it, and joining the others back at the palace, she'd felt herself fall into a type of reverie. A determined focus she had never felt before.

This was it. All her journeying had been leading to this moment—to find the final segment of armor and unite the pieces of the goddess so that she might once more join her kin in the heavens.

It all waited beyond that door. She had an excited buzz in her gut like a child waiting to go downstairs and discover what Santa had left for her and her siblings.

"The final chapter," Chloe murmured. "One last venture into the unknown before it all ends and we go our separate ways."

"Our separate ways…" KieraFreya repeated, sadness in her tone.

Chloe moved her attention from the wobbling rift and to the top of the forest canopy. As usual, it wouldn't be as easy as she'd hoped. Of that, she was sure. Somewhere out there, the darkness was gathering for one last revolt. One final, desperate attempt to block the reunion of KieraFreya and her mother and father in the heavens.

Just what secret were they hiding?

Why were they so determined to keep KieraFreya down here?

What in the hell was lurking beyond the curtain into the Nether Realm? In that bleak orange and purple landscape, where could a powerful goddess' steed be hiding?

And what other horrors awaited them there?

Character Sheet

Bio

Character name: Chloe (click to select a new character name)

Level: 16

Class: Battle Mage (Novice)

Titles: Chief Guardian of the Queen, Mage of the Academy

Race: Human

Stats

HP: 518/518

MP: 837/837

Stamina: 492/492 Active effects: Null

Boons: +15% luck to experimental magicks, 5% proficiency in skill-learning, spell cost dramatically reduced

Attributes

Strength: 22 (+53)

Intelligence: 10 (+55)
Dexterity: 20 (+61)
Endurance: 25 (+38)
Etheric Potential: 9 (+76)

Skills

Languages: Human
Acrobatics: Lv 5
Armed Combat: Lv 5
Charismatic: Lv 4
Climbing: Lv 2
Cooking: Lv 2
Crafting: Lv 1
Creature Identification: Lv 5
Dark Vision: Lv 4
Dual Wielding: Lv 3
Entrepreneur: Lv 1
Etheric Manipulation: Lv 5
Experimental: Lv 2
Fishing: Lv 1
For the Queen!: Lv 1
Hand of the Gods: Lv 2
Herb Identification: Lv 2
Monster Slayer: Lv 1
Mounted Combat: Lv 1
Reckless: Lv 7
Saddler: Lv 5
Scholar: Lv 1
Sneak: Lv 5
Swimming: Lv 3
Tutor: Lv 2

Available Points: 0

Skills-dex

Skill increased: Acrobatics (Lv 5)

You're taking enormous strides—literally! Bounce and spring your way to battle or adventure and savor the moments spent in the air!

Bonuses: +7 dexterity

(NOTE: Increases in skill override any previous bonuses gained from the skill).

Skill increased: Armed combat (Lv 5)

Damn. Hack, cut, slice, and wield that sword like it's your second arm. Keep on leveling in this skill to learn new combinations that will be beneficial in the heat of battle.

Bonuses: +5 strength

(NOTE: Increases in skill override any previous bonuses gained from the skill).

Skill increased: Charismatic (Lv 4)

You've really worked that tongue loose. Now let's see what you can do with it.

Purrr...

Bonuses: +4 intelligence

Skill increased: Climbing (Lv 2)

Cling to the rocks like a lizard, scale to the highest heights. Or...just not get so tired when climbing up walls. Keep practicing, and soon you'll be jumping up cliff faces with the best of them.

Bonuses: +2 dexterity

· · ·

Skill increased: Cooking (Lv 2)

You've developed something akin to taste buds. Now you can get a little bit more experimental while lowering your chances of food poisoning!

Bonuses: +2 dexterity

You've unlocked a new skill: Crafting (Lv 1)

Those who can craft gain a fair advantage in Obsidian. Create your own armor from leather. Make your own weapons. Or continue paying others to do it, because at this level, your chances are still relatively slim.

Requirements: Create your first item

Bonuses: +1 dexterity

Skill increased: Creature Identification (Lv 5)

Congratulations on reaching level 5 in this skill. You'll now be able to access the basic strengths and weaknesses of your foes, as well as additional nuggets of information that might be of use to you.

Bonuses: +7 intelligence

(NOTE: Increases in skill override any previous bonuses gained from the skill).

Skill increased: Dark Vision (Lv 4)

The night is fast becoming your mistress. Dark shapes become more refined, night terrors lose their fuzz, and oh, the pranks you can play as you dissolve into the darkness and lead your friends astray.

Bonuses: +5 intelligence, +8 etheric potential

(NOTE: Increases in skill override any previous bonuses gained from the skill).

. . .

Skill increased: Dual Wielding (Lv 3)

Many don't understand the diversity of battle style that dual wielding has to offer. Some stumble across this by chance. Like you. You're a chancer, right? Now you can combine both magic and the physical in battle. Boop!

Bonuses: +3 dexterity

(NOTE: Increases in skill override any previous bonuses gained from the skill).

You've unlocked a new skill: Entrepreneur (Lv 1)

You've set up your first business! There are many ways to make money in Obsidian, but only a few learn the glorious benefits of letting the money make you. The more passive income you make, the higher this skill will increase.

Requirements: Start your first business

Bonuses: +5 intelligence

Skill increased: Etheric Manipulation (Lv 5)

Congratulations on reaching level 5 in this skill. You are surely working your way down the path of magedom, and with that, you can reap a host of rewards.

You will now be able to learn basic spells by observation. Simply watch another mage use a spell, and you will be able to absorb that spell's knowledge and set yourself on the path to taking that spell farther. Not only that, but specialization bonuses are now in play. Should you choose to narrow your skills to a specific elemental path, you will progress in these spells twice as fast. You will also have the option to change your title to reflect your specialty and reward yourself with bonus tuition from the academies and schools across Obsidian to further your skill set.

Should you wish not to specialize, you will find that combining spells and playing with experimental magic will have its rewards.

Bonus buffs will be available any time spells are combined, and any new spells unseen before in Obsidian will be labeled with your name as the founder and creator.

Bonuses: +12 etheric potential, spell cast cost dramatically reduced, immunity to friendly fire

(NOTE: Increases in spells override any previous bonuses gained from the spell).

Skill increased: Experimental (Lv 2)

You've discovered a new way to manipulate a spell! Keep pushing the boundaries of common thought to discover bigger, better, and more efficient ways to enhance your abilities and further your knowledge of Obsidian.

Bonuses: +2 intelligence, +1 dexterity, +1 endurance, +2 etheric potential

(NOTE: Increases in skill override any previous bonuses gained from the skill).

You've unlocked a new skill: Fishing (Lv 1)

See those things in the water? They're fish. You can catch them. Well done.

Requirements: Catch your first fish

Bonuses: +1 dexterity

You've unlocked a new (unique) skill: For the Queen!

Unite and inspire any and all allied fighters surrounding you in battle with a war cry, backed by the queen herself.

Fighters will rally around you, finding courage in their hearts to fight longer and with increased strength for a limited time.

Bonuses: +5% strength, +5% stamina, +5% endurance, +5% mana regeneration, +5% health regeneration.

Duration: 3 minutes

Skill increased: Hand of the Gods (Lv 2)

You clearly have the favor of the gods. Guiding your strength, the gods can lend you unique skills and abilities to aid you in a pinch. Don't rely on this skill unless you're ready to live a reckless life. The gods take vacations, too, y'know.

The results of this skill may vary.

Bonuses: +10 etheric potential

(NOTE: Increases in skill override any previous bonuses gained from the skill).

Skill increased: Herb Identification (Lv 2)

The surrounding foliage is beginning to talk to you. Discover new ingredients for food and potion recipe by experimenting with combinations of Obsidian's plant life.

Bonuses: +2 intelligence

You've unlocked a new skill: Monster Slayer (Lv 1)

There are many horrors that haunt Obsidian's lands, some big, some small, some *enormous*. With this skill, you'll now gain proficiency in defeating larger monsters. Once you have stumbled upon the monster's weakness, you'll be able to identify the weak places of all future monsters of this type.

Requirements: Defeat 3 dreyda

Bonuses: +2 strength, +2 intelligence

You've unlocked a new skill: Mounted Combat (Lv 1)

Attacking while riding is a whole different kettle of fish. Get used to the motion of your steed and counterbalance the overeagerness of its trot to learn to deal vicious blows.

Or, fall off a lot and hope you land on an enemy. Always worked for me.

Requirements: Battle a monster while riding a steed

Bonuses: +1 dexterity

Skill increased: Reckless (Lv 7)

Okay, okay. We get it. You're *craaazy!* Since you're determined to risk your neck and go down unwise routes, you have gained an exclusive "time-slow" buff anytime you do something considered reckless.

Bonuses: +17 strength, +12 endurance

(NOTE: Increases in skill override any previous bonuses gained from the skill).

Skill increase: Saddler (Lv 5)

You've tamed the impossible, finding a way to ride a legendary beast and make it your bitch. Additional experience has been added to this skill to reward your bravery and boost you further on your way as you tame and ride the creatures of Obsidian.

Bonuses: +5 dexterity

You've unlocked a new skill: Scholar (Lv 1)

Your hunger for knowledge is insatiable. Whether you're learning from people, experiences, or books, you can now take comfort in knowing that you will learn faster from this point on.

Requirements: Read a book that's above your level

Bonuses: +1 intelligence, skills can now upgrade 5% faster

Skill increased: Sneak (Lv 5)

The darkness has become your friend, your feet lighter than

feathers on air. GREAT! As always, be sure to use your powers for good.

Who knows what horrors a silent battle mage can create when sneaking...?

Bonuses: +5 dexterity

(NOTE: Increases in skill override any previous bonuses gained from the skill).

Skill increased: Swimming (Lv 3)

Slicker and faster, you're becoming more streamlined. The water loves you. I wonder what delights you'll find way down in the depths of Obsidian?

Bonuses: +3 dexterity

(NOTE: Increases in skill override any previous bonuses gained from the skill).

Skill increased: Tutor (Lv 2)

Although you prefer your own methods, you've left the path open for your students to choose their own way. The key to being a solid instructor is to nourish your students, not push them in one direction. Keep this up and the benefits will continue to grow.

Bonuses: +4 intelligence

(NOTE: Increases in skill override any previous bonuses gained from the skill).

Quest-dex

Open Quests

Quest unlocked: A Fallen Goddess

The Goddess of Retribution, KieraFreya, has fallen from grace. Her form has been divided and scattered across the land of Obsidian. For eons she has lain in wait, hoping for an adventurer who is brave enough and strong enough to unite the pieces of her armor once more and restore KieraFreya to her former glory.

Find all [x] pieces of KieraFreya and return her to the gods.

Difficulty: 10/10

Rewards: 100,000 exp, + rare items (locked).

Accept quest: Y/N

————————

Complete Quests

Quest complete: Walk the Deathwalk of the Gods

You've done it! You've outwitted the trolls, trodden through the realm of fire, swum the unforgiving lake, and emerged victorious through the fractal labyrinth of death. You've truly proven yourself—

#ERROR404

—a champion among champions—

MISSING_SEQ

REBOOT_POPUP

—Carry on, adventurer Untitled, and soar to ever great heights!

Bonuses: 10,000 experience + Bracers of KieraFreya

Quest unlocked: We didn't start the fire.

Some idiot has lost control of his flames. Help him put out the fire before the whole house is burnt to cinders.

Rewards: 50 exp

Quest complete: We didn't start the fire.

Smarts, cunning, quick wit, and the intelligence to solve a problem. These were none of the things you used as you launched water on the fire and jumped headfirst into a smoke-infested building.

You somehow managed it, though. Hooray!

Reward: 50exp

Quest complete: Crossing the language barrier

You took the easy way out. Well, why not? It certainly speeds things along now, doesn't it? Even if you don't get that glorious glow of knowledge.

Reward (Interpreter): 100 exp

Quest complete: Where's the shaman?

You didn't turn away when the going got tough. Congratulations. You've made a new friend and a powerful ally.

Rewards: 500 exp, Final slumber potion recipe

Quest complete: Chasing Nightmares

You've reunited the stableboy with his steeds. Unfortunately, the cost was high, since you lost favor with Jacob. Experience still awarded, but no horses for you.

Rewards: 1,500 exp

Quest complete: An unlikely pairing

Rosaline and Derren are a match made in heaven. Congratulations on uniting them and letting love blossom in this barren world.

Extra points awarded for copulation within the first 24 hours of meeting.

Rewards: 1,300 exp, + 500 exp (copulation bonus), + map location unlocked.

Quest unlocked: A most bloody request

Someone has it out for you. Find the sender of the death note in Nauriel and discover what truly lies behind this request.

Rewards: 2,000 exp

.   .   .

Quest complete: A most bloody request

You've found the sender of the death note, now track down this 'Tohken' and see if you can unravel just exactly why he has it out for you.

Rewards: 2,000 exp

Quest complete: A Woman in Need

You've discovered the truth about Lady Gwent. Quite a web has been woven, now, let's see if you can conquer part two.

Rewards: 3,400 exp

Quest updated: A Woman in Need (Part II)

You've united the town and brought peace to Gallen Hollows. Not only that, but you've earned the undying affection of Lady Gwent. Powerful allies are good to have, my friend.

Rewards: 7,000 exp + unknown items

Quest complete: A Willing Student

The Mages' Academy is stringent with who they accept into their order. Prove your worth and earn the respect of the tutors to unlock the benefits of the globally revered academy.

Difficulty: 4/10

Rewards: 1,000 exp

Accept quest: Y/N

Quest complete: Opposite of Gods

For the last few weeks, a strange phenomenon has been affecting Killink View's mages. A shrine dedicated to the gods of the darkness has reportedly been seen to be surrounded by demons. These demons have been spilling into the daylight, threatening to enter the city.

The guards have been vigilant, firing and deflecting the demons in their attempts to break into the city, but their arrows only keep them at bay. More must be done to eradicate this nuisance before the threat grows.

Visit the Shrine of the Damned within the mountain's caves, discover where the mages have been disappearing to, and uncover the source of the disturbance.

Difficulty: 6/10

Rewards: 5,000 exp

Accept quest: Y/N

Party quest unlocked: A Call to Arms

You've destroyed the dreyda and emerged as the triumphant party of the task! The King and Queen are very impressed and wish to bestow many rewards upon you. Look out for additional party quests as the game continues to grow, and the populations build.

Rewards: 20,000 experience to each team member of the party who contributes the greatest progress to this task (3,000 to each member of every other party) + favor with the city of Killink View + an audience with the king and queen.

Quest complete: We don't take kindly to strangers

Track down the ringleader of the grumblers within Rustfields and change their opinion of the blessed.

Bonus points not awarded.

Rewards: 1,200 exp

Quest complete: Who's been goblin?

Your goblin companion is missing, and you have a hunch that

someone in this town knows something about it.

Find out what happened to Huk and return him safely to your party.

Rewards: 800 exp

Quest complete: Horsin' Around

No steed can outmatch your power! Congratulations on acquiring a new steed (and with unmatched finesse, impressive...)

Rewards: 50 exp

Quest complete: Stubborn Llamas

You did it! Wow, was that one easy. Still, every good deed deserves a reward.

Rewards: 500 exp

Quest complete: Get the chick in the wagon

Don't get cocky, kid. Even my grandmother could have completed this one, and in less time. With more skill. I mean... they're chickens, not basilisks.

Rewards: 400 exp

Quest complete: The Rift to Nether Realm

You have unlocked the entrance to the Nether Realm—congratulations!

This was deemed an impossible task by those who came before, but you managed to unite more magic-users than the city has seen together. You have found the tear in the fabric of reality and can now access the Nether Realm.

Celebrate your victory but tread carefully. Explore the unexplored. Strange paths lie ahead, but for now, rest up a bit...

If you can.

Rewards: 50,000 exp

——————————

Failed Quests

Quest failed: One of us

Rewards: 5,000 exp, Title unlock (Oakston Villager), New language (Tribal: Primitive)

——————————

Spells-dex

New spell acquired: Aqua Orb (Lv 1)

A spell for even the sunniest of days. Conjure the Aqua Orb to protect yourself from heat and heat-related monsters. This ball is the ultimate addition to any high-society party or is perfect when in a pinch in dry environments such as deserts.

Requirements: n x 20MP per second (where n is equal to the number of seconds taken to cast the spell)

Spell power increased: Creepers Crawlies (Lv 2)

Now that your spell has leveled up you can—*you guessed it*—control vines and foliage with a slightly greater level of efficiency. A wider range of plant life is available to your manipulation, too.

Requirements: n x 17MP per second (where n is equal to the number of seconds taken to cast the spell)

Spell power increased: Deic Light (Lv 2)

The gods have treated you kindly, and you have channeled their light well. Now enemies in the darkness will cower before your might as you blast through shadow and harness the power of the gods.

Requirements: n x 50MP (where n is equal to the number of seconds taken to cast the spell)

Spell power increased: Healing Hands (Lv 2)

A studious mage would be nothing without a little healing power. Lay your hands upon an injured comrade and help bring them back to health. Lay hands on yourself to fix those bumps and bruises and return to the battle as if nothing had ever happened.

Requirements: (on others) n x 15MP (where n is equal to the number of seconds taken to cast the spell)

(on self) n x 18MP (where n is equal to the number of seconds taken to cast the spell.

Spell power increased: Ice Shard (Lv 2)

Ice may melt, and ice may thaw, but you can guarantee that it'll do some damage before it fades into oblivion.

The ultimate spell for stealthy kills, fire an ice shard into your opponent's heart and watch the baffled faces of the investigators when the shard melts without a trace....

Requirements: n x 10MP per shard (where n is equal to the number of seconds taken to cast the spell)

New spell acquired: Mind Manipulation (Lv 1)

You've mastered the art of combining spells in order to screw with people's minds. Now you can actually try digging your hands into other characters' brain matter and affecting their biology on a cellular level.

Mind Manipulation is a spell in the Illusion branch of magic. With this spell, you'll be able to affect what people see and influence their decisions.

Warning: There are many who frown upon the manipulation of people's minds. Use with caution to maintain good standing among those within Obsidian.

Requirements: n x 20MP

Spell power increased: Purple Blaze (Lv 4)

You're on FIRE! You've found a new way to manipulate your spell. Your spells-dex will keep a record of any and all manipulations you discover. Continue with your experiments to unlock bigger and better forms of your Purple Blaze spell, Hot Stuff.

Manipulations:

- Fireball: Summon a fireball to throw at your enemies. Size varies dependent on focus and mana invested in the spell.
- Scorching trail: Mark your territory, create barriers, or just draw pretty pictures with the purple flame. Size and duration dependent on focus and mana invested in the spell.

Bonuses: +1 etheric potential, reduced cast cost (n x 18MP)

New spell acquired: Resurrection (Lv 1)

There are a great many forces at work in this realm. Though many choose to pursue the path of the light, magic can be found in the path of the darkness. While life is sought and clung to with iron claws, death is the inevitability that comes to all.

Or so it would seem.

Summon the powers within this spell to bring the dead back to the living. Higher tiers of this spell will allow control of the dark forces of the dead, while lower tiers will allow the resurrection of fallen comrades.

A note of warning: there are those within the realm of

Obsidian who frown upon the dark arts. Be wary of your surroundings before toying with the gods of darkness and snatching away their prizes.

Requirements: 100% of player's MP

(NOTE: The Spell of Resurrection can only be cast once within a 48-hour period)

Spell power increased: Shadow Tweak (Lv 2)

Ever thought of producing puppet shows? Just an idea. I suppose there are better ways to manipulate the shadows (extra points for creativity and innovation).

Requirements: n x 12MP (where n is equal to the number of seconds taken to cast the spell)

Spell power increased: Telekinesis (Lv 3)

You've done it! Now you can manipulate multiple objects at once. Use this spell to confound and confuse your enemies, as well as helping yourself out of sticky situations.

Requirements: n x 30MP (where n is equal to the number of seconds taken to cast the spell)

Spell power increased: Volt Shock (Lv 2)

Is it me, or can you feel a spark between us? Maybe harness that power and zap the hell out of enemies with it. Who knows the limits of your potential?

Requirements: n x 30MP (where n is equal to the number of seconds taken to cast the spell)

New spell acquired: Whisper of the Wild (Lv 1)

Have you ever wanted to communicate with animals? To have them listen to your whispers and wishes? Well, you better start increasing your rank in this spell, then, eh? For now, you might be able to talk to insects and possibly a squirrel, but train this up and you'll have even the most fearsome predators obeying your will.

Requirements: n x 20MP (where n is equal to the number of seconds taken to cast the spell)

CONNECT WITH THE AUTHOR

Connect with Michael Anderle

Website: http://lmbpn.com

Email List: http://lmbpn.com/email/

Social Media:

https://www.facebook.com/LMBPNPublishing

https://twitter.com/lmbpn

https://www.instagram.com/lmbpn_publishing/

https://www.bookbub.com/authors/michael-anderle